"Rising star Meding offers up the first book in a new series with her twist on the world of superheroes. . . . This story follows the journey of a young woman finding her place in a world that is about to grow much more treacherous."

—*RT Book Reviews*

"Meding successfully captures the action-packed pace of superhero team comics with her group of colorful young adventurers."

—*Publishers Weekly*

"Dark and gritty, heroic and horrifying, not to mention intense, aptly describe Meding's work. . . . I can honestly say that I loved this book more than any other I have read by Meding. Her love of comic books, *X-Men*, and the like comes through every single page. She pulls no punches, takes you to the heart of her characters so that you share their joy and their sorrow. . . . I can't wait to see what else is in store for Trance and the gang!"

—*Night Owl Reviews*

"The first book in Meding's Meta Wars series sets the tone for further exciting, death-defying adventures. . . . It is heartening to know that amid the life-and-death struggles, there is still time for romance. Excellent, compelling reading for all fans of urban fantasy."

—*Single Titles*

"What a great world Meding has built with her new Meta Wars series. . . . The story line was fresh and engaging. I had NO clue who the villain really was. It was a total shock to me. . . . Definitely a great opening to a new urban fantasy series."

—*Urban Fantasy Investigations*

"I loved the complete break from traditional urban fantasy mythology that *Trance* introduced. There is a real *X-Men/ The Incredibles* vibe to this story that really worked. . . . There is certainly a lot of fun to be had in a world like this."

—*All Things Urban Fantasy*

"Meding provides an entertaining superhero vs. supervillain urban fantasy. Filled with action from the moment the young MetaHumans begin to realize their powers returned . . . fans will enjoy this fun thriller."

—*Alternative Worlds*

"A well-written book by a talented author. . . . I can't say there is a character I didn't enjoy. . . . And the villain was just crazy! . . . This book is so cool. I can't think of a better word to describe it."

—*Yummy Men and Kick Ass Chicks*

Praise for Kelly Meding and the Dreg City novels

"A fast-paced adventure."

—Charlaine Harris, #1 *New York Times* bestselling author

"Gritty, imaginative, and a terrific read.... A real storyteller."

—Patricia Briggs, #1 *New York Times* bestselling author

"Dark, dangerous, and delectable.... Impossible to put down!"

—Gena Showalter, *New York Times* bestselling author

"Action-packed, edgy, and thrilling.... You won't want to miss this one."

—Jeaniene Frost, *New York Times* bestselling author

"A phenomenal story ... utterly addictive."

—Jackie Kessler, critically acclaimed author

"Thrilling.... Especially impressive are her worldbuilding skills."

—*RT Book Reviews*

"[An] excellent series."

—*Bitten by Books*

"Will keep you on the edge of your seat."

—*Book Lovers Inc.*

ALSO BY KELLY MEDING

Trance

Available from Pocket Books

KELLY MEDING

CHANGELING

POCKET BOOKS

New York   London   Toronto   Sydney   New Delhi

Pocket Books
A Division of Simon & Schuster, Inc.
1230 Avenue of the Americas
New York, NY 10020

This book is a work of fiction. Names, characters, places, and incidents either are products of the author's imagination or are used fictitiously. Any resemblance to actual events or locales or persons, living or dead, is entirely coincidental.

First Pocket Books paperback edition July 2012

POCKET and colophon are registered trademarks of Simon & Schuster, Inc.

For information about special discounts for bulk purchases, please contact Simon & Schuster Special Sales at 1-866-506-1949 or business@simonandschuster.com.

The Simon & Schuster Speakers Bureau can bring authors to your live event. For more information or to book an event, contact the Simon & Schuster Speakers Bureau at 1-866-248-3049 or visit our website at www.simonspeakers.com.

Manufactured in the United States of America

10 9 8 7 6 5 4 3 2 1

ISBN 978-1-4516-2093-1
ISBN 978-1-4516-2095-5 (ebook)

For the dreamers who dare to look beyond the obvious,
and wonder "What If?"

Acknowledgments

Thank you to the usual suspects: my agent, Jonathan Lyons; my editor, Jennifer Heddle, and her intrepid assistant, Julia Fincher; Erica Feldon and all the folks at Pocket who've shepherded this series from the start.

My thanks to Nancy and Melissa, two of the amazing and patient people who read multiple drafts of this book, and who didn't kill me dead for changing the ending at the last minute.

And to my loyal readers: thank you so much for following me on the next adventure in the Meta Wars world. I couldn't do this without you.

Introduction

My name is Dahlia Perkins, but on the job I go by Ember. Six months ago, I was a struggling journalist for a small gossip paper. Now I'm a superhero. Freelance superhero, to be specific. Specifics are important. In our line of work, it's all in the details. Details keep you alive.

Consider this detail: fifteen years ago, superpowered humans, or Metas, worked for a subbranch of the Bureau of Alcohol, Tobacco, Firearms and Explosives called the Meta-Human Control Group. They were the Ranger Corps—the good guys. They kept the peace against their malevolent counterparts, the Banes, who used their powers to terrorize the general public. Then everyone mysteriously lost their powers for the next fifteen years. Six months ago those powers returned, and it was discovered that the MHC kept a fail-safe on hand, just in case the Meta population got out of control. Their fail-safe solution to global safety was death for all Metas—Rangers and Banes alike.

During the chaos of these events, my own hitherto unknown Meta powers came to the attention of the surviving Rangers, and my career as a reporter came to an abrupt end.

Long story short: the former Rangers and I bid the ATF farewell and took to freelance work. The Banes are still in prison, but the goal of our leader, Trance, is to see all of them eventually set free. Unfortunately, the majority of Americans don't want to see them set free, so Trance's inroads keep hitting dead ends.

On a personal note, it's finally useful to be the illegitimate daughter of a well-known billionaire. Trust fund money bought our new headquarters, is funding its renovations, and will keep us afloat for a while longer—barring any serious disaster that results in the city of Los Angeles suing our asses off.

Big trouble, that.

One

Settling In

W ho's got the friggin' fire extinguisher?"

Renee's shout echoed all the way down the main staircase, punctuated by a foot stamped down on the ceiling above me. I dropped my paint-soaked roller into its pan a little too hard and splattered eggshell interior latex all over the legs of my jeans, adding to the preexisting splats of burgundy, sage, white, navy blue, and two different wood stains.

I was downstairs in the foyer of the mansion we were hip deep in renovating, trying to get a second coat onto the walls of the spacious entry. Even after a primer and first coat, the garish blue-green paint job the home's previous owners subjected themselves to—in a fit of drunken misguidance, one can only hope—continued to peek through. The home in mostly deserted Beverly Hills had been on the market for seven years before we bought it; real estate in California anywhere south of Santa Barbara was hard to sell. Everyone was moving north, just as they had been in the twenty years since the outbreak of the Meta War, which had ravaged Los Angeles, among other major cities. With the last four major film studios located in Vancouver, half of the city's population had defected to Canada.

Several million residents remained, though, including us six—the last of a defunct group of superheroes once called the Ranger Corps.

The house we settled on—and after much discussion named Hill House, in memory of a fallen friend—was huge. More than twenty rooms, a perimeter fence with a built-in security system, an interior courtyard, outdoor pool and tennis court, and plastic pipes that didn't need replacing. Everything else was superficial and could be fixed with time and patience.

More foot stamping above. Renee and Ethan had gone upstairs to work on the front room, which was destined to be our common lounge. I darted toward the main staircase on my right and took the steps two at a time, past the first landing and up to the second floor.

The lounge was on my immediate right. Its floor was bare, stripped of its old carpeting, and sanded smooth of ancient carpet glue. The walls were painted a pleasant lemon yellow and trimmed with walnut molding. It was a large, L-shaped room, and I stood at the entrance to the short end.

Ethan "Tempest" Swift sat on the floor by the far wall, next to the open balcony doors. Morning sunlight glinted off his red hair, seeming to set it on fire. He clutched his left hand to his chest and scowled at the far end of the room. I rounded the corner to the longer end of the L and was assaulted by the odor of scorched plastic. Renee "Flex" Duvall hovered in the center of the room, staring up at the ceiling. A dusty, broken light fixture lay in pieces at her feet. Above her, exposed wires dangled and sparked, and light gray smoke twisted out of the hole in the ceiling.

"Are you two trying to burn us down?" I asked. I strode over, accidentally bumping Renee sideways with my hip. She grunted. I extended my hands toward the exposed wires and concentrated. The heat pulled into my body, absorbed through my fingertips to settle deep in my belly. A warm flush filled my cheeks. A few sparks leapt from the hole to me—little caresses of warmth—and then the threat passed.

"Yeah, we were hoping to cause a nice fire," Renee said. Her berry-red lips twisted into a wry smile, the only bit of her skin that wasn't ash blue. "Because I love burning down the headquarters I've barely had a chance to live in."

For a moment, I didn't know if she was serious. Renee and I had an awkward relationship, to say the least. I discovered the awesome extent of my powers during the same fire that killed a good friend—possibly a lover—of hers. I hadn't grown up with her and the others, and she often seemed to view me as an annoyance, rather than a teammate.

"My fault," Ethan said, hauling ass to his feet. "I should have turned off the circuit breaker before I decided to try some rewiring."

I blanched. "You think?"

"I'm just trying to be helpful with this whole renovations thing, Dal. I like to think I can do more than just help paint dry faster."

Renee's mouth twitched. "You know, people might line

up for that kind of assistance. Blow a lot of wind, dry the paint in ten minutes flat. Contractors would pay good money for you."

"Not contractors who get paid by the hour."

Ethan's particular power was control over the air. His code name, Tempest, fit the ability perfectly. He could concentrate a whirlwind to drill a hole into the ground, and aim a blast of air at an object to knock it loose from a great height. His most impressive (to me) talent was gliding on air currents to simulate flying. He looked so free when he flew, as close to happy as he ever seemed to get. Ethan often played peacemaker among our disparate personalities, but he never seemed to find any peace for himself.

I blew air out through my nose. "Look, guys, I know that Teresa is all gung-ho about us doing as much as possible ourselves, but there are reasons people hire professional electricians. Painting is one thing, but electricity is tricky. Let's just pay someone and get it over with. We can—"

"If you say we can afford it one more time, I'll gag you," Renee said. She planted her hands on her hips, and I half expected her to stretch her limbs into crazy proportions in order to intimidate me. I admired her power. She could stretch her body like taffy, at least ten times its original length. All I did was absorb heat.

"Well, we can," I snapped. Our decision to break away from government oversight and go freelance had hinged on accessing the trust fund my father left in my name. It was money I'd ignored my entire adult life, until I finally found a way to put it to good use. "What we can't afford is Ethan constantly electrocuting himself, or us burning this place down around our ears. He's not an electrician."

"Just a windbag."

Ethan grunted. "Funny."

Renee blew him a kiss. "Look, Dal, bring it up with Teresa again. If she wants to hire out, fine. Great. Go for it. Just don't get your hopes up."

"I just don't understand why she's so averse to using the money," I said.

"It's not about the money."

I stared. "What do you mean, it's not about the money?"

They had both known Teresa "Trance" West longer than I had; they had grown up together, along with Marco "Onyx" Mendoza and Gage "Cipher" McAllister. The five of them, elder heroes by all rights, worked together like a single entity. As much as I tried, I never felt like one of them. Yes, I was MetaHuman just like they were, but I wasn't part of their shared history. It made me an outsider.

They knew what else bothered our venerable leader, and I hadn't a clue.

"Well?" I asked. "Throw me a bone here, guys."

"She's being cautious, is all," Ethan said. "Any electrician we hire would be a stranger. This is our sanctuary, Dal, and we can't let just anyone inside."

I understood Teresa's reasons for extreme caution, having lived through the events that culminated in our separation from the MetaHuman Control branch of the ATF. Her sense of betrayal over the fail-safe plan. The literal betrayal by Dr. Angus Seward, who was once considered a valuable ally and had, in the end, tried to annihilate all Metas. Knowledge that attack could come from any direction, as it often did when we ventured into the city. Heroes to some, villains to others, but feared by all—this is what we had become to the people of Los Angeles.

"I'm not suggesting," I began, picking my words carefully, "that we grab contractors off the street and give them a key to the front gate. We check them out, they have escorts while on the property, and no access to certain rooms." Rooms that housed our personal history and, like the War Room, were not for public viewing.

"I could agree to that."

We all turned toward the door nearest us, at the top of the L. Teresa stood in its frame, arms tight across her chest. Her violet-streaked hair was pulled back into a tight ponytail, the tips frozen with blue paint, and more blue paint decorated her cheeks, forearms, and jeans. It created a palette contrast with the natural violet hues that framed her forehead, jawline, and elbows, and sunk deeply into the wells of her collarbone.

The coloration made her look like a domestic abuse victim—a laughable thought to anyone who knew Gage McAllister. They loved each other in a messy, passionate, eyes-wide-open way I thought existed only in the cinema. Few people found that kind of love, and being around them made me alternate between sugar shock and longing for it in my own life. I had low expectations; relationships and I did not go together.

Teresa smiled at me, brightening up the room with such

a simple gesture. She was only three years older than me, and the youngest among the others, but her leadership was unchallenged. She created intense energy orbs that could knock someone senseless, or shatter entire brick walls. Power led, and she possessed great power, tempered by equal amounts of humility. Her gentle approval was worth more to me than a thousand words of encouragement.

"I take it you have someone in mind?" Teresa asked.

Oops. "I'll find someone we can trust." The haziest bit of memory poked at my brain without coalescing into something useful. It would come to me.

She nodded, taking me at my word. Her violet gaze turned past me, to Ethan. "Let me see it," she said, walking to him.

He held out his hand, frowning like a kid who'd had dessert taken away. The tips of his fingers were red, his index finger starting to blister. She held his hand gently, gazing at the burns with a mother hen quality she'd displayed more and more frequently these last few months.

"Just don't say I told you so," Ethan said.

She quirked an eyebrow. "Would I say that?"

"You're thinking it."

"There's some burn ointment downstairs in the infirmary."

"I'll patch him up," Renee said. "Come on, Windy, I'll give you the hot-pink bandages."

Ethan blanched. "That's supposed to be an incentive?"

She slung her arm over his shoulders and steered him toward the door. Their idle teasing followed them out of the room, leaving me and Teresa alone. She gazed up at the dangling wires and blackened hole. A shadow of fatigue stole across her face, and then disappeared behind a mask of thoughtfulness.

"Was this Renee's brilliant idea, or Ethan's?" she asked.

"You got me. I just came when someone yelled for a fire extinguisher."

Laughing, she said, "Good thing you were home, then, because I don't believe we own an actual extinguisher. Something else to add to our growing list of needs." Her voice dropped on the last bit, humor overtaken by frustration. No one, least of all Teresa, had believed striking out on our own would be so exhausting.

Give her something positive to think about, Dal.

"The lobby is almost finished," I said. "I have one more wall to cover and then we can lay down the new floor. The laminate arrived at the store this morning, it just hasn't been delivered yet."

"Good news." Something still distracted her. Couldn't be a fight with Gage. They didn't know how to fight without resorting to makeup sex within ten minutes of the argument. The upstairs walls were pretty thick, but not the doors.

"How's your room coming along?" I asked, trying again.

"Almost done." The edge in her voice softened at the topic of her shared room. Definitely not a fight with Gage. "I never thought I'd be the type to spend so much time picking out curtains, especially at twenty-five. Literal curtains and metaphorical ones."

It was a simple statement that said so much about her,

probably without meaning to. She rarely gave up details about her life during the last fifteen years she and the others had spent without powers. Fifteen long years separated from her childhood friends, from anything remotely like her old life, forced to pretend she'd always been normal; had never been the daughter of two decorated heroes.

From idle conversation, I knew she'd done things she wasn't proud of in those years, even spent a little time in jail, and she hadn't found happiness until getting her powers back. It had been a rebirth for everyone, including me.

She had lost her powers as a child of ten, torn away by a pair of mysterious Wardens, then restored when the Wardens were murdered. I discovered my powers during a freak accident at my old apartment, two days after. I spilled sesame oil while attempting a stir-fry and caught the pan's contents on fire. It sizzled, splattered, and ignited the sleeve of my blouse.

I had screamed, startled less by the fire than by the lack of heat on my skin. The flames licked at the blouse and my hand. As I watched, the fire absorbed right into my body. It remained hot for the next hour, and then faded completely. I'd explained it away as a panic-induced hallucination—even after news began to spread of the Meta reactivation. I hadn't entertained the idea that I was a Meta until the day the Channel 9 broadcast station blew up, and I really came into my abilities.

No, I couldn't compare our pain, or hope to understand her feelings of alienation and isolation. Trying to was patronizing.

"I haven't even thought about wallpaper," I said, "much less curtains."

Teresa laughed, and I basked in the warmth of her smile. "You have time to settle in, Dahlia. With any luck, we'll be here for a very long while." She picked at a fleck of dried paint adhering to her arm. "So, do you know any good electricians?"

An alarm clanged in the hallway, like an old-fashioned school bell. We turned toward the door in perfect unison.

"Something tripped the security system's perimeter alarm," Teresa said, then took off running.

I dashed after her through the door, around a curve in the short hallway, and back down the main staircase. She took them two at a time, moving faster than me, and disappeared. I crossed the lobby, still running, and turned down the left corridor. I ran past the interior courtyard exit on my right, to the first door on the left. Our appointed War Room housed a long oak table and eight chairs. A digital monitor took up four feet of the opposite wall, situated between the room's two windows. Maps and a dry-erase board decorated the wall on my right.

To my left, another door stood open and voices filtered out. Research and security. Half the size of the previous room, it contained only two computer systems so far. More were expected to be delivered next week. At the moment, the monitor on the right desk was for online research and connecting to our intranetwork, a program that Marco had written for us, after admitting his pre-repowering job was as a computer programmer (it still felt odd to think that any of us once had real jobs). It collated and integrated all of our combined information about known Metas, unsolved crimes, and even allowed us access to certain protected government databases.

On the left desk, the computer displayed eight different camera angles of our property. The perimeter fence had twenty-four different views and it monitored almost every single inch of the fence line. With that much acreage, it was quite a feat. The display monitor switched views every four seconds, recording everything into our database. I knew the views by heart, since I'd helped Marco install all of the cameras two months ago—right before that friendship went all to hell.

Teresa, Renee, and Ethan were hunched over the monitor.

"Did something trip the alarm?" I asked.

Teresa had taken the desk chair, and she punched a series of command codes into the keyboard. A search box came up. Moments later, the eight angles disappeared and were replaced by one large scene. I recognized the length of fence behind the pool house. A grove of trees created a natural curtain between our property and our rear neighbor. Teresa pressed Play.

Wind rustled the leaves of the trees. Seconds passed and nothing happened. Two birds, about the size of wrens, swooped down from the trees. They chased and danced back and forth across the screen. Then they angled sideways and flew right between the narrow iron bars of the fence. Red letters appeared on the bottom of the screen: Perimeter Breach Detected.

"Hell, T," Renee said. "I thought it was some kind of emergency and it's just a goddamn bird?"

"It's a sensitive system, Renee," Ethan said. He tapped a few keys and new words popped up: Perimeter Sensor Eight Deactivated. "We need to find a middle ground with the sensors so it doesn't get tripped by birds but will still pick up on small objects being lobbed at our house."

"Yeah, we don't want to be woken up in the middle of the night by a runaway parakeet."

"It's fixable, okay?" Teresa said. "There are going to be glitches, folks, we're still feeling this out. But we responded to the alarm, which is its purpose."

"What about the earthquake that set it off two days ago?" Renee said.

"The earthquake, really?" I said. I wasn't home for the 5.2 that shook the town. Earthquakes set off car alarms and such, so our system really wasn't a stretch.

"We'll have false alarms, guys," Ethan said, stepping in as peacemaker. "I'd rather have false positives than a system unable to detect a real threat. Am I alone?"

"No, you're not," Teresa said.

Renee grunted, and the others took that as her agreement. Their scrutiny fell on me, and I nodded.

Teresa's intense, violet-eyed gaze continued to study me, until she finally asked, "So what are your afternoon plans, Dal?"

"Hadn't really thought much past painting the—" Oh, wait, I had a new assignment. "Electrician hunting, right?"

"Bingo."

"I'll get on that," I said, and darted from the room.

As I passed through the lobby I tossed a guilty look at the paint pan and roller, drying to a tacky mess by the wall. Someone would finish it later. Half the house still needed fresh coats of paint. Thank goodness it was June and not the middle of L.A.'s rainy season. We had the windows wide open and box fans blowing fresh, if somewhat humid, air around to rid the place of the cloying odor of new paint.

My room was on the second floor, like the others. Unlike them, I'd chosen a room in the front of the house, second door on the left, on the opposite side of the house from the rooms of my elders. It's funny that I still thought of them that way, even though, at thirty, Gage was as old as we got. Unless you counted Simon Hewitt, a former bad guy and current Teresa West Pet Project. He lived and worked in New York, though, with his son, Caleb, and wasn't technically part of the team.

They were all elder compared to my experience, I supposed, and in bloodline. My mother hadn't been a Ranger, nor had anyone else in her family. My father—such as he was—had no powers. Someone in one of their family trees had to have been Meta, but I had no idea who and really didn't care enough to research it. The direct descendants of the Ranger Corps were the five people I worked with every single day. Stories circulated about newly powered people popping up across the country. We'd publicly invited them to contact us. So far, they were keeping to themselves.

I popped into my bedroom to change. Its meager contents included a well-made bed, littered with overstuffed pillows, and a matching dresser. My favorite wicker rocking chair had followed me from my old apartment. An oversize, peeling white monster with a flat, faded cushion, it was the only thing from my mother's house I'd kept.

Sentimentality wasn't my strong suit. I had a shoe box of snapshots packed up in a carton along with the rest of my meager belongings—mostly books and a few academic award certificates. Spiffing up my personal space was less important than getting the rest of the house in order. No one would ever see the crappy interior of my bedroom, but the lobby and downstairs rooms presented an image to others. It had to be a good one.

I stripped out of my paint-splattered jeans and tank top, then did a quick skin check in the closet mirror, as had become a habit. Teresa had smudges of purple on her body, some more noticeable than others. Renee was completely blue. Marco had black and brown patches of velvet-soft fur all over his face, torso, and legs. Sections of Gage's hair reflected the same silver in his flecked eyes. Only Ethan had escaped noticeable discoloration.

So far, I had an orange streak that no brand of hair dye managed to hide, but no other major colorations on my body. Thank God. Even my eyes had remained light blue.

I slipped into a pair of clean, dark blue jeans and a white silk camisole. A brush through my hair separated the dried-together bits. I twisted the orange section into a rope, tucked it behind my right ear, and secured it with a barrette. Not too bad. Nothing like the timid journalist I'd been last year.

I opened the door and jumped back, barely missing Ethan's fist knocking into my nose. His other hand sported bandages on three fingertips.

"Hey," he said, "change your clothes. We've got a job."

Two

Sunset and Laurel

The "job" turned out to be a dead body on Sunset Boulevard. Two LAPD squad cars were double-parked on the street, lights flashing, when Trance parked our SUV behind them. Tempest and I tumbled out with her. The midday humidity felt like dragon's breath after the chill of the car's AC.

The Dream Parlor provided just what it advertised, in the form of exotic dancers and cheap booze. Housed in an old comedy club—as were many of the businesses on this strip of Sunset—its façade was painted in garish shades of yellow and green, with the silhouette of a naked woman parked between the *m* and *P* on the sign. Tacky, tasteless, and perfect for the neighborhood.

One of the uniformed officers pointed us left, toward an alley between the Dream Parlor and the vacant building next door. Trance started to thank him, but he'd already turned away. The snub didn't hurt, not like it had the first time I realized we were no longer city celebrities. We had become, without realizing it, people to fear. The public wanted us to help them out when needed, but otherwise stay far away.

Fear does strange things to people.

The alley reeked of stale beer, rotting food, and the general odor of human waste, all twisted up into one great, sickly stink. I bit down on the tip of my tongue, willing breakfast to stay put. I could handle broken bones and gushing blood; bad smells would not get the better of me.

A dozen yards down, past a collection of plastic trash cans and rotting cardboard boxes, stood a trio of people. A well-dressed man in a pressed blue suit and expensive shades hovered nearby, jotting something on a notepad. At his elbow was a brown-haired woman, conversely dressed in jeans and a tight, three-quarter-sleeved blouse. Detective partners we worked with occasionally—Pascal and Forney, if I recalled correctly. Another uniformed officer stood nearby, trying his best to melt into the brick wall. He saw us first, another trio in our own unique uniforms.

After quitting the Ranger Corps and the MHC payroll, Teresa had brainstormed a new idea for our uniforms: simple, slick black pants with a variety of zippered pockets, tank tops in our preferred color, woven through with armored thread, and matching black jackets. My color was orange, Trance's was silver, and Tempest's green. The stretchable Kevlar in our tank tops was a gift from the brain trust that was ATF Agent Rita McNally. She could come up with some unusual toys, and it made me glad she was on our side.

Trance approached the scene with confidence in her stride. Tempest and I flanked her, creating a perfect triangle.

My palms were sweaty and not from the day's heat. I schooled my face into the perfect picture of calm as we approached. The wall of human bodies parted, and I gazed down at my first murder victim.

And almost lost my breakfast.

It wasn't a body as much as it was a body's case. Skin, hair, and nails, in the perfect replica of a human being. The pink-and-tan body looked like an inflatable doll that had gone flat, but it wasn't plastic. The details were too perfect, from the lines around the empty eyes to the warts on the tops of the man's feet. There was no blood, no gore, no sign of the eye-balls or anything else that wasn't external.

A human slipcover.

"Oh boy," I muttered.

"You okay?" Tempest asked, a little pale himself. His good hand squeezed my shoulder.

I tore my eyes away from the graphic—yet, oddly, not gory—sight. "Yeah, I think so. Wh-what could do that to a person?"

"That's why we called you people in," Detective Forney said. She wore shockingly red lipstick and matching nail pol-ish. A scar ran the length of her left cheek, from ear to chin, thin as a pencil line, but noticeable in the bright daylight. Heavy makeup covered her face, thickest under her eyes and across the bridge of her nose, which seemed slightly swollen.

"You people?" Trance said, shoulders tensing.

"Yes, you guys, you people," she said. "Christ, don't be so touchy. We're doing you a favor by bringing you into this case."

Trance squared off with the mouthy detective. "Funny,

I assumed you brought us in because you don't have a clue what did this, or why, or how you'd fight it if you met it in a dark alley. Am I anywhere close, Detective Forney?"

Forney sneered. Detective Pascal placed a warning hand on her shoulder. A good six inches taller than his partner, he was an intimidating presence, and she backed off. Her hand brushed mine as she swept past and stalked down the alley to the street.

"She's not very good with people," Pascal said. "That's why she works homicide. Gets along great with dead bodies."

Tempest snickered.

Trance crouched over the skin. "I take it your forensics team will inform us of anything they find? Any indication of how the skin was removed and why."

"Of course," Pascal said. "Forney might not like you, but this is far beyond our abilities to solve alone. Maybe if there was some sign that the skin had been cut, some evidence of a knife or scraping tool, but there isn't. Everything that was inside the skin is just . . . gone."

Trance studied the scene with more control than I could have managed in her position. "I wish I had a quick answer for you. I can't recall any registered Bane with the power to do something like this." The majority of our repowered enemies were still living in Manhattan, on the island that had been turned into a prison at the end of the Meta War, and no one had been reported missing.

"Unregistered Metas have been popping up across the country," Pascal said. "This could be someone you've not encountered before."

"Possibly."

Tempest cocked his head to the left. "You have a theory, Trance?"

"Not yet."

Pascal's pocket jingled. He fished into it and retrieved a phone, flipped it open with his thumb, and pressed it to his ear. "Yeah, Mike?" Pause. His eyebrows arched. "Where was that again?" He wrote something on his pad. "Who?" Writing. "Okay, thanks, Mike."

Pascal enlightened us. "That was a pal over in the County Sheriff's Office. Eight days ago, they found one of these skin jobs in a Dumpster behind a diner out near the foothills. It was partially decomposed, and they guessed the time of death was two days earlier."

This wasn't an isolated incident. Someone was out there skinning people. Or sucking their insides out. Neither idea appealed to me.

"Did they identify their victim?" Trance asked.

"Yeah, a man named Ronald Jarvis," Pascal said, checking his notes. "Thirty-two, divorced, no kids. He worked for a place north of Studio City called Weatherfield Research and Development."

"Weatherfield?" I said. It was a name I'd not heard in years, and it made horrible, fascinating sense that Weatherfield could be involved, even tangentially, in something like this.

"Ember?" Trance said. "What is it? You look ill."

I swallowed. "Weatherfield R and D is a biological research center fronting as a hospital facility. They were the subject of my senior investigative piece. I wrote a thirty-page article on that place and got a failing grade because all I had to substantiate my claims were rumors."

"What claims?" Pascal asked.

"Genetic meddling, biological enhancement, cloning experiments, you name it. It's entirely possible, given what they're known to do, that one of their projects is our skin remover."

"What do you know, exactly?" Trance asked.

She crossed her arms over her chest, gazing at me like a professor challenging her student. I squared my shoulders, not intimidated by the familiar stance. For the last two years I had fought hard to get my dignity back, to rise above graduating last in a journalism class of one hundred and eleven students because I chose to write the article. I hadn't started my career writing for gossip rags for fun.

"When I was a junior at Cal State, I dated a guy," I said, nervous under the gaze of my attentive audience. "His name was Stan. He was an art student who worked two part-time jobs to make tuition. One day close to Christmas break, he answered an ad in the paper. Five hundred dollars cash if you volunteered for a five-day experiment. He didn't have family, and we weren't that serious, so he did it.

"He didn't come back for the winter term, and when I saw him again in the spring, he was different. Nervous, always pale and tired. He stopped eating, stopped doing his art. Eventually he dropped out. Over the summer I tracked him down at a mental hospital in Reno. He'd completely lost it. During cogent moments, he talked about Weatherfield. The experiment had killed a participant, and they'd all been paid to keep quiet.

"A lot of it was delusional rambling, but it got me interested in Weatherfield in a huge way. I talked to more students who'd signed up, but they wouldn't tell me anything. No one would go on the record. Weatherfield never returned my calls."

My heart was pounding faster than was healthy. Adrenaline had kicked in at some point during my story. I hadn't thought about Stan for ages. He and Weatherfield were no longer part of my conscious mind—just part of my past mistakes. My skin felt warm, flushed, the air around us a few degrees cooler.

"Ember?" Tempest said.

"I know." I closed my eyes and concentrated on my emotions, squashing the anger back into place. Every time I thought I had a handle on my powers, something took that control away. The flush dispersed. "Sorry."

"It's okay," Trance said. She turned to Pascal, who had distanced himself from me. "Did your friend question Jarvis's employers at Weatherfield?"

Pascal nodded. "He said Jarvis had no enemies at work. No high-priority projects that might incur jealousy among fellow employees. Everyone was surprised he died, and no one noticed him missing because it was a weekend." His gaze flickered toward the ground. "Mike said he got fingerprints off his vic, so we should be able to get an ID on ours."

"I hope so, because you don't have any teeth to check against dental records."

"You sure you're not a cop?"

She smiled. "I read a lot, Detective, and I have a lot of smart people around me. I assume you brought us in for a reason, so if we choose to investigate independently, will I have the support of the LAPD?"

"I'll vouch for you."

"What about your partner?"

"She will, too, even if she doesn't know it yet."

"Thank you. I promise to not abuse your trust."

Pascal nodded and left the alley, already dialing a number on his phone. Trance squatted over the shell of skin, near the remains of the face. I forced myself to look, to learn and understand what she was doing.

Five holes dotted the face: two eyes, nostrils, and the mouth. The lips were gone, only smooth flesh indicating where they had been. Eyebrows and eyelashes were intact, as was the shadow of an unshaven beard. Nothing about the body was ragged or violated. Everything in perfect order, just empty.

"Did you mean it before?" Tempest asked. "When you said you couldn't think of a single Bane who could do this?"

"Of course I meant it," Trance replied. "I have no reason to lie to him."

"So you would have told him if you could think of a Bane?"

Her violet eyes flashed. "Yes, Tempest, I would have. As much as I want the Banes to be forgiven for their past crimes, that does not extend to present ones. If one of them is killing now, I want them brought to justice."

"Just checking, boss."

The near fight ended as quickly as it began, but something had sparked between the pair. Tempest and Flex openly disagreed with Trance's position on the imprisoned Banes. Trance wanted to see them pardoned, released, and allowed to live regular lives. Many of the Banes had expressed similar wishes over the last few months. They no longer had a leader to fight for; many had established some semblance of a life on Manhattan Island and desired to stay—with freedoms intact and supplies made readily available.

In Trance's eyes, we were all MetaHumans. She reserved the term *Bane* for those still operating outside of the law, rather than a blanket label for the sixty-odd adults who once opposed our predecessors. A fresh start, she called it.

Tempest and Flex stood in the opposite corner of the boxing ring. Both had been terribly hurt—the former physically, the latter emotionally—six months ago. No one expected the hurt to go away quickly, but they clung to it like a safety blanket. The Banes had not changed, and they never would. In their eyes, evil never died. It only hibernated awhile before rearing its terrible head.

I didn't take sides in the argument. I never felt I had the right. I could never hope to walk in their shoes. Everything I'd done, every move I'd made over the last six months had been about making my own path.

Rangers and Banes were things of the past. All we had now was the present.

"So what's our next step?" I asked. "Weatherfield?"

Trance stood up. "Definitely Weatherfield. They're connected to this case, even if the killer isn't from their facility. One of the victims definitely is, and for all we know, there are more than two."

A sense of triumph settled warmly in my chest. After all these years, a chance to finally set foot inside of the Weatherfield facility; enter the walls that had destroyed Stan's mind and spirit and left an empty husk in its place.

"We should bring Cipher along," Tempest said, and Trance agreed. She had her com out and dialing as we headed back to our car.

Three

Weatherfield

To save time, we picked up Gage "Cipher" McAllister a few blocks from the house; we still had a good twenty minutes of traffic maneuvering between us and Weatherfield. He climbed into the backseat with me, in his blue-topped uniform, and Trance sped off toward the freeway.

Cipher's hyper-enhanced senses would make any interrogation expert turn green. He could hear heartbeats a hundred yards away, had a vision range of a quarter mile, and possessed the sensitive nose of a bloodhound. He'd also taught himself to combine his senses and create a unique organic lie detector. Changes in blood pressure, heart rate, sweating, and body temperature were all easy clues in the game of deceit.

Though the heart of the film industry had moved north years ago, music remained a cash cow in Los Angeles, along with other entrepreneurial enterprises. Traffic on the freeways remained heavy as citizens traveled north to south, from Van Nuys and Burbank down to Pasadena, and farther south to Long Beach. Most of the exits to and from West Hollywood, Chinatown, Inglewood, and Santa Monica saw little use, and sat cracked and empty. The center of old L.A. was for the poor, the hiding, and people like us—outsiders, all.

The Weatherfield compound took up an entire city block. Double rows of chain-link fence ran the perimeter, topped with razor wire and security cameras. A four-story parking structure occupied the north corner. Two large buildings took over the rest. The second and fourth floors were connected by glassed-in walkways. It looked like a hospital or office building, with no outward signs of its sinister interior. A single gate emerged out of nowhere, and Trance had to hit the brakes to avoid shooting past.

She paused at the guard hut and rolled down her window. The guard, sweaty and red-faced in his black uniform and hat, took one look at her, a quick look into the van at the rest of us, and dashed back into his concrete and glass hut. He picked up a phone, said something, and nodded. The phone went back into the cradle and he poked his head outside.

"Visitor parking is on the first level," he said. "Dr. Kinsey will meet you there."

The gate buzzed and parted. A thrill danced up my spine as we drove through. Years ago, I had stood on the sidewalk across the street, desperate for a way in, never dreaming I would be invited inside to poke around.

The parking structure was dimly lit and chilly. It reeked of gasoline, exhaust fumes, and something else. Something darker, mysterious. Dank places like basements and garages give me the creeps. We walked back into the brilliant sunlight, and I basked in the glow. Much better.

Past an immaculate flower garden and a tended lawn, we found the main entrance to Weatherfield Research and Development. A revolving glass doorway welcomed us inside. Passing through the spiral was like entering another world.

The odor of antiseptic hit me hard and tempted a sneeze. I pinched my nose and squinted under the glare of bright fluorescent lighting. The lobby floor was polished white marble, the walls painted a sparkling silver-gray. A stark white security desk took up the center of the room, punctuated by a bank of monitors. Black and white leather sofas created a small waiting area immediately to the right, near a long line of tinted windows. On the left was a bank of elevators, four in a row, each gleaming chrome surface reflecting our images back to us with perfect clarity.

The desk guard stood up. He looked just as uncomfortable in his black uniform as the guard outside had, and I suddenly smiled. Even the guards matched the décor. Not a single potted plant or hint of color anywhere.

"Dr. Kinsey will be with you in a moment," the guard said. His name badge read Smith.

Yeah, right.

Smith stared openly. He either didn't know he was being rude, or plain didn't care.

The elevator dinged; the doors to the first on the left slid open. The man who emerged wasn't the stodgy, bespectacled scientist schlub I'd expected to see running the show. Dr. Kinsey had a lean, swimmer's body that he showed off beneath brown slacks, a royal blue shirt, and immaculate tie. No lab coat, no clipboard or spectacles. Just thick brown hair, cut short in a style almost spiky and modern. His pale eyes might have been hazel. He had a neatly trimmed mustache and goatee that showed no trace of gray, even though he had to be at least forty, if not older. The only giveaway that he might be a doctor at all was the silver stethoscope looped around his neck.

His attention moved around the room, landing on me last. He narrowed his eyes and practically snarled, "No press. You can ask your questions, but no press is allowed in here."

My throat squeezed. I was so taken aback by his anger, I couldn't utter a word in my own defense. His voice had a dry, sandpaper quality that was at once commanding and frightening.

Trance took a step forward, unafraid. "She isn't a journalist anymore, sir, she's one of us."

He didn't seem to hear her. "I remember you," he said, still glaring at me. "You caused a lot of trouble a few years ago. What is it with you, girl? You get off on this?"

"Hey!" Trance snapped her fingers. A violet orb the size of a grapefruit hovered above her hand, twirling and crackling, and finally got his attention. "That's better. Now, if you would curb the attitude for a minute, I will reiterate that Ember is a member of my team. She is not a reporter, and if you deny her access, you can just explain to Detective Pascal and the LAPD that you are not cooperating with an official investigation. Understand?"

He narrowed his eyes at Trance, then at the orb. "Put that thing away. We're not here to fight, just share information."

"That's what I thought."

Turns out he *was* Dr. Abram Kinsey, head of the biogenics lab and our tour guide for the afternoon. Trance introduced everyone; Kinsey barely nodded in our direction. Trance was in charge, which made her the one with whom he wanted to speak.

"You're here about Ronald Jarvis," Kinsey said.

"Yes, we are," Trance replied.

"Then let's take this into my office."

He gestured at the elevator, and we boarded it one by one. I hid in the back, trying to stay away from Kinsey and his angry eyes. Just because I'd tossed around some careless accusations two years ago did not mean I was the same person. I knew better now. Knew to have evidence to support my claims, and I knew the devastating effects of not having any.

No one spoke during the ride up to the sixth floor. The doors opened on a corridor as silent as a tomb. Sky-blue linoleum floors, ivory walls, and intermittent oak doors lined the hall. Polished brass nameplates hung on each door, and we passed half a dozen before Kinsey produced a plastic card from his pocket, swiped it, and pushed open a door.

His office was homier than I expected. A heavy walnut desk took up half of the open space, flanked on both sides by wall-to-wall bookshelves overloaded with texts—books, binders, manuscripts, all sorts of words on paper. More than I'd read in my lifetime. Thick blue drapes were pulled back from the room's twin windows, letting in shafts of afternoon sunlight.

Kinsey sat in a high-backed leather armchair and waved his hand at the only other two chairs in the room. Tempest and I stood by one of the bookshelves, allowing Cipher and Trance to sit. They were there to engage; we were backup.

"You mentioned the LAPD before," Kinsey said, leaning forward on his elbows. "I thought the L.A. County sheriff was handling the Jarvis investigation."

"They are," Trance said. "But our contacts are in the LAPD."

Not quite a bald-faced lie. She was playing him, hoping Cipher could tell if Kinsey was playing her. They had a system worked out, which I had witnessed only once. Cipher sat loosely in his chair, right ankle on left knee, hands flat on his thighs. If the interviewee was lying, his left hand clenched into a fist. If it was the truth, he kept his palm flat. If he couldn't tell, he curled the fingers up.

Kinsey seemed to buy her explanation. "So, has there been any headway into Mr. Jarvis's death?"

"Not so far." Trance settled back, getting comfortable. "Tell me about Mr. Jarvis, Doctor."

"He was a lab assistant, a position that is two rungs up from janitor. He had no enemies that I knew of, and everyone seemed to get along with him. Dr. Morrow was his supervisor. He never attended social functions, but I think it's because he suffered from acute adult acne. He wasn't an outgoing man."

Cipher's palm remained flat.

"Did he have access to any of your projects?"

"And what projects would those be?" He smiled, but it was disingenuous and very creepy.

"You tell me, Dr. Kinsey."

"No, I don't think I will, Trance, not without a warrant."

"Warrant?"

He nodded, a slow tilt up and down. "Yes, a warrant. You see, our success here at Weatherfield requires a certain amount of discretion. Our work is often under contract, and our employers count on secrecy. If we started chatting up top secret work to everyone who asked, we'd be out of a job very quickly."

"We're trying to capture a killer," she said. "Isn't a little indiscretion worth a man's life?"

"Not to me, no. Jarvis is already dead. His life is now worthless to me."

I bristled, standing up straighter. *Son of a bitch, how dare you call a human being's life worthless!* Tempest clamped a hand over my wrist. His perfect calm kept me cool.

Trance sat up straight and slid forward in her seat. "What if I said it was no longer just about Jarvis's life, Doctor? What if I said there was a second victim?"

Kinsey's face went slack. "Who?"

"We don't have a positive identification yet, but it's another male. If I were you, I'd start checking if any other employees never showed up this morning."

"Jarvis has a coincidental connection to this place," Kinsey said. "You have no proof that the killer has anything to do with Weatherfield, and until you have more to go on than the suspicious nature of a former reporter"—he glared directly at me—"you should watch what accusations you're throwing around."

Cipher's fingers curled, tapped on the leg of his jeans. He was uncertain, confused by mixed signals.

"I apologize if I offended you," Trance said. "But the second victim was killed in the exact same fashion as Ronald Jarvis. Skin left behind, every bit of blood, organs, and bone completely disintegrated. Or removed. The point is, we don't know how or why or who, which means there's a chance the killer will strike again."

Kinsey settled. Some of the fight drained away, and he just seemed tired. "Why are you involved in this?"

"The nature of the deaths means it could be Meta related. We have to follow every lead."

He snorted. "Follow every lead, or try your best to prove it wasn't one of yours by making up stories about this facility?"

"Touché, but to be fair, I don't know what this facility does." Trance stood up and clasped her hands behind her back in a demure pose. "Perhaps you could enlighten us. Change my mind, Dr. Kinsey."

Kinsey's mouth opened, closed. Trance had spun a perfect web and captured him in it. "If any of this shows up on the front page of some—"

"It won't. You have my word."

He stared at me. "Mine, too," I said. "I'm not a reporter anymore."

"Fine," he said after a brief pause. "Come with me."

We took the elevator down to the second floor. The doors opened on a very different scene, a waiting room decorated with vivid colors—blues and greens and reds and yellows, splashed on the walls and chairs and carpet. Picture books and games were stacked neatly on tables shaped like insects. On the other side of the room, novels and magazines littered a simple oak coffee table.

A lime-green front desk guarded a set of double doors, all steel and reinforced glass. The attendant, a woman in pink nurse's scrubs, smiled when she spotted us. No one was in the waiting room, but I caught the faint hum of music.

"Good afternoon, Dr. Kinsey," the woman said. "You brought visitors?"

"Yes, I did, Sasha," he replied. "These Rangers are looking into Ronald's death, and they wanted a quick look around."

Sasha's face fell. Sadness bracketed her round eyes. "So sad, what happened to Ronald. He was such a good guy, you know? He brought cookies for the kids."

"What kids?" Cipher asked.

"No one's out here now," Sasha said. "It's therapy time, so everyone's together, but sometimes they have to come out of the rooms for a while." That explained the little waiting room.

"Is it okay if we go inside?" Kinsey asked.

"Sure, just don't go into the rooms. Like I said, therapy time." She looked past him, at us, like she was sharing a secret. "We don't like to disturb therapy. It could contaminate the results."

Kinsey swiped his card, punched in a code, and the doors unlocked. He pushed and went inside. Tempest and I continued bringing up the rear. I liked the support role; it gave me time to observe.

We walked down a short corridor and stepped out into a circular room at least thirty feet in diameter. The curved walls were glass panels, marked every couple of yards by a glass door. Curtains were drawn everywhere, cutting off any view into those rooms, but I suspected that's where the therapy happened. The center of the room held an assortment of tables and chairs. Chess and checkers games, stopped mid-play. Card games equally interrupted. Drawing paper and stubby crayons, storybooks and construction paper littered the floor nearby.

"This is our psychiatric ward," Kinsey said. "All of our patients are volunteers, or are here under the written consent of family members. We use unorthodox methods to reach adults who are mentally handicapped through illness or accidents, and our results are promising."

"What does unorthodox mean?" Trance asked.

"It means we don't feed them stimulants, get them to talk about their feelings, and then call it treatment. Beyond that, until we have enough research to patent those methods, you'll need your warrant."

"Alternative therapy seems legitimate to me," Tempest said. "Why not put that in your brochure?"

"Because we don't advertise for patients, Tempest," Kinsey said. "The ones we can help have a talent for finding us without assistance."

"So you have a flair for psychiatry," Trance said. "What else do you do?"

"Research." Kinsey smiled, as unsettling as the first time. "And development."

The interview ended soon after. I didn't start to relax until we hit the sidewalk, back under the kiss of the afternoon sun. That place stifled me, like a hand closing in and squeezing tight. Some of their work sounded promising, but the things Kinsey wouldn't talk about scared me the most. He was hiding something behind a warrant, and we had no grounds to get one.

"He was pretty honest," Cipher said as we entered the parking garage. "He was probably protecting their other projects, but he wasn't lying about Jarvis. I hate to say it—"

"But you're going to," Tempest said.

Cipher frowned. "He may be right about the coincidence. The killer could have no connection to Weatherfield, other than his choice of victim."

"You know that from a ten-minute conversation?" I asked, unable to keep the snap from my voice. Amazingly, I didn't blush or back down.

"First impression, Ember, that's all. And it's possible Jarvis wasn't even the first victim, just the first one found. I imagine after a while, skin gets harder to recognize as human than an entire corpse would."

My stomach clenched. "That's so gross."

"So what now?" Tempest asked.

"Home," Trance replied, unlocking the SUV. "I'll check in with Pascal, see if he's got anything new, but—"

"What time is it?" I asked, a mental lightbulb flaring.

Trance hopped inside, turned the key, and checked the clock. "A few minutes after three, why?"

I slid into the back, sort of wishing I hadn't asked. With two related deaths to investigate, my other assigned task seemed superfluous. "I, um, still need to find us an electrician and most places close at five."

"You wouldn't rather concentrate on finding the manufacturer of human pillowcases?" Tempest asked as he climbed in next to me.

"Here I thought you and your singed fingertips would thank me."

"Says the Human Fire Extinguisher."

"Windbag."

He winked. "Thank you for refraining from a very bad pun."

Cipher twisted around in the front seat, amusement dancing in his silver-flecked eyes. "You mean by saying you're full of hot air?"

I groaned. Tempest blew Cipher a kiss. Cipher blew a raspberry. The pair looked more like feuding siblings than adult superheroes. I started giggling.

"Children," Trance said, watching us in the rearview mirror, "I will turn this car right around—"

"He started it," we three said in perfect unison. A moment of utter silence preceded a long dissolve into laughter. After the horrors of the human skin and the unsettling nature of Weatherfield, the release felt wonderful.

I relaxed into the backseat, still grinning, and pondered our electrician problem. That, at least, I could solve.

Four

Scott & Sons

After a quick change back into street clothes and a glance through an outdated phone directory, I left Hill House in one of our tinted-window Sport utilities, air-conditioning blasting full speed, and music pumped up. One of the things I missed most about my old apartment was listening to anything I wanted at any volume that I wanted. My neighbors were either deaf, stoned, or never at home, so no one complained. No one ever noticed my presence, as a matter of fact, unless rent was late. Then the landlord noticed plenty. Working for a struggling gossip rag and writing free-lance articles is no way to earn a living in this gasping-for-life town.

Growing up here, I knew the area by heart and had no trouble navigating my way into West Hollywood. My intended destination was Scott & Sons Electrical, and I hoped it still existed. The ad had caught my attention and jogged my memory. I'd attended high school with a boy named Noah Scott, until I changed districts in the middle of my junior year. I vaguely recalled him saying his parents owned an electric supply store. If I was going to trust our sanctuary to anyone, my first choice was someone I had a quasihistory with—as long as his parents hadn't sold the shop to someone else, or closed down along with hundreds of other businesses during the post–Meta War years.

I turned onto Vine and spotted the colorful storefront situated between two discount liquor stores, each advertising the lowest prices in town. The walls were relatively free of graffiti and seemed freshly painted. The red-and-white sign over the glass-and-iron doors announced Scott & Sons Electrical.

The windows were papered over, as was the front door, giving the place an air of disuse. But a plastic sign said Open and listed the business hours. I pulled the handle; an interior bell chimed.

Nerves settled into my stomach like a cloud of butterflies. I pulled harder and the door squealed as it opened. To my immediate left, a long row of fixtures dangled from the ceiling, each one apparently connected. On the wall was a bank of switches, each labeled with a code, probably for the individual chandeliers and lanterns. All shapes and sizes, from gaudy jeweled monstrosities to simple curved bamboo balloons.

On the right was a wall of inset shelving, and dozens of lamp displays. Most of them were the kind you attach directly to the wall, but several were table lamps.

Two more steps in and a warm vanilla-sugar scent sent the nervous butterflies packing. It could have been incense, or a crock of scented oil. At the far end of the narrow room, an empty sales counter stared back at me. A door stood open behind it, a gaping black hole. No music, only the gentle squeaks of my sneakers on the polished wood floor.

"Hello?" I said, too softly. I cleared my throat, making a point of it. "Is someone here?"

A thud directly above my head promptly preceded the sound of footsteps thundering down a flight of stairs. I watched the door behind the counter, waiting halfway between it and the door. My fight or flight reflex was starting to kick in, and flight was winning.

Dirty sneakers descended from the darkness, followed by tight, ripped jeans and a T-shirt clad torso. An unbuttoned flannel shirt, sleeves rolled up, flapped in the wind he created as he charged forward. I looked up, past a narrow jaw, and into the brightest green eyes I had ever seen on a human being (except for Marco, but his eyes weren't quite natural).

If he wasn't Noah Scott, he was definitely related. He was about my age, with spiky auburn hair and a light smattering of freckles on his sharp nose. He stood about my height, thin-waisted, muscles rippling beneath his tight T-shirt. A runner, maybe, or a swimmer. Nothing like the skinny, gangly boy I remembered from high school. That boy had enjoyed loose clothes, kept his hair shaggy and long, and he couldn't possibly have been so handsome. Even his eyes seemed a brighter green than before.

Of course, a distance of eight years can change your perception of a person.

Slim eyebrows arched as he studied me back. Wide lips

puckered into a silent question, and he tilted his head to one side.

"Can I help you?" he asked. His voice had a rough quality, like sandpaper.

I licked my lips, trying to calm the butterflies in my stomach. "Yes," I said. "I, um, need lights." I could have slapped myself. Obvious and stupid.

His smile broadened, baring bright white but somewhat crooked teeth. Some small amount of recognition had crept into his eyes—it could have as easily been knowing me as Ember as remembering me as Dahlia from school.

"You're in luck, because that's all we sell here," he said.

I laughed, feeling like an idiot, and walked confidently up to his counter and squared my shoulders. His eyes dropped briefly to my chest, and I had the sudden, irrational urge to flee this shop and never look back.

"What kind of lighting do you need?" he asked.

"All kinds. We're, um, remodeling an older home and a lot of the ceiling fixtures need to be replaced. That's our biggest need right now. And installation. Ethan's not so good at it."

"Your boyfriend?"

"My what?"

"You said Ethan isn't good at installation. Is he your boyfriend?"

Laughter bubbled in my chest, but I tamped it down. Maybe-Noah was much more Ethan's type than I was. "No, he's not my boyfriend. One of my roommates. A bunch of us are fixing up the house together."

He walked around the counter and stopped an arm's length away. I liked that we were the same height; I didn't have to strain my neck to stay under his intense gaze. His eyes roamed all over. Most days, I would have walked off in a huff after being openly appraised like that. With this maybe-not-a-stranger, I rather enjoyed the attention. Even living with five other people, I was often lonely.

"Do you see anything you like?" he asked.

"Oh, yeah." His eyebrows shot up, and I realized what I just said. "I mean, I haven't really looked at your lights." Eyebrows higher. "What you have to offer, I mean." Lordy, there was nothing coming out of my mouth that didn't sound like innuendo. Teresa would kill me if I screwed this up.

"How about some track lighting?" he asked, indicating the wall behind me. "Brightens up a room pretty quick, and you can set it on a dimmer switch. How many rooms?"

"Quite a few." Good, simple answer to a simple question. I was back on track to having an intelligent conversation. "We don't need all of them done at once, but there are half a dozen rooms downstairs, and at least six on the second floor."

"The house sounds huge."

"It's in Beverly Hills."

His lips parted in surprise. "Wow, that's an interesting neighborhood to pick. Few people can afford those houses."

Dollar signs danced between us, taunting. It was a social barrier that I'd never dealt with, growing up—at least, not from the rich side of the line. I never wanted money from my father, and I ignored my trust fund when I turned eighteen. Mom's insurance paid most of her medical bills. Everything I had, I earned on my own. I was no different than this man in front of me, self-made and struggling to be independent. But the squint in his eyes, the harder line of his mouth, indicated he didn't know that. He just knew I had money. Money he could make.

"It's a group effort," I said. I wanted him to understand and didn't know why. "We needed a big place with good security. A bungalow in Inglewood wasn't going to do it for us."

"So you're looking for at least a dozen fixtures," he said, as though I hadn't spoken. "Plus installation and any necessary rewiring. Some of those old places can have exposed wires that cause shorts. Fires. You should definitely have a thorough inspection."

I bristled. Yeah, he was milking those dollar signs. Ass. "Do you provide those services?"

"As a matter of fact, we do. Why don't—" Footsteps thumped down the back stairs, cutting off his train of thought. We both turned toward the sound.

A girl appeared behind the counter, maybe eighteen or twenty years old. She had long black hair and equally long legs that disappeared beneath a short, white skirt. "Hey, Noah, how come I always—" Her almond-shaped eyes landed on me. "Oh, sorry. Didn't realize you had a customer."

Okay, so he was definitely my old schoolmate. Someone I obviously hadn't made an impression on, since he'd yet to indicate he remembered me.

Noah eyed the girl's outfit, from the white stiletto sandals to the low-cut orange tank top barely reining in her breasts. "Are you going out in that?"

"Sure." She twirled, the flared skirt riding up a little too high for decency. "Why the hell not?"

"You look like a hooker."

She belted out the perfect flirtatious giggle. "You think I'm going to go out and pick up some strange man to bring home? Be serious."

"Just be careful." He sighed, and I wondered if he'd had this conversation before.

She blew a kiss and flounced out the front door.

"Sorry about that," Noah said.

I shrugged. "What were you saying?"

"I was going to suggest I make an appointment to inspect the property. I'll be able to get a better idea of your needs, see the wiring as it is, and know where things are going to fit. Then I can order what I don't have in stock, and we can start getting you guys set up."

"Sure. What's good for you?"

"How about right now?"

Right now? "Um, can you just leave the shop?"

"I kind of run it myself, so I make my own hours."

"Your brothers don't help?"

He stiffened. No longer a businessman, he tensed up like an animal who'd been spotted by a predator. Stupid me.

"You don't remember me, do you?" I asked, hoping to put his mind at ease so he didn't think I was some crazy stalker. "Parker High School?"

A light came on behind his eyes and he blinked. His lips parted, and I finally saw recognition. He relaxed in the space of a breath, going from attack-ready to laid-back with the ease of someone used to putting up a strong front. "I knew you looked familiar, I just couldn't place you. Darla . . . no, that's not right. A flower. Dahlia."

I grinned. "Yeah, Dahlia Perkins."

"We had a lot of classes together in ninth grade, didn't we? Not so many in tenth."

"Yeah, and then I moved." Mom's job necessitated the move farther south to Anaheim. It was still years before she realized six of her organs had been eaten up by cancer.

It occurred to me that if Noah was running a family-owned shop at his age, there had to be tragedy in his recent past. Had his parents died?

"Yeah, I wondered about that." He waved one hand to indicate the shop. "My younger brother, Jimmy, helps out when he can, and Aaron, the older one, he . . . isn't in the city anymore. He likes to travel." He cleared his throat. "So, do you want me to follow you back to your place?"

And just like that, we're off Memory Lane and back on topic. "Sure, I'm a block up in a black SUV."

"Give me three minutes to lock up and get my van."

I leaned back in the driver's seat, cool air trickling from the Sport's vents, trying to catch my breath. Noah Scott. Just thinking his name made my heart race with all of my pent-up loneliness. My relationships were few and far between, the last one ending with acute mental illness. It made sense that I'd be attracted to a cute, former-friend electrician who looked great in tight denim.

It didn't hurt that we had a history. Sort of. Between keeping up with classes and nursing my mother through to the end of her illness, I hadn't maintained an outside social life. No friends called me on weekends. No guys were lining up to take me out to nice restaurants. My entire dating history for the last year consisted of two awkward dates with Marco and a nonbreakup that nearly destroyed our working relationship. I just hadn't returned his feelings, and even six weeks later I couldn't shake the feeling that it was all my fault. That if I'd just tried harder, I wouldn't have broken his heart.

But Noah . . . I could easily be attracted to him, if I let myself.

Doubt crept in on stealthy feet as I remembered the Asian girl and her mile-long legs. Him asking about her outfit meant she kept clothes there. The banter was familiar, protective. And the look in his eyes when he realized I had money—a wall had gone up immediately, putting a distance between us where none had existed.

Why are you worrying about this when there's a job to do?

A white service van trundled down the block to my vehicle. Work was my priority; everything else had to wait.

Five

Noah Scott

Fifteen minutes later, I entered the security code on the gate at Hill House and it squealed open. I drove forward and waved out the window for the van to follow. His engine ground. He backed up a few feet, and then made a sharp turn toward the driveway. I watched in the rearview, amused, wondering if he had just learned to drive in the last few days. He pulled up behind me and hopped out. He wore the same jeans but had changed shirts, swapping the flannel for a blue polo with his name stitched over the right breast pocket in yellow thread. Sunlight glinted off his eyes, making them radiate emerald fire.

I climbed out of the Sport and met him by his van door.

"Hey," he drawled, and then whistled low. "Nice digs, Dahlia."

Those dollar signs hung between us again. "Um, thanks."

He opened the side door and rummaged around until he produced a white toolbox, then followed me up the front steps. I still wasn't certain if he recognized me as Ember, or if he suspected who lived here. The mystery wouldn't last long if we ran into Renee or Marco.

The house had a long wraparound porch across the entire front and halfway down the east side. A peeling, rusty porch swing shifted in the breeze. Our footsteps creaked the boards. One of the double doors stood open, allowing light to filter through the stained-glass insert. Dots of red, blue, and green hit the porch and created a mosaic of color.

We entered to the overwhelming odor of fresh paint and the steady thrum of music. Distant, but not upward, it had to be coming from the kitchen located at the very back corner of the main floor.

Noah gazed around the spacious foyer, glistening with its new paint and polished baseboards. It would be impressive when we got the floor finished, furniture moved in, and a few items added. Teresa had commissioned a glass case to display several items very personal to the old Rangers, including a shadow box that held one of her father's uniforms.

Noah walked to the center of the lobby and stared straight up. His neck stretched gracefully, creating a perfect line with back and spine. It was the purposeful stance of someone seeking—

"Dahlia?"

I jerked my head. He was asking me a question. "I'm sorry, what?"

"I asked if you would be replacing the fixture here in the lobby."

"What do you think?"

He raised one shoulder in a half shrug. "I think it's in good working order and doesn't show signs of age. As much as I'd like the commission on one more installation, I'm not afraid to admit I think you should keep it."

Wow, more honesty than I expected. "Then we'll keep it."

Footsteps approached from the hall leading back toward the dining room and kitchen. Gage came through the arch. He stopped, a question on his lips, eyes glued to Noah.

Noah gazed back, curiosity shifting to something that looked a lot like recognition. "Hey. Noah Scott, Scott and Sons Electrical."

After a brief pause, he said, "Gage," and shook Noah's hand. "You seem young for an electrician."

"I am. Took over when my dad passed away. It seemed important to keep the business in the family."

Gage considered him a moment longer—I recognized the signs. He was reading him, checking his pulse rate for signs of deception. Having a human lie detector on the team was useful, but having one as a roommate could be a little invasive.

"Have fun with the tour," Gage finally said. He continued past, to the opposite hall, toward the War Room.

"How many others live here with you?" Noah asked.

"Five, so there's six of us total," I said. His jaw twitched, eyes darted in the direction Gage had just gone. "We're all like a family."

"I'd imagine so."

"Why's that?"

He froze, as if unsure of his next move—admit what he suspected, or play dumb. "Just that, you know, after everything you guys went through earlier this year . . ."

"Right." My smile seemed to quell his nerves a bit.

"So are you going to show me?" he asked.

I blinked. "Show you?"

"The rest of the rooms that need fixtures."

Duh. "Of course, come with me."

Beneath the main staircase, we followed the right hall past the infirmary and a small alcove, through another door to the dining room. We had two folding tables and chairs set up, with plans to get something nicer and more permanent when construction was finished. The room was painted, the laminate floor laid down. All it needed was curtains and a chandelier of some sort. Exposed wiring hung from a gaping hole in the middle of the room.

"You know what you need here?" he said. "Two smaller fixtures instead of one big one. It'll disperse the light more, make it look brighter and bigger. We have some classy ones in the shop. I think they'll look nice in here."

"Okay."

He put down the toolbox and retrieved a notepad from his back pocket, jotted something down, then looked back up. "Next?"

The kitchen was a spacious area with two islands, a gigantic walk-in refrigerator, and two huge cupboards. We could store two years' worth of food in there, easy. I imagined the previous owners liked to throw lavish parties with tons of food. He suggested only a few minor tweaks, and we moved on. Two small storage rooms were empty, so we left them alone for now, and continued.

Our path cut back around toward the lobby, down the left passage and past the War Room and archives. I steered him along with no real explanation, and he didn't ask.

"Are we just looking at the first floor today?" he asked. He sounded so professional I kept forgetting he was my age. Part of me wanted to ask why he was running the shop alone. The tactful part of my brain knew it was none of my business.

"No, we can go up. We haven't really started working on the third floor or the attic yet, so we don't have to check them out today."

First upstairs stop was the lounge, site of that morning's fire hazard. Noah inspected the hole and surrounding wiring.

"It won't all have to be replaced," he said. "Just a few of the wires, where they got singed. This one will need at least two ceiling fixtures, maybe a floor lamp or two for ambient lighting, in case you just want to curl up with a book and read."

"I used to love that," I said.

"Used to?"

I thought of my favorite chair, residing in my current bedroom. I'd pull it close to the dirty window in my dingy old apartment, curl up with a blanket and mug of tea, and read anything I could get my hands on. I wanted a library here one day, rife with the scents of wood, polish, old leather, and dusty paper.

Fingers snapped in front of my eyes. "Where'd you go?" he asked.

"Just thinking."

"From the way you were smiling, it must have been a good thought."

I looked away, embarrassed, but controlling the heat I allowed to escape to my face.

"Hey, you two!" Renee's voice blasted through the room moments before she bounced in. And bounced was quite literal. She was so proud of her boob job, and her low tank top showed every curve and jiggle.

"Just wanted to catch you," she said. "The light switch in my room doesn't work. I mean, I have a lamp and that's fine, but just so you know, it's either the switch or outlet."

"Thank you," Noah said. He stared right at her. I couldn't tell if it was her skin, her breasts, or both. If he had any doubts that we were the old Rangers, they should have been thoroughly squashed by her blue bustline. "I'll be sure to check it out when we get there, Miss . . . ?"

"Renee."

"Noah."

"Very nice to meet you," she purred. To me, she added, "Boy, Dal, when you pick them, you know how to pick them. The last electrician I met couldn't keep his jeans up past his butt crack."

He laughed, a pleasant sound that rumbled deeply in his chest. "I assure you, Renee, I don't have that problem."

I couldn't imagine he did. As nice as he looked in his clothes, though, they didn't seem quite right. He was at work, same as me, therefore in uniform—one he didn't seem completely at ease in, despite his professional attitude. Did he wear a costume, as well? Was the real him somewhere underneath that embroidered polo, waiting to be off the clock and free?

"Well, don't let our Dahlia bore you too much, Noah."

The barbed statement stung, even if Renee meant it as a joke. She flounced—bounced?—out of the room, long blond hair streaming behind her. She was a force, a presence in my life as strong as a thunderhead and as pleasant as a sleet storm. I drifted toward one of the large picture windows and gazed out onto the front lawn. It was badly in need of a mow and some grass vitamins—or whatever you give grass to make it green and thick.

"Does she always get to you like that?" Noah asked, so close that I jumped. His hand brushed my elbow.

"I am boring." My breath created little clouds of vapor on the glass.

"You're a superhero, Dahlia. How could that be boring?"

"I haven't done anything heroic in my life." The day I "came out" as a Meta, all I did was hide and cower while an explosion burned a news station to the ground. I let Teresa and Gage save me. I did nothing while their friend William Hill died—a death I could have prevented if I'd come out of my shock and tried to stop the inferno that had trapped him. How could I expect Renee to forgive me when I hadn't forgiven myself for my part in William's awful death?

Noah spun me around, gentle but firm, and searched my face. "I don't think that's true."

"You don't know me." *Way to be defensive, Dal, great job.*

"I'd like to." Something unspoken lingered in his gaze,

strong enough to make me uncomfortable. I stepped around him and retreated a few steps.

"We should finish the inspection," I said.

His eyes flashed, something hard, tired. "Yeah, sorry."

On that note, we continued.

Noah took copious notes on the rooms as we came and went. Our circuit took us the long way back around toward the staircase. The shared bathrooms were there, a feature left over from the days of taking in borders. It certainly showed the age of the mansion. He inspected another empty bedroom, and then turned toward a door in the corner of the hall, diagonal from the bathrooms.

"We missed one," he said.

Quite on purpose. I had avoided taking him into my bedroom, fear pushing me into every other room on the floor first. It wasn't until we were there that I realized my mistake. How would he interpret my actions in leaving my room for last? As if I expected to spend an inordinate amount of time there, alone with him.

Hell, Dahlia, he's not going to try anything in a house full of people with enough power to pound him into a bloody pulp if he lays a hand on you.

I drummed up enough courage to turn the knob and push open the door. I said nothing as I stepped inside, followed closely by Noah. The door remained open, and he made no move to close it. My nervousness level dropped a few notches.

He wandered to the center of the room, eyes roving over every detail. "It isn't very personal."

"I don't have a lot of stuff." I pointed to the three cardboard boxes taking up space by the closet. "My life is in there. Mom and I didn't have a lot of money. Old habits, I guess."

Okay, so that was only partly true. My earliest years had been spent in a nice bungalow in Malibu, mortgage and rent free, and within walking distance of everything. I don't recall it, because the entire neighborhood was destroyed in a mudslide when I was four years old. We lost the house, all of our possessions, including baby pictures and anything Mom once owned of sentimental value. I vaguely recall her crying herself to sleep in a cheap hotel room night after night, worrying about money and keeping us fed.

We survived, though. Come hell or high water, Mom made a good life for us. Staring at those cartons in the corner of my current bedroom made me miss her again. Miss her terribly. To cover, I indicated my monstrosity of a rocking chair. "I was thinking of a reading lamp to go with that. What do you think?"

He stroked the smooth, aged wicker of the chair's back. "I like it. You need soft lighting, Dahlia. Frosted bulbs and ambience, not glaring overhead fluorescents. They don't suit you."

"How do you know what suits me?" I asked, more defensive than intended, but it rolled off him.

"Intuition. You learn how to read people in my line of work. After a while, it stops being about their choice of overhead or wall fixture, and it becomes about them. Expectations and needs. They desire something and I provide it."

"Makes you sound like a pimp."

"A pimp's just another kind of salesman. Only what I sell isn't illegal in thirty-seven states." He chewed on the corner of his lip. "You know, of all the people I knew from school before I got sick, I remember you the most."

My pulse rate increased. "Really?" *Wait, got sick?*

"You took the accelerated classes, and you always sat on the west side of the cafeteria during lunch, closest to the exit. You always had a book in your hands, even if you weren't reading it. You seemed to know what the hell Mrs. Sharpe was talking about in chemistry when I didn't have a clue. People liked you, but you didn't care about being popular."

He remembered more about me as a teenager than I did about myself.

"When you moved over the summer, I was mad I never got up the courage to ask you out," he said.

My lips parted, but no words came out. "Um, wow, thanks."

He smiled warmly. "I want to make up for that and take you out to dinner tonight."

Hello, conversation curveball. Dinner? He was asking me out now? Eight years later? I gaped at him a moment before opening my mouth to reply. A bell tone came out.

Out of the hall. Once, twice, it sounded. Then static came from the intercom box mounted in the high corner of the room, installed for specific moments of crisis.

"War Room, everyone," Teresa's voice crackled over the box. "We've got a chemical fire downtown. Police are requesting our assistance containing it."

Moment of crisis, check..

I exhaled hard. "Maybe I can get a rain check on dinner? This could take us a while to sort out."

"Breakfast?" he asked, grinning since I hadn't shot him down. "I know a great little diner, Mallory's Table, out in Studio City. Good eggs, great coffee."

"It's a date."

We headed downstairs, and I escorted Noah to the door. He glanced back once, as he climbed into the truck cab, and smiled. I waited for him to drive away, then turned and headed to the War Room and the job that awaited me.

Six

Crystal Street

Why is it always a fire?" I asked, watching smoke curl up into the blue sky, streaks of dirty gray against an otherwise cloudless atmosphere. Still two blocks away, and I could already smell it, hot and toxic and bitter.

In the seat next to me, Tempest shrugged. "Because flash floods are less common in the middle of big cities?"

"Smart-ass."

"He's not completely wrong," Flex said from her seat in the very back with Onyx.

It was our first team outing in weeks, and everyone was suited up for it. Flex had poured herself into her fake-snakeskin stretch suit that moved with her ability to contort her body to serious extremes. Marco "Onyx" Mendoza's uniform, manufactured by Rita McNally as a gift, was a new synthetic blend that worked with his shape-shifter abilities. Instead of ending up stark naked after a transformation, he would return to human form still fully clothed. It fit him like a second skin, showing every ripple of muscle and potential bulge. He worked hard to maintain his physical perfection, almost to an obsessive level.

Everyone had hobbies.

No matter what we found at Crystal Street, I knew the majority of the work would ultimately fall to me. I could absorb massive amounts of heat, and a chemical fire would produce it in spades. Probably more than I could safely handle, and Trance had been very clear about that—only take what my body could absorb. Don't overdo it, don't hurt myself.

It was amusing advice coming from a woman who returned from almost every job with at least one wound. She wore her scars with pride, though, and never complained. Unless one of us got hurt; then we never heard the end of it. Endless lectures about taking care, using caution, et cetera.

"Don't go begging for a natural disaster," Trance said. "We live in a seismically unstable city, and you're tempting an eight-point earthquake. We're due, you know. That little shaker we had two days ago was nothing."

We knew. Thirty years had passed since the last earthquake over six points on the Richter scale. Mother Nature was either moving house, or saving up for a big show in the near future.

Around the next corner, the disaster site came into clear view. This part of town housed dozens of warehouses, storage centers, and abandoned buildings and created perfect squatter housing. Just off I-5, the Crystal Street strip lined the southern side of the Arroyo Seco section of the Los Angeles River, providing a natural barrier against spreading fire. The

Southern Pacific Railroad cut a black line on the opposite riverbank.

We only had to keep the blaze from moving forward and sideways. A single warehouse about the size of a football field burned and smoked, flames leaping toward the sky. A brick building—a deserted factory, maybe—stood at the north, and a second warehouse of equal size bordered it on the south.

Police cars and a dozen uniforms kept the gaping crowd a safe distance from the blaze. Trance honked. They cleared a path. Heat struck me in the face the moment I opened the door and climbed out. Sharp odors of smoke and sulfur and gas curled the inside of my nose. My eyes tingled and teared up.

Captain Hooper strode toward us, his deep-wrinkled eyes red from the smoke. I felt a strange sense of nostalgia, remembering the first time I'd met my teammates face-to-face. Hooper had been managing a building collapse. I'd been there reporting on the story. So surreal now, to be part of the team offering assistance.

"Our hoses aren't doing much except keeping the other buildings wet," Hooper said, his voice a thunderhead over the roaring blaze. "Whatever they had stored in there, it's burning like jet fuel. We've got a foam truck coming."

"Are the neighboring buildings empty?" Trance asked.

Hooper coughed. "The other warehouse isn't under contract to store anything right now. The factory there should be empty, but sometimes people set up house and don't want to leave."

"Risk burning to death rather than being arrested for squatting," Cipher said.

"No doubt." Trance turned to our assembled group. "Cipher and Onyx, sweep the factory and make sure no one is holed up inside. Tempest and Ember, you're on the fire. Do what you can to settle it down." She looked right at me and only me. "Flex and I are on crowd control with Captain Hooper. Coms on, everyone."

Next to me, Onyx began to transform. His legs shortened, thinned out. Arms sprouted feathers. Nose sharpened, turned hard and yellow. Black feathers began to cover everything, head to torso, as his body shrank to less than one-fifth its former size. In moments, a green-eyed raven lit off to the sky and soared toward the factory. Cipher jogged after him, tossing a supportive wink to Trance as he left.

A hand touched my shoulder. Trance lowered her voice. "Only what you can handle, Ember."

"I know," I said. "I'll be careful."

"How come you never worry about me like that?" Tempest asked.

"Because you're cautious enough for ten people."

"How about we all be careful?" Flex said.

It was something everyone agreed on.

Tempest and I approached the blaze from the west. Water from the fire hoses flowed around our feet in gray streams. The thick odor of damp pavement warred with the smell of smoke, making it difficult to breathe properly. I sucked in deep breaths through my mouth. We took position twenty feet from the leaping flames. Firetrucks surrounded us. Firemen wrangled their hoses and ladders and kept the crowd at bay.

None of that mattered. We had to concentrate.

Side by side, we gazed up at the inferno. Tempest raised his hands above his head. Cooler air swirled around us, creating a bubble within which it became easier to breathe. The fresh air energized me and helped me focus.

"I'll suck the oxygen out of the interior of the warehouse," he shouted. "Take away the fire's fuel and kill the source."

I nodded. "Go for it. I'll see what I can do about this heat."

The fresh air disappeared as Tempest concentrated his powers elsewhere. I closed my eyes and opened up to the heat, welcoming it inside my body. To my very core. Hundreds of degrees, thousands of individual flames. Out of the wood and metal and chemicals, into me.

In, in, deeper in.

Superheated, but unburned. Surrounded, but not smothered. Constantly in motion, but unmoving. I descended into the bowels of hell, where fire and brimstone and ash thrived, heat blazed in all its glory, and cold had no chance of survival. The inferno glowed like embers, the innards of a piece of coal. Sharp and bright and red.

My heart pounded. Blood raced through my veins, hot like a lava flow. Energizing and exhausting all at once—the perfect adrenaline rush. I skated along the edge, terrified of going too far, of losing myself, of making a deadly mistake. Of hurting someone else.

So much fire, almost too much. Closer to the ember, deeper into the flames.

The edge of reason narrowed, and an abyss loomed. My chest hurt; my heart was pounding right through my ribs. I couldn't see, couldn't smell, couldn't breathe.

And then I fell. Down, down, unable to stop.

No.

I pulled out of it, but didn't quite make the jump. The hard pavement scraped my hands. All I saw was flame— bright and scorching, sweeping over and into me. My lungs seized; I couldn't breathe. Someone touched me. Shouted. Pulled. Shouted again.

Skin burned. Sizzled. Too hot, too much. I screamed, soundless and never-ending. Still couldn't breathe.

Air whipped, cool and fast. Wrapped me in its chilly embrace. Lifted me up and out. Flying. Descending.

The flames were gone, but the intense heat remained. My body radiated it, unable to absorb anything else.

Come on, girl, come out of it. You've got a breakfast date tomorrow, remember?

Frigid wetness enveloped me in its slick embrace. I latched onto that sensation and held on tight.

I woke up in the back of an ambulance, soaking wet and covered with blankets. The gurney beneath me was drenched. Nauseating odors of smoke and burned plastic lingered, and set my stomach roiling. I coughed, lurched to the side, and tried to vomit onto the floor. Nothing but dry heaves, as my angry lungs forced old air from my body. I retched until my throat burned and my stomach threatened to turn inside out, then I collapsed onto my back, rattling the gurney.

The roof of the ambulance tilted and swirled. Sirens still wailed outside, mingling with dozens of voices. One sound was gone: the roar had ceased.

It worked. Yay, me.

The gurney wobbled. Concerned violet eyes gazed down at me, framed by soot-streaked hair and more purple. A heavy frown creased her face. "What did I say, young lady?" she asked.

"Be more specific?" I slurred, knowing full well what she meant. My throat was dry, voice hoarse. Water. Definitely needed water.

"Only what you can manage."

"Caught me by surprise." I licked my parched lips and tasted ash. Gross. "Must have been the chemicals, whatever was burning. It's never gotten away from me like that before."

"It was a damned big fire, Ember. I should have known better."

"Not your fault."

A smile ghosted across her face. "I'm in charge. Everything is my fault."

"I'm alive."

"And probably poisoned."

"Nah." I tried to sit up and the ambulance tilted. "Okay, maybe. Everyone else all right?"

"Everyone else is fine." She sat down on the ledge next to the gurney. Ash smudged her cheeks, giving them a hollow, carved-out look. "The blaze is almost out, thanks to you and

Tempest. Captain Hooper is laying down foam, though, just in case. Cipher and Onyx chased a few squatters out of the building next door, but I'm sure they'll be back inside tonight. It didn't spread."

Good news. I loved good news.

"Any idea what started it?"

She shook her head. "The arson investigator hasn't been able to go inside yet. Onyx flew a few rounds overhead once the smoke cleared, but couldn't get a good look at anything. It's an old building. Bad wiring and barrels of flammable material do not go well together."

"No kidding."

The nausea had subsided, along with most of the dizziness. Now all I needed was to get out of those wet blankets.

"So you're quite taken with the electrician," she said.

I blinked. How in the world did she—?

"Your body temperature spiked to one hundred four for a few minutes. His name came up." She grinned and seemed more like a girlfriend than a concerned boss. "In relation to eyes and lips, if I recall correctly."

My cheeks burned. Good God, what had my delirious brain let loose for her to hear?

"Relationships are tricky things," she continued. "I won't tell you to not see him, just to be careful. Not everyone really gets what we are, or how that affects our lives. There's more to it than physical attraction. Hill House is our sanctuary."

Good advice, but not something I wanted to hear at the moment. It was easy for her to lecture about our love lives;

her boyfriend was one of us, and therefore understood things by default.

Trance smiled. "Don't worry, no lectures. At least not until you look a little less like a drowned rat."

"Or feel less like one. Do we have fresh clothes?"

She reached out of my line of sight and produced jeans and a navy-blue sweatshirt. "Found these in the car. I think they're Flex's."

With a lot of patience, time, and careful maneuvering in a tight space, I sat up and peeled out of the wet uniform. Some of the odor left with the clothes, and I used a dry blanket to towel off. Modesty didn't even occur to me. The rear of the ambulance faced the side of a firetruck and no one passed by.

The navy sweatshirt—"Princess" emblazoned on the front in fuchsia stitching—fit, no problem. I rolled the cuffs of the jeans several times. Flex wore tall; I went back and forth between petite and regular. I felt strange bouncing around without a bra or panties, but it was either discomfort or a big wet spot on my butt.

I ran the blanket through my damp hair. "Should get Tempest over here for a quick blow-dry," I mused.

Trance scooted to the end of the ambulance and twisted my clothes, wringing out the excess water. Each motion was an exercise in deliberation. Twist, squeeze, drip. Repeat. Motherly and kind, taking care of her people. She was the heart of our team, the blood in its veins. We were hers, and she was ours; in that moment, I knew it more fiercely than ever.

I finger-combed my hair. The orange lock flipped down in front of my face, and I batted it away with a huff of irritation.

"You'll get used to it," she said.

"What?"

"The color change. One day you'll look in the mirror and won't be able to remember what you looked like without it. The change becomes part of you."

"Your experience, right?"

"Of course. It would be disingenuous to try to relate someone else's."

"Does Flex like being blue?"

"You'd have to ask her."

Her diplomatic response hinted at "sometimes" as an answer. Flex was always confident and on top of things, as secure in her blue skin as anyone I'd ever known. She had the body of a model and personality of a game show host. The idea of uncertainty, of Flex disliking anything about herself, was unsettling.

"Maybe I will," I said.

"Good." Trance rolled my clothes into a bundle and tossed them at me. "You okay to walk?"

"Yeah, the dizzy spells are gone. Now I'm just thirsty and hungry."

"We'll get you fixed up at home."

She slid out of the ambulance. I followed and was immediately confronted by an irritated paramedic. After a brief argument about going to the hospital for treatment that ended with my signing a form that said I refused, we went to join the others. Trance didn't look happy with my medical decision, but she didn't try to override me.

My jeans and sweatshirt were too warm for the late-afternoon humidity. I pushed up the sleeves as we walked around the fire engine, toward the scene of organized chaos.

The basic frame of the warehouse still stood, with its blackened walls stretching dark fingers toward the sky. Water ran in small rivers across the uneven pavement, trickling past us toward the river basin. Firemen poked at the debris with axes, testing its doneness. A flock of reporters had taken up residence near a police car, reined in by a trio of uniforms. The reporters started shouting questions when we appeared. Trance was a favorite of journalists. She knew how to give repeatable quotes and good copy.

I knew that from experience.

She ignored them and navigated her way to an emergency rescue truck. Captain Hooper was holding court with Cipher, Tempest, and Flex. A shadow darted across the ground in front of us; Onyx swooped through the sky, still scouting from above. I always envied him his bird form and the freedom to fly unfettered through the air.

Tempest noticed me first. "Hey, Golden Girl, how do you feel?"

"Like I've been through the spin cycle," I replied. "How'd you do?"

"One of my best performances yet, I think."

"Yeah," Cipher drawled, "no one blows hot air quite like you, Tempest."

Tempest rolled his eyes and clutched his heart, pretending to be wounded. "Hey, Trance, your captive audience awaits. They need their sound bites for the evening news."

Trance gazed over her shoulder at the flock. "Is it wrong to feel like a circus ringleader when I talk to them?"

I started to giggle. It caught in a cough and turned into an abbreviated snort.

"Good answer," Flex said.

"I think Ember just volunteered to do reporter duty with me," Trance said. "If you feel up to it?"

The other side of the microphone and minirecorder. This should be interesting. "Sure, but do you think my sweatshirt will give the wrong impression?" I asked.

Flex giggled successfully. "I think it'll give you an image. Former journalist becomes superhero diva, film at eleven."

I rolled my eyes at her. "Flex, if I ever become a diva, you have my permission to tie me up, put me in a barrel, and dump me into the Pacific Ocean."

"Sweets, if you ever become a diva, I'll eat my tongue."

I decided to take that as a compliment and just leave it alone. Trance whispered something to Cipher—it made him grin like a loon and tweaked my curiosity—and then strode toward the gaggle of reporters. I double-timed it to catch up and fell into step next to her. Questions flew at us the moment we were within shouting distance. I lost track of who asked what.

Good Lord, did I ever sound like that?

Trance stopped a few feet away, hands clasped loosely behind her back. I took a similar position slightly behind her on her right. The questions ceased almost immediately; they knew how this would play out. Trance's violet gaze danced over the crowd for almost a full minute before she selected someone.

"Go ahead, Shannon," she said.

A middle-aged woman with a mop of unruly brown curls thrust her microphone forward. "Shannon Milton, Channel Four. The Rangers have kept a pretty low profile this past week. What brought you out today?"

Something flashed across Trance's face, there and gone so quickly I couldn't identify it, and I doubted anyone else noticed. "First of all, there hasn't officially been a Ranger Corps in fifteen years. Six months ago, we separated from the former MetaHuman Control Group arm of the ATF, and we are now an independent organization. As you well know, but thanks for asking." Shannon seemed unaffected by the barb. "As for why today, because we were called and our help was requested. We do what we can, when we can, and if someone asks, we respond.

"It was a difficult fire, one fueled by chemicals and uncontrollable with water. We brought skills that helped contain it long enough for the Los Angeles County Fire Department to put it out completely." To the short, balding man on Shannon's left: "Andy, go ahead."

"From where we were standing," Andy said, "it looked like Ember there put the fire out on her own. Is she that powerful?"

My heart thudded. *Don't single me out, please don't do that.*

Trance's eyes narrowed. "Ember's skills kept the fire's heat from increasing and the flames from spreading. Tempest pulled oxygen away from its core. Captain Hooper's men did the rest. It was a complete and total team effort."

"Ember, why did you pass out?"

I blinked, surveyed the crowd, but could not locate the source of the question. No one owned up, so I ignored it.

"So what are you calling yourselves?" Shannon asked, nudging in another turn.

"Labels only serve to pigeonhole people," Trance said. "You all know who we are. Does it really matter what we call ourselves?" A murmur spread through the gaggle. "Now, if there is nothing else of pressing importance—"

"I have a question." A distinctly male voice rose up from the crowd. Heads turned, trying to locate the source. Bodies shifted and allowed a young man to step forward. He wore colorful surfer shorts and a T-shirt under a loose, too-large Windbreaker, and didn't look like a reporter. No notebook, no recorder or camera. Just a dim-eyed stare and thin, grim mouth. He moved toward the front of the barrier, hands in his jacket pockets.

Everything about him set me on edge. Instincts screamed to keep him at bay, don't let him get too close. Next to me, Trance tensed. We both sensed it keenly, like a scent in the air: danger.

"What is it?" Trance asked.

He smiled. His right arm moved faster than should have been possible, faster than I could react, and his question came in the form of a single gunshot.

Seven

Aftermath

The gunshot report rang in my ears, which were further deafened by the cacophony of screams and shouts from petrified reporters. Someone knocked me to the ground. I smacked my funny bone on a chunk of gravel and bit my tongue. Blood and pain blossomed in my mouth, adding to my disorientation. I tucked my legs up to my chest to prevent the feet stampeding around from trampling me, and mentally tested my other extremities. Arms: check. Chest and stomach: check and check. Head: check.

Nothing else hurt. I wasn't shot.

Men shouted, ordering him to drop his weapon. Footsteps scuffled in all directions, around me, over me, and other voices shouted my name, Trance's name. I peeked one eye open and found myself gazing into a purple one. Face-to-face with Trance, laying flat on her back on the damp pavement, head sideways. She blinked. Neither of us moved.

"Trance!" Cipher's voice, getting closer.

Something red had splattered Trance's cheek. Farther down, just above her right breast, where the silver armored tank top failed to cover flesh, blood flowed in a thin stream under the slick fabric of her uniform and puddled on the cement by her arm. Near my hand. I sat up, a surprised yelp dying in my throat. She was shot. Trance was shot.

"No," I said, clamping my hands down on the wound. The blood was hot on my skin, pulsing from the small hole beneath my palm, unwilling to be stanched. "Help me! Someone help!"

Screaming and shouting became a whirlwind of sound. Cipher appeared on the other side of Trance, his mouth open and silver-flecked eyes wide. He clasped her left hand to his chest. She turned her head with some effort. The violet colorations on her forehead and neck seemed to glow against the new pallor of her skin. Like bruising on a corpse.

No! Don't you dare think like that.

A paramedic nudged me to the side, and I released my hold on her wound. He shouted things to a second paramedic. Blood sticky on my hands, I could only sit by Trance's head. Sit and watch. Panic poked at the edge of my consciousness. I did not allow it in. Could not.

A hand touched my shoulder. Tempest crouched directly behind me, an anchor to the unfolding events. Someone blurred past us, a streak of blue and black, and was quickly restrained by two police officers. They could not, however, restrain Flex's amazing talent or her anger. Her arms snaked past the cops, toward the young man already facedown on the ground, secured by handcuffs.

Flex screamed and tried to hit him. Onyx got in her way, said something I couldn't hear, and she relented. Her arms retracted, and the cops let her go. Onyx steered her back, away from the shooter, who seemed unconcerned with the goings-on around him. He just lay there, disinterested in his immediate fate. Uncaring that if he hadn't just dropped the gun after firing his single round, the dozens of police officers on scene would have shot him to death.

The first paramedic had trouble cutting through the top of Trance's uniform to further expose the dime-size wound. Blood continued oozing in steady streams. He gave up on cutting and placed a square of gauze against the wound, and then another. I caught a scent, something sharp and sterile. Both pads soaked quickly. His partner handed him another.

My stomach churned and twisted; and I looked away. Trance continued to hold Cipher's gaze. He whispered things, told her to be strong, be brave, it was just a scratch, and you've survived worse. Her chin trembled as her breathing became more labored. Her expression didn't change—pain, fatigue, acceptance. Never fear. We were terrified for her, while she seemed downright calm.

Perhaps merely having Cipher nearby kept her that way. They complemented each other in a way I had never seen, one drawing strength from the other when needed most.

Someone brought a gurney and collapsed it down. Tempest looped his arms around my waist and helped me stand up. My head spun. I stumbled; he held tight. Bloody hands away from my body, I let him back us up. Cipher stayed glued to Trance's side while the paramedics loaded her onto the gurney and wheeled it toward the back of a waiting ambulance.

They were saying things about starting IVs, labored breathing, and O_2 levels, scientific stuff I just couldn't follow. It sounded like an episode of a bad television soap opera. Fake and overly bright and too simple. Cipher climbed into the back of the ambulance. None of us moved until it peeled away, lights spinning and siren wailing.

"Why?" It took a moment to realize I'd asked the question. I pulled away from Tempest, intent on the man still on the ground. Strong arms held me back.

"I don't know, Ember," Tempest said in my ear. "We can't do anything now. Let the police take care of him."

I brought my hands up, hoping to use my elbows on Tempest and gain freedom with a few sharp jabs. Crimson glinted off my fingers and palms, slowly congealing, darkening. Trance's blood. It shouldn't be on my hands. It needed to be inside of her, keeping her whole and safe and with us. She was our heart; our heart needed its blood.

Fear crashed down on me for the first time, hard and fast. My hands shook. Tension knotted my stomach. Tears rose up and closed my throat, but I couldn't dislodge them. I couldn't cry here in front of everyone.

Tempest shouted something and moments later, a police officer appeared with three bottles of water. I held my hands out, then rubbed them together while Tempest poured the warm water. I tried to block out the voices, the talking, the people shouting orders and asking questions. Just think about getting my skin clean. Wash it off, then we can go to the hospital.

"Where did they take her?" I asked.

"Someone said City of Angels," Tempest replied as he poured a second bottle over my almost clean hands. "It's a few miles from here."

When the blood was finally gone, I wiped my hands on the seat of my borrowed jeans. I drank from the third bottle, grateful for the moisture. It was fortifying, even energizing, as I finally paid attention to what was happening.

Tempest stayed nearby and I appreciated that, more than I could tell him. Onyx had cornered Flex against the side of a firetruck, still trying to calm her down. Anger sparked from her like fireworks and radiated from every pore. Roses blossomed on each cheek, harsh smudges of color on her blue skin. No tears, only unadulterated fury.

Behind us, two uniforms were pushing the shooter into the back of a police car. One of them slammed the door shut, said something to his partner, and then walked toward us, shoulders squared. Flex paid me little mind, but sprang to attention when the officer—Ortega, from his name tag—stopped a few feet from our tattered group. Onyx also turned, releasing Flex from his grip. His eyes shimmered with emotion.

Ortega looked at each of us in turn, clearly at a loss. Trance was in charge, everyone knew that. If she wasn't around, we defaulted to Cipher, but after him there was no clear chain of command. No third to step up when the other two were absent.

Tempest cleared his throat. "Did he say anything, Officer? Anything at all?"

"I'm real sorry," Ortega said, shaking his head. "He's not

talking. He either isn't interested, or he's waiting for a lawyer, I don't know. He's not giving any trouble, so we're taking him to the local precinct. You can find him there."

"What makes someone do that?" I asked. The question slipped out.

Ortega hesitated, then said, "Lots of things, miss. He could be mentally ill. We won't know until our detectives interrogate him."

"I want to be there," Flex growled.

"That's up to—"

"Talk to Detective Pascal, Fourth Division, he knows us."

"I'll put in a call."

"Thank you." She spared one more venomous glare at the squad car, pivoted on her heel, and then stalked back toward our Sport.

"We'll have to get statements from everyone," Ortega said, looking right at me. "Especially you."

"Can you do it at the hospital?" Tempest asked.

"Of course."

As if that ended things, Tempest grabbed my hand, poked Onyx in the shoulder, and steered us in the direction Flex had gone. We walked back to the car at a clipped pace, eager to be gone from this place and dreading what we might find once we reached the hospital. Believing that Trance was alive and fighting seemed better than knowing if she had died. I didn't want to know.

Six months ago, these people had been faces in the media, names on a printed page, no more real than the other strangers I wrote about daily. They'd quickly become the siblings

I'd never had, the family I hadn't realized I wanted—even if I didn't always feel like one of them. I needed them.

I didn't know what I'd do if Trance died.

Detectives Pascal and Forney arrived at the ER waiting room ten minutes after we descended on it. Everyone else waiting for word had migrated to one side of the rows of chairs, leaving a small corner to our smoky quartet. One by one, reporters from the fire scene began to arrive. They kept their distance and their cameras off, choosing instead to linger near the entrance.

They fired off a few questions at the detectives as they passed. Pascal returned fire with a handful of obscenities that would have made a sailor blush, and they left them alone. He strode toward us, a welcome presence, tall and commanding, black coat swirling around his legs. Forney followed at a slight distance, present but not engaged. Considering her hostility toward us, I was shocked she'd come at all.

"Any word?" Pascal asked. Flex's contemptuous glare answered. He spoke again before she could fire off a litany of questions. "I only know what Officer Ortega told me, which isn't much. It's not my case, so I'll have to talk to their captain about allowing any of you to sit in on the interrogation."

"Do we at least know his name?" Tempest asked.

"Arnold Stark, we got it from his driver's license. So far his record is checking out clean. Ortega said he'd let me know if anything new came up." He sat in the chair opposite Flex, and his attention shifted to me. "You okay, kiddo? You look green."

I shrugged, mostly because I was still pretty numb. I knew the symptoms of trauma, knew I was somewhere in the middle of shock, edging toward denial. I wanted to curl into a fetal position and suck my thumb until the nightmare went away. I wanted to crawl into my bed and sleep for days. I wanted to cry, bawl, sob, and scream. Anything to unplug the dam and get this pressing weight off my chest.

"I absorbed some chemicals earlier." My voice sounded hollow, not quite mine. If anyone suggested I see a doctor, I'd slap them silly. "I should wash my face."

He pointed down the hall, past the admitting desk. "There's a bathroom that way."

Leaving showed weakness. It didn't support Trance. Then my bladder contracted insistently. Hell.

"Someone will come if there is news," Onyx said. "Go."

I gave him a soft smile that he didn't return, then left. I ignored the few reporters who tried asking me questions. Definitely not in the mood to do more than lob a few heat waves in their general direction. Two women were washing their hands and chatting about pores or the poor, or something, but stopped when I entered. One look at me, and they scooted out of there. I darted for a stall, did my business—to my body's eternal relief—and then hazarded a look into the bank of mirrors.

Gunmetal gray streaked my blond hair, giving me a zebra-do that was more freakish than punkish. Soot covered my forehead and throat in odd, war-paint patterns. Flecks of red dotted my left cheek. I brushed at one splotch that was adhered to my skin. A bit of work removed the dried blood.

More of her blood. On my face, flecks on the sweatshirt and my throat.

I turned on the faucet and let the water run hot while I pushed up the sleeves of the sweatshirt. Over and over, I plunged cupped hands beneath the streaming, steaming water and splashed it over my face. Pumped out some pale pink soap, scrubbed it into a thick, white lather, and scrubbed it over my hot skin. Scrubbed and splashed and scrubbed some more.

My face stung and tingled. A bit of soap landed in my eye, and it began to water. I muttered a curse and rubbed. Rubbed until the tingle spread and the tears began in earnest. They trickled down my already soaked cheeks, mingling with the clean, cooling water that had splashed into my hair. With shaking hands I gripped the edges of the porcelain basin and held on.

It wasn't enough. My knees gave out, and I slumped to the tiled floor, water dribbling down my face and into the sweatshirt's collar. My lungs seized and a sob erupted, echoing around the small public bathroom. A second followed. I slapped both hands over my mouth, but couldn't stop the torrent.

I cried on my knees, as silently as I could, for what felt like hours. Maybe only minutes passed, I didn't know. It didn't seem to matter. The tears burned my eyes, unnaturally hot. It could have been my powers, or my body expelling the chemicals it had absorbed, ridding me of them the only way it knew how. The body expels its poisons, heals itself.

The soul takes a little more work.

The bathroom door squealed open. I scrambled to my

feet, heart pounding, nose stuffed. Flex stepped around the divider, took in my state with a single, careless once-over, and frowned.

"Pull yourself together, Ember," she snapped. "She's not dead, and you're in here bawling like you're planning her funeral."

Her words stung. I turned away, facing the mirror and sink. She continued to watch me with a disapproving glare. I didn't have the energy to wage a verbal battle with her. Let her think whatever; I no longer cared.

"I'll be right there," I said.

"Good. The doctor's coming in a few minutes. Wipe your face and come out when you don't look like you'll break into a hundred pieces." With those precious parting shots she was gone. The door squealed shut behind her.

I stared at my own reflection, at my red-rimmed, bloodshot eyes and puffy cheeks, and couldn't manage any anger. Flex could hate me for crying. She could hate me for showing weakness, but at least I had emotions. I showed my emotions, instead of keeping them bottled up like warm champagne. Sooner or later, Flex would pop, and the mess would be ugly.

Water adjusted to cold, I splashed it a few more times, and then patted my skin dry with paper towels. I blew my nose, relieving some of the pressure in my aching head. Aspirin was definitely next on the list of required items. I also wanted a rubber band to secure my dirty hair up and away. A pencil would do, but the bathroom offered nothing useful. Second thing to find right away.

My appearance was as good as it would get without supplies. I left the restroom, bypassed the growing gaggle of reporters, and navigated back to our corner. Our group had grown by one. I froze when the new arrival stood up, struck dumb by her presence.

Agent Rita McNally stood there, in a gray skirt and suit jacket, her silver-blond hair as perfectly coiffed as the first day we met. She continued to work for the Los Angeles branch of the ATF, which kept her nearby, a loyal friend to our squad of freelance heroes. Seeing her there made the situation seem much more dire.

"Hi, sunshine," she said. "I hear you were quite the hero today."

"So they tell me," I said.

Heads turned. A female doctor in bloodstained scrubs strode toward us with a very pale Cipher in tow. He walked stiffly, hands by his sides and clenched into white-knuckled fists. Tension bracketed his mouth and lined his eyes. He seemed breakable—a description I'd never before associated with Gage McAllister.

"She's stable," the doctor said. "And she's on her way up to surgery to repair the damage. The bullet missed major arteries. However, it nicked her right lung and caused minor internal bleeding. We're transfusing her, and we're very hopeful."

"What's hopeful?" Flex asked.

"The odds are in her favor. I don't want to get specific until after she's through surgery. Now, there's a waiting room upstairs that one of our interns can take you to, if you'd rather have some privacy." She glanced around the filling ER waiting room. "Dr. Patrick Shelby is Trance's surgeon. He'll speak with you when it's over."

"Thank you, Doctor," Cipher said mechanically. He seemed to be running on autopilot, not quite aware of his surroundings.

She nodded and removed herself from the group. Flex started to follow. Cipher put his arm out, stopping her. She glared at him. Some of the frost in her stare melted a bit when she met his eyes. They were heartbreaking, raw.

"We don't all have to stay," he said. "She'll probably be in surgery for a couple of hours, if anyone wants to go home. Change or eat or something."

No one volunteered. Hours or days, we were there until we had news. Good or bad. Our leader's fate lay in the hands of the City of Angels surgical team.

Eight

Surgical Floor

The waiting room on the surgical floor was devoid of good distractions. Maybe they did that on purpose, so nervous families could huddle together and talk, offer up prayers, and think good thoughts about the patients in the surgical suites down the hall. It was an enclosed room, with a single door and two rows of chairs. A central coffee table held an array of nature and household magazines, and a few old newspapers. The blinds were drawn, save the single panel on the door, keeping prying eyes out.

Detective Forney placed a pair of uniformed officers at both elevators, checking everyone without a hospital ID before they were allowed near the waiting room. Reporters were known for doing pretty sneaky things, and we didn't want guerilla photographs ending up on anyone's front page tomorrow. Forney herself had taken a call twenty minutes ago and headed out, promising that she or Pascal would call if something else turned up on . . . well, anything.

Gage filled the room with his nervous energy. He'd removed his uniform jacket, and pounded the length of the floor in a blue undershirt that displayed every tense, bunched muscle in his torso and arms. He wouldn't engage in conversation; he just paced. The scar on his throat, a pale reminder of a near-fatal wound of his own, fairly glowed against the agitated flush on his skin.

Renee, Marco, and McNally huddled in one of the corners, chatting quietly. Too quietly to pick up any hint of the topic, but the frequent, furtive glances in my direction suggested one. I wanted to know why I was so interesting. Perhaps because I was on the floor, in the opposite corner, arms wrapped tight around my knees. I'd given up on the magazines, and at least from that position, I couldn't watch the clock tick down endless minutes.

Three hours had passed, and nothing. Not even a whisper from the nurses' station.

The door opened and Ethan shouldered his way in, arms loaded with vending machine snacks and sodas. He nudged the door shut with his foot, and then deposited his load onto the center table. My stomach growled. I didn't reach for the food. I'd shown weakness to Renee in the bathroom. I would not lower myself to grab a snack first, not with her watching me so closely.

Cellophane crinkled and can tops popped. I kept my eyes fixed on the carpet and its beige diamond patterns. A shadow passed. Marco sat down next to me and ripped open a bag of cheesy crackers. He offered them; I shook my head, even though their salty-sweet scent increased the rumble in my stomach.

"You are allowed to eat, too," he said softly, concern in his gently accented voice.

Ouch. Was I that transparent? "I'm not hungry."

"Liar." He tossed a second bag of crackers into my lap. "Eat."

I tore into the bag, swallowing mouthfuls without really chewing. It had been a long, strange day, and I couldn't remember the last time I ate. Breakfast, probably. The crackers went down dry. A can of cola found its way into my hands. I drank it too quickly. The bubbles made my eyes water.

"Renee is not really mad at you, *Ascua*," Marco said, voice almost too low. I almost smiled at the familiarity of his nickname for me—the Spanish word for ember. "She is scared, and she does not do scared well."

"Could have fooled me."

"She fools a lot of people."

I appreciated Marco's words, even though I found little truth in them. Renee hadn't liked me from the day we met, and she'd made it very clear tonight. I arrived the day William Hill died, and she would always see me as a cheap replacement, weak, no matter what I did to prove myself.

A stray thought niggled at the back of my mind, something I hadn't realized was bothering me until now. "Teresa didn't make a shield," I said.

Marco frowned. "I don't understand."

"You know the force fields she can make with her orbs. She's used them to stop bullets before, but she didn't this time. Why didn't she?"

"Perhaps she did not wish to risk the bullet ricocheting into the crowd."

True, and definitely a possibility. Even in the midst of a

split-second decision, Teresa had been thinking of everyone except herself.

The waiting room door opened again. This time a cop poked his head in. He looked around until he found me. "Sorry for the interruption, folks," he said, not sounding the least bit apologetic. "But there's a young man out here asking after Ember."

My heart sped up. "What's his name?"

"Noah Scott. You know him?"

I nodded, but made no move to stand. Marco stiffened. Across the room, Gage locked his eyes with mine. He tilted his head. I took it as silent permission and stood, dusting cracker crumbs from my hands. I slipped out of the room, Renee's eyes drilling holes into my back.

Noah stood across the hall from the door, next to a water fountain. Concern ghosted across his face, replaced quickly by relief. I took a few steps forward, then faltered. Had he come all the way out here for me? He closed the distance between us, eyes searching for . . . what? I didn't know.

"I'm glad you're okay," he said.

"I'm not hurt," I said, "but I'm not okay." How could I just open up to him like that, when I clammed up around Marco? Someone who had been a dear friend for months. No, I felt safer with a near stranger.

Noah stepped closer and warmth wrapped around me. I tensed, surprised by the embrace. His arms were loose, offering comfort without force, and that melted the last of my objections to his presence. I inhaled deeply as I relaxed into the luxury of being held. I had no reason to be strong for Noah.

"The news keeps saying one of you was shot, and you both went down, but the police aren't confirming who or saying if anyone else was injured." He pulled me back, hands on my forearms, and gazed at me with his emerald eyes. "Trance?"

My chin trembled.

"I'm so sorry, Dahlia. I can't imagine how scared you are."

"Not nearly as scared as Gage is. He loves her so much."

His eyes narrowed. "Don't compare your pain with his. You both feel things differently, and you're allowed to be upset." Maybe, maybe not. "Um, can we go somewhere and talk?"

"Afraid to be seen in public with me?"

He missed the joke. "No, the guy with green eyes keeps glaring at me through the window. He looks like he wants to turn into a jaguar and rip my throat out with his teeth. It's a little disturbing."

Marco. Damn. "Don't take it personally, Noah, it isn't you."

"He doesn't like you?"

"Kind of the opposite."

I tugged Noah's hand. This wasn't a conversation for the middle of the hallway, where any pink-scrubbed nurse or lab-coated intern could be a spying reporter. I found an open door and empty room. Rows of shelving held boxes of surgical supplies, scrubs, masks, and other things I didn't recognize. I closed the door so only a sliver of hall light remained.

"He has feelings for you?" Noah asked.

"He did," I admitted. "I don't know if he still does, because we don't really talk much. Onyx—Marco and I were very close when I first joined the Rangers. He was the first one to befriend me, and we got along so well. He was my best friend."

Those memories came to life in my mind. Helping me choose my first uniform. Late-night snacks and cheesy movies we religiously tore apart and made fun of. He was there when I called my estranged father and asked for control of my trust fund. Marco came to the bank when I put down the deposit on our current house. He laughed at my bad jokes and cheered me up when I needed it.

"He wanted more?"

I nodded and started to turn away. Noah grabbed my hands and squeezed. "I tried, I really did. I care about him so much, but I wasn't attracted to him. We haven't really spoken about it since."

"How long ago?" His expression remained unreadable, interested by way of detachment.

"A month and a half, maybe."

"You should talk to him, Dahlia, because I'd hate to spend our relationship wondering if a pissed-off superhero is out for my blood."

"Relationship?" The word released the butterflies again. "We just met. What makes you think we'll have one?"

His mouth quirked. "Well, technically, we've known each other for years."

"That doesn't count, and you didn't answer my question."

He grew serious. "I've lost a lot of people I care about, Dahlia, I know how short life is. When I see something I want, I go for it. I can't afford not to."

Afford—a loaded word and he didn't even see it. Or did

he? Did he really see me, or did he see a girl with money and power?

"Anyway, that's not entirely why I came here tonight," he said.

Oh. "No?"

"I brought something I thought you should see." He rifled around in the pocket of his jacket and produced a handheld recording device. I eyed it, immediately suspicious. "It's okay, Dahlia. Most of the footage shot by the reporters was confiscated as evidence, but I got this from a friend who was in the crowd. I thought you'd want to see it."

I recoiled from the device. "You just happened to have a friend in the crowd?"

"He works for one of those online conspiracy websites and thinks all Metas were originally possessed by aliens, or something. He isn't technically press, so the police didn't search him."

"What's it show?"

"What do you remember about the shooting?"

Everything and nothing. So many of the details had blurred together. "The gun firing. Someone pushed me down. A lot of screaming, and then Trance bleeding. Why?"

"Do you know who pushed you down?"

It never occurred to me, and I shook my head no. My stomach twisted, eager butterflies replaced by cold fear. Noah turned on the recorder. A paused image of the back of someone's head popped up. He held the recorder out. Long seconds passed before I took it and pressed Play.

The angle changed, moved past the head and fixed on myself and Trance, standing in front of the gaggle of reporters. I looked downright silly in that sweatshirt. Trance was speaking, letting them ask questions. I studied how we stood, me just behind her and to her right, Trance perfectly relaxed. In her element. Alive.

"So what are you calling yourselves?"

"Labels only serve to pigeonhole people. You all know who we are. Does it really matter what we call ourselves?"

The camera wobbled, as though someone had jostled the elbow of the person holding it.

"Now, if there is nothing else of pressing importance—"

"I have a question."

I swallowed hard. A shoulder moved into the foreground. The videographer stepped sideways, giving the asker more room. His voice was so loud, right next to the recorder. I cringed, wanting desperately to stop watching.

"What is it?"

The muzzle of the gun glinted in the foreground of the screen. In the background, Teresa stepped to her right, and the bullet struck. She fell backward, hitting me in the chest, and we both went down. The camera jostled hard and went out of focus. The recording stopped.

Pain blossomed in my lip, and I loosened my jaw before I bit right through. Bile scorched the back of my throat, tinged with the flavor of cola. I swallowed, unwilling to vomit in front of Noah.

"Did you see it?" he asked.

"No, I basically saw what I remembered." Except for the part about Teresa slamming me to the ground. It happened so fast the first time.

Noah took the recorder, pressed a few buttons and handed it back. "Watch it, slow motion. Look at how she moves."

I did, and this time it sunk in with heart-wrenching clarity: as Arnold Stark raised his gun, Teresa stepped in front of me. The bullet struck her and knocked us both down, missing its intended target: my heart. Me.

Noah caught the recorder before I dropped it. I slid to the floor, numb, cold. He crouched in front of me, reaching out to clasp my hands. My head swirled and tumbled, and I was tottering on the edge of passing out altogether. I clung to him, to his warmth and presence.

"He was trying to kill me," I choked out. "She saved my life. Saved me."

"She did."

"Why, though?" Tears stung my eyes, threatened to pour out again. "I don't know Arnold Stark, why did he want to kill me?"

"I don't know, Dahlia, but you had to see this."

The tears stuck in my throat. "Do the police know?"

"I'm sure they do. Everyone's camera caught the same thing as this one. I just didn't want them to hit you with that when they interview you."

I found little comfort in his words. Arnold Stark had tried to kill me, and I didn't know why. Could be he hated Metas on principle. Maybe he was having a bad day, and it seemed like a good idea at the time. I had to know, and the only one who could tell me was sitting in an L.A. County jail cell, not talking.

Yet.

"Thank you, Noah, for bringing me this," I said, finally finding my voice and my resolve.

"What are you going to do?"

"Talk to Gage and see what he thinks."

Noah's jaw twitched. "Is he your boss now?" Something new crept into his voice, hollow and annoyed. Had he expected me to handle this on my own, without involving my peers? I didn't work alone. I needed guidance.

"With Trance hurt, yes. We don't have an official chain of command beyond Trance in charge, but it's understood that he's her second." Ethan was who I really wanted to tell and receive direction from. He was the only other person who knew what happened between me and Marco, and he'd confided his own personal secret, his sexuality, to me once. I never felt judged by Ethan.

Noah stood, pocketed the recorder, then offered his hands. I let him haul me to my feet. Blood rushed to my head; I swayed. He caught me around the waist and brushed a chunk of dirty hair from my face. "Can I come with you?" he asked.

I hesitated, then thought of how much it would annoy Renee. "Sure, you brought me the recording."

We left the storage closet. A passing orderly gave us a funny look, but didn't comment. Heat rose in my cheeks. Noah's step faltered as we approached the waiting room. I tugged him forward, drawing confidence from him and his statement about taking what he wanted. I wanted him with me. The officer at the door stepped aside without question.

Heads turned. Ethan, my best ally in this, wasn't in the room. Another food run, maybe, or the bathroom. Dirty looks from Marco and Renee sailed right past me, flung over my shoulder at Noah. Agent McNally glanced up from her novel, as though expecting to see a doctor with news.

"Have we heard anything from the police?" I asked, directing the question at Gage and no one else.

His head listed to the side, confusion clouding his expression, followed quickly by curiosity. "No," he drew out. "Why?"

I took a few more steps inside, Noah matching me pace for pace. The irritation radiating from our resident shape-changers was stifling. And a little satisfying. "Can we talk to you for a few minutes? In private?"

Gage frowned, eyebrows knotting. He nodded. "Can we have the room?"

For a moment, I thought he wanted me to leave. Then Agent McNally stood up without a word, tucked her book under her arm, and slipped past us. Renee and Marco didn't argue the request. I hadn't expected Gage to make them leave, but they followed his order without question. If only he could tell Renee to lay off.

Gage leaned forward, elbows on his knees. Tension knotted his forehead. Dark smudges deepened the set of his eyes, making him look ten years older. The unnatural silver streaks in his hair only added to the illusion. "What is it, Dal?"

Noah gave me the recorder. I sat down next to Gage and

handed it to him. "The police have to have seen this by now, but they haven't said anything to us about it."

"What is it?" The grim line of his mouth indicated he knew. He just needed to hear it.

"The shooting."

He watched the scene twice. His skin was a few shades paler when he handed the recorder back. He looked up, his suspicious, silver eyes fixing on Noah. "Where did you get that?"

"I know someone who was there," Noah said. "The cops confiscated everyone else's tape for evidence. They didn't know he had this one."

Gage's attention flickered to me. "This doesn't prove he was targeting you, you know."

"He was aiming right at me." A worm of fear wiggled into my stomach. So close to dying. So very close.

"What do you want to do with it?"

"Talk to him." The admission came without thought. "Talk to Arnold Stark and ask him why he tried to kill me."

Gage nodded. "How about you?" he asked, gazing up at Noah. "What's your angle?"

"I don't get what you mean," Noah said. Bright spots of color appeared high in his cheeks. He shifted his weight, no longer relaxed or comfortable. The change in his entire demeanor occurred in the space of a breath.

"You're our electrician, Mr. Scott. You've known Dahlia for less than twelve hours. She's like a kid sister to all of us, which makes me a little protective. So forgive me for sounding like an overbearing creep, but . . . ?"

I cringed.

"Are my intentions honorable?" Noah finished.

God. I wanted to hide behind a chair.

Noah considered the question without ever breaking Gage's stare. "I'm not a crazy stalker, and I'm not a serial killer. We were classmates once, so I'm not a perfect stranger, either. I'm just a guy who runs his dead parents' lighting store and tries to take care of his family. I want to get to know her again, even if it's just as a friend. Most of us don't have enough friends nowadays."

Silence. Gage said nothing, and the pair stared at each other. My heart thudded so loudly I knew they could both hear it. Certainly Gage could. More likely, though, he was listening to Noah's heart, judging his truthfulness. I wanted assurance that Noah was being honest, and that I wasn't making a huge mistake befriending him. Trusting him.

After several long minutes, Gage blinked. He turned his head, finally looking at me. He winked, grinned. Relief drenched me like ice water.

"Do you want anyone to come with you to the police station?" he asked.

"I'd rather do this on my own," I said. "But you'll call me as soon as we hear from Teresa's doctor?"

"You know I will."

I did. I still had to ask. Leaving the hospital felt wrong, but I couldn't do anything more to help her in the waiting room than I could out in the city. At least this way, I was seeking answers. I needed answers, even if I might not particularly like the ones I found.

Nine

Arnold Stark

Noah offered to drive. We walked silently to the parked van, side by side. I replayed his words over and over, awed by them. And they were all true. Unless Noah was the most skilled liar Gage had ever encountered, which I seriously doubted.

He unlocked and opened the van's passenger door, then waited for me to climb inside. I reached across to pop the other lock. He cranked the engine and backed out of the parking space.

"I'm sorry about that," I said.

"About what?"

"Gage."

Noah chuckled, shifting into drive. "I've never been interrogated like that before, but it's understandable. He cares about you."

"I always thought dads were supposed to ask those kinds of questions."

"Will he?"

I turned sideways in my seat. "Will who what?"

"Will your dad ask those kinds of questions, too?"

Hah! "My father and I don't really have a relationship. He wasn't around when I was a kid, and I don't want him in my life now. Seems like a betrayal to my mom, and she doesn't deserve that."

"You're close to your mom, then?"

"I was. She died two years ago."

"I'm so sorry, Dahlia, I didn't mean to bring it up."

"It's okay, I can talk about it now without bursting into tears."

Not so just six months ago, when even after a year and a half, the pain of her death was still fresh, sharp. Agonizing. As Noah navigated the freeways, taking us toward the police station in Pasadena, I described my mom's short, painful bout with cancer. Tired and fluey for a whole year, but too concerned with my college tuition to bother paying for a doctor's visit. Collapsing at work. Dying at home over the summer, pale and weak and worried I wouldn't survive on my own.

Noah didn't ask questions, just listened. He clutched the steering wheel in a white-knuckled grip, his jaw clenched, muscles tight. As if knowing my horrible secrets was painful for him. I left out the worst details. The rotation of colorful pills and night nurses, the diarrhea and skeletal weight loss. He didn't need to know those things. Hell, I didn't particularly like knowing those things, but no amount of time could make you forget certain details. They were burned into my mind, forever.

My com beeped. I fished the earpiece out of my pocket and plugged it into my ear.

"Ember. Go ahead."

"It's Cipher. We just got a call from Officer Ortega concerning Arnold Stark."

I didn't like the waver in his voice. "And?"

"He's dead."

"What?" I slammed my palm down on the van's dashboard, eliciting a surprised yelp from Noah. "How?"

"They aren't sure yet. All that's left is his skin, just like Jarvis and the body in the alley."

My head throbbed. "Did Stark have any connection to Jarvis or Weatherfield?"

"Other than cause of death? No, not that anyone is telling me. Listen, Ember, I sent Tempest and Onyx out to meet you guys. Detective Pascal is also on his way. I want you to wait outside the precinct until he arrives."

"But we're almost—"

"Wait outside, Ember. Please."

I scowled at the windshield. "Fine, we'll wait. How long?"

"About fifteen minutes."

"Okay. Anything on Teresa?"

"A nurse came by and said that the surgery is going well and they should be done within the hour."

"Call me."

"I will."

The earpiece went back into my pocket as Noah turned into a parking lot on the edge of Old Town Pasadena. Across the street, a bright sign announced Police Station in black letters. People still wandered up and down the avenue, even though it was almost midnight. Mostly couples, and small groups of young folk about our age. Living lives of feigned simplicity, pretending the rest of the city wasn't in ruins.

"What was all that about?" Noah asked. He parked the van in a front-row space, giving us a good view of the station. He cut off the engine but left the keys dangling in the ignition.

I told him, taking extra time to describe what I'd seen that morning on Sunset. His eyebrows arched higher and higher. Silence filled the van when I finished, while Noah pondered the information I'd just tossed into his lap.

"That's . . . well, bizarre is the only word that sounds right."

"Agreed." I tapped my finger against my chin. "But that's three victims within the same ten-day time period, and it can't just be a coincidence that victim number three is the guy who tried to kill me."

"You're assuming there are only three victims, because you've only found three bodies."

"Skins."

He grimaced. "I like bodies. Skins just sounds wrong." He turned, putting his feet on the floor between our seats. I likewise shifted, until we sat face-to-face. "This is really your day job?"

"Sometimes. It's not usually this gruesome, but Detective Pascal has worked with us before. Given the nature of the deaths, it seemed likely the killer was a Meta."

"Do you still think so?"

"Has to be, although I hate to think it is. We'd hoped the last serial-killing Bane was dealt with back in January."

"When you killed Specter?"

"When Onyx killed Specter," I said.

"I mean a general you, not you specifically. The news reports about the incident didn't give a lot of details about who did what."

Thanks to Rita McNally and her ability to spin crap into gold via the media. "Well, I was unconscious and rolled up in a mat during that last big battle. It was really all Trance and Onyx. But I feel like all I do is talk about me. We have time to kill. Tell me something about you, Noah."

"What do you want to know?"

"Tell me about the 'sons' part of Scott and Sons."

A muscle in his jaw twitched. "I have two brothers."

Duh. I waited for more. He didn't seem eager to give up information without a little prodding. "Do you get along with your brothers?"

A smile ghosted across his face. "Sometimes we get along. Jimmy is a year younger and Aaron is a year older, so we've been pretty close our whole lives."

"Wow, three in a row. Your mom must have had some stamina."

The smile fled, and I could have kicked myself. *He said his parents were dead, you idiot. From the looks of it, it's still damned painful.* I leaned forward and squeezed his knee. "You don't have to talk about your family if it makes you uncomfortable."

His fiery green gaze met mine—family was definitely a

sore subject. I made a mental note to avoid it during light-hearted moments.

Headlights flashed through the windshield. I opened the door and jumped out on slightly wobbly legs. Our Sport followed a blue sedan into the parking lot and took two spaces behind our row. Pascal exited first, his nice suit somewhat wrinkled. He had a cup of drive-through coffee in one hand and his badge out in the other. Forney climbed out of the other side, as disheveled as her partner.

Tempest waved me over to the Sport.

"What?" I said when I arrived at his side. He tossed a clean uniform at me. I took the hint and got in the back, while Onyx exited from the front. I was glad to be out of Renee's clothes and that ridiculous "Princess" sweatshirt. At least now the cops could take me somewhat seriously. I found a pen under one of the seats and used it to twist my icky hair up into a coil at the nape of my neck before I climbed back out.

"Who's he?" Forney asked as we joined the detectives, jacking her thumb at Noah.

My lips parted to reply, but Onyx beat me to it with, "Civilian."

Forney scowled.

Pascal shook his head, his angular face particularly harsh beneath the glow of the streetlights. "Then he stays here. I'll vouch for you three, not for some kid I don't know."

Noah stiffened. "I'm not a kid."

I flinched inwardly. Bringing Noah hadn't been a smart move on my part. The detectives probably thought I was an idiot.

"Uh-huh." Pascal strode across the street, suit coat flapping wide in the gentle breeze. Forney, Onyx, and Tempest followed.

"I'm sorry," I said.

"He's right, Dahlia, I don't belong in there. You still on for breakfast?"

"Can we make it lunch? I don't know when I'll get to bed tonight."

"Lunch, then. Noon, same place."

"I'll be there."

I wanted to be excited about our lunch date—my first real date in almost a year—but I couldn't find it beneath the weight of so much uncertainty and fatigue. With a burst of waning energy, I bolted across the street and caught up with the others just as the outer door swung shut.

Stark's skin lay much the same way Jarvis's had, crumpled like a pile of wet laundry. There was no blood and very little fluid of any kind. Fingernails, eyebrows, eyelashes, chest hair, all outer details were still intact. Muscle, bone, tissue, and organs were gone. No one else had shared the multiple-occupancy cell with Stark, and both cells directly across were empty.

Onyx took one look and retreated to the safety of the corridor. Pascal squatted and poked the fingers with the tip of a pen. Officer Miguel Ortega hovered nearby, a little green around the edges. Forney had remained in the front room to interview the night officers.

"No one saw a thing?" Pascal asked.

"Ramirez and Jones were on duty," Ortega replied. "We checked on Stark twenty minutes before we found the body—er, skin—and they said he was fine. Sitting on his cot, staring into space. No one came in the front door, let alone down into holding."

"They both still here?"

"Down the hall, front desk. What the hell does that, Detective?"

"That's what we're here to find out."

"You said there was another—"

"Officer Ortega, thank you." Pascal waved his hand, dismissing the younger man. "We've got it from here, but if we need you, we'll call."

Ortega flushed red and stalked out of the cell in a rush of warm air. I considered staying, but there was little I could glean from the small cell. It was empty, save three people and human remains. Remains that still contained every inch of leg hair and a mole on the left ankle—wait.

"Wait a minute," I said. "He's naked."

Pascal nodded slowly. "Yes."

"He was in a locked cell, Detective. Where did his clothes go?" Understanding dawned on his face, so I kept going. "All along, we've what? Been assuming that whoever killed Jarvis and our other guy—do we know who he is yet?"

"Still a John Doe," Pascal said.

"Jarvis and John Doe, we've assumed they were skinned or gutted, and their skin left behind." My stomach rebelled just saying it, but I tamped down the nausea. "No one was in this cell with Stark. No one besides the officers on duty was even in the building to clean him out."

Tempest let out a strangled sound. "Whoever killed him was already inside," he said. "Stark brought him in with him when he was arrested."

"What, he was possessed?" Pascal scoffed, standing. His skepticism, now that he was at his full height, seemed to fill the room. I wasn't deterred. He was used to fighting regular bad guys who killed with knives and bullets. He was allowed to be skeptical.

"Something like that," I said. "It could be some sort of telekinetic, at a level we've never seen before. Maybe the killer was finished with Stark, so it was time to go elsewhere." The possibilities excited me almost as much as they terrified me. An incorporeal killer who inhabited bodies, sucked the life out of them, and then discarded the skin? Gross.

Pascal pursed his lips. "Why remove the clothes?"

"I don't know." I tapped my finger against my chin.

"They were restricting," Onyx said. He stepped into the cell's doorway, still seeming uneasy at the sight of the skin. He looked directly at Pascal. "Perhaps it cannot leave the skin while it is encased in clothing."

"So where did Stark's clothing go?" Pascal asked. He lifted the cot's mattress—nothing. There was nowhere else to stash clothes and a pair of sneakers.

"Someone had to have carried them out, right?" Tempest said.

"Or put them on."

Fear wormed up my spine and sent chilly fingers across the back of my neck. "Did Ortega say which officer specifically checked on him twenty minutes before they found the skin?" I asked, afraid to voice what instinct was screeching.

Tempest shook his head no.

I dashed out of the room to the sound of several shouted questions, all of which I ignored. Detective Forney leaned over the front desk, reading a report in a manila folder. Two officers sat behind the desk. A quick look at their name tags identified Ramirez and Jones. One person was missing.

"Where did Officer Ortega go?" I asked.

"He didn't come back this way," Forney said.

I turned and fled past three perplexed faces. Past the holding cells, I came to two doors. One said Locker Room. One said Exit. Someone was behind me. Onyx's face started morphing into cat form. The nose flattened and darkened, and whiskers sprouted on his flat lips. He inhaled sharply, using his feline senses, then pointed at the exit.

I pushed through, noting two cut wires next to the alarm trigger. We came out in a narrow alley, less than six feet between us and the back of the next building. Strewn with trash, the length of the alley ran the entire block, with splashes of light from dozens of back doors and side alleys.

Ortega was our killer. Or was possessed by our killer. Same difference, at the moment, because we needed to find him.

Onyx loped past me to the south, completely morphed into a muscled, full-grown panther. Faster than I could run, he was soon out of sight, hanging a sharp left down an alley leading back toward the main drag. Footsteps pounded the pavement behind me.

I hit the junction and turned, skidding in a puddle of slimy goo I didn't analyze too hard—just caught my balance and kept going, panting, out of breath. I needed to get into a gym and work a treadmill. Onyx stood on the sidewalk, just outside the mouth of the alley. He sniffed, turned left, sniffed again. Paused.

The sheer ease with which he passed between forms amazed me. His feline body lengthened, black hair disappearing as mottled skin emerged. His face flattened, tail drew away, paws split into fingers. In seconds, he flexed his shoulders, human once more. He turned, breathing hard through his nose. His green eyes glowed unnaturally bright in the streetlight, brighter than normal. The same hurt—barely concealed annoyance—with which he'd gazed at me for the last six weeks was gone, replaced by . . . respect?

It lasted only a moment, but I bathed in its warmth for the time I was given. I had missed his calm acceptance, the friendly smiles and gentle jokes. I missed the friendship we'd shared. And in that instant, I believed we could have it again.

Tempest, Pascal, and Forney finally caught up, red-faced and flustered. Before anyone could ask, Onyx beat them to the punch line. "The scent is gone," he said. "There is fresh oil here. Someone picked him up."

"Ortega, you mean?" Forney said, panting.

I nodded. "He ran. He had to have taken the clothes and hidden them, and then done whatever it is this . . . thing, this . . . Skin

Walker does. He fooled all of us. I mean, I spoke to him back at the fire, we both did, Tempest."

Forney's eyes narrowed, and she looked up and down the street. It was deserted, those last lingering couples long gone home. We were two blocks down from the precinct. No one would have noticed a vehicle down here. She grunted and looked at Onyx. "You were chasing his scent?"

"Yes, his cologne and the burrito he had for dinner. It gave him gas."

I scrunched my nose.

"Did you notice anything else?" Pascal asked. "Anything odd? Or even familiar?"

"No." Onyx shifted his eyes, turning them into catlike slits. "I can try again, perhaps search for a scent shared by Ortega and the body."

I bit the inside of my lip to keep from screaming in frustration. Ortega was missing, potentially possessed by a killer—what had I called it earlier? Oh, yeah—Skin Walker. Arnold Stark, the man who shot Trance while trying to kill me was, likewise, dead and all skin. And we still hadn't heard news on her surgery.

Glaring at the Closed sign on the café across the street, I followed the quartet back to the precinct. I wanted coffee. It promised to be a long damned night.

Ten

News

Just when the constant motion of the car had rocked me into a blissful sleep, it stopped. I jerked awake and almost fell off the seat. I didn't remember lying down, but I must have, because it took a conscious effort to haul my aching body back into a sitting position. It was after one in the morning and—chemical poisoning aside—way past my usual bedtime.

Ethan twisted around from the front passenger seat, started to say something, and stopped. He frowned. "Dal, you okay? You look really pale."

"Long day," I said. I could still smell smoke in my hair. A shower would be a blessing. "Where are—?" I recognized the hospital parking lot.

We used a side entrance and bypassed the reporters still hanging around hoping for a scoop—or at least an update on the condition of the wounded Meta. Their constant presence infuriated me. They were not there because they cared if she lived or died. They didn't know her or want to know her. They wanted their story. It was that simple. Murder played better than survival, so it was easy to guess their desired result.

I just wanted my mentor back.

The same uniformed officer still guarded the elevator, sleepier since the last time. He nodded as we passed. The waiting room door was ajar and low voices drifted out. Marco reached for it at the same time as Ethan's com beeped. The door swung open, revealing Gage with his own com out, placing the call. He put it down when he saw us, eyebrows arching in surprise.

"Hey, you're back," he said.

Ethan snorted. "Did your supersight tell you that?"

"Why were you calling?" I asked, ignoring the sarcastic remark.

Gage didn't, though. He took a moment to glare at Ethan, and then acknowledged my question. "The surgeon came by a minute ago. Teresa is out of surgery. He said she's doing well, and they'll know more after she's rested awhile. We can see her when she's out of recovery."

A hand of joy squeezed my heart, threatening to burst it. Impulsively, I wrapped my arms around Gage's shoulders and hugged. He surprised me by returning the embrace, hard and fierce. His body practically vibrated with tension, shoulders knotted, heart thrumming. He began to shake and inhaled a shuddering breath. And another. I blinked, then held him tighter.

He was crying. Actually crying. Releasing the pent-up frustration and consuming relief of knowing the hard part was over and recovery was just around the bend. That everything would be okay. I held him, letting him cry silently on my shoulder. Ethan and Marco left us alone, and after a while, I realized they were the only other people in the room.

Renee was missing.

She returned to the waiting room halfway through our story, right around the part that made me look pretty smart for figuring out Ortega was the new host. Renee slipped through the door, eyes on the floor, straw-blond hair falling in a loose curtain across her pale blue face. Only Marco raised his head to acknowledge her arrival; I just kept talking.

"He had a head start, though, and we lost him," I said. "Marco said his scent trail stopped back on the street, so he must have gotten into a car and driven off."

Gage inhaled, held it, and then blew the air out through his nose. He scrubbed both hands over his face, through his hair. "Okay, so now we've got three victims. Jarvis was first, then our John Doe, and now Stark."

"Jarvis is still our first link," Ethan said. "Which is keeping Weatherfield near the top of my suspects list, evidence or not."

"Mine, too," Gage added. "We need to find out who this John Doe is, and if he has any real connection to Jarvis, or if the Skin Walker took him at random. Same thing with Arnold Stark. Details about him, if he was just the next body or if there was a reason he was taken."

He started to add something, but stopped. We were all thinking the same thing. Was it Stark who tried to kill me, or the Skin Walker possessing him? Because if it was the Skin Walker, he may not be finished trying. It made all of us open targets, especially if anyone on the street could be possessed by this creature.

"I'm sure Pascal will share whatever he gets," I said. "He knows this isn't just a job for us anymore."

Gage nodded his agreement. "Pascal is a good man, but I don't want to rely on him for information. We're not private investigators, but near enough."

"What do you suggest?" Ethan asked.

"Sleep." Gage took the time to look at each of us, his silver-flecked gaze hard and tired. "Go home, get a few hours of sleep. Then we'll do our own checking on Arnold Stark."

Ethan's eyebrows furrowed. "But—"

"We won't be effective if we're all exhausted."

Everyone conceded the point.

"Look," Gage continued, "I'm going to stay here. You guys, just go home. It's been a long-assed day, and I am reserving the right to be the stiff-upper-lip guy who stays behind and pretends he isn't bone tired, too." Conviction couldn't mask his exhaustion; it did do a moderate job of making me believe him. He looked old and so damned weary.

Renee stood up. "You'll call if—?"

"Yes."

She left first and quickly. My annoyance meter rose a few notches. She hadn't been there ten minutes ago when Gage needed comfort, and now she was dashing as quickly as possible toward the elevator. Marco and Ethan followed her out.

I reached over to squeeze Gage's hand; I didn't want to leave him there alone.

He squeezed back. "Where did your friend go?"

"Home, I guess," I said. "Pascal wouldn't let him go into the station with us, so he left. We made lunch plans, though, as long as I'm not passed out in bed."

"If you are, he'll understand, Dahlia. I was serious before, about feeling protective, so bear with me if I start to take his interest too personally. Especially now, with someone out there targeting you. Promise me you'll be careful when you go out tomorrow. Keep your eyes open."

"I promise." I was a little surprised he hadn't ordered me to stay home, insisting I not go out in public where Ortega—or someone else, if Ortega was shed just like the others—could finish what he started. Going out wouldn't be the smartest move of my life, but I couldn't let this Skin Walker cow me, or make me afraid of the outside world.

I would not.

"Well, I appreciate the concern." And I did, more than I could ever express. "I never had siblings, let alone a big brother."

A smile quirked the corners of Gage's mouth. "How about three big brothers and two sisters?"

"That either." Sometimes Renee reminded me more of an evil stepsister, but I kept that to myself. No sense in analyzing our inability to get along at one in the morning, with someone who was as emotionally exhausted as I was physically. Renee and I had time to work out our problems.

Right now, Teresa and the Skin Walker were our biggest priorities.

"Look, try to rest a little bit." I released his hand and stood up. "She'll be fine. Teresa is the strongest person I know. She's a warrior, and warriors don't die when a coward shoots them with a gun. It's not her style."

He seemed to sink back into his chair, shrinking in front of me. "I know. I guess I thought I was finished sitting by her hospital bedside, worrying if she was going to live or die. I got quite enough of that back in January before she learned to control her power surges. I didn't think I could ever worry about her more than I did then, but I was wrong." He waved his hand in a dismissive gesture. "Go on, they're waiting for you. I'll see you in the morning."

On impulse, I kissed his cheek. He winked at me as I departed, and then settled back into the chair for a long wait.

I caught up to the others at the elevator and got a good look at Renee in the fluorescent light. Her eyes were bloodshot, the rims bright red and swollen. She turned away when she caught me staring. Anger rose, heating my chest. She had displayed the same weakness that she berated me for and was now trying to hide it.

Let it go, Dahlia, just let it go.

Oddly, I was able to, and chose to just ignore her for the entire trip home.

As much as I longed to take an extended shower and wash the last smoky remnants of the warehouse fire out of my odorous hair, I was just too damned tired to bother. We trudged upstairs as a unit and retired to our separate bedrooms. I peeled out of my uniform jacket and pants and crawled into bed.

Sprawled out on my belly, pillow bunched up beneath my head, I closed my eyes but could not sleep.

Images of the shooting kept replaying. The glint of light off the muzzle of the gun; the flat look in Stark's eyes; the surprise in Teresa's. The blood on the pavement and on my hands, oozing through my fingers, and the stink of smoke and water and damp concrete. Tears stung my eyes and I forced them away—no more tonight.

I refocused my thoughts on the best part of yesterday: Noah Scott. The short, spiky pattern of his auburn hair, and his mesmerizing green eyes, a shade so startling they didn't seem real. The way his mouth curled at the corners when he was trying not to smile. He gazed at me like I was the most precious thing on Earth. Only Marco had ever looked at me like that before; I hadn't been able to return his affection.

I hadn't been attracted to Marco, no, but the idea of loving someone scared me, too. Noah said it himself—life was short, and we lost people we cared about. My mother had her heart broken and was left alone to raise a child. Renee lost William. Gage loved Teresa, and now she was fighting for her life. Love seemed easy to fall into, but did it ever last? I could easily lose my heart to Noah.

The question: Is it worth it?

Eleven

Wild Cards

The sharp, intoxicating aroma of freshly brewed coffee enticed me out of a deep, dreamless sleep. I woke slowly, curled on my right side, one bare leg draped over the edge of the mattress. A blue porcelain mug hovered directly in my line of sight, and I followed the attached hand up to Ethan's face.

"Good morning," he said.

I grunted, still trying to form coherent thoughts in my sleep-deprived mind. Light streamed in through the single window, pale and low. It was definitely morning; good or not remained to be seen. And the person they'd sent to rustle me out of bed was the one most likely to succeed.

It wasn't any one thing that had cemented my fast friendship with Ethan. He'd been horribly injured by a collapsed ceiling when we first met, so we hadn't spent a lot of time together until I'd been with the team for a month. Maybe it was that he would never make a romantic overture, and he didn't play the part of the overbearing big brother. He didn't judge me like Renee did. He was just Ethan—funny, understanding, good friend Ethan. The guy who had advice for any problem, but never dumped his own stuff on me.

And sometimes I really wished he would. All of the bright smiles and sunny conversations couldn't completely hide the shadows in his eyes or the weight of the secret he still hid from the others. I knew he trusted his friends with his life, and he had his own reasons for keeping that secret from them.

Ethan swayed the coffee mug back and forth in front of me. "We've got a big pot going downstairs, and a mug waiting for you. After a shower, because, my dear, you reek."

I blew a raspberry and sat up. "I'll be down in a few minutes." He made it halfway to the door before I called out with a question: "Anything new on Teresa?"

"She's still unconscious, but her vitals are strong." Ethan glanced over his shoulder. "You know, I always thought of you as more of a lacy thong type of girl."

I stared blankly until I realized I was sitting there in an orange tank top and pale yellow panties, and nothing else. "Out!"

He laughed and closed the door behind him. Lacy thong, indeed. I worked hard enough to find panties that didn't ride up my butt; I wasn't about to purposely spend money on ones that did.

I rolled out of bed and into my robe. The custom-made bathroom was conveniently across the hall, and empty. A three-basin sink and long mirror covered the wall on the right, and a curtained entry at the very end hid a row of toilet stalls. On the left, across from the center sink, was another curtained doorway. I stepped through, ignoring the mirror and my reflection. I didn't want to know how bad I looked.

The shower unit had four separate stalls, each with a small changing area and bench. The design was better than what I remembered from college. Those dorm showers didn't have a separate spot for drying off and dressing. We'd agreed on this style, instead of several private baths, on the off chance that our resident numbers increased in the future.

I kept my things in the last stall, nestled together in a plastic basket. The cloying odor of smoke washed away quickly with my shampoo, and I took care to scrub every single inch of skin with the body wash. I wanted to linger beneath the steamy spray for hours, allowing the heat to soothe tired muscles and comfort the hurts, only there wasn't time.

I ran the lathered sponge down my left leg, over a pattern of small bruises. Two more dotted my right, just behind the knee. Bruises popped up all over the place lately. Teresa was pushing me hard in my physical training, helping me develop my self-defense skills. Bruises came with the job.

Hair wrapped up in a towel turban, I padded back to my room to dress. We were officially on a case, so I pulled on a fresh pair of black pants and orange tank and swept my wet hair up into a tight bun. Jacket tucked under my arm, I headed downstairs, refreshed and somewhat energized.

I approached the kitchen by way of the dining room, but found both empty. The coffeepot was half full, so I poured a large mug, added sugar, and grabbed a slice of wheat bread from the open package on the island. With breakfast in hand, I padded down the second hallway to the War Room.

Voices drifted toward me. Ethan and Renee were hunched over a pile of printouts, their own coffee mugs nearby. Only Ethan raised his head to acknowledge my arrival and wave me over.

"What did you find?" I asked.

"A lot on Arnold Stark," Ethan said. "Pascal e-filed us what he had on Stark, which was enough to get our own search started. So far we've got quite a profile going, but irritatingly, not a thing that connects him to Jarvis or Ortega."

"Besides the fact that Ortega arrested him," Renee added. "We can't discount John Doe until we identify him."

"So who is Stark?" I asked, sitting on the edge of the table and biting into my slice of bread. Should have put some butter on it.

"Freelance journalist," Ethan said. "He used to make a living doing security at music galas, while writing on the side."

Renee slid a paper toward me. It was a photocopy of a letter. "Seems Stark has amassed quite a few enemies by writing about those galas under a pseudonym," she said. "Even earned himself a few death threats, and he was definitely fired from the gig when he was found out. He's got a thing for raking celebrities over the coals in his articles, which could explain why he was at the fire yesterday. Maybe he was looking to throw some dirt at us."

"But it doesn't explain why he shot at us," I said.

"Why he shot at *you*," Renee said. "He's got no history of violent behavior, no recorded anti-Meta statements, nothing to indicate he'd do what he did."

I nodded, glancing over the scrawled words on the page,

and silently told him to perform an anatomically impossible action on himself. "So we're going on the assumption that the Skin Walker is the one targeting us, not Stark."

"Looks that way, Dal," Ethan said. "And whoever this Skin Walker is, he or she knew exactly which host to pick in order to get close enough to shoot."

"But why? Why try to kill me? How could I have possibly made someone hate me this much this fast?" I desperately wanted to find the son of a bitch and lock him (or her) away for a very, very long time. Stark was, in the end, as much a victim as we were, another pawn in someone else's sick scheme.

"If he's picking hosts at random," Renee said, "it's going to make tracking this guy, or thing, that much harder. He knows we know he's in Officer Ortega, which means he'll dispose of Ortega pretty quick."

"And kill Ortega in the process," Ethan said.

My stomach tightened, the bread no longer sitting well. Another in a long line of victims, drained of his insides and left as nothing more than a sack of skin and fingernails. Dead because he was doing his job. Did he have a family? Would they mourn him when he was gone?

"Where's Marco?" I asked, refocusing my thoughts to something a little less (but barely so) depressing.

"Telephone," Ethan said. "Gage called a few minutes ago, and Marco is filling him in."

"So do we have a plan for this morning?"

Renee shook her head. "So far, we're doing it." Her attention darted over my shoulder, prompting me to turn around.

Marco stood in the doorway, phone in hand, mouth drawn into a tight line. Worry bracketed his eyes.

"Gage had to hang up," Marco said to us, words clipped. "Teresa had a seizure."

Dread washed over me. I nearly dropped my coffee mug when Renee slammed her fist down on the tabletop near my hip. Ethan reached for her arm, but she yanked away from him.

"We should get to the hospital," she said. "We should be there."

Marco took a step toward her. "Renee—" The phone in his hand rang, its shrill tone cutting him off like a warning bell. He looked at the receiver's display, frowned, but pressed Receive. "Headquarters, Onyx." We watched in curious silence as his expression changed from confusion to surprise, and finally annoyance. "Fine, we will be there in twenty minutes." He hung up.

"We'll be where in twenty minutes?" Renee asked.

"Weatherfield," he said. "Dr. Kinsey has something more to tell us about Jarvis and the person who may have killed him."

"What?" Renee stalked toward him. She stopped an arm's length away, apparently realizing Marco was not her enemy. "He was lying to you the first time you spoke?"

"Es posible," Marco replied. "Or he was carefully omitting details. We will not know until we speak with *el bastardo.*" He narrowed his eyes at Renee. "Are you coming with us?"

She hesitated. Shaking her head no, she said, "Someone needs to be with Gage. You guys go."

I guzzled a few gulps of scorching coffee—thankful it didn't seriously burn the inside of my mouth—plunked the mug down on the table, and followed Marco out, Ethan on my heels. Anger built with each step toward the front door; anger directed entirely at Dr. Abram Kinsey. For lying to us before, and for dragging us away from Teresa's side when she needed us most.

We were at a disadvantage during our second visit to Weatherfield. With Gage otherwise occupied, our lie detector was out. He'd either missed something during the first interview, or Kinsey was an accomplished liar who no longer distinguished reality from lies. We would get the truth from Kinsey if I had to force it from him with pliers.

He didn't meet us in the lobby. A different desk guard pointed us toward the elevator and said we were expected in Dr. Kinsey's office. We found it easily, the corridors as empty as the first visit. I was tempted to stop at the treatment ward, just to see if everyone was "in treatment" again. The entire building gave me the creeps.

Tempest banged his fist on the closed office door. A terse "Enter" gave us permission, and he yanked on the knob, maybe too forcefully. I walked in behind him, Onyx bringing up the rear. He hadn't been with us the first time and was taking in the scenery, making his own observations.

Dr. Kinsey sat behind his desk, hands folded flat on top

of each other. His lab coat hung on a rack behind him, and he was dressed in a simple suit and tie. He indicated the two chairs with a sharp nod. Tempest and I sat down, mirroring the way Trance and Cipher had sat just twenty-four hours ago. Onyx stood behind my chair, hands squeezing the vinyl material.

"I hear you've had a change of heart, Doctor," Tempest said, his voice dripping with ice and anger. "Care to tell us what you couldn't elaborate on yesterday?"

Kinsey's eyes narrowed, taking time to study each of us in turn before speaking directly to Tempest. "I will, of course," he said. "But first, I want to convey my sincere condolences about Trance. I do hope she pulls through."

Tempest's jaw flexed, and I wondered if he was holding back a sarcastic response. My first words would have been along the lines of *You don't know her and you don't care about her, so shut the hell up, you patronizing ass.* Something in Kinsey's tone kept me silent, and likely also kept Tempest on his best behavior. The icy façade Kinsey had displayed yesterday was gone, replaced by fatigue and concern. Genuine concern.

"Thank you," Tempest ground out. We hadn't heard back from Gage or Renee since leaving the house and could only hope the seizure was under control and Trance was stable again.

"I apologize for my manners yesterday." Dr. Kinsey reached across his desk, toward a black box the size of a baseball. He touched a button and a gentle, whirring sound filled the room, quickly melting into the background. White noise.

"I was under direct orders from my superiors not to discuss Ronald Jarvis."

"What changed their minds?"

"They haven't," Kinsey said. "They think you requested this interview, hence the white noise. I don't want them to know what we're about to discuss, and I couldn't risk meeting you in public. They're probably following me now, outside this building."

"Why?" I asked, sitting up straighter in my chair. "What do you know about the person who killed Jarvis and at least three other people?"

"Three?" Dr. Kinsey paled, something I had never actually seen a human being do before. White as paper, just like that.

Tempest nodded slowly. "Our John Doe, a man named Arnold Stark, and when he's finished with the body, Officer Ortega of the LAPD."

Dr. Kinsey squeezed his eyes shut, pinched the bridge of his nose. "I never expected them to go this far, I swear I didn't."

"They?" we said in unison.

"Yes." He pulled open a desk drawer, removed a sheet of photographic paper, and slid it across the desk. "They."

I picked it up. It was a picture of three people, teenage boys by the looks of their clothing, standing in a cluster, as though mugging for the camera. But they couldn't be, because they had no faces to mug. I brushed my finger over the image. Had their faces been smudged out? Altered in some way? No, certain features like the brow ridge and slight bumps where eyes, nose, and lips should be still existed.

Holes appeared where ears and a mouth should have been. No hair anywhere I could see.

"What is this?" Tempest asked.

"Your suspects," Dr. Kinsey said.

"Is that some kind of joke? Those aren't people, they're mannequins."

"I assure you, they are as real as you and I."

"Why don't they have faces?" I asked, not sure I wanted to know the answer.

His gaze flickered up to Onyx, and then back down to me. "Because they are Changelings, Ember. Hybrid Changelings without faces of their own."

He said it as though it explained everything; instead, it left me mystified. I didn't know what a Hybrid Changeling was, and judging from their silence, Tempest and Onyx didn't, either.

"You're going to have to explain what that means, Doctor," Tempest said.

Dr. Kinsey eyed the white-noise box on his desk, and then began to speak. "When I was hired twenty-five years ago, it was for their Recombinant-DNA project. For decades, like several other companies at the time, they tried to dissect, understand, study, and re-create Meta powers. They failed, so they went another route with Recombinants. It took countless trials, but we were finally blessed with five healthy infants—two girls and three boys. This was twenty years ago.

"They were all Changelings, born with no physical features of their own. For some reason, the girls' DNA was less stable than the boys." They were often sick, and they both died within days of each other at age five. But the boys were strong and capable, and they learned fast to use and control their powers."

I listened with a strange mixture of shock, awe, revulsion, and fascination. I'd heard rumors of DNA experiments before, from all over the country. Never in my career as a journalist had anyone ever confirmed those rumors and admitted to participating in their creation. Scientists playing God, trying to re-create what nature had blessed us with, and the results were . . . well, loose. And murdering people.

"Tell us about their powers," Tempest said.

"As Changelings, they have no identities of their own, but possess the ability to mimic others. With just a touch, they can perfectly reflect someone's outward appearance, from height and weight to hair and eye color. Everything external is re-created to the last detail. They can pass as anyone, and as teenagers, often did, and got themselves into trouble."

"Everything external," I said, thinking of the skins. "What about other things, like voice? Could they mimic that?"

Dr. Kinsey's face darkened, coloring with anger. "No, not with just a touch. We discovered this ability the hard way, I'm afraid. If they choose to, they can physically possess the body of any person they touch. Their own body becomes one with the host, but in that moment of possession, the host . . . well, two souls cannot coexist in one body, and the stronger of the two is always the Changeling. The possessor absorbs the memories, knowledge, and life experience of the host, down to voice patterns and food preferences. The host doesn't die, exactly, but he's no longer an individual. The Changeling can exist this way indefinitely if he chooses to assimilate the host, rather than fight his personality."

Onyx growled low in his throat. "So when the Changeling is finished with the host, he moves out and leaves an empty shell behind. They are the skins we have found."

"Essentially, yes, I'm afraid you're correct. It was a difficult ability to test, because there was no going back for the possessed victim, and we discontinued its practice very early. The boys were taught never to use that particular talent against another person."

"Looks like someone forgot a lesson or two," I said. "So, how many of them escaped, Dr. Kinsey? Just one, inside Ronald Jarvis?"

Kinsey shook his head. "No, all three are missing. It would take only one complete possession, that of Jarvis, to get them out, which is what our security cameras picked up. Him leaving with two of our janitors, who were later found tied up in a utility closet."

Three Changelings, out there taking over bodies and killing people. The journalist in me was salivating at the story potential. The hero in me was just plain pissed. "So let me guess," I said. "This breakout occurred the night Jarvis died? Once they were out, he wasn't needed anymore?"

"Yes."

This just kept getting worse and worse.

"You said they were Hybrid Changelings," Tempest said. "What does the hybrid part mean?"

Dr. Kinsey pursed his lips, seeming to weigh his answer.

"Each of them also possesses a secondary ability, one that sets him apart from his brothers."

"Which are what?"

"Ace possesses telekinesis. He can move objects with his thoughts. Joker is telepathic, which is fairly self-explanatory. He can listen in and place suggestions in your mind but only has two-way telepathy with his brothers. And King is fast. He can run upward of eighty miles an hour given an open space and lots of room. The ability also gives him a slightly denser muscle and skin mass, to protect him from wind pressure, so he has increased strength and endurance."

Just like William.

The thought came unbidden and with it, the guilt that never completely went away.

"Ace, Joker, and King?" Tempest said.

"Yes, their sisters were Queen and Deuce. My Wild Cards." He spoke so fondly of them, he could have been a doting father bragging about his child's seventh-inning, game-winning home run.

"Why would they break out, Doctor?" Onyx asked. "If they've been here for twenty years, why leave now?"

"I have no answer for you," Dr. Kinsey said. "Perhaps they no longer felt safe. Perhaps your reappearance made them feel unimportant to the world. Recombinants were meant to aid you, understand, and then replace you after the War took away your powers."

Tempest snorted. "Well, running around killing people is not the right way to prove your worth."

"I do not believe blind murder is their motive, Tempest.

Please understand, I worked with these boys their entire lives. They are not violent by nature, and they do not kill for sport."

"Have they contacted you since they escaped?"

"Why would they?"

"You just said you raised them, Doctor. Why wouldn't they? I can't imagine they were prepared for living in the outside world without any sort of guidance."

"They are more well equipped than you think."

"Why would they want me dead?" I asked.

Dr. Kinsey blanched, stared. "What?"

"You know about yesterday's shooting?"

"Of course." His confusion concerned me.

"Arnold Stark was the one who pulled the trigger, aiming at me and hitting Trance instead," I said, measuring his reaction with every word I spoke. So far, he was following, just not comprehending. "Stark was our third victim. He was possessed by one of your Changelings at the time of the attack."

The man actually grew paler. His hands clutched into fists so tight his knuckles popped. "That's impossible," he whispered.

"Really?"

"Look, I've already told you more than is safe for me to say. How you extrapolate the data is up to you, but those boys are not murderers. Not in cold blood, not like you think. They are trying to survive, and we are trying to bring them home. I told you all of this so you might help me do so."

"Not happening," Tempest said. "If we catch them, they're going to jail to face charges. They don't get to run around killing people in our city, and then go home like nothing happened, so you can forget that fantasy right now, Doctor."

Dr. Kinsey's eyes narrowed. "If you take anything I've just told you to the police, I will deny it wholly and under oath. This is a good-faith interview, Tempest, not a confession."

Tempest glared. "My only concern is for the safety of the people left in this godforsaken, rotting city, Dr. Kinsey. Saving your job and your precious Recombinant project is nowhere on my list of priorities. Just so you know where we stand."

"I am asking you, please—" Kinsey tried again.

"No." Tempest stood up. "Unless you have some other information for us that will be useful in apprehending three suspects now wanted for murder, I think our interview is over."

Dr. Kinsey also stood, nostrils flaring. "You'll be able to tell them apart by their birthmarks," he said. "They are absorbed by the host body, sort of like a fail-safe switch in case we lose one of them. It's a brown mark, about the size of a quarter, located in the small of the back. It's shaped like Australia."

Of all the random shapes . . .

"Thank you, Doctor," Tempest said. "We'll be in touch."

"I appreciate that." He switched off the white noise and silence settled back over the room. "Good day."

"Fat chance," I muttered.

Twelve

Simon Hewitt

A heated argument over what exactly to relay to Detectives Pascal and Forney filled the first ten minutes of our drive to the hospital. Oddly, Marco and I found ourselves pitted against Ethan, both of us in favor of telling them nothing—for now.

"We're not saying keep them in the dark forever," I said. I had scooted forward between the front seats. Marco drove, so I had to take point on our side. "But Dr. Kinsey took a calculated risk telling us what he did. If we go to Pascal, he'll turn Weatherfield inside out looking for information on the Changelings."

"And why is that a bad thing?" Ethan asked. His eyes flashed angrily. Surprisingly so. "You of all people should want the cops to bust down the doors and put that place out of business."

"I do. But this isn't the way, Ethan, and you know it. Something about today's conversation makes me think Kinsey is on the level. He wants us to find the Changelings before the cops do. The cops won't be able to stop them without killing them."

"The Changelings have killed."

I blew hard through my nose. "And you really think I've forgotten that? Look, we don't work for the police. We work for ourselves. Isn't that why we left the ATF? So we wouldn't have suits breathing down our neck, waiting for results?"

"She is right, *hermano*," Marco said. I braced as he negotiated a sharp left turn. "Teresa said we would work with the police, not for them. If we handle this ourselves, it is likely to stay out of the media. The public is already afraid of us, and knowing our kind—"

"They aren't our kind," Ethan said. "They're experiments."

"They're still living beings," I snapped. "Maybe they had donated DNA, but they're alive. And something tells me they didn't break out of Weatherfield solely to try to kill me, so there's another reason we aren't seeing."

Ethan quirked an eyebrow. "Chili cheese fries?"

"Ass." I punched his shoulder, but it was lighthearted. He was coming around, and I needed to work that so it was three of us talking if Gage needed convincing, too. Renee wouldn't; she didn't like working with the police. Period.

"Brat."

"Windbag."

"Fire-eater."

Ethan's com rang, interrupting my turn at jabbing an insult. He plugged in the earpiece. "Tempest. Go ahead." Pause. "Really? When?" Eyebrows furrowed. "Okay. Listen, we've got a lot to talk about when we get there." Pause. "Maybe ten minutes. See you then."

Call over, his attention diverted back to us. "Teresa's fine. The seizure was mild, some sort of reaction to the pain medication, and she's resting again. They could move her out of ICU as early as tonight, if she keeps doing well."

My chest felt lighter. In my book, no seizure was a mild seizure, but getting out of ICU was a great sign. She was getting better. She'd be fine.

"And you'll never guess who's in town," Ethan continued. "Our old friend Psystorm."

Simon "Psystorm" Hewitt was a formerly imprisoned Bane-turned-ally, and Teresa's liaison with the current residents of Manhattan Island. He was working with her and the government to gain pardons for many of the residents and to establish their own community on the island that had once been their prison. He had a five-year-old son named Caleb, and the unlikely pair doted on each other, the son taking care of the father as much as vice versa.

Both also had strong powers. Simon was a telepath, and his son was already a high-level telekinetic. I had never personally seen their powers in action, but had heard the stories. They made me glad the pair was on our side.

"Social call?" Marco asked.

"Not strictly," Ethan replied. "Sounds like he's heard about our little problem and wants to assist."

"Which is good news for us, right?" I said. "Maybe he can help us distinguish who's real from who's a Changeling."

"Let's hope," Ethan said.

Marco hit another turn too hard, tossing me into the side of Ethan's seat. I crossed my eyes at him in the rearview mirror. Next time, I was driving.

The waiting room outside of the ICU wasn't as private as the surgical waiting area. Another couple was there, so once Simon Hewitt joined us at the hospital, we held our little meeting down the hall in a storage room. It wasn't ideal and left six people crammed in together.

Ethan and I took turns narrating the interview with Dr. Kinsey, accommodating occasional questions from our audience. Gage seemed more relaxed than he had last night, even though the circles under his eyes had darkened. Fatigue, more than fear, hovered around him like a storm cloud. Renee listened attentively, glaring in all the appropriate places and biting her lower lip to stop errant comments.

Simon asked the most questions as he caught up on a new case. Renee had filled him in as best she could before our arrival, but he was still missing salient details. He hadn't changed—still balding, holding on hard to the last of his light brown hair. He had kind, gentle eyes and a narrow face that lit up when he smiled. Something we all did too rarely.

"You can't take this to the police," Simon said, once we'd finished.

"Agreed," Marco said. "Dr. Kinsey took a large risk in telling us—"

"I don't give a good goddamn about Kinsey," Simon said.

"He made his bed, he can lie in it and get boils on his ass for all I care. This isn't about him or his company, it's about how the public will react."

"The public?" Ethan asked.

Simon nodded. "It's bad enough the media is starting to report the bodies and that a Meta could be responsible. How do you think people will react when they learn there are three of these Changelings out there? And the police, for that matter? They'll get jumpy and innocent people will get hurt."

Gage tilted his head, regarding Simon for a moment. "This isn't Ocean City, Simon," he said. "We don't shoot first and ask questions later."

"You don't," he replied, "but some people still do, and this isn't about me, Gage. It's about catching these kids before they do any more damage, either on purpose or by accident."

"By accident?" Renee repeated. "You think leaving three people's skins out to dry is an accident? Shooting Teresa was an accident?"

Simon narrowed his eyes. "You know what I mean, Renee. They don't know how to be anything other than what they are." He held up a hand. "And before you snap, no, I don't condone what they've done, but I'm in a better position to sympathize. I don't wish to see them dead."

"So we don't tell the police," Ethan said. "What do we do instead?"

"Gage is going home for a shower and some sleep," Renee said. Her tone left no room for argument, and judging by the slump of his shoulders, she wouldn't get one. "I'll stay and keep an eye on Teresa if you guys want to . . . you know, do investigative stuff."

"I'll go back to the house with Gage," Simon said. "I want to go over the information you've pooled together and get a better feel for things. Then I'd like to talk to your detectives."

"What for?" Ethan asked.

"As much as I don't want to see a human corpse that's been reduced to a pile of skin, I may be able to get something from one of the bodies. A feeling or an image, something to help me locate one of the Changelings' minds."

"You're looking for a needle in a stack of needles."

"Yes, but occasionally one of them rusts and becomes distinguishable from the rest."

"Good point."

"Glad we agree." Simon grinned. "Because I'm going to need an escort. I don't know this city, and your detectives don't know me from Adam."

Ethan groaned. He'd just been volunteered and he knew it. "Want to tag along, Dal?"

The pleading look in his eyes made me smile. "I think—" Wait a minute. "What time is it?"

Simon tugged back the sleeve of his shirt. "It's half past eleven. Something wrong?"

Crap. "No, I just need to make a call and cancel something."

"Don't cancel, Dahlia," Gage said. He shook his head, jaw set. "We don't need you until another lead stumbles across our path, so do your thing this afternoon. Don't cancel it."

I wanted to throw my arms around his neck and hug him,

but he looked fragile enough to shatter into a dozen pieces if I even poked him. Instead, I poured my gratitude into a hundred-watt smile. I wanted to have lunch with Noah. I craved the sense of normalcy I'd get from such a simple thing. It beat pacing the house with nothing to do, or having to look at those skin piles again. Gross.

The frown creasing Renee's face voiced her silent disapproval. I smiled at her until she looked away. I neither needed nor wanted her approval anymore.

"Who wants me?" Marco asked.

"Keep me company until they need you," Renee said, slipping one arm through his.

We continued to stand there, a ragtag corps of Metas, united by our shared knowledge and pain and by our determination to see this thing through to whatever end. It hummed through the room like a bass vibration, an invisible thread binding us. Another moment passed, and then we parted company.

I rode back to the house with Gage, Simon, and Ethan, impressed that Gage didn't fall asleep in the backseat. He walked stiffly into the house and up the stairs. I followed at a distance, waiting until his bedroom door clicked shut before heading to my own room to change. I didn't want to show up in uniform and scare the locals.

I also didn't want to tempt fate, since someone was obviously trying to kill me, so I put a plain black blouse on over the armored tank top, and switched out my pants for denim shorts. I let my still-damp hair down, and it spiraled around my shoulders in soft waves. No makeup, though, as I rarely wore it. The fatigue circles under my eyes weren't too visible, so I ignored them. He knew I was tired, and he knew why.

I opened my bedroom door and stepped back, a startled yelp rising in my throat. Ethan stood against the wall across the hallway, arms folded over his chest. Struggling to keep my pounding heart from blasting out of my chest, I glared at him. "Hover much?"

"Are you sure this is safe?" he asked. "Going out alone, when we know someone is targeting you?"

"Gage seems to think so."

"Gage is exhausted."

I stepped past him and started down the hall toward the main staircase. He caught up, grabbed my arm, and spun me around. I yanked out of his bruising grip, and he backed off a few steps. "I do not need a chaperone, Ethan."

"No, you need an automatic Changeling detector, but since we're all out of those, chaperone is the next best thing."

"Forget it."

"What if someone attacks you?"

"What if I get hit by a bus while crossing the street?" He flinched; I pinched the bridge of my nose. "Look, I appreciate the concern, I really do, but Noah's an old friend, not a crazy stalker-man. And I swear I will be careful and alert. I don't need you guys to protect me. I'm a big girl."

"You're twenty-two."

Windbag was pulling the age card on me? "So what? Teresa is only twenty-five."

"But she . . ."

He stopped. I didn't relent, knowing precisely where that line had been headed. "But she what?" I said. "Had parents who were Rangers? Grew up around this sort of thing? Is our default leader and therefore the only female in this group capable of taking care of herself?"

"That's not fair, Dal."

"Tell me one damned thing about all of this that is fair. Go on, I dare you."

Nothing. Good. Hoping the discussion was over, I turned and stalked toward the stairs. He caught up again at the top of the landing. This time, he didn't grab me. He bolted down two steps and cut me off.

"Can I at least say be careful?" he asked.

"You can say it," I replied. "But I already knew it." He finally smiled, and my annoyance melted. "Have fun with Simon," I said.

"An afternoon reading files and inspecting dead bodies." He rolled his eyes. "What could be more fun?"

Thirteen

Mallory's Table

After stopping three times for directions, I arrived at the diner twenty minutes late. Everyone in Studio City had heard of Mallory's Table, but no one knew the exact street name or block number. I drove past it twice before spotting the hole in the wall, tucked between a Laundromat and an adult-video store, bordering the hospitable part of the neighborhood. I found a public parking lot two blocks down and ran the entire way back.

The exterior looked like nothing more than a simple storefront. Inside, the ambience assaulted me the moment I entered. The walls were painted a rich amber, accented with deep burgundy curtains and carpeting. Fake mahogany tables and chairs were set with small lamps, each mosaic shade different from the one next to it. So much elegance, completely unknown from the outside.

I spotted Noah in the back, hunched over a mug of coffee. Judging by the empty sugar and creamer packets, he'd been waiting and drinking for a while. I bypassed the waitress and dashed over to his table, red-faced from both running and embarrassment.

He looked up and a grin lit his face. "Hey," he said, bolting to his feet, "I thought you changed your mind."

"No, just work." We had an awkward moment, caught between issuing a handshake or a friendly hug. In the end, he pulled out my chair and I slid in.

"How's Trance doing?" he asked as he sat across from me.

"Better. She could get out of ICU as soon as tonight if she keeps improving."

"That's great news."

A pink-haired waitress snapped her gum as she approached the table and grinned over the edge of her wrinkled notepad.

"Can I getcha a drink?" she asked.

"Iced tea, please," I said.

"Sure." She scribbled on her notepad. "Appetizer to start you guys off?"

I didn't see a menu on the table, so I deferred to Noah. "Do you like clam strips? Best in the city," he said.

"I'm allergic to shellfish."

"Oh, sorry." He puckered his lips, thinking. "Potato skins with the works?"

"Perfect."

The waitress nodded, scribbling. "Coming up. Specials are on the board, and I'll be back with your tea."

"Do they have menus?" I asked after she'd gone.

Noah reached behind a basket boasting an array of

sauces and bottled spices, and removed a printed card. "It's mostly a locals' place. Once you've been here a few times, you get to know their food, but they keep these on hand for the new folk."

"Like me." My fingers brushed over the shade of the small lamp on our table. Chips of red, orange, and purple glass made nonsense patterns that cast sparkles of light across the marred tabletop. "How did you find this place?"

"I used to come here with an old girlfriend."

My hand fisted. Jealousy slapped me in the face. Jealousy over a woman I didn't know, and maybe he didn't even like all that much. I was acting like an idiot. This was our first date. Why get upset over past girlfriends?

Because you don't have anyone for him to get jealous over, and you hate that.

Maybe so.

"What did she like to order?" I asked.

His jaw muscle twitched. "House salad, no dressing." Four simple words, said like a curse.

"What would she never order?"

He considered the question, starting to smile. "Double cheeseburger and seasoned fries, with a side of cole slaw."

Sounded like heaven. "I'll get that, then."

"You don't have—"

"The great thing about my powers is they keep my metabolism high," I said. "I can eat pretty much anything I want."

"Except shellfish."

"Right."

The waitress returned with my tea, and we both ordered

the double cheeseburgers. Instead of cole slaw, he asked for extra fries, and away she went again, still snapping her gum. Not something I usually saw in a restaurant, but Mallory's seemed to run on its own rules.

"You looked out of breath when you got here," Noah said. "Everything okay?"

"Yes and no, and I'm so sorry I'm late." I squeezed a lemon slice into my tea.

"It's okay, I only drank six cups of coffee waiting."

My head jerked up. He was grinning. For the first time, I noticed he had tiny dimples in both cheeks. "Anything you can talk about?" he asked. "Something to do with Arnold Stark?"

"Very definitely about Arnold Stark." I swirled my tea with the straw, unsure how much to tell Noah. We didn't really have rules about discussing our cases, because we hadn't had many. We also didn't have many civilian friends.

"It's okay if you can't," he said. "Talk about it, I mean."

"I probably can, but it's a long story. The long and short of it is that we know who we're after now, both for the shooting and yesterday's dead bodies. We just don't know how to catch him. Or them or whatever."

"Bodies? Plural?"

Oops. I told him about Stark, that he was found in his cell skinned, just like John Doe. I did, however, leave out the part about Officer Ortega. It seemed more along the lines of "need to know," and Noah didn't really need to know. Simon's words about civilian panic were still too fresh in my mind. I also left out our morning visit to Weatherfield.

Noah followed along, nodding in all the right places. He didn't press for details, respecting the boundaries without hesitation, which I appreciated.

"So how did you manage the afternoon off?" he asked.

"We're waiting for new leads. I couldn't do much sitting around the house or the hospital, so I thought lunch with our electrician would help pass the time nicely. It was either the pleasure of your company or helping Simon play catch-up all afternoon."

"Simon?"

Double oops. "Um, Simon Hewitt, he's an old friend of ours."

"A Meta."

"Yes, a Meta. He has abilities that might help us track down our killer. He and Tempest are working on it today. If we're lucky, we'll get a bead on this guy and get a serial killer off the street."

"Serial killer?" Something in his tone rang of displeasure, annoyance.

"Three bodies and counting, Noah. It's not a pretty term, but it seems accurate to me."

"I didn't mean to upset you, Dahlia." He reached across the table and squeezed my hand. "I guess I don't like the idea of you out there with people like that. I know it sounds like macho bullshit, or something."

"Thank you, Noah, that's sweet." But if he wanted to be protective, he'd have to get in line.

We chatted nonsensically until the potato skins arrived, steamy and oozing with cheddar cheese and crispy bacon.

Little dishes of sour cream and guacamole were nestled on the plate in a bed of lettuce. Our waitress left a pair of small plates, and we dug in. I slathered my potato skin with sour cream until the orange cheese disappeared under a layer of white.

"So tell me something about you," I said, blowing on my steaming appetizer. "You don't talk too much about yourself, you know."

"I find myself pretty boring," he replied, applying equal amounts of guac and sour cream. "That's why I keep asking you questions. What would you like to know?"

"Did you grow up here in Hollywood?" Even though we'd gone to the same high school, the cobbled-together school district still had three different elementary schools scattered around. Eventually, all three student bodies matriculated together at Parker High.

"Yep, my whole life. The shop's been around for about four generations of Scotts, so we've been in the area in some form or another." I bit into my potato skin. Hot grease dribbled down my chin. Noah reached out with a napkin and wiped it away. "My dad used to tell us stories about the Rangers, things he remembered from his childhood. Stories about . . . I guess they would have been your grandparents, and all the things they did."

"Not my grandparents," I said. "At least, not that I can figure. I don't know a lot about my family history, so maybe there's a Meta somewhere else down the bloodline. Teresa's theory is that new Metas are waking up, ones without powers before. Kind of a cosmic balancing act, since so many died during the War."

"You never knew you had powers before?" he asked, eyes widening a bit.

"Not until everyone got them back, no. I was a reporter, just trying to make my rent. Bonus points for me, though, because if I hadn't had these powers, I probably would have burned down my apartment six months ago." Even though my experience the night all Metas got their powers back was a little different from my friends', the timing was the same.

"Thank God for small favors. What made you want to be a reporter?"

A short, uncomfortable laugh filled the long pause. "That's a long story, actually. I wanted to do something to help people, but I wasn't brave enough to even consider police work. Journalism seemed like the next best thing. Digging for the truth, keeping people informed. I was pretty good at it, too."

"You're wrong."

I blinked. "What?"

He backpedaled quickly. "Not about being good at it, about being brave. Just seeing what you've gone through in the last twenty-four hours, you have more strength and courage than you give yourself credit for, Dahlia."

Only sheer force of will prevented a puddle-of-goo moment. Heat flamed in my cheeks. The remnants of my potato skin held my complete attention. I watched a drop of yellow grease dribble down the side and plop onto the plate next to a bit of bacon.

"I didn't mean to embarrass you."

"It's okay." I looked up and returned his smile. "I just don't get those kind of compliments very often."

"I'll have to make sure I compliment you as often as possible."

"Don't you dare."

"Try and stop me."

"Is that a challenge?"

"Most definitely."

I held his gaze for several long minutes, engaging in an unofficial stare-off. He stuck out his tongue and waggled his eyebrows, trying to distract me with funny faces. I pursed my lips and held on, determined to win. Unfortunately, our lunch arrived and we looked up at the same time, ending the battle in a draw.

The affection I'd seen in his eyes dangled in my memory for a long while as we ate.

During the consumption of two greasy cheeseburgers topped with lettuce, tomato, and pickles and heaps of spicy fries, we covered every first-date topic imaginable. Favorite color (mine, orange; his, green); why we both preferred spring over fall (birth versus death); the best place to watch the sun set in Los Angeles (the Santa Monica Pier, if you dared to brave the trip to that side of town); our mutual love of the hokey pokey and inline roller skates; and perhaps most important of all: regular or extra-crispy.

I didn't press about his family. He mentioned his two brothers a few times, but avoided parents. Hints came out in memories and story snippets as we chatted, but not enough to draw a clear picture. Not enough to know how or when they died. He reciprocated by not asking about my father—whom I had not once mentioned—and by keeping topics light. Enough darkness surrounded my life. I needed this break.

We also discovered a mutual fondness for white-water rafting.

"Three times," he said, proud that he'd bested my two trips. "Twice in North Carolina and once in Colorado. The first time was a family trip. Mom, Dad, and my brothers, we all went up on vacation. I think I was eleven. We were all so scrawny back then, and pale. So damned pale. We burned in a reflection of the sun."

I giggled at the image of him, a sunburned, gangly youth with flaming skin that matched his auburn hair; freckles darkened by sunlight, mischievous green eyes that never stopped watching.

"We only had money for rafting or tubing," he continued. "Mom and Jimmy wanted tubing because it was safer and more relaxing. Dad and I wanted rafting, of course. Which meant Aaron was the deciding vote."

"How'd you get him to pick rafting?"

"I bribed him with a candy bar I stole from a convenience store."

My mouth fell open, and I started laughing. "So you're a thief, are you? I may have to do my civic duty and place you under a citizen's arrest."

He quirked one eyebrow, tilting his head to the side. "Citizen's arrest? And what does that entail, exactly? Home confinement?"

"That could be arranged," I played along, still grinning. "I don't know if home confinement is a stiff enough penalty for such a crime. I mean, candy bar theft is serious business, Noah."

Pretending to think it over, he said, "What's your suggestion?"

"Confinement to one room seems fair."

Both eyebrows rose into twin arches, broadcasting amusement. "Any room?"

"I was thinking the smallest and least-used room in the house."

"Ah, yes, the bedroom."

My heart jumped. Okay, not quite what I was thinking.

He continued, "Tell me, Citizen's Arresting Officer Perkins, does house arrest allow visitors?"

"Only if you found a willing visitor." I stumbled a little with the banter. "Have someone in mind?"

Emerald eyes stared at me, seemed to look right past my joking exterior to the woman hiding inside, too nervous to come out and play. "There's just one person I'd ask," he said, so serious from just a moment ago.

Breath hitched in my throat. I barely managed, "Anyone I know?"

His lips parted.

"Dessert?" The tinny, gum-smacking voice of our waitress broke the spell. She stood at the head of the table, pen poised over pad.

"We were just discussing dessert," Noah said, frown clearly telegraphing his annoyance. "I think we've decided to have something at my place."

My heart pitter-pattered. His place. Dessert. House arrest. *Oh boy.* Had I sent out the wrong signals without realizing? I was interested, sure, but we'd known each other a day.

"Enjoy." She slapped our bill facedown on the table and sauntered off. In most places, I would have called her rude. I watched her go, in her short denim skirt, white blouse, and green apron. Nah, just the right kind of attitude for a place like this.

Noah snatched the bill before I could see the totals. He removed cash from a worn leather billfold and tossed it onto the center of the table between our plates.

"I have to say, Dahlia, I'm impressed."

"By what?"

He pointed at my ketchup-smeared plate. "At your ability to pack away more food than me." His own plate still sported half a dozen fries and two bites of burger.

"Lightweight." I plucked a stray sandwich dill off the corner of his plate and popped it into my mouth, savoring the salty tang.

He stood and offered his arm. I tucked mine through it, and we walked outside into the afternoon sunshine. I spotted his van at the back of the lot; I'd been too harried before to notice it there.

"Do you want to follow me back?" he asked.

I stared, uncomprehending. Wait, his place. I tried to cover my flub by scratching a pretend itch on my ankle. I wasn't ready for our date to end. I also wasn't sure if I was ready for his place. It was an ideal distraction from the multiple problems stressing me out. Someone wanted me dead. Pulling Noah into my crazy world only put him in danger. No. "Maybe that's not a good idea."

He blinked. Hard. "Dahlia, I'm not asking you home to have sex with me. We just met. Sort of. And I really do have dessert at home. Store-bought blueberry pie and canned whipped cream."

"I didn't mean to imply . . ." Okay, yeah, I had. "It's just . . . people near me keep getting hurt."

"You can't blame yourself."

"I can when the shooter was aiming for me."

Anger simmered in his eyes—at me, at my intended killer, I didn't know. "Just for pie," he said quietly. "I don't have a lot of friends. The, ah, shop keeps me pretty busy now that Mom and Dad are gone."

I couldn't help remembering the skimpily dressed Asian girl I'd seen at the shop, or from wondering how she fit into his schedule. Not that she was any of my business at this point. Noah and I had been on exactly one date. Personal histories and ex-girlfriends could wait.

Noah's sincerity convinced me to follow him. "Yeah, okay, I'll follow you. In case someone calls or something happens." *Or in case you chicken out and run away like a startled pigeon.*

"Okay."

Noah's cell rang. He fished it out of his pocket, frowned at the display, then answered. "Jimmy?"

I looked at the pavement, trying to not eavesdrop until Noah said, "Yeah, she's right here, why?" I gave him a sharp look. He held up his hand, and I barely kept silent long enough for him to finish the brief call. "Thanks, Jimmy, I'll tell her." He hung up.

"What?" I asked, nearly bursting with anxiety.

"Jimmy said your friend Onyx called the shop looking for you."

Marco. Figured he would—wait. "He called the shop?" I patted myself down, seeking a familiar bulge. Well, hell, I'd left my com in the car. "Why?"

"He said to tell you Tempest and Psystorm were in an accident and to get home."

If Noah added anything else, I didn't hear it over the roar in my ears.

Fourteen

Nadine Lee

The moment rubber hit the road, I was on the phone, dialing the house. Noah had kindly offered to drive me. I think I mumbled an apology and thank-you before fleeing the parking lot. I drove with a white-knuckled grip, trying to keep a cap on my panic until I knew exactly what was happening. Marco said to go home, not to the hospital, which was a good sign. Unless they were dead, in which case the hospital was pointless.

No, they were fine, just shaken up or bruised. No big deal. Had to be no big deal.

Someone picked up on the third ring. "Where the hell have you been?" Renee asked.

"What's going on, Renee? What happened to Ethan and Simon?"

"Hold on." Muffled voices on her end. "Dahlia? It is Marco. They are fine, but Gage is calling a team meeting. Are you coming home?"

They are fine. The best words ever, but they left me with a smoking kernel of anger in the pit of my stomach. Why all the panic if they were fine and it was just a meeting? Furious words nudged at the back of my brain, but I reined them in. No sense in screaming at him over the com.

"I'm in the car, maybe ten minutes away," I said. "And don't you ever leave a freaking message like that again, you ass. That was cruel."

"I apologize, *Ascua*. I did not mean—"

"Yes, you did."

Silence. "I am truly sorry." Penitence coated his words, pouring a little water on my smoking anger.

"See you in a few." I smacked off the com and gripped the wheel. I should have asked what exactly had happened to Ethan and Simon. Now I had to spend the rest of the drive wondering. Briefly, I considered calling Noah to tell him everything was okay. Only, I didn't know what was actually happening, or if it really was okay.

Ethan was sitting on the porch when I drove up. Only one Sport was in the driveway, which struck me as odd. He stood, the sun glinting off a white bandage taped to his forehead. His nose was red, swollen, and one eye had darkened. He was out of uniform, in khaki shorts and a blue T-shirt that read "Get Real." I parked, palmed the keys, and practically flew into his arms.

"For a minute I thought you were dead," I said, words muffled against his shoulder.

One hand stroked my hair. "I'm fine, Dal, just a little sore."

I pulled back. "I'm so sorry, did I hurt you?"

"No, just don't punch me in the ribs or anything, okay?"

Not a problem, since someone else with greener eyes and cat-shifting abilities was currently on my list of people to punch.

We ascended the porch steps, and I pushed open the front door. My roller still lay where I'd dropped it yesterday, dried to the paint pan.

"Did you enjoy your afternoon?" he asked.

"I was starting to." The way I ran off, I'd be lucky if he wanted to see me again. The joys of being an on-call superhero. "So what happened, anyway?"

He lingered in the lobby, casting furtive looks down the left hall, toward the War Room. "Simon was caught up on the details of the case, so we called Pascal and got permission to visit the morgue, to see the Stark and John Doe remains. We decided to shortcut across town by using the freeway. Someone came up behind us on the exit ramp and smashed right into the bumper. I was so surprised, I couldn't hold the wheel."

He cringed, probably reliving the still-fresh memory. "We went over the embankment, flipped a few times. I guess there's a great example of why one should always wear safety belts, because we both walked away from it." He seemed to notice my expression for the first time. "What?"

"Someone drove you off the freeway and nearly killed you."

"He gave me a splitting headache, but I'm nowhere near almost killed. Neither is Simon. He just got a bloody nose and glass in his hair."

"Do you think it was a Changeling?"

"Gage does, which is why he wants a team meeting. Everyone in one room."

One room. "Who's at the hospital?"

"Agent McNally's keeping an eye on her."

Voices bounced back and forth in a heated discussion, drifting out of the War Room's open door long before we reached it. Words died and arguments stopped as we entered. Gage, Simon, and Renee sat on one side of the long table; Marco kept the other side warm. Simon sported a swollen nose and bruise across his left cheek.

"Did Ethan fill you in?" Gage asked.

"Yes," Ethan replied.

He sat down next to Marco, and I took the neighboring chair. Right across from Renee, whose intent gaze drilled into my head. I ignored her and focused on Gage.

"I don't like the word *coincidence*," Gage continued. "Teresa never believed in it, and I don't think it applies here. I think they were purposely run off the road, because of their destination and intentions."

"It seems impossible, no?" Marco asked. "That the Changelings would know precisely where they were going and when to cut them off?"

"Not if they were following them from the house," I offered. "We didn't exactly keep Simon's presence a guarded secret, so people know he's here. They know who he is and what he can do."

Gage nodded. "My thinking, exactly. We haven't been careful enough, and we've underestimated our enemy. They know what they're doing, and they also seem to know what we're doing."

"Which means they see me as a threat," Simon said. "My powers could find something useful to us and damaging to them. It's even more important that I see those bodies. Get a feel for them, see if there's any residual aura I can trace. Especially Stark, since it's been just over twelve hours since he was killed."

"Have we learned anything new about Stark?" I asked.

"Actually, we do have a lead on that," Renee said. She pushed a sheet of paper across the table. A police report. "He had a girlfriend named Nadine Lee, who worked part-time at a coffee shop down in Anaheim. She didn't show up for work yesterday or today."

"I take it that's not like her."

"Her boss said you could set a watch by her schedule. She does things down to the minute. Obsessive-compulsive disorder, he said. Less the counting thing, and more keeping things organized and tidy."

"And I don't suppose," Ethan said, "there's anyone in Nadine Lee's life who's gone missing? Someone who could be our John Doe?"

"We're still digging into that angle," Renee said. "But so far, nada."

"What's our timeline on this so far?"

Gage stood up and walked over to one of the dry-erase boards. He picked up a marker and wrote as he spoke. "Eleven days ago, the Changelings break out of Weatherfield using Ronald Jarvis. His skin must have been shed as soon as they get out, because he's two days gone when his body is found. There's an unknown period of eight days between finding him and John Doe, the next victim, who died yesterday."

"The same day Lee was noticed to be missing," Renee added.

"Right." Gage scribbled that down. "From John Doe, we go to Arnold Stark, who was used to get close enough to try to kill our people." I squirmed; he studiously avoided eye contact. "From Stark, we get Miguel Ortega and now we're stuck. He could still be in Ortega, or the body could be out there waiting to be found."

"Doubtful," Simon said. "They know you're onto them now. They won't leave any more bread crumbs, not if they're smart, which they seem to be."

Scary good point.

Ethan drummed his fingers against the table. "We're also assuming the same Changeling is moving through all of these people, but there are three of them."

"That's true," Gage said. "But I don't think any of these host choices are coincidental. They were all chosen for a specific reason, like stepping-stones toward another destination."

"But why do all of this?" I asked. "They're Changelings, for God's sake. They could become anyone they want to be, and no one would be the wiser. They could settle down and live normal lives, right under our noses. So why this elaborate charade? Why a public assassination attempt and uncontrollable road rage? It doesn't make sense."

"Lots of good questions, Dal," Gage said. "On the list of things I'll ask when we catch these sons of bitches, believe me. As far as easy escapes go, theirs ranks up there, but they didn't stay under the radar. They're doing this for a reason."

Renee snorted. "Another anti-Meta statement?"

"Maybe." Gage drew a star above the line that represented the eight days between Jarvis and John Doe. "This is what I want to know more about. And I want to find Nadine Lee. Pascal has another detective looking into her disappearance, and he's agreed to copy us on anything he finds."

"You guys trust this Detective Pascal to do right by you?" Simon asked.

"Absolutely."

"Good enough."

"Do we know what Nadine Lee looks like?" Ethan asked. "In case we see her on the street or something?"

Gage shuffled through a stack of papers and withdrew a photograph printed out on a half sheet. He slid it down the table to Ethan. I scooted a bit closer and peered over his arm. A pretty Asian girl with long black hair and about my age grinned off to the left of the picture taker. I studied the oddly familiar image, but couldn't place—

Are you going out in that?

Sure. Why the hell not?

You look like a hooker.

My stomach seized. I tried to inhale and choked. My vision blurred, obscuring the photograph. It couldn't be, it was just a coincidence. My mind was playing tricks, that's all. It couldn't be the same girl.

"Dal? You okay over there?"

Gage's voice, concerned. I stood up, sending the wheeled

chair rolling backward into the wall. *Lie, you idiot, just get out of there.*

"Lunch," I ground out, gasping for air. "Not agreeing with—oh no."

I bolted from the room, tearing ass down the hall to the bathroom near the kitchen. I shoved the door open without bothering to turn on the light, skidded to my knees in front of the toilet, and vomited up every bit of that burger and fries. Acid scorched my throat. I swallowed hard, gagged, and retched a few more dry heaves into the bowl.

It wasn't possible. Nadine Lee had no reason to be in the Scott apartment. No reason whatsoever. I had to have confused the mystery girl with Nadine. My imagination was working overtime. They just looked alike. Everyone had a twin, that's what they said.

That's what who said?

My hands gripped the sides of the porcelain bowl. Tears spilled across both cheeks and dripped down my chin and neck. I couldn't breathe. I didn't want to think. Noah was not involved in this; he couldn't be involved. It was a coincidence. Maybe Teresa and Gage didn't believe in coincidence, but it did exist. It had to exist.

I spat and flushed, desperate to rinse out my mouth. The sink seemed so far away. I crawled toward it on shaking limbs, but collapsed against the wall before making it halfway. My entire body trembled, as much from the violent vomiting as from shock and fear. Noah wasn't a killer. I knew deep down, in a place where logic didn't go and instinct ruled. I knew it like I knew the sky was blue and the Pacific Ocean was just a few miles west.

A shadow fell across the square of light created by the open door. Human-shaped shadow. I looked up at the backlit figure. Girl-shaped. Renee. Just what I needed.

Hoping to stave off more accusations of weakness, I offered a wan smile. "I'm never getting a cheeseburger at Mallory's Table again."

She flicked on the light. I recoiled from the sudden glare. She took a hand towel off the rack by the sink and soaked one end under the faucet. She crouched in front of me, an unfamiliar wrinkle of concern on her blue face. I sat quietly as she wiped my cheeks with the cold towel, brushing away sweat and tears and cooling my flushed skin. I was so surprised I just let her do it.

It was an oddly tender moment—the first we'd ever shared. It felt like a silent apology, and I found myself wanting to forgive her for last night's harsh words. We carried different kinds of pain, but it was still pain, and in pain we could find common ground.

"You should go lie down for a while," she said.

It was a wonderful idea, but there was no time. I had to get back to Noah's place and ask him about the woman I saw at his shop. He had to tell me that her name was anything except Nadine Lee, and that he and his brothers—*three brothers, oh dear Lord no*—had nothing to do with this. They aren't Changelings. They can't be Changelings.

"Rest sounds like a good idea," I said.

Renee tossed the towel into the sink and slipped an arm around my shoulders. As she helped me stand, she said, "Nothing like ending a first date with a case of food poisoning."

First date, maybe a last date. "Next time I pick the restaurant."

She guided me upstairs to my room, though I could have made it on my own. The intense shaking of limbs had subsided. I played up the weakness, anyway—the more spent she thought I was, the longer they'd leave me alone. I needed a few hours of alone time. I collapsed into bed and kicked off my sandals as I rolled toward the wall.

"Do you want anything?" she asked. "Glass of water or juice?"

"Just some sleep. And maybe a bodyguard on the door, to keep out inquiring minds."

"I'll tell them to leave you alone for a while. Do not disturb, unless something huge happens."

"Right, thanks."

"No problem."

Footsteps whispered away. The door clicked. I rolled back over and sat up, glad to be alone again. Now I just had to figure out how to get off the property without being caught, and across town without a car. I'd brought Noah into our lives and into our home. I had to know that I hadn't made a huge, irreparable error in trusting him.

And if, by some horrible twist of fate, I had, then I'd fix it. I didn't know how, but I'd fix it.

I peeled out of my date ensemble and slipped back into my uniform pants, tank top, and boots. I left the jacket on my bed. This was only a semiofficial visit, and walking across town in the entire getup on a hot day like this would probably make me faint. Having thrown up everything I'd eaten in the last two days wouldn't help, either.

The challenge of getting out of the house still remained. Gage had supersensitive hearing when he chose to use it. If he was listening, I was screwed. My main challenge lay in the stairs. The house had one main staircase leading from the second floor to the first. An old servants' staircase existed behind one of the locked doors above the kitchen, but we had never bothered renovating it. Trying to open it now would be noisy and obvious.

Think, Dahlia, think.

The lounge. An enormous maple tree grew outside, just to the east of the lounge's balcony. If I could get to that tree, I could climb down into the yard. I hoped. I'd never had to sneak out of the house as a teenager, so dangling from trees was pretty new.

I opened my bedroom door a crack. Listened. Nothing. They could still be downstairs in the War Room. I crossed mental fingers and slipped out, silently closing the door behind me. I tiptoed down the hall and darted into the lounge. It was in the same disarray as yesterday. Funny how our lives had gone from house repairs to fighting for our lives in only a matter of hours.

The balcony door squealed. I cringed, expecting shouting voices at any moment. Nothing happened. I slid through, closed it. More squealing. The balcony floorboards creaked under my weight as I crossed to the far corner. I hated this.

I wanted to tell them, to ask permission to go talk to Noah. They wouldn't let me. At the very least, Gage would insist he and someone else go with me.

No, if Noah was going to talk, it would be with me. And only me.

I eyed the grand maple tree. Its nearest branch was still a foot away. I could jump and miss and break my neck. I could jump and grab hold . . . and still slip and break my neck. Or I could . . . something metal caught my eye, running up the length of the house, perpendicular to the balcony and porch below. Drainpipe. I almost laughed. The perfect cliché to get me out of here.

Swinging both legs over the balcony rail, I gripped the sides of the metal pipe. It groaned. Held. Hand over hand, I shimmied to the ground and hit the grass. So far, so good. Open ground lay in front of me, marked with the occasional tree. Praying no one was in the dining room looking out, I bolted, my heart jack-hammering in my chest. I ran from tree to tree until I hit the property line. A tall hedge grew on our side of the fence. I stuck to it, crouched low, and darted toward the back of the property. More trees there, up against the fence.

One bonus of helping Marco install the perimeter sensors was that I knew where they were placed. And unless Ethan thought to reactivate it after the false alarm, Sensor Eight was still off—the fence had a weak spot. Then it would be a matter of hitching a ride or walking. And then getting the answers I needed.

I just hoped they were also the answers I wanted to hear.

—————————

An hour passed before the aging Scott & Sons sign loomed down the block. Sweat trickled down the back of my neck. I had twisted my hair up and secured it with a twig. Waning sunlight glared down, baking through my long pants and tank top. A few cars honked at me; I ignored them, too tempted to salute with my middle finger if I acknowledged their admiration of my assets.

I stopped at the end of the block, debating my approach. Storm in through the shop, or go around back and hope what I assumed to be an upstairs apartment door was open? Demand answers, or use a more subtle approach? I hesitated to accuse Noah of anything. I didn't know what exactly he had or hadn't done, not with any great certainty. However, going in with guns blazing and catching him off-guard also had its merits. Less time to think up a lie.

If he's been playing you this whole time, he's had plenty of time to come up with lies. He took you to lunch while his brother ran your friends off the road.

No proof. No proof. It became a mantra in the back of my head. Innocent until proven guilty. It was the only way to get through this with my sanity intact.

Halfway down the block—"Hello, Dahlia."

I yelped and nearly jumped out of my skin. As I spun around, my ankles caught and I pitched forward—right into Officer Miguel Ortega's arms. His hands gripped my shoulders, squeezing painfully. Panic hit, and I raised my knee. He avoided the groin shot and gave me a shake.

"I'm not going to hurt you," he said.

"How do I know that?" I glared at my shoulders.

He let me go, his dark eyes flashing. "Because Noah told me not to. Come inside, Dahlia. We need to talk."

Something in his voice prevented me from arguing. It had a keen, dangerous edge. Even though he wore his sidearm holstered with safety snapped, I remained acutely aware of its presence as I led the way. Slow, tentative steps drew me forward. The shop was silent, empty. He locked the door, turned the sign to Closed, and then indicated the back stairs.

They creaked beneath my feet, groaning their age and announcing our arrival to anyone listening from above. The top of the dusky stairwell ended at a wooden door. I half expected it to swing open, admitting me into the bowels of my own personal hell.

"Go on," Ortega-but-not said.

The cool knob turned. I pushed. It swung easily, and I walked into the apartment hall. On my right and left were closed doors. Without further prompting, I followed the corridor to the end. A quick glance discovered an empty living room. Sunlight streamed in through half a dozen open windows, allowing in humid air. Two box fans circulated, doing little to cool the place. The sofa was worn, the tables nicked and scarred, the rug threadbare. Dozens of trophies for various sports lined the built-in bookcases. Someone had been an athlete.

Something about the living room was odd, though, and I didn't have time to stand there and puzzle it out. My guide pointed. I stepped into the sunny kitchen, greeted by the scent of brewed coffee. Mugs and a blue carafe decorated the tabletop, along with a scattering of plastic spoons and a bottle of nondairy creamer. A slightly younger, ganglier version of Noah—Jimmy?—sat on the far side, by the door.

Noah stood next to the wall, mug in hand and eyes on the floor. He didn't look up, just stayed hunched next to a window. The sight of him sent fury rippling through me. He looked like Noah Scott, but he wasn't. Not the Noah I'd known in high school. This person I was looking at had taken him, used him—used me.

The word *fool* didn't have nearly enough letters to describe how I felt about myself.

A third person sat at the table with his back to me, showing only brown hair and tailored suit. I stopped, more afraid of this stranger than of anyone else in the room. Ortega remained at my back, destroying any chance of fleeing. Not that I would have. I came for answers, and it looked like they planned to oblige. If they didn't kill me first.

Jimmy's attention flickered to me, then away when I returned the look with a poisonous frown. He deferred to the man whose face I couldn't see but still seemed familiar.

"Please, have a seat," the man said.

My heart nearly stopped at the sound of his voice. It made perfect sense and no sense. Information given, information hidden. Obfuscated. All to this purpose. I should have seen it coming, but I hadn't. None of us had. And no one at home knew I was here.

I walked to the chair farthest from Noah, closer to the

man in the chair, amazed at my ability to take steady, unhindered steps when I wanted to fall apart. The man stirred his coffee with a plastic spoon, calm and unbothered. He looked up, meeting my glare inch for inch, never giving.

"Well," Dr. Abram Kinsey said. "We have a lot to talk about."

Fifteen

Abram Kinsey

W as anything you told us true?" I pulled out a scarred wooden chair and sat down, folding my hands neatly in my lap. Amazed at my self-control—for now.

Fear, annoyance, confusion, and wrath clambered over each other for dominance, none winning the battle quite yet. I tried to ignore the three other men in the room and focus on Kinsey. He was a scientist; he thought things through rationally. Surely, if he meant to kill me, I'd be dead already.

"Yes, my dear," Kinsey said. "Most of it was true, in fact. Certainly everything I told you about the Changelings' escape and their powers. I only failed to mention my part in that escape."

"So why admit it now?" It took every ounce of concentration I possessed not to look at Noah; to pay sole attention to Kinsey and ignore the very near presence of my supposed friend. Had our entire adult friendship been predicated on a lie? Just another façade stolen by someone with no identity of his own?

"Mistakes were made." Kinsey turned his head to deliver

a deliberate look to Ortega. "You and your friends are getting too close to the truth, and I feel we have no choice but to approach you."

I narrowed my eyes. "Why me?"

"Noah says we can trust you, and that's good enough for me."

The response broke loose the fury inside me, and it rose to the surface in a furious blush. "Does he? That's very interesting, because I don't trust *him*."

Noah winced.

I didn't relent, imagining each word striking him like a firm kick to the nuts. "That was an interesting way to keep tabs on what we knew. Let's befriend the youngest, she's sure to fall for it and blab their secrets for a few compliments and a pity date from an old schoolmate. It's too bad one of your brothers decided to run my friends off the road, so you never got the chance to go for dessert. So sorry, Noah. Try again with the next poor soul you want to con."

His mouth twisted into something ugly, and he launched his mug at the wall. It sailed end over end, spilling coffee across the linoleum floor and smashing against the refrigerator door. The crash echoed through the small kitchen. A chair scraped. Noah glared at the mess he'd made, not moving or speaking. My heart sped up a bit more.

"Noah," Kinsey barked.

"What's his real name?" I asked. "Which one is he?" I wasn't letting this go, now that I had my anger revving.

"Ace," Noah said, finally adding to the conversation. His voice was tight, harsh. "They called me Ace."

Jimmy raised his hand. "I was Joker, in case you were wondering."

I looked over my shoulder at Ortega. "So you must be King." To Noah, I snapped, "Is Aaron Scott even real, or was the whole three brothers thing just for show?"

"Aaron Scott is quite real," Kinsey said, taking the question. "The Scott siblings created the perfect cover for the boys to blend in and disappear. It almost worked out perfectly."

"So what went wrong with this perfect cover of yours?"

Kinsey sipped his coffee. "It's extremely complicated, Miss Perkins, so let me start from the beginning. Everything I told you about the Recombinant project was true. I oversaw the project, and I raised the Hybrid Changeling children. I trained them and nurtured them. Only I failed to mention I was one of the genetic-material donors. They are, genetically and spiritually, my sons."

The admission tempered my anger a smidge. I recalled the photograph he'd shown us in his office, of the three faceless teenage boys. What did it take to look at your children every day and see nothing of yourself in them? Never see anyone in them, except the masks they chose to wear.

"They are my sons," he continued. "But to Weatherfield, they were still projects. Objects, owned and operated, and about a month ago they decided the project no longer had merit. With the Metas reactivated, our research was meant to go in a different direction. They told me they could no longer justify the expense of the Hybrids' training program. In short, they were to be terminated."

"You mean killed?"

Kinsey nodded. "Put down like unwanted strays, and nothing I said could change their minds. The board didn't understand my feelings, so we four came up with an alternative to death. We decided on freedom."

"An alternative to death? By killing Ronald Jarvis?"

"His death was an unfortunate circumstance, but it became unavoidable. Voice recognition software is used on all except the main entry gates. Their powers do not allow for voice change without the full possession of the host. It was the only way to get them out, and for that, I am truly sorry."

"I don't think a judge is going to care that you're sorry."

The snide remark rolled right past. "We thought the escape through very carefully, planning contingencies for any unforeseen emergencies. Everything was going well. Noah and James were in place, but Aaron was nowhere to be found. We had King's cover prepared, and no body with which to veil him. The other boys had to pretend for a bit."

In place. Covers and veils. He spoke with such clinical detachment, he could have been discussing cold symptoms. These were the lives of human beings, not toys to be played with. But, as with a three-car pile-up on the 405, I found it impossible to ignore the things in front of me.

"Where's the real Aaron Scott?" I asked.

"We aren't certain. He was tightly wound even before the death of the boys' parents, and he lived his life selfishly. He couldn't be bothered to leave a circuit party to attend their parents' funeral. Six weeks ago he told Noah he was going to Colorado with a group of ex-boyfriends to do some mountain climbing. He hasn't been heard from since."

"So he could just show up at any moment?"

"Yes."

I waved one hand at Jimmy. "And he won't notice that his little brothers aren't his little brothers anymore?"

"We *are* his brothers," Noah snarled. His words struck like punches, furious and intimidating. "It's impossible to explain, Dahlia, but this is me. This person I am, he's both Noah Scott and Ace the Changeling. You don't stop being one to be the other, you become an amalgamation of the two. I am me, brother to Jimmy Scott and to King, in whatever form he has chosen."

I wouldn't look at him. Looking at Noah made me want to throw hard objects in his general direction—which was not a good idea while surrounded by people I didn't really know, one with a gun and a temperament to kill. But I might as well press my luck while they were talking.

"So if Aaron shows up in an hour, what happens?" I asked. "King just takes him over, whether Aaron agrees to it or not? They become some amalgam of two people and he gets no say?"

"Our lives change without our permission, Miss Perkins," Kinsey said. "You of all people should understand how that's possible. You weren't given a choice about your powers. Aaron Scott will become greater than he was as an individual. He was selfish, distant from his family, and a recreational meth user."

"By choice."

"He made the wrong choices."

I snorted, blowing air hard through my nose. "And you get

to judge him? To take away his free will to blow his brains on meth and probably die young from an overdose?" The "group of ex-boyfriends" comment came back to me. "Are you going to take away everything that makes him an individual?"

"His life will become more than it was. My boys made the choice to embrace the personalities of the Scotts. Everything Aaron is, so will King be, but stronger and wiser, and with amazing abilities. The Aaron who destroys his mind with crystal meth will thrive in this partnership."

"What gives you the right to decide he needs to change?"

He didn't answer. Maybe he didn't know how to explain what was so obviously correct in his mind.

"So how long will they make good use of the Scotts?" I jerked my thumb over my shoulder at King-Ortega. "Because King there doesn't seem real keen on keeping one body for any lengthy period of time. What happens when he's bored with Aaron, or maybe decides he doesn't like being gay, and leaves his skin in a back-alley trash heap?"

King-Ortega didn't speak until Kinsey nodded. "Everything Aaron Scott is, so will I be."

"You make it sound like being gay is a choice."

"Hardly. It's just not something to be afraid of. Aaron will be my last identity. Unless we're hunted"—he gave me a hard look—"I won't need another. None of us will."

"So you say. And while we're on the subject of bodies in trash heaps," I continued, "who exactly was the John Doe we found yesterday?"

"His name was Joel Stevenson," King-Ortega said. "He was supposed to be my veil until we found Aaron Scott.

He came into the shop that first day to get an outlet in his apartment fixed. Noah did the job, asked questions. Joel lived alone, didn't have many friends. I didn't want to hide in the apartment without a face indefinitely, so I became him."

He spoke carefully in Ortega's moderately accented English, but the tone belonged to someone else. A tone so detached it frightened me. Something about King was different from the other two boys, and I couldn't put my finger on it. "How is that not murder?" I asked. "Taking over someone's life and then discarding their body when you're done?"

"Because Joel isn't dead, not really," King said. "When we take a host, we take their memories and traits. We know things they know, possess their skills. I still remember everything about Joel's life. You found his skin, but his . . . I don't know, his essence? It's still in me."

"And that makes it okay?" At the very least it was violent assault.

He shrugged. "Maybe not, but it is what it is."

"Why did you leave Joel's skin behind and take another?"

Silence. It hung over us like a humid blanket, stifling and thick. Everyone looked away, including Kinsey. I'd struck another nerve. We were getting to the heart of my business here, and suddenly no one wanted to talk. I knew I wasn't going to like any of the answers (not that I'd liked them so far).

"Well, somebody is going to have to answer the question," I said. "You knew I'd ask it, so stop pretending you don't know what the hell I'm talking about. Why did King possess Arnold Stark and try to kill me?"

Noah choked, a strangled sound from deep in his throat. He wrapped his arms around his torso, hugging tight, still staring at the remains of his shattered coffee mug. The odor of it tingled my nostrils and churned my stomach, reminding me of its emptiness.

I tried to glare, to intimidate, but no one would look at me. "Well?"

Their silent consensus meant either they weren't ready to answer that now, or they weren't answering it at all. The former I could work with. The latter? Not a chance.

"Fine," I said. "Let's try an easier question, since you're having a hard time with this one. Why was Nadine Lee here yesterday?"

Noah's head turned, his eyes drilling holes through me.

I stared right back, unfazed by his surprise. "What? You thought my memory was so bad I wouldn't remember her? You saying she looked like a hooker? Or was she another one of King's veils?"

Jimmy slumped lower in his chair, eyes focused on his lap. He worried his lower lip with his teeth. They were very telling signs.

"That was you?" I asked.

He ducked his head lower. Noah ran a hand through his spiky auburn hair and blew hard through his nose.

To Kinsey I said, "I thought they couldn't hold more than one host at a time?"

"Only Joker can. Their training always focused on producing a physical glamour from touch, as it was less invasive and not permanent." Kinsey's eyebrows furrowed. Tense lips communicated his annoyance at this conversational turn. "Joker discovered his ability to possess two quite by accident. King had taken over Stark and discarded Stevenson the night before last. Nadine was a very jealous sort, and when Stark didn't come home, she tracked his car down. She found it parked on the street outside."

He shot another withering look at King. "She beat on the apartment door until Jimmy opened up. She assumed . . . well, something, and she attacked him."

"It *was* an accident," Jimmy said. "I swear it happened while I was trying to get her to stop. See, I'm a telepath and I was trying to connect with her mind and calm her down and it just kind of happened."

The plaintive tone hurt my heart. Venom still fueled my response. "So Nadine is dead, too?"

His chin trembled. He seemed so young, almost innocent—too innocent to be a murderer. Maybe it had been an accident. Noah approached and squeezed his brother's shoulders, genuine affection in the gesture. Brother. The identification was easier to stomach, if still confusing. Unreal, even.

"Where's the skin?" I asked.

"Gone," King replied.

I swiveled around, no longer afraid of him and his gun. He'd had a chance to kill me once and failed. "Same place this one will go when you're finished? Some backyard incinerator or garbage dump on the other side of town?"

"You're a mouthy broad, you know that? Want me to wear you next?"

"King!" Noah roared.

The instant fury lit a fire in the room, changing the tone from tense to downright aggressive. The pair shared a silent exchange across the table, communicating on a basic level I couldn't share. Almost a full minute passed. Jimmy started nodding along, and I got it—telepathy. They were talking right in front of me and doing a terrible job of hiding it.

I kept silent, unwilling to further provoke their wrath. They'd possessed people without their permission. They had killed, even if they described it more as a forced partnership. Everyone in the room had a problem with the extra hosts, except King. He showed little remorse over the people he'd destroyed—certainly a point of contention among the quartet of men.

King grunted and stalked to the other side of the kitchen, where he sat down on a step stool. Tension remained in the room, but a bomb had been defused, and I didn't take it for granted.

"Please understand something, Dahlia," Noah said. "They were going to kill us. We are living beings, as deserving of freedom as you."

The abject misery in his voice and stance cut like a blade. On the outside, I saw the teenager I once knew and wanted to go to him—to offer comfort, to tell him I understood. But I didn't; he wasn't really Noah. Was he? Unable to answer that, I turned to Kinsey and asked, "Why didn't you go to the authorities?"

"Weatherfield would have denied their existence. They have no birth certificates, no social security numbers. To anyone outside of the Recombinant project, they are ghosts. Objects on paper. Part of the inventory, not living and feeling people. At least as the Scotts, they were protected. No one could detect them, no one could force them out. It was the only logical choice."

Dr. Kinsey did what he had to do to protect his sons. The two Scotts were sacrificed—in the most bizarre interpretation of the term, since both were still technically alive—so Ace and Joker could live. An argument could be made for the Changelings acting in self-defense in the cases of Jimmy, Noah, and Nadine. Maybe even Ronald Jarvis.

I could not, however, excuse Joel Stevenson, Arnold Stark, or Miguel Ortega. Not to mention the giant coincidence that I'd stumbled back into Noah Scott's life right around the same time that he was taken over by a Changeling. Or the fact that Noah and Jimmy hadn't been given a choice in their possessions.

"You did what you had to do to save your family," I said. "I get it, I really do, Dr. Kinsey. And I think my friends would get it, too."

"But?" Kinsey prompted.

"But King tried to kill me yesterday, and instead, he shot Trance. She nearly died because of him, and no one in this room will tell me why." I stood up, knocking my chair over backward with a hard thump. I pivoted and kicked the chair away with my boot, then glared across the room at King. He tensed but didn't stand. "Why?"

Nothing.

I drew the heat around me inward, pulling it out of the

air. King sensed the change and cocked his head to the side, observing. "Why?" No answer. The heat filled me, pooling in my core, creating a pulse of energy I had every intention of blasting at King's smug head. "Why, dammit? Why did you try to kill me?"

Power coiled. Pulsed. Ready to be expelled. It felt good— the buildup to a release of energy and emotion that I desperately needed right now.

"Stop!" Noah slid into my line of sight, blocking my straight shot at King. Muscles rippling, jaw set, Noah took a single step toward me, so close he could reach out and touch. "Just don't, please."

My power dissipated, blown out like a candle's flame. Fatigue and frustration replaced it, filling the void created by the need to simply shatter something. Tears stung my eyes, and I blinked hard. I would not show weakness in front of them. I held Noah's gaze, caught in its spell, eyes both familiar and foreign. I fisted my hands, keeping them pressed to my sides so I didn't punch him in the face.

"Why won't you tell me?" Something new came through in my voice, propelled by the gamut of emotions roiling around in my head: despair. "Please, just tell me why."

He reached out, his hand ghosting the air near my face. "I could give you a thousand reasons, Dahlia, but none of them would make you feel better."

"I don't want to feel better. I just want the truth. Don't I deserve that?"

"You deserve that and more."

I pushed him, hard. He stumbled backward, tripped over

his own ankles, and hit the floor flat on his ass. "Go to hell."

Over him, toward the living room, I bolted down the short hall. The door to the shop downstairs wouldn't budge. I kicked it when panic set in. There had to be a way out of here. Window! I turned around. Noah stood at the opposite end of the hallway. I darted into the nearest room—bathroom, of course—and slammed the door with a satisfying crunch. I fumbled for a light switch. Two shaded bulbs blazed to life. No windows. *Freaking figures.*

It was oddly clean for belonging to three men. The tile floor sparkled and the freestanding sink was polished and mildew free. I rummaged under the sink for some sort of weapon and came up with a bottle of spray bleach. Not ideal, but it would burn like hell. So far, no one had stormed the bathroom.

I had to get out of this. How? They hadn't given me ultimatums, or made me promise anything before revealing their secrets. They told me things on faith, while withholding the one answer I needed more than any other. The one "why" haunted me. I owed it to Teresa to get this answer. She deserved to know why she took a bullet.

"Dahlia?" Noah's voice, muffled behind the door.

"I'm armed."

"With what, bleach?"

How the—?

He opened the door and poked his head inside. "Can I come in?"

"No."

"Glad we agree." He stepped in, closed the door, and

leaned against it, hands behind his back. I kept the bleach at waist level, nozzle facing him, too angry to risk pointing it directly at his eyes. I might squeeze. "I'm so sorry, Dahlia."

"They're just words, *Ace*." I had to stop thinking of him as Noah, no matter whose face he wore, the deceitful bastard. "You can say them again a thousand times over, and it won't change that you lied."

"I never lied."

"No?"

"Name one thing I ever told you that wasn't true."

"Your name."

"My name is Noah Scott. We are one person now, Dahlia. Forever."

"Or until you get sick of being him."

His lips puckered. He pushed away from the door and crowded my personal space. Annoyance danced in his eyes and radiated from the tension in his shoulders.

"I want to make you understand, but I don't know how," he said. "Growing up, I never had an identity. I was Test Subject 0983, also known as Ace. My brothers were Test Subjects 0982 and 0984. We never had parents, friends, a family, or a future. We didn't even have faces, unless we borrowed them from other people. I never had a real life until now."

"Until you stole Noah's," I said.

"No, until I saved his." He pinched the bridge of his nose. "We saved each other. Noah Scott was dying, Dahlia. He battled lymphocytic leukemia before, and it recurred again last year. Treatments failed. He gave up. It was one of the reasons

Dr. Kinsey chose him, chose all of them. Noah would have been dead in a month."

"So you stole the rest of his life?"

"No, he gave it up willingly when I asked him."

I felt faint. Completely unseated by the statement. "You what?"

"I didn't want to make our father responsible for the choice to absorb the Scotts, so I went to Noah. I told him what I was and what would happen when we joined. I promised he and his brothers would all be stronger, healthier, that we were immune to human disease. They would all live long lives."

"As other people."

"Not exactly, no. Noah was afraid to die, but more than that, he was afraid to leave his brothers. He'd always tried to take care of them, and he was terrified that if he wasn't around, Jimmy would die of an overdose, and that Aaron would eventually self-destruct. He wanted to save them. He made the choice for all of them. It's my burden, not my brothers'."

"So, Noah's cancer?"

"Gone."

He freaking cured cancer. Jimmy was a recovered heroin addict. Two lives put on the straight and narrow, given a second chance at a good life. Memories were still intact, remembered as though actually lived. Emotions and desires keenly felt, experienced through new eyes. Amalgamated eyes.

"What about your feelings?" I asked. "Am I the old Noah's former schoolmate, or Ace's obsession?"

He shook his head and grabbed my hands. The touch sent a strange tingle up my arms. I didn't pull away. "Neither," he said. "And both. I was always me, from the second you walked into the shop and my heart started racing. I had Noah's memories of you from school. He had a crush on you since junior high, Dal. He never forgot you. I never forgot you, and it's killing me to see you look at me like I'm a stranger. Like you think I'm going to hurt you."

"You have hurt me."

"I know. There were so many times I wanted to say something, to point you in the right direction, but I have to protect my brothers. This has all been about protecting them."

"And I have to protect my friends. I have to tell them what I know."

"You can't." Panic washed across his face and widened his eyes. He gripped my hands painfully tight.

"Why not?" I challenged.

"Because I'll never see you again."

"You'll live."

He took a step back as though physically struck, radiating frustration and hurt.

"Will you tell me why King used Stark to shoot at me?" I asked.

"I can't."

I glared at him, my right hand tucking into a fist. "Then you and your fucked-up family can go straight to hell." I punched him square in the temple. The action sent a shock of pain up my knuckles and wrist. He stumbled sideways and cracked his head off the wall. He crumpled to the floor in a heap. I felt no satisfaction—only wrenching guilt.

I yanked open the door and shrieked. Dr. Kinsey loomed in the doorway, cold and resigned. Something stung my arm. I saw the flash of the syringe tip and King standing just over the older man's shoulder.

"I'm sorry it came to this, Miss Perkins," Kinsey said.

His image blurred into a Picasso of colors and shapes. Sounds muffled. I pitched forward, against something warm. Giving. And floated down. Down. Darkness.

Sixteen

Comprehension

Consciousness returned slowly, through a haze of scents and sensations—the odor of earth, heavy and dense, and the sharp tang of grass. Wetness had seeped through my shirt, soaking my back. I swam upward, past the throbbing at the base of my skull. I pulled, reaching for the light, and found only darkness.

I blinked the night sky into focus, blurred by light pollution, yet still dark blue and cloudy. The twisted green and brown of a tree branch invaded the left corner of my vision. No breeze stirred the air, as thick and humid as during the day. Daylight. Hours ago.

How long had I been here? Where was here, anyway?

They knocked me out. Cowards. Bastards. Scum-sucking trolls.

Noah said he'd never see me again. The memory of that statement brought fresh tears.

A sound drifted around me, carried from a great distance. I concentrated. It repeated, louder. Again. A single word, over and over. Not just a word. No, someone was calling my name.

I tried to reply, managing only a croak. My mouth was dry, tongue thick. Water. Spit. Anything wet. I collected a bit of energy and rolled onto my left side. Found myself face-to-face with a stone wall. Chinked and mossy, it ran at least six feet high, and the length of whatever yard I lay in. It seemed familiar. A neighbor, perhaps. I was close to home. Noah hadn't dumped me across town where I'd be hard to find—not that I planned on thanking him.

Forgoing any attempt at actual words, I let loose a scream of frustration, anger, sorrow, and hate. It echoed off the stone wall and bounced around, fleeing on the night air. The other voices drew closer. I flexed my hands, feet, legs, and found them all in working order. I rolled over the other way, toward the open lawn, and was greeted by the sight of three pairs of feet racing in my direction.

"Dahlia!"

Marco, Renee, Gage—streaks of black, blue, and brown flying toward me. I licked my lips, grateful for the rescue and ashamed of its need. Ashamed at sneaking out. Getting caught like this. For being weak and young and stupid. And grateful that both Marco and Gage had excellent senses of hearing and smell.

I managed to prop up on one elbow before they descended upon me. Questions blurred together, a cacophony of words that made no sense, and only served to make my head ache harder. Someone shushed them. Blissful silence.

"Ascua?" Marco's face hovered in front of mine. I focused in. His eyes moved so fast, checking me everywhere, it made me dizzy. "Are you all right?"

I'm so far from okay it'll take a week to get there. Okay and I aren't even on speaking terms right now. What the hell kind of question is that?

"No, I'm not," I said.

Strong arms slipped around my torso. I launched into Marco's embrace, desperate to hold something, anything, as long as it was solid. He pulled me tight. I anchored to him for a while. My head throbbed and my chest hurt, but that pain was bearable.

The ground rushed away. I let him carry me, too exhausted to protest. I pressed my face into his neck, against velvet-soft hair that caressed my cheeks, and just held on.

I told them everything over two large glasses of water and a plate of saltine crackers. Story time took place in my room, because that's where Marco deposited me once he walked three blocks back to the house, never once complaining. I immediately felt better out of the heat and in air-conditioning, and the effects of the syringe wore off fast.

They sat in a circle, listening and asking few questions. Ethan, Gage, Renee, Marco, and Simon, an attentive audience I couldn't look at for most of the story. I didn't want to see the anger or accusations, not if I was going to get through it all and leave nothing out. Every single detail, from my recognizing Noah that first day in the shop, to Noah's confession about choosing to join with Ace, all the way to Kinsey poking me with a needle. No stone unturned, no truth untold.

As I described waking up in the yard without any idea how I got there, the natives grew restless. Butts shifted, clothing whispered. Someone cleared their throat. I fiddled with my water glass, waiting for a verdict to fall.

Or at the very least, someone to speak. Fill the void. Break the silence. Put me out of my damned misery.

Marco was the first to speak. "That is unbelievable."

"Which part?" Renee asked.

"*Todo*."

I dared to look at him and saw no judgment. Only keen interest, curiosity, and mostly a sense of understanding. The same expression was shared by everyone else in the tight circle, occasionally tempered by a flicker of annoyance. I had expected their wrath. Unbridled fury at being left in the dark, lied to, and danced around. Righteous indignation at furthering the investigation on my own. I didn't deserve their calm acceptance.

"That was pretty brave, Dal," Ethan said. "Brave and kind of stupid, going back there on your own."

"I know it was stupid."

"In a way," Gage said, "it worked out in our favor. They may not have been so forthcoming if we'd descended on them like a flock of swarming buzzards over a warm carcass. They trusted Dahlia enough to confide in her."

Noah trusted me. King did not. He'd openly threatened to turn me into his next suit of clothing, and I didn't doubt for a second he would have done it. "Not all of their secrets,"

I said. "They outright refused to talk about the shooting."

Gage sucked his lower lip into his mouth, a nervous gesture he never seemed to consciously notice. "Which makes me think there's more to the shooting than we know."

"They admitted to so many other things," Renee said. "To taking the lives of four people and lying about it, and a mass deception on a scale I've never seen before. What's one more attempted-murder charge?"

"Remind me to ask them when we catch them," Gage said.

"If we catch them," I said. "They won't go back to the apartment. Kinsey can't go back to Weatherfield. If they're smart, they'll leave the city and go into hiding somewhere else far away from here."

"No." Gage offered a wan smile. "They won't be smart about this. They still have one brother, Aaron, missing. I don't see them leaving him behind."

"So what now?" I asked. "Would it do any good to let Simon take a look at the apartment?"

"It probably couldn't hurt," Simon said, joining the conversation at last. "They were there in the last few hours, so any psychic residue will be fresh. I can't guarantee anything, except a good old-fashioned try."

"I want to go with you," I said.

Simon shook his head. "Dahlia—"

I swung my legs over the side of the bed, still woozy but stronger. "I'm going. This is my mess, and I'm going to help clean it up."

"You're going to need a big mop," he said. "So what do we tell Detectives Pascal and Forney about all of this?"

Five heads, including mine, swiveled toward Gage, waiting for his decision. He remained silent for a few moments, worrying his lip.

"Nothing, for now," Gage finally said. "We don't know if Ortega is still being used, or has been discarded, and the minute they hear this, they'll think of King—King?"—he looked at me for confirmation, and I nodded—"as a cop killer. They'll have all four of them posted on every bulletin in the city."

"Shoot to kill," Simon added.

"Precisely."

My stomach tightened at the idea of Noah being hunted down by a mob of angry police officers. Wounded, beaten, and strung up as an example, all for making the choice to live. He had not taken anyone against their will, not like his brothers.

"Simon, Dahlia, and I will go check out the apartment," Gage said. "Renee, I need your ears on the police scanners, in case something turns up. Marco, Ethan, think you can do a little scouting from the air? We may get lucky."

"We haven't been very lucky so far," Ethan said. Off Gage's glare, he held up his hands in surrender. "Air scouting, absolutely." Ethan's ability to manipulate and channel the wind allowed him to glide along on the air currents and fly just like the raven form Marco morphed into.

Gage stood up. "Five minutes," he said to me and Simon, and then strode from the room.

I remained on the bed, wanting everyone to leave before I attempted to stand. Just in case I wobbled or fell or something equally weak. Only Marco lingered, thwarting my plans. He scuffed his boot on the floor. Great, no lecture from Gage or Renee. Just him.

"Well?" I said.

"I am sorry, Dahlia, so sorry."

I gaped. Not what I expected. "For what?"

"For being a self-centered ass these last few weeks," he said. "You were my best friend and I could not respect that enough to accept your . . . rejection. I should never have been so rude to you. I wish to be your friend again."

On my feet without difficulty, I walked to him and pulled Marco into a tight hug. His arms looped around my waist in a crushing embrace. We had shared so much laughter and joy, tears and sorrow, and every other emotion in between. It was impossible to stay angry or withhold forgiveness. Face pressed against his lightly furred neck, I inhaled his cologne, a musky fragrance I associated solely with him, and started to feel better. Not great, but better.

"You care about him, do you not?" he asked.

"I do. Is it stupid?"

"No, just human. He is a fool, you know, *Ascua*. He did not know what he had."

Noah knew exactly what he had, and what he gave up the moment Kinsey tranquilized me and they dumped me in an abandoned yard. "You're wrong. Thanks, though."

He pulled back, bright green eyes searching mine. "*¿Todavía amigos?*"

"Always. Ass."

He grinned.

We parked behind the store. Both vans were gone and the lot was empty. Gage stood at the base of the stairs for many long minutes, letting his senses do their job. Sniffing the air, listening to the creaks and groans of the old wood. Simon did his thing, too, searching for leftover psychic imprints. They found no sign of anyone home. Gage began a slow ascent of the wooden staircase to the apartment door above. I went up last.

Gage stopped at the door, still listening. Nose wrinkling. He tested the knob, then opened the door. Hot vanilla- and coffee-scented air filtered out.

Into the kitchen, one at a time. The mugs and carafe were still on the table. Noah's shattered mug and spilled coffee had not been cleaned up. Even my kicked chair still lay on its side by the far wall. They'd fled in a hurry.

"There's a lot of anger in here," Simon said. "From a lot of different people."

Gage wandered into the living room. I followed, lingering in the doorway. He walked around, studying the room. Watching him, I finally realized what it was about the living room that had bothered me the first time. The one thing missing from every other lived-in space I knew: photographs. Not a single picture of anyone, anywhere.

I wandered down the hall to a bedroom. The door was open. It was small. A bed and dresser, some music poster tacked to the wall over an old desk. Piles of magazines and albums on the floor. The desk held neatly stacked books, a pile of loose-leaf paper, sharpened pencils and ballpoint pens. A framed quote about living each day to the fullest.

I opened the top drawer. Paper clips, erasers, scraps of paper, and a few foil-wrapped sugar candies. Nothing exciting or telling. Next drawer was more of the same. Down to the bottom drawer. It stuck, squealed, and I tugged it open to discover stack after stack of photographs. Three boys, about ten or eleven years old, with matching grins. I recognized Jimmy and Noah. The third boy, his eyes closer set and squinting, had to be the elusive Aaron.

Dozens more photographs of the three of them, all ages and combinations, filled the drawer. Near the bottom, I found one of their parents—a nice-looking couple, happy and kind. The boys got their looks from their father, and their glimmering green eyes from mom. One of the last pictures was of Noah, dated six months ago. He was bald, cheeks sunken, skin sallow. He lay in a hospital bed, surrounded by flowers, holding a two-foot-tall birthday card with a cartoon dog on the front. Pain and exhaustion bled through his forced smile.

Noah Scott was dying, Dahlia.

And he let Ace save his life. They were one and the same now. They were Noah Scott. *He* was Noah Scott.

"Dahlia?" Gage stood in the doorway, arms folded over his chest. "You should see this."

I put the pictures back in the desk and followed Gage to the room across the hall. It was stark, unlived-in. Aaron's room? Simon hovered over the bed and a slew of photos. He moved aside to let me see them, twenty or so in all. My chest tightened with each image I studied. One after the other, photographs of me—in uniform, in civilian clothes, on the street, at jobs, with others or alone. In each one, I had the familiar orange streak in my hair. All of the photos had been taken since January.

My eyes were drawn to one near the top of the bed. I picked it up with trembling fingers. The stained jeans and old sneakers. Hair piled up in a messy ponytail. Standing on the sidewalk, one can of paint in each hand. "This was taken three days ago," I said.

"They were targeting you from the start," Gage said.

"They couldn't have been. They were in Weatherfield until two weeks ago. Kinsey said the Changelings had no contact with the outside world. They could not have been stalking me since January, it doesn't make sense."

"Then someone else was, Dahlia. How else do you explain this?"

"I can't!" I wanted to curl into a ball and scream until logic returned and reared its lovely head. "I can't explain any of this, Gage, and it's driving me crazy. It's like I woke up this morning and the world stopped making sense."

"They could have left this behind on purpose," Simon said. "Maybe some clue as to why she was targeted at the warehouse fire. They couldn't talk about it openly, but that didn't prevent them from leaving bread crumbs."

"Leading back to what, though? Some mysterious third party who wants me dead?"

Simon nodded.

I sank down on the edge of the bed, pictures crinkling beneath me. The world seemed gray, fuzzy. "I think I'm going to be sick."

"We'll take the photos with us," Gage said. "The fire marshal still hasn't declared the fire an accident or arson. If it was arson, then we know someone set it to draw us, particularly Dahlia, out into the open."

"Why would someone want me dead?" Shivers racked my body despite the heat in the apartment. "Why?"

Gage crouched in front of me, silver-flecked eyes boring into mine. Determined and strong. "That's what we're going to find out, Dal, I promise."

I trusted his promise—when Gage gave his word, he meant it. I just didn't trust the people around us, particularly the unknown party who wanted me dead. Even if Gage fulfilled his promise and found out why, nothing prevented the would-be conspirator from following through with his intentions.

Nothing.

Except three Changelings and a scientist. We just needed to find them.

Seventeen

Leads

Gage's com rang while he negotiated our exit from the parking lot. He accepted the call, swerving a bit before carefully maneuvering the Sport back into its proper lane.

"Cipher." His grip on the wheel tightened. "Following up on some leads, Detective Forney, same as you, I'm sure." He looked into the rearview mirror, right at me, and winked. "Unfortunately, I don't have anything new I can share with you." Messing with fire, playing with words.

"Yes, my people did interview Dr. Kinsey again. . . . We didn't believe he told us the entire truth during our first conversation." He started to speak, but was cut off. Then, "He did? That's good to know." Pause. "I'll do that."

He ended the call and rolled his eyes. "She and Pascal have less to go on than we do. I just hope we can figure this out before she calls again and I really have to lie."

"Me, too," I said. "What was the second part of the conversation about?"

"Apparently Kinsey's boss at Weatherfield has sworn out

a complaint against Kinsey, accusing him of conspiring to steal top secret materials and for embezzling funds from corporate accounts. Dr. Abram Kinsey is now a wanted man."

"Damn."

"Yeah."

"Forgive me for voicing an unpopular opinion," Simon said, "but now that Kinsey has been implicated by his own people, wouldn't it be better to tell Pascal what you know? Two thousand more eyes in the city looking for the Changelings is better than just our five pairs."

"We can't," I said. "Even if the police find Kinsey first, he won't give up his sons."

Simon twisted around in his seat to look at me. "How do you know that?"

"Because I saw them together, Simon. He's their father. Is there anything you wouldn't do to keep Caleb safe?" It was a low blow. He turned around without another word.

Gage made a left onto a one-way street. "Dal, call Tempest and see if he's got anything."

I put my com piece into my ear and speed-dialed. Crackling, then the whirring rush of wind blasted over the channel. "Tempest, you there?"

"Yeah, I'm here, Ember. I'm above Burbank right now. Nothing but me and the birds. I don't really know what the hell I'm looking for."

"Suspicious activity?"

"I should stay away from Santa Monica, then, or I'll be chasing people up and down the street." His teasing tone made me smile. "How'd your house call go?"

"The good news is, the place wasn't rigged to explode the minute we opened the front door. We found a few bread crumbs, but no pieces that make any sense."

"So, no sign of them?"

"No, and there's a pretty good chance someone who isn't Kinsey or the Changelings is responsible for the shooting, in a roundabout kind of way."

"You mean they were hired to do a hit?"

"Yeah."

"Whoa."

"Yeah."

"So what's your next move? House-to-house searches?"

"You say that like it's a bad idea." Streetlights whirred by in a blur of color, making the nighttime city streets as bright as normal daylight. "Don't stay out too late, okay?"

"Yes, Mom."

He hung up. I settled back against the seat, catching a glimpse of the clock. Had it really been only a day since Teresa was shot? It felt like a lifetime had passed. So many things in such a brief period, combining to turn the world on its head. Normal was a freshly foreign concept.

"I'm guessing Ethan has nothing new?" Simon asked.

"You guessed right."

Gage's com chimed again. He grunted as he accepted the call. "Cipher . . . what?" The tone of his question made me sit up straight and take immediate notice. "We're on our way." He leaned forward, checked the street signs, and made a hard right onto another block.

I slammed sideways into the door. "What the hell, Gage?"

He looked into the mirror, a new pallor drawing color from his skin. "They had to take Teresa back into surgery."

I buckled up and held on as Gage navigated the city streets, sparing neither speed nor safety to get to the hospital.

He stormed the surgical floor's nursing station. A woman with tidy brown hair and pink scrubs saw us coming, and didn't flinch when Gage began asking questions, demanding to know what was going on, without ever raising his voice. Simon flanked him, a little scary in his intense silence.

I hung back by the elevator, observing without interacting. Useless.

Gage started gesturing, apparently not receiving the answers he wanted. I watched, concerned now, as his expression grew more and more confused. He asked to speak with a doctor, someone in charge. Not good.

"You're Ember, right?"

I jumped, head snapping toward the voice. An orderly stood next to me, his linen uniform stained and rumpled. His face was lined with age and too many emergencies, but he regarded me kindly. Almost curiously, without threat.

"Yes, I am," I said.

He put his hand in the pocket of his trousers. "Someone asked me to give you this."

My heart nearly stopped. Stark. The gun. Chaos and the odor of wet pavement. All of it flashed through my mind in a symphony of images and memory. I struggled to react, to summon up some measure of my power in order to defend myself.

The orderly produced a flash drive. I stared. My heart started beating normally again. *Paranoid, much?*

"Here," he said.

I took it carefully between two fingers. "Who is this from?"

"Punk kid gave it to me, along with fifty bucks to wait here until you came along, and to make sure you got it."

"Did he have green eyes?"

"Yeah."

I turned the memory stick over in my hand. Something was on here Noah wanted me to see. So that meant—

"She's not in surgery," Gage announced, unexpectedly standing next to me, Simon next to him. He didn't acknowledge the orderly. I half expected his head to explode from the sheer force of his fury. "What kind of sick joke is this? The nurse said no one here placed the call."

"Someone wanted to get us here," I said, holding up the stick. "I just got a gift."

"From who?"

"I think it's from Noah." I slipped past him, down the hall toward the nursing station. The woman in charge tensed. I tried to charm her with a smile. "This is going to sound weird, but do you have a computer I can use?"

"Is it an emergency?"

"It could be." I held up the flash drive. "This could have important evidence in an ongoing criminal investigation, and I need to view its contents right away. I just need the computer for a minute."

She eyed it. "What if it has a virus?"

"I'll buy you a new computer network," I said. "I'm rich, I can do that. Please?"

I hated pulling the money card, but it seemed to work. She relented, waving me toward the room at the back of the station. It led into a small lounge, with a table and chairs, refrigerator and coffeepot, and a computer workstation. Gage and Simon followed me inside, heads lowered and eyes averted. I could only imagine the tense conversation they'd had with the head nurse a minute ago.

"Thank you so much"—I glanced at her badge—"Alice. I promise I'll take care of the computer."

She sniffed and retreated from the room. I glared at Gage over my shoulder. He shrugged, chagrined. Rolling my eyes, I sat down in the desk chair and inserted the flash drive into an appropriate port. It initiated, and in a few seconds, a video program loaded.

The image opened on a shot of Cipher, Trance, Onyx, and Tempest, all in their original Ranger uniforms. I knew it instantly. Remembered the way they stood there, Trance and Tempest facing off against the crowd of reporters. Firetrucks and rescue workers in the background, frozen in midmotion.

"Is that when I think it is?" Gage asked.

"Yes," I said, and pressed Play.

It was six-month-old footage of the very first press conference given by the reactivated Ranger Corps. A demolition accident had brought them to Inglewood, and the quartet worked together to rescue four trapped construction workers. They all made it out successfully and chose to speak to the throng of reporters desperate for the hottest scoop in town.

I had been in that crowd, only two months on the job as a cub reporter for the *Valley Gazette*, which was little more than a gossip rag. Trance had chosen me, of the dozens of people there, to ask her questions. The questions on all of our minds. The questions and answers were as fresh in my memory as the day they happened, reinforced by hearing and seeing it all again. I heard the awe in my own voice, the fear and excitement.

The camera was jostled, and a man's shoulder came into view. The angle changed, getting out of the man's way even as he spoke. Asking a question out of turn. Alan Bates, Channel 4 News. He cheated, and Trance ended the interview. The footage ended a few seconds later. It wasn't raw, probably part of a news feed from six months ago, the same section the initial newscast would have aired.

"This was the first time we met," I said. "For some reason, Teresa picked me, before any of you knew I had powers. It was the second most surreal day of my life."

"What was the first?" Gage asked.

"Two days earlier, when I discovered my powers."

"So what does this mean?" Simon asked. "How does this interview help?"

"Maybe it's the starting point," Gage said. "Some of those photos of Dahlia go all the way back to her first week with us. Maybe whatever vendetta this person has against her started that day, with someone who was there."

"That has to be a hundred people," I said, boggling at the idea of narrowing the list down.

"We'll start with Alan Bates," Gage said. "Maybe he's still at Channel Four."

I closed the video program and yanked out the flash drive. "There's only one way to find out," I said, standing up.

Instead of leaving the hospital right away, we detoured to ICU to check on Teresa. Despite the assurances of the staff, Gage wouldn't truly believe she was okay until he saw her with his own eyes. Simon volunteered to wait in the visitors' lounge and call Renee with our latest update, while Gage and I went inside.

It was past visiting hours, but they let us in. Trance and Cipher's romance had been briefly played up by the media back in early February. It was a good press angle, and it didn't hurt that they were an extremely good-looking couple. Gage could have had the entire nursing staff eating out of his hand if he'd put any effort into it. But Teresa was his whole world, and I don't think he remembered how to flirt with anyone else.

I hovered near the door outside Teresa's cubicle, content to keep her in sight and let Gage have time alone. She looked so small on the hospital bed, surrounded by machines and equipment I couldn't name, doing jobs I didn't understand. Her left arm was nearly buried beneath wires and tubes—an IV, a pulse monitor, something else that seemed to be either draining or giving blood. The purple marks on her face were incredibly dark against her pale, pale skin.

She seemed at peace, no hints of new trauma.

And I hated seeing her in that place.

Gage crossed to the right side of her bed and gently took

her hand in his. His touch was so light, tender, as though afraid of squeezing too hard. He stroked her hand, her arm, then bent closer to brush his knuckles across her cheek. Whispered something I couldn't hear.

"You're scaring the hell out of me," Gage said. His voice was quiet, but audible. "I need you back, baby."

Teresa's face scrunched, and he jerked. I stepped a bit closer to the door, heart pounding with excitement. She was waking up.

"Teresa? Can you hear me?" he asked.

She moved her lips, and he bent down lower. Listened. Smiled.

"We're all fine," Gage said. "Everyone's too busy worrying about you to get into much trouble."

It was a lovely sort of lie. She didn't need to know how complicated everything had gotten. She'd want to try and help, and the only thing Teresa needed to do was get well.

"Even Simon came out to make sure you were okay," he said. "Once you're out of ICU, everyone can come visit."

Teresa studied him. She said something I didn't hear, but her face betrayed her disbelief. She knew he was hiding things. Her lips moved, and I swore she asked, "What's really going on?"

"It's nothing we can't take care of, and this time you don't get to override me. All you get to do, love, is heal. Understand?"

She seemed poised to argue, and when she opened her mouth, words became a yawn.

"It's late," Gage continued. "And you need to rest. I just wanted to see you and to say good night."

She mouthed, *Good night.*

He bent low and pressed a kiss to her forehead, and I knew I was intruding on a private moment. I just couldn't look away. He kissed her forehead and both cheeks, then brushed his lips over her mouth.

"I love you," he said.

"Love you, too," she replied.

Gage kissed her again, and I walked away from the cubicle, giving them the privacy they deserved.

Simon had information for us the moment we stepped into the visitors' lounge.

"I called Alan Bates's old boss at Channel Four," Simon said as we headed toward the elevator. "He was fired right after the incident at the construction site. It seems at least a dozen other producers made angry phone calls to the station, so they canned him."

"How'd he react to that?" Gage asked.

"He was furious. He made threats and stormed out of the office, and no one at Channel Four has had contact since. The boss said he was a mediocre reporter, at best, so he was probably blackballed from the industry."

"For asking a question out of turn?" I asked.

"It was a pretty important interview," Gage said.

"True."

Simon hit the elevator button. "His firing certainly gives him motive for shooting at Dahlia."

I opened my mouth to respond to that, and it turned into a yawn. A forceful, eye-watering yawn. "Sorry, I haven't slept much," I said.

Gage's phone rang just as the elevator arrived. Three other people were already on it, so we spent the entire ride down to the lobby listening to him make the occasional comment on a mostly one-sided conversation. As soon as the doors opened and we got off the elevator, he hung up.

"Well, this just keeps getting better and better," Gage said.

"No good conversation ever started like that," I replied.

"Renee ran a current address on Alan Bates."

"Dead?"

"Worse. He's in jail."

"Where?"

"Here."

"For what?"

"Aggravated assault." Gage wrinkled his nose. "He beat up his girlfriend and the guy she was cheating on him with. Put the other guy in the hospital and gave her a bloody nose and a cracked rib."

"How long has he been in?"

"A week. He couldn't post bond so he's in custody until it goes to trial."

"Sounds like the man has a temper," Simon said.

"He does," Gage agreed. "He even took a swipe at his arresting officer."

I tilted my head to the left. "Something in your tone tells me we know the arresting officer."

"We do, and we even know the girlfriend."

"Do tell, the suspense is killing me," I deadpanned. I wasn't going to like what he had to say, but it was another puzzle piece in this slowly widening mosaic of images and events.

"Detective Peter Pascal arrested Bates, and the girlfriend is Pascal's partner, Liza Forney."

I stared. "Seriously?"

"Yes."

The day in the alley, when we first found John Doe's—no, Joel Stevenson's—body, Forney had been there. Annoyed and quiet and wearing too much foundation beneath her eyes, she had moved slowly. Cautiously. Hindsight was twenty-twenty on the memory, no doubt. It also made me wonder about the scar running the length of her left cheek. Had Bates been responsible for it, too? Was Liza Forney just attracted to the wrong kind of guy?

"So," Simon said, "can we chalk Bates up to a big fat coincidence and move along to our next dead end?"

"I don't like coincidences," Gage said. "But I also don't particularly like the idea of invading Detective Forney's personal life, especially when we'll have to explain why we're investigating Alan Bates in the first place." He sucked in his lower lip. "It's still on the table, but I want to hit any other possible leads harder."

"We'll go over the footage and collate a list of names of the people at the construction site that day. We'll go over them one by one, and hope someone can lead us to the next stepping-stone."

"In the morning?" I asked, hopeful. No, more like desperate.

"Yeah." Gage slipped his arm around my shoulders. "In the morning sounds good."

Morning sounded great, in fact. And so very far away.

Eighteen

Glamour

Morning was further away than I expected. Sleep avoided me, offering no relief from the storm of emotions at war inside me. I dragged my tired, battered body out of bed and curled up in my comfy chair with a blanket.

Someone out there wanted me dead. I didn't know why, and I didn't know how he or she had convinced King and his brothers to help. They knew, but they refused to tell me. Noah refused, a fact that hurt more than anything else. It was a betrayal of my feelings and of the trust he claimed to have in me. I didn't return his trust. How could I?

A shaft of silver moonlight trekked slowly across the unfinished wall in front of me, inching its way toward the door. Branches from the tree outside created spiderweb patterns that tricked the eye. They bent, shifted, thinned, and thickened as they traveled.

Footsteps shuffled in the hallway outside. It was probably someone heading for the bathroom, the one downfall of choosing the room directly across from it. A shadow fell across the bottom of the door. The footsteps stopped, followed by a gentle knocking.

I sat up straighter. Who would be coming in this late? I ignored the knock and waited for the intruder to leave. I wanted sleep, not a conversation. But the shadow remained, and the hand knocked again. I growled, mentally telling them to go the hell away.

The doorknob turned—too late I remembered I hadn't locked it. It squealed, and the door pushed open. I froze, watching the shape enter the dim room, his face in shadows. He closed the door, and a bit of moonlight identified the visitor: Gage.

The hell?

He looked first at the bed, and then around the room until he spotted me on the chair. His head tilted to the side, observing. He didn't move. He didn't seem upset or panicked, so I didn't suspect anything had happened to Teresa. I was both curious and annoyed at the intrusion.

"Something that couldn't wait?" I asked, voice low even though we were on the other side of the house from the rest of the occupied rooms.

He stepped forward. "I had to talk to you," he said.

The voice chilled me. Butterflies tore through my belly. He continued to walk through the shaft of moonlight. Silver-flecked eyes melted into emerald. His entire body shimmered and went out of focus. The jaw narrowed. Hair spiked out and brightened into a deep auburn. His muscles became more streamlined, sinewy versus toned, even beneath the tight white T-shirt and jeans. Panic set in and my heart caught in my throat.

Noah-Ace crouched in front of my chair, and I couldn't move. Shock and fear held me in place like iron cuffs, refusing to let me react. Run. Shout an alarm. He didn't speak, just knelt there like a penitent churchgoer. Did he want me to forgive him? Six Hail Marys and an Act of Contrition? As if.

He sported a cut on the left side of his cheek, puffed up by a purplish bruise. I did that to him. Good. One small wound for all the things he'd done to hurt me.

Oh God, what had he done to Gage?

He must have seen and understood the panic on my face, because he said, "It was just a glamour. I shook his hand yesterday, so I could use his image to get inside."

I exhaled hard, relieved. Until anger crept in and took over. "How'd you get through the gate?"

"I slipped in when you arrived home earlier, right before it closed. Nearly caught my foot in it, too."

"Too bad."

"I can't believe you punched me." He smiled.

I didn't return the smile. "There's a lot of things about the last two days I can't believe, and punching you doesn't rank anywhere on the list of things I'm sorry about, Noah. Or Ace, or whoever you are."

He flinched. Good.

"I just came to talk, Dahlia."

"We don't have anything to talk about."

"Yes, we do."

I wanted to bolt out of the chair and climb into bed, pull

the sheet over my head, and pretend it was all a nightmare. He wasn't really here. I was imagining him in my sleep-deprived, drug-addled mind. Hallucinations. Everyone had them at some point in their life, right?

He touched the blanket, very close to my knee. I jerked, and he withdrew his hand, hurt very clear in his eyes. Hurt was good.

"Fine, we do have one thing to talk about," I said. "But you and your brothers refuse to discuss it."

"We have our reasons."

"Of course you do. So why don't you take your reasons and shove them, you unforgivable ass."

His jaw tensed. "Did you get the footage I sent?"

"Yes. And thank you so much for almost giving Gage a coronary with the whole Teresa's-back-in-surgery thing. Real nice touch, that."

"I'm sorry, but I needed to be sure you'd go."

"Congrats. It worked, but I don't really know what you wanted me to see. There are a hundred different people in that footage, Noah, so if one of them is who hired you, I'm going to need a little help narrowing it down."

"I've given what help I can right now. There's more at stake here."

"More than just my life?"

"Yes."

I narrowed my eyes, caught off-guard by the venom in his voice. Undiluted wrath, and it was not directed at me. "What else? What else is at stake that's more important?"

"I can't." While his tone was adamant, his expression held

less conviction—were Noah and Ace battling this one out? Or did he (they?) really want to tell me and couldn't? It didn't matter. It was information I needed, and he continued to withhold it, the jerk.

"Right." I lurched forward. He scuttled back, avoiding potential hits to the head. As I stood, I pulled the blanket tighter around my body, very aware of the flimsy tank top and short-shorts I had worn to bed.

He scrambled to his feet and then inserted himself between me and the door. "I don't know how to make you believe me," he said.

"Oh, I believe you. I believe there is something else going on that's more important than my life and telling me who wants me dead and why. For you, but not for me." And I was sick of it. I sucked in a deep breath and prepped a good scream. It lodged in my throat, along with my ability to breathe. Or move, for that matter. Crap.

Ace was telekinetic. He could kill me with a thought.

"Don't. Scream." He released my lungs, and I exhaled hard. He allowed me nothing else. I couldn't even blink. His ability had no power over my mind, though. I leached the heat from the room, lowering the temperature by fifteen degrees in seconds. Twenty degrees. Twenty-five. Goose bumps rose visibly on his arms.

He reached into his back pocket and produced a slim cell phone. He tossed it onto the bed. "Keep that close tomorrow. I have to do something, and if I can . . . if it works, I'll call you and tell you everything. Everything, I swear." He released control of my head; the rest of my body remained frozen.

"What if I need to contact you?" I asked.

"Speed-dial one."

"Is what you're doing dangerous?"

"Keeping you frozen?"

"That, too."

"I need to do it, Dahlia, and if it works it takes care of both of our problems. It gives us a chance."

I snorted. "A chance for what?"

He lifted his hand as if to touch me. Stopped. He let his hand fall. "For a lot of things."

He walked to the door, and by the time he reached it, he was a glamour of Gage again. He turned back. I glared. A sudden pressure against my neck first stunned, then alarmed me. I couldn't get away or shout for help. Blood rushed against a blocked artery and found no escape. My vision blurred. A telekinetic sleeper hold.

This was getting ridiculous. . . .

Nineteen

Coming Clean

Fists pounded on the door. I pulled my fleece blanket tighter around my head. No interruptions, just another ten minutes. Ignore the peasants storming the castle gate. Back to that nice dream about a white-sanded beach somewhere warm, and far, far away. I rolled over, surprised to discover I could roll at all. Hadn't I fallen asleep in my chair?

No, I hadn't fallen asleep.

The door creaked open. "Dahlia, is there . . . ?" Simon's voice and a rough hand on my shoulder, shaking. "Wake up!"

Head throbbing, I untangled the blanket and blinked against the glare of the overhead light.

Simon loomed above. "I could sense his aura in the hallway. Where is he?"

"Who?" Last night trickled back in vague bits and fuzzy pieces. The hospital . . . no, that was two nights ago. Wait, yes, we did visit the hospital last night. Me and Simon and Gage. An emergency that really wasn't.

"Who?" Simon parroted with some serious sarcasm.

"He was here," Gage said. Where had he come from? His

nose wrinkled, and he didn't venture out of the doorway. "I can smell him."

"Huh?"

Granted, not the most intelligent rebuttal of my short superheroing career, but genuine. Smell him? Noah. The ass knocked me out and then put me to bed. I touched my throat. Something akin to fear must have flashed across my face, because Gage thundered across the room.

"Did he hurt you?" he asked.

"No," I said, shaking my head. Not exactly, and I didn't need my surrogate big brother going crazy over the sleeper hold.

"But he was here."

I squirmed. "Yes."

"Why didn't you alert someone?"

"At first I was too frightened to call out for help." And that was the honest truth. His arrival in my room had shocked the hell out of me, and was the only thing that had kept me rooted in my chair instead of beating him senseless. "Then he wouldn't let me."

"Wouldn't let—telekinesis?"

I nodded.

"So you let him go?" Simon asked.

"I didn't let him do anything. I couldn't freaking move!"

Simon frowned. "You went to sleep after he left, Dahlia."

I blanched, my anger growing by leaps and bounds. So much for keeping this one to myself. I just couldn't stomach Simon's condescending tone or his silent accusation of recklessness. Maybe he had twenty years of life experience on me, but he wasn't always one of the good guys. "I didn't let him go, for God's sake, he knocked me out. You really think I'm that big of an idiot?" Heat rose all along my skin, sucking what little warmth it could out of the air. In seconds, Simon's breath puffed out in pale clouds of vapor.

"I would have kept him here if I could, but I couldn't, so take your judgment and shove it up your—"

"Dahlia!" Gage slipped between us, his body creating a physical barrier that broke my concentration. The heat fled from me. Room temperature returned to normal. Gage glared at me, frustration flashing in his speckled eyes. "Simon, go downstairs."

Simon grunted but followed the command, and seconds later the bedroom door slammed shut. I jumped. Gage grabbed my robe out of the closet and tossed it to me. I stood and slipped it on.

"Are you okay?"

I perched on the edge of my cozy chair. "Slight headache."

"Not what I meant."

Of course it wasn't. My throat felt tight. "I feel like an idiot, Gage. He was in the house and I let him get away."

He was quiet for several seconds, and then said, "I got this leadership thing by default, Dal. I spend my days going, 'What would Teresa do?' and half the time, I think I've got the right answer."

"What about the other half?"

"I muddle through it, just like she does when she's uncertain."

The idea of Teresa West admitting to uncertainty made

me smile. "So, if she was here with us now, what would she say to me?"

He scratched his chin with one finger, grazing over a day's worth of blond stubble. "Well, first she'd threaten to beat Noah to a bloody pulp for hurting you."

My lips twitched. "That sounds like her."

"Then I think she'd remind you about your family here and the people who love you. That you aren't in this battle alone."

"I know." *Do I really?*

I would never betray my friends, but I was hiding things from them. Trying to be all things to all people. I couldn't keep protecting Noah. He wasn't my family. He had his own to think about. Family was something to protect, no matter the cost. No matter who else got hurt.

Family.

My mouth fell open. It seemed too simple, and yet perfectly logical, and it had been right in front of me the entire time.

"What's wrong?"

I tried to work my jaw and probably looked like a gasping fish.

"Dahlia?"

"He's protecting Aaron," I said.

"Who is?"

I scrambled out of the chair and dove onto the bed, fumbling beneath the rumpled sheets for the cell phone. "Noah and Jimmy and King," I said. "They're protecting Aaron, that has to be it. It's why Noah can't tell me who wants me dead.

He isn't hiding it to protect me. He can't, because withholding the information protects Aaron."

Gage bobbed his head up and down, trying to follow along with my speeding train of thought. "Aaron is the brother they haven't found yet, right?"

"Yes, the one King was supposed to take over as a permanent host to make them a trio again. Noah told me Aaron disappeared while on a skiing trip with friends, and he hasn't been seen in weeks. It makes perfect sense that the one thing keeping Noah from being totally honest with me is his brother."

"But who would do something like this?"

"Still the big question," I said. "The good part is, Noah didn't break any promises he made, because I figured it out on my own, which means we can help them get Aaron back from whoever's holding him."

"They may not want our help, Dal."

I finally found the phone tucked between the mattress and the wall. "We can at least offer it, can't we?" I stilled, alarmed by his lack of response. "I'll do it myself if you don't think the team should get involved."

"I don't know what I think yet." He eyed the phone. "If you can get Noah to confirm your suspicions, that his actions and King's actions have been made under duress, I'll get the others to help. If it's something else, anything else, we have to bring the Changelings in."

"They'll fight before they let us capture them."

"Then let's hope it doesn't come to that." Gage nodded his head toward the phone, offering silent permission to go ahead with whatever plan I had in mind. It couldn't be easy for him, allowing me to take such a risk. He wanted someone to pay for Teresa's injuries. He knew King was directly responsible, and now he practically promised he wouldn't seek vengeance if it turned out King had been coerced into it.

My respect for Gage McAllister tripled.

He left. Voices began arguing immediately behind my closed bedroom door. They eventually moved away. I turned on the phone and speed-dialed, heart thudding in my ears. What was I going to say to him? Would he even answer?

This is a really bad idea.

It rang twice, and then clicked over to voice mail. "Dahlia." Noah's voice, prerecorded. "Meet me on the corner of Hollywood and North Sycamore, one hour from the time you're about to say after the beep. Do I have to say come alone?" Beep.

I looked at the phone's display. "It's quarter to eight in the morning. I'll see you in one hour."

After snapping the phone shut, I threw open the closet doors and started dressing. Back in civilian clothes, with my hair tucked up under a matching green bandana to hide the orange streak. The phone went into my back pocket, along with the team com. Wallet—check. Shoes—check. Courage—working on it.

Courage to see this through and do the right thing. Courage to face my friends and teammates if anything went wrong. I had to know the truth of things; until I did, nothing else mattered.

———————

Cipher and Tempest dropped me off three blocks from the meeting place. They were both in full uniform, coms in place. Onyx was already staking out the corner from a building across the street. He flew in as the raven, but had likely shifted into his third animal form and was prowling the rooftops as a black housecat.

As we pulled up to the curb, Cipher's com rang. "It's Cipher," he said.

I waited, hand on the door handle. Good news or bad, I couldn't figure out from his face.

He listened for less than thirty seconds before saying, "Thanks," and hanging up. "Scott and Sons Electric burned to the ground last night. Looks like they had something on timer to get rid of their trail."

"Looks like." They'd just added arson to the list of charges piling up against them. Fantastic.

Neither man spoke as I climbed out of the Sport. They had offered every bit of imaginable advice during the drive over, voiced their concerns, and offered contingency plans if things went south. I listened, nodding in all the right places.

I forced myself to walk slowly down Hollywood Boulevard, pretending I belonged there like the dozens of other people wandering the street. The sidewalks had been torn up and repaved ten years ago, but already the concrete was cracked, pitted. Tourist traps were closed up, or converted into cheap diners and cheaper bars. The night life never really left this section of old Hollywood; it was just sleeping off last night's bender.

Another block, and I made a right. At the designated corner was a parking structure with public access. Street level boasted a boisterous clothing store. Down a side street, the ramp led up four parking levels. I crossed the street against traffic and stood on the requested corner. Precisely on time.

I watched the foot traffic, resisting the impulse to look at the buildings across the street. To seek out Onyx and know my backup was as close as a well-timed scream. I wasn't alone, no matter how isolated I felt.

The cell phone chirped. I palmed it. A text message appeared on the display. *Parking garage. Second level. Now.*

Onyx wasn't the only one watching.

Phone in hand, I strolled toward the garage entrance, every step loud in my ears. Up the ramp, into cooler air reeking of oil and exhaust fumes. My stomach churned, unhappy I'd only eaten half a wheat bagel for breakfast. Even that had been forced on me by Renee. I'd been too scared to eat, too anxious to get this over with.

Walking up toward the second level of the parking structure, I wanted to run—away from the fear and uncertainty, from the warring emotions and disjointed desires. Conflicting stories, scientific experiments, human pillowcases, jailed reporters, and missing persons. All of it gone. Every single thing that prompted me to run also kept me walking straight ahead. The need to make sense of it all pushed my feet forward, step by step, toward a necessary goal.

The level was half full of parked vehicles scattered around

the dozens of available slots. Vans, trucks, and cars—nothing stood out.

Chirp. Another message. *Blue pickup.*

I spotted the vehicle and approached. It had dark-tinted windows. I cupped my hands against the glass and peered inside. Empty.

The cellular's shrill tone screeched across the lot. I fumbled, then hit Receive.

"Yes?" I said.

"It's me." Noah. "When I hang up, put this phone and your team com in the bed of the truck. Then walk in the opposite direction, to the gray food truck next to the west wall." Click.

Food truck? I spotted it and deposited the phones in the pickup as ordered, ridding myself of the tracking mechanism planted in my personal com. Not good. Certainly smart of him. I approached the gray truck, slowing a fraction with each step, nerves getting the better of me. It had two back doors with vents instead of windows. The passenger side sported a long, narrow counter and sliding glass window, all covered and locked. I checked the cab—empty. A plastic accordion curtain blocked my view of the interior.

The driver's side had another vent, but no windows. I circled around to the rear. The latch on the back door turned on its own and swung open. I climbed in, swallowed whole by the sickly-sweet odor of grease and fried foods. The interior was lit by a single, center bulb, casting orange shadows on the two people inside: Noah and Dr. Kinsey. They sat on overturned plastic crates, their backs against a long grill. A third crate was set up across from them. Waiting for me.

"I continue to underestimate you, Miss Perkins," Kinsey said. He reached behind him and touched the small black box on the grill's surface. White noise again. "We didn't expect to hear from you so quickly. What changed your mind?"

"Domestic dispute," I replied.

Noah tensed. "What happened?"

"Cipher caught wind of your after-hours visit and got a little pissed." To Kinsey, I said, "I suppose you know Weatherfield swore out a complaint against you, and both the local police and L.A. County Sheriff's Office are looking for you."

"Yes, and?"

Time to see if I was as good a guesser as I hoped. "And I want to help you get Aaron back."

Noah's hand jerked. Kinsey closed his eyes, then re-opened them a moment later. The men shared a silent stare, communicating something, maybe via Jimmy hiding somewhere else in the parking structure. It didn't matter, because the declaration had struck a nerve, grabbed their attention, and I had to hold on to it.

"You didn't break any promises you made," I continued. "I guessed on my own, and it looks like I'm right."

"How?" Noah asked.

"Family is the only thing that would make *me* do what you've done against my will and my better judgment. Who has him?"

"We don't know."

"Noah," Kinsey said.

"What, Dad?" Noah threw his hands into the air, relief

relaxing the tension in his body. "She figured it out, why can't we just tell her everything?"

"You're risking Aaron's life."

"We don't know for sure they'll hold up their end and give Aaron back to us."

"They haven't lied yet."

"Yet."

The exchange happened so rapidly I almost missed the point of the argument. They didn't know who had Aaron. They didn't know how much the kidnappers knew about their current activities, or if Aaron would be released when they did what they were told. It was all on faith—to get Aaron back alive, they had no choice.

"How do you know Aaron is alive?" I asked.

Noah dug into his pocket and pulled out a phone. He pressed some buttons and brought up a picture. "They send us a new one every day."

The image showed a newspaper in the foreground with yesterday's headline about the warehouse fire and shooting. Past that was a young man, similar to Noah in size and build, with dirty-blond hair and piercing green eyes. He was tied to a chair, gagged. Blood had dried on his upper lip and stained the cloth around his mouth. Older now, but still the same boy from those photographs.

"You have no idea who's holding him?" I asked. "Or where?"

Noah shook his head as he put the phone back in his pocket. "The photos are too dark. Whenever they call, the voice is electronically filtered. We don't even know if it's a man or woman. They make demands, and we try to follow them."

"Do they know what you can do, Noah?"

"They know we're Changelings, yes."

"How?"

"I don't know."

Kinsey's eyes narrowed at me. "What are you thinking, Miss Perkins?"

I was thinking he needed to stop calling me Miss Perkins. "When were you first approached by these people and told they had Aaron?" I asked.

"Two days after they escaped Weatherfield," Kinsey said. "The kidnappers called me at work. Demanded I go to a public telephone booth a few blocks away and wait for further instructions. The caller told me they knew about the Changelings, they had Aaron, and were sending me proof. The first photo was sent to my cellular that afternoon. I showed it to the boys. A few more days passed before they contacted us again with their demands."

"Which were what?" I asked.

"Money," Noah said. "And three favors, the specifics of which we'd be told about as they were needed."

"You agreed to three blind favors?" *Favor* seemed like the wrong word. *Demand*, maybe, or *blackmail orders*. *Favor* implied a willingness to go along with it—help given without threat.

"We had to, for time if nothing else. We've spent this last week scouring the city, hoping for some trace of Aaron, some hint as to where they might be keeping him."

"Have you given them the money yet?"

"No," Kinsey said. "The money is only to be given at the exchange. That was our one demand they compromised on. Favors first, then money for Aaron."

That was something, at least. "How many favors have you done?"

"Two," Noah replied. "We're waiting on a call for the third."

A chill wormed its way up my spine and tingled across the back of my neck. "Was I one of those favors? The shooting?" Their silent inability to look at me confirmed the question. "Did they hurt Aaron because King missed?"

Noah's head snapped up, fury narrowing his eyes. He hesitated. "Yes. We got the call five days ago, demanding a very public assassination of you." His voice wavered as he fought for the words to explain. "We knew of the Rangers through our dad and our combined Scott memories. We didn't know why they wanted you dead, and they wouldn't tell us when we asked. At first we refused, so they sent us video footage of them tor-torturing Aaron."

His voice broke under the weight of the memory. "When I realized I knew you from school and that it could be our way into your life, Jimmy manipulated you into coming into the shop. He put the subliminal suggestion into your head the day before, when he saw you buying paint. We thought if we got close enough, we'd get the opportunity. I just never expected . . . I never thought an old crush would affect me so strongly."

My stomach ached. I wanted to bolt from the truck, call for help, and get them out of my life. I needed to make my tumultuous emotions cease once and for all. Clear my head completely of Noah Scott.

"Do the kidnappers know we're . . . ?" What? We weren't anything except at odds with each other's goals.

"I don't know," Noah said, understanding my meaning when I didn't. "Lunch was a mistake."

I flinched.

He realized how that sounded. "I should have been more careful to limit who saw us together. I don't know who I'm looking out for. None of us do."

"What about Weatherfield?"

"What about them?" Kinsey asked.

"Did anyone outside of Weatherfield know the Changelings existed?"

"No, and I've done thorough checks on all of our high-level employees, everyone involved in any aspect of the project. There is nothing to suggest anyone I worked with is involved in this."

Figures. Only an intelligent, high-ranking scientist would forget the most obvious suspects, because he never gave much thought to those below his status. "You only checked high-level employees? What about the janitors? I don't know about medical research buildings, but in my high school, the janitor heard and saw everything. You wanted dirt, you went to him."

Kinsey's skin went ashen. Nope, it hadn't occurred to him, even after using low-level Jarvis to facilitate the Changelings' escape. Self-centered bastard.

"We'll have to look deeper into that," Noah said.

"Let my people do it," I said. "They want to help, Noah. We have good equipment and access to police records. They can check it out and get back to us fast."

Father and son exchanged looks. Kinsey nodded. Noah handed over his phone. I dialed the house number.

"So," I said as I pressed Send, "what was the second favor you did?" The phone hissed in my ear. The line went dead. "The hell?" I tried again. Same result.

Kinsey plucked the phone from my hand and tested it. "Someone's blocking our calls."

"Who?" Noah and I said in tandem.

Kinsey climbed over Noah, rushing toward the accordion curtain blocking the driver's cab. He pushed it aside, slid into the seat, and cranked the engine. Noah leaned across me and peeked through the blinds covering the sliding counter window. I twisted around to look.

A shadow moved two rows away. Light glinted off metal. Several new cars were in the lot, each one a dark sedan. Also an unmarked black van. I'd seen vans like that before, when the city's SWAT team didn't want to be seen coming.

"How did they find us?" I asked.

"Ask your friends," Noah snarled.

"Get down, you two," Kinsey said. He shifted and backed up so quickly that Noah and I went sprawling.

I hit the floor on my back, and Noah landed on top of me. Before he could move, Kinsey changed direction. A cupboard opened above us, raining down packets of ketchup, mustard, and mayonnaise. Noah braced on his elbows, covering me from the avalanche. Arms around his waist, I held on tight and we huddled on the floor.

A sharp rat-a-tat-tat sound was punctuated by loud pings against the sides of the truck. Gunshots. The truck swerved. Plastic utensils showered down from above, cans and boxes rolled in their cupboards. More gunshots banged against the back door. I screamed.

Kinsey kept driving. The truck bounced and swerved again. Glass exploded up front. I peered over Noah's shoulder and saw a gaping hole in the windshield. Kinsey had his hand up, shielding his face. We sped up. Turned again. Our tires squealed. I closed my eyes and held Noah tighter.

"It's okay, I've got you," he whispered. His voice burned my ear.

After all his speeches about trust, had Gage betrayed me? Sent me in alone, only to call the cops? I couldn't believe he would do that. Simon was the more likely candidate, but he hated cops. Calling them made no sense. None of this made sense.

The only thing I was certain of was that someone had betrayed my trust and used me as bait to catch Noah and the others. Damn them to hell for not trusting me.

The ride smoothed out, still dangerously fast, but the sharp turns stopped. We must have made it out to a freeway. Noah sat up, debris falling all over the place. He offered his hand. I took it, letting him pull me up.

"You okay?" He opened his arms, and I fell into them.

"Not even a little bit," I replied. My hands bunched in the

fabric of his T-shirt. We swayed with the truck. Air blasted through the broken windshield, hot and humid. I lifted my head and pulled back to look him in the eye. "As far as high-speed chases go, this one isn't so bad."

He chuckled. The sound vibrated in his chest and in mine. The truck jerked sideways. We both crashed into the side of the grill, letting go of each other to keep ourselves upright. Noah stumbled toward the cab.

"Hey, watch the turns," he said. "Where are— Dad?"

His abrupt change in tone alarmed me. I picked my way forward, stepping on and breaking a dozen different condiment packets in the process. Noah leaned over Kinsey, gripping the wheel with both hands, eyes straight ahead. At first I couldn't figure it out. Then I saw the blood.

Twenty

Getaway

Noah pressed one hand against Kinsey's chest, just above his heart. Blood oozed between his fingers and had already soaked Kinsey's shirt. The older man continued to drive—ignoring us or spaced out from blood loss—intent on the road. From bits of scenery, I guessed we were on I-101 heading south. Traffic was heavier going the other way and sparse in our lanes, which wasn't surprising given the neighborhoods we were heading toward.

I climbed around Noah, getting into the small space between the two front chairs and the dash. Noah shifted to the rear, his hand still pressing against the wound. I grabbed the wheel with one hand, glad we were on a pretty straight section and not boxed in with cars.

"Keep your foot on the gas, Dr. Kinsey," I said, easing his hands off the wheel. "I'll steer, just don't stop pressing the gas pedal."

"'Kay," he said. His eyes were glassy, unfocused.

"Okay," I said. "Noah, when I say, I need you to pull him out of the driver's seat. We're going to switch places." I didn't wait for confirmation of the plan. Instead, I slipped across Kinsey's lap, keeping all my weight on the balls of my feet, practically straddling the steering wheel. My hand slipped and the wheel jerked. Someone in the next lane honked long and loud.

I got us going straight again, then situated my right foot near Kinsey's leg. Took a deep breath and, "Now, Noah, pull."

Noah grunted. Kinsey shouted. The body below me moved, brushed, nudged me forward over the wheel. More grunting from beside me was followed by a heavy thud. The instant the seat was empty, I sat down and put my foot on the gas. So far, so good. I inched into the next lane, hoping for a halfway-decent exit ramp in the next few minutes.

On the floor between the front seats, Noah cradled Kinsey in his lap, still pressing hard against the bleeding bullet hole in his father's chest.

"He needs a hospital," Noah said.

"No, no hospital." Kinsey waved one hand in the air, too weak to do little more than verbally protest. "Not too bad, just need rest."

"What about my house?" I asked. "We have medical facilities, he can get attention there."

Kinsey growled. "No, back to the hideout. They're waiting for our call. Aaron. The third favor."

They still hadn't clued me in on the second favor, but now wasn't the time to ask. Once we were safe and Kinsey was out of immediate danger, I'd poke into that viper's nest.

"No matter where you want to go, we can't stay in this truck," I said. "Every cop in the city will be looking for it."

A bright red import careened into my lane from the left. I hit the brake to avoid rear-ending it, then mashed my hand down on the horn. It bleated like a dying cow. The driver flipped me off and zoomed sideways into the exit ramp.

"What was that?" Noah asked.

"Road rage." I sped back up, alert for the next exit. We were smack in the middle of one of the worst neighborhoods in Los Angeles, heading toward the big East L.A. Interchange. South toward Huntington Park and Compton was our best bet. Even the city police stayed out of those ravaged neighborhoods.

We needed a car. Finding one was easy. The hard part was getting it to run. "I don't suppose either of you knows how to hot-wire a car?" I asked.

"King can," Noah said.

"Not helpful."

"He can?" Kinsey asked. Pink flecked his lips, making them stand out brightly from his ashen face. His eyes blinked rapidly. Every pavement crack I hit put him in more pain, and I couldn't do anything to stop it.

A peeling billboard, half covered with graffiti and paint, advertised Used Cars, Cheap! at the next exit. Not helpful—wait. A plan formulated. It was a little out of my usual repertoire, and I wasn't much of an actress, but then Kinsey made an awful sound, something between a cough and a wheeze, and I made up my mind.

I pulled onto the next exit ramp, mindful of every single bump and shimmy. The truck had bad brakes, and they squealed and rattled when I slammed my foot down—the stoplight at the bottom of the ramp seemed to come out of nowhere. I peeled my aching fingers off the steering wheel. Panic attack was so not on the day's docket.

"What are you doing?" Noah asked.

"Improvising," I said.

No traffic, right or left. Nearly a full minute passed; the light did not change. I checked again, then made the left turn, anyway. Half a mile down, I made a right onto a slightly busier street. Foot traffic and beat-up cars, many with rusted roofs and doors, mismatched hubcaps, and dented exteriors. Multifamily homes and the occasional convenience store lined the street.

A few residents waved at the truck, probably hoping for a hot, cheap meal. I kept going, ignoring their taunts and swears as I passed. Houses turned into apartments, apartments into businesses—adult-video stores, groceries, cheap and resale clothing shops, a bowling alley. Farther up, another billboard: Used Cars, Cheap! Bingo.

Kinsey had closed his eyes and seemed to be sleeping in Noah's arms. The dutiful son just held him, his chin resting on the unwounded shoulder, whispering things over and over into the older man's ear. I ached for both of them, and for their intense bond. I had loved my mother that way, but she was gone. I wanted to love someone like that again—in an all-consuming way.

I drove past the car lot. It took up half a city block, sandwiched between a Korean deli and a used bookstore. Red and yellow plastic flags adorned every streetlight, strung between them like a party banner. The word *sale* was printed on every available surface. Another block down, I turned into a narrow alley, barely able to fit the girth of the food truck.

A dozen yards down, a pile of metal trash cans blocked half the alley. I stopped, shifted into park, and turned off the engine. Noah looked up, curious but silent. Fear for his father was his entire existence.

"I'll be back in less than ten minutes, I promise," I said. "I have an idea to get us another car."

His lips parted as if to protest, but he didn't. He nodded. I winked and then climbed out, slamming the door shut behind me.

Jeans pulled down lower on my hips and shirt rolled up above my navel, I strolled onto the lot showing midriff and swinging my hips, mimicking Renee's sexual ease and camping it up. I had let part of my hair down, careful to keep the orange streak beneath the bandana, while still showing enough blond to catch interest.

Sure enough, five feet onto the lot, a man was beelining toward me. His gray hair glinted in the sunlight and sweat patches darkened both armpits of his blue shirt. The sleeves were rolled up, and he hastily fixed his tie as he walked. Perspiration rolled down the sides of his face. He made no attempt to hide his open appraisal of me.

I twisted my lips into a teasing smirk. "Hot day, isn't it?"

"One of the hottest so far." His voice was high and reedy, mismatched with his bulk. Not overweight, just big without being muscular. "Anything I can show you today?"

"Depends on what you're offering." I ran my hand over the hood of the nearest car, no idea of its make or model. Just that it was light green and rusty. "Got anything with good air-conditioning?"

"Working air costs a little more," he said to my breasts. "We have cars that come with it. Some of the others ran out of freon, and you know how hard it can be to get around here."

"Oh, yeah, you learn quick to sweat it out." I toyed with my hair, lifting it up away from my neck and letting it tumble back down in yellow waves. He watched, already squirming on the hook. Too easy.

"You looking to buy today or shopping around?" he asked.

I grinned, pretending to be shy. "I was hoping for a long, cool test drive."

His eyes glistened. "I see. I've got just the car in mind for your test drive, Miss—?"

"Wright," I said, grabbing a name from the air. Miss Wright? Good grief.

"I'm Bill." He indicated the cars ahead of us, and I started walking. His hand found its way to the small of my back. I managed not to twist his roaming hand off his wrist like a New Year's party cracker. "I've got just the car for your test drive. Good air, wide backseats."

My stomach twisted at the very notion of being in a backseat with him. Apparently the sleazy salesmen around here had no problem sharing their precious air-conditioned cars with willing females who needed out of the blazing heat for just a little while. Not a bad way to go to work and get your whoring done all in the same eight hours.

He stopped in front of a tan station wagon. The paint was decent, the interior clean. I would have preferred something with tinted windows, but this would do.

"I'll be right back," he said, shuffling off toward the office to get a key.

I lounged on the hood, playing my part and fanning myself with one hand. Less than a block away, Noah and Kinsey were waiting for me to come back. I prayed no one had noticed the bullet-riddled truck illegally parked down the alley. They had no weapons to protect themselves, except for Noah's telekinesis.

A door slammed. Laughter followed Bill out of the office. I couldn't drum up any annoyance at what he'd probably bragged about to his pals. He would pay for it with a nice, fat headache in just a few minutes. He approached, walking fast, obviously excited about his prospects to get a good lay for a free test drive. I tried not to roll my eyes.

He unlocked the driver's door and held it open like a gentleman. I slid inside. The interior reeked of disinfectant, the heavy air hotter than Hades. I put the key into the ignition and turned the battery on enough to lower every single window. Warm, fresher air blasted inside. Bill climbed into the passenger seat, and the entire car rocked.

"Ever driven one of these babies?" he asked.

I grinned, batting my baby blues. "Never one quite so big." My gaze flickered to his lap. He twitched.

Hook, line, and sinker.

I cranked the engine while he fiddled with the air-conditioning controls. Sweat rolled down his cheeks in torrents and dampened the front of his shirt. The salty-sweet odor tested my gag reflex. Once satisfied that cool air would blast us soon, he let his hand drift down to my right knee. I managed to not cringe, vomit, or crash the car on the way out of the lot. Pervert.

Tease.

I turned left.

"I haven't seen you around town before," he said, hand squeezing a bit.

"I just moved into the area." The alley was fast approaching. "And I like to make an impression when I can."

"You'd be hard to miss in a crowd." Nice compliment coming from a guy trading a car ride for sex. I couldn't help noticing the gold band on his wedding finger. I hoped she was screwing around on him, since he obviously screwed around on her. "Hey, where are we going?"

"It's a surprise," I said, negotiating the turn into the alley. The truck was still ahead, its back doors closed. The bullet holes and impact dents were more obvious in this light.

"This isn't very private," he said.

"I wouldn't worry about it." I parked behind the truck, left the engine idling. "Because you aren't having sex with me."

"Huh?" His face shaded scarlet.

Calling on a move Teresa taught me, I hit his throat with the tendon between my thumb and forefinger, right below the Adam's apple. He croaked and clutched at his throat, eyes bugging out. I punched him in the temple. His forehead hit the dash. He didn't move. Fist aching, I threw open my door and bolted to the front of the food truck.

Something by the trash cans caught my eye. Moved. Stood. A man in grimy clothes, hair so greasy I couldn't decipher the color, inched out from behind the haphazard stack of cans. Brown fingers betrayed years of street life. Pockmarks on his face and nose painted a life of poverty. He watched me with rheumy eyes, no sign of hostile intent.

Considering the wallet hastily stuffed into my back pocket that morning, I asked, "You want to make fifty bucks?" He nodded. "There's a guy in the car back there. Can you get him out and put him in the back of this truck?"

Another nod. I left him to his task—hoping he actually did what I asked, because moving the hefty car salesman on my own was a near-impossible task—and yanked open the driver's door. Noah blinked over the edge of the seat, sweating. Shit. The interior blazed like a furnace.

"I have a car." I climbed up, the faux leather seat hot through the knees of my jeans. "Can you wake him? We have to move."

Gentle prodding roused Kinsey to semiwakefulness. Enough to get him up and across the seat. He groaned, trying to fold his long body over and tuck his legs beneath the steering wheel. I got an arm under his shoulder, earning a sharp yelp from him. I pulled. He stumbled on the landing, and we crashed to the slick pavement. My bare elbow smeared something damp and yellow, scraping skin across rough stone.

Noah jumped out of the cab with a startling preternatural ease, hitting the pavement without making a sound. A Changeling ability, perhaps? The truck rattled. Noah sprinted to the rear.

"Hey!" he said.

"It's okay, he's helping." At least, I hoped so. Witnesses weren't ideal, but we didn't have much choice.

Noah hesitated, then came back to assist me. Kinsey couldn't stand on his own (pain delirium or blood loss, take your pick) so we supported him, one of us on either side. I got the wounded side and did my best to hold both Kinsey and the wound. The blood flow had slowed, but not completely stopped. At the back of the wagon, I grunted. The keys were in the ignition.

Noah raised his free hand, palm out toward the wagon. The back hatch popped open. Telekinesis. Duh. Noah pulled down the tailgate and climbed in first. He sat down facing me. We gently turned Kinsey around and helped him sit. With arms hooked around Kinsey's chest, Noah crawled backward inch by inch, pulling the weight. Once their feet were in the car, I pushed it shut. I turned around and yelped.

Hired Helper stood directly behind me. The food truck doors shut, hopefully with the car salesman inside. I fished into my pocket and retrieved a wad of bills. My sweaty, trembling hands couldn't count properly, so I shoved most of the money at the stranger.

"Help yourself to what's inside the truck," I said, hoping he'd find more food than just spilled condiment packets.

He nodded, pocketed the money without counting, and

shambled to the truck. I got in the station wagon, shifted into reverse, and then started backing up. Out of the hot, stinking alley.

"What did you do?" Noah asked.

Assault and grand theft auto. "Taught a guy a lesson in why it's bad business to assume a pretty girl wants more than a literal test drive."

Checking traffic in both directions, I backed out into the main avenue, and off we went. I fiddled with the dials and then rolled the windows up. Chilly air blasted through the vents, cooling my sweaty skin. I directed the passenger vents toward the back, hoping the air reached them quickly.

"Now what, Noah?" I asked. "You don't want to go to Hill House, so I hope you have a place."

"We do. Can you get back to I-5 from here?"

Still pretty familiar with the area, I nodded, only to realize he was facing backward and couldn't see me. "Yeah, I can."

"Good, do that."

"Fine." I slowed for a traffic light, applying pressure to the overly sensitive brakes. We were sitting targets, even in our borrowed—stolen!—car. Every passing moment seemed like a blessing, and also an opportunity for a random cop to get suspicious. Or decide we were part of his daily quota and pull us over for no good reason.

Stop being so paranoid.

Easier said than done. My attention divided itself between the road in front of me and the rearview-mirror angle I had of Noah's head. I started to speak several times, to ask random questions just to kill the utter silence in the car.

Radio seemed like bad form, almost rude given our dire situation, but I needed a distraction.

Silence came with too much time to think. Time to ponder my current situation and how in blazes I ended up driving a stolen car across town, hoping to avoid police capture. I had climbed into the truck on my own, but the police—and my own people, for that matter—had every reason to think I was being held against my will.

I had done the right thing. Noah and Kinsey had placed their trust in me by setting up the meeting in the parking garage. Someone else had betrayed us and called the police. I hated pondering the implications—would much rather ponder a root canal—but could not avoid them forever.

Sooner or later, I had to call home.

Twenty-one

Hideout

Y ou should have just said Sun Valley, Noah," I said, negotiating a right turn onto Farmdale Avenue. "I'd have
gotten us here a lot faster than by your directions."

Noah twisted his head around, and I met his gaze in the
rearview mirror. "I know my way around the city, I grew up
here," he said.

"Yeah? So did I, in case you forgot."

He grunted. "It's the blue house at the end of the block."

Our destination came into view, nestled behind a thick
hedge of holly, an unusual bush to find growing in Southern
California. Most of the run-down houses in this neighborhood sported dying orange trees or transplanted cactuses.
Some had a tree or two, but most were chopped down, torn
down, or ripped apart for the firewood. Peeling blue paint
covered the outside of the adobe cottage, while its terra-cotta
roof was still its original shade. The mismatch gave the place
character.

The front end of my stolen wagon dipped hard in the
cracked driveway. I winced. No sounds of protest came

from the rear. Good sign or bad, I didn't know yet. Dr. Kinsey hadn't made a peep in the twenty minutes it took us to get to this side of the city.

No other cars occupied the short, narrow driveway. It ended at a dilapidated wooden garage, both doors chained and rotting. I turned off the engine.

"Where are we?" I asked.

"Ronald Jarvis's house," Noah said.

"Why?" Something whispered through my mind, like a chilly breeze caressing just below my skull. It lingered only a moment before passing by completely. I shivered.

"It's just Jimmy, making sure it's us."

"He shouldn't walk through people's brains like that." I climbed out and darted around to the back, keys in hand to unlock the hatch. The side door of the house banged open. I yelped and jumped back from the noise.

Jimmy strode toward me in the same rumpled clothes he'd worn yesterday. He barely glanced in my direction. His eyes were fixed on the interior of the car as he came around. "What happened?" he asked.

"The police knew where we were meeting," I said. "I don't know how, but they did. Dr. Kinsey tried to get us out of there and the police shot him."

Noah inched forward. Jimmy and I grabbed Kinsey's ankles and pulled, our combined strength moving the unconscious man. We kept our places, Noah's arms remained wrapped around Kinsey's chest, and we carried him toward the house. I had only a fraction of the weight, but felt the strain immediately in my shoulders and arms. Jimmy huffed and puffed, his thin body not used to the weight. I almost asked Noah about telekinetically moving Kinsey, but figured he'd be doing it if he was able.

The sagging screen door had stayed wide open, a blessing for our straining band. Up the stairs backward, Jimmy and I struggled not to drop our burden. Only Noah seemed unaffected, his face grim.

In the kitchen, someone shouldered me sideways. Startled, I dropped Kinsey's foot. A six-foot, medium-build body slipped in and took over. King, I had decided before I got a look at his face. A scream died in my throat, terror choked out by utter fascination.

It was King. Changeling King, not King in possession of anyone else. He wore simple blue jeans and a man's sleeveless T-shirt, showing off his muscled arms and torso. His face was a blank slate. Pronounced ridges where eyebrows, nose, and mouth would have been, hinted at the man inside. Not a speck of hair anywhere. Only two small holes for nostrils and a larger one for a mouth, without any cartilage or lips, and earholes without lobes. A living mannequin's head.

The three brothers continued through the kitchen, toward a hallway.

"Do you have a first aid kit?" I asked, trailing after them.

"Dad left a medical bag in the living room," Jimmy puffed.

They struggled down the hall, while I doubled back. Next to the kitchen was a dim living room. Heavy drapes were drawn across the windows, allowing little natural light into the room. The furniture was old, mismatched, and smelled of mildew. I circled past a worn sofa. Air from a window unit caressed my face.

The bag revealed itself in the far corner, a black satchel seeming better suited for a blackmail payday than medical supplies. I unzipped and sorted through the array of bandages, syringes, medicine bottles, tape, and instruments. Perfect. Shouldering the bag, I quick-stepped it back down the hallway. Past a dingy bathroom and one bedroom, to the only other room in the small house.

Kinsey was laid out on the bed with his feet propped up on a pillow. Noah hovered by his chest, one hand still applying pressure to the wound. Jimmy and King stood by the foot of the bed, tense. Worried. A nice feat for a man with no face.

"The bullet didn't go clean through," Noah said.

"He needs a hospital," I replied.

"No."

"He could die."

The pain in his glare told me he knew that without me saying it. He was willing to risk Kinsey's life over not getting caught. From what I knew about the family in front of me, it had been Kinsey's choice. Maybe whispered to Noah in the back of the wagon, maybe decided on before they met me this morning. Either way, nothing got in the way of getting Aaron back safely. Not even their father's death.

King shimmered, his entire body fading out like a camera gone out of focus. I blinked, sure it was an illusion. He cleared, and had taken on the appearance of Miguel Ortega.

"Ortega had emergency medical training," King said. His

voice was no longer Ortega's, but some strangled, scratchy sound somehow formed into words. Like a synthesizer wheezing out its last few chords. He no longer possessed Ortega; he couldn't pull off the complete show, just a glamour. I could only imagine where the poor officer's remains ended up, but did not want to ponder that right now. All things in their proper time.

"Can you remove a bullet?" I asked. "If it stays in, he could get an infection."

King shook his head. "I don't know."

"You have to try," Jimmy said.

"Jimmy, get rid of that car for me," Noah said. "We'll take care of Dad."

"But—"

"Please, it can't sit out there and draw attention. Find a hiding place a few blocks from here. Make sure you can't see it from the street."

Jimmy opened his mouth, poised to argue again, but didn't. I sympathized with his desire to stay and make sure everything went okay with—

"Dahlia, can you go with him?" Noah asked.

I blinked, stunned. He wanted me to leave. I caught his gaze, free of anger or annoyance, and understood. He didn't want Jimmy there to witness the guerilla surgery, and he didn't want Jimmy running around alone. Noah and King could handle the medical side of things.

"We'll take care of it," I said.

He tried to smile, but couldn't seem to manage it. "Thanks."

"We'll be careful," I said before he could.

With a confident smile, I grabbed Jimmy's wrist and tugged him out of the bedroom. He let himself be led and that surprised me. I expected more resistance, but he seemed resigned to following orders given by his older brothers. In that way, we were very much the same. I allowed Teresa and Ethan and the others to dictate my actions and control my world, because they were older. They knew more about being heroes and living with superpowers and, in those things, I didn't mind being led.

But this was new territory, and I was stuck in a situation that was—if not completely of my own making—partly my fault. I was cut off from my friends. This time I had to take the lead and fix it.

I released Jimmy's wrist as we passed through the kitchen. He maintained momentum and followed me outside, jogging around to the passenger-side door. I slammed the back of the wagon shut, then climbed into the driver's seat. The odor of blood tingled my nose.

"They treat me like a child," Jimmy said as I backed down the driveway. "They always have, both of them, but I'm not a child."

"It's just because they're older." I checked traffic before easing out onto the street. "They want to protect you, Jimmy."

"Noah's worse than King is, but once he and Aaron are together, he'll be just as bad."

It took a moment to process that line of thought. The whole "two people in one" concept remained elusive. "So are the Scotts more protective of each other than the Wild Cards were?" I asked.

"About the same, I guess." Jimmy pressed his forehead against the window. "But when you combine the two, the instinct grows. It's kind of hard to explain."

"I think I understand." I made a left turn onto the next block, eyeing every shadow for movement. "And I think more people will understand than you think, Jimmy. What you did was an accident, and what Noah did was an act of mercy."

"What about King?"

A car drew near, driving in the opposite direction, coming right at us. I squinted into the bright morning light. My stomach twisted, palms instantly sweaty. An LAPD cruiser, bearing down on us. Mouth dry, I clenched the wheel, resisting the sudden urge to urinate.

Jimmy sat up straighter, probably sensing my distress. His eyes widened. "Holy shit."

"Just relax, act natural," I said. "It's probably a routine patrol."

"In this neighborhood?"

Excellent point. I slowed just a bit, hitting the speed limit on the dot. We still had dealer's plates, so no crime there (except for the small fact that the dealership was halfway across town). He had no reason to pull us over. Hot even under the blast of the air-conditioning, I kept my eyes forward.

The cruiser drove right on by. I didn't chance it and made a right turn onto the next block, exhaling hard the moment the cruiser was out of sight. We had to ditch the car before the dealer I'd assaulted woke up and reported me—if he hadn't already.

Three houses down, I whipped into an unpaved driveway. The house was a two-story, boarded-up wreck, probably home to a dozen or more squatters. I drove right into the overgrown yard, past a broken-down swing set, and angled the car as close to the rear of the yard as possible. I wiped the handles and steering wheel as best I could with the edge of my shirt, then climbed out.

I couldn't see the road from here. "This'll do," I said to Jimmy.

He followed me back down the driveway to the uneven neighborhood sidewalk. We had a bit of a hike back to the Jarvis house, and it left us both completely exposed. I tucked my arm through his and leaned close.

"Just pretend we belong here," I said.

He nodded, easing his stance a fraction. It wasn't the most natural gait. The summer sun glared down at us, baking the pavement and scalding my exposed skin. We were both sweating by the time we reached the end of the block. I had half a mind to simply bolt, run as fast as I could back to the hideout and the safety of those four walls.

"Can I ask you something?" My question invaded the tense silence around us.

Jimmy shrugged one shoulder. "Sure."

"Why'd you burn down your store? It had to be hard, destroying something that was part of your life for so long. Jimmy's life, I mean."

He stopped walking and gaped at me. "It burned down?"

"Yes." I turned to face him. "Last night. You didn't do it?"

"Of course not." His eyes shimmered, adding to the illusion of extreme youth. He was twenty-one, but seemed stuck on sixteen. If they hadn't set the fire, who had?

"I'm sorry," I said. "I just assumed . . ."

We continued walking, surrounded by an uneasy silence broken again by a question. This time, Jimmy asked it. "Do you love him?"

"Who?"

"Noah."

I stumbled. "Jimmy, I barely know him. I mean, I do like him, and I don't want to see him hurt."

"He said he fell in love with you the first time he saw you."

Stumble number two almost landed me flat on the pavement. The air was suddenly too hot, too humid to breathe properly. "No, he didn't." Impossible.

"Noah wouldn't have asked King to shoot your friend and risk Aaron's life if he didn't love you."

This time I stopped walking completely, too stunned to trust my feet any longer. The world grayed out around the edges as I struggled to process Jimmy's words. I'd obviously misunderstood something. "Noah did what?"

Jimmy looked at me with wide-eyed fear, splotches of red brightening both cheeks. "Crap."

"King didn't miss?"

"Um, no."

King had shot Teresa on purpose. Which meant Noah had lied. Again. White-hot fury settled in the pit of my stomach, sending acid into my throat. Let him try and talk himself out of this one. I wanted him to try so I could make his right eye match his left. Never in my life had one person managed to infuriate me so often in such a short span of time, his actions disguised as . . . what? Good intentions?

Hah!

Jimmy jumped. Had I said that out loud? Or was he poking around in my head?

"What are you going to do?" he asked.

I started walking, uncertain until the moment he asked. "I'm going to go back and make sure your dad is okay."

"I meant to Noah," he said as he scrambled to catch up.

To Noah? I could think of a list of things guaranteed to be loads of fun. For me. "We're going to be having a serious discussion in which he convinces me why I should continue helping you three, instead of going straight to the police."

We walked the rest of the way in silence.

The arctic air-conditioning felt wonderful when we entered the house twenty minutes later. King sat at the kitchen table, back in his original form, sipping soda from a can. He didn't look up, but he didn't need actual eyes to tell me where exactly he was looking. I had trouble imagining Noah faceless and hairless, just a swatch of skin over a skull and the few odd holes. I almost preferred King masquerading as Ortega.

"How'd it go?" Jimmy asked, pausing long enough to lock the door.

"He's resting," King replied in that artificial voice. His jaw and tongue worked without lips to move and form sounds and syllables.

I glared at the doorway. "Noah?"

"Bathroom, washing up."

Leaving them behind, I crept down the hallway, past the bathroom and sound of running water, to the last bedroom. The peeling wood door stood halfway open. I peeked around the side. Kinsey still lay in the middle of the bed, pale as the dingy white sheets around him, his shoulder bandaged. Blood had seeped through, probably stimulated by their field surgery. The medical case rested on top of a nearby bureau. Intricate wood patterns matched the bed's headboard and side tables. The furniture that had once cost a pretty penny now sat in ruin, remnants of a lifestyle the city of Los Angeles hadn't boasted in twenty years.

Water stopped running in the aged pipes. A door squealed. Footsteps whispered closer, stopping right behind me. The scent of generic soap mixed with sweat greeted me. My entire body went rigid. Lucky for his fingers, he didn't touch me; I'd have broken them.

"Will Kinsey be okay?" I asked.

"I don't know," Noah replied. "We gave him a little morphine, but I'm afraid to give him more. He's lost a lot of blood."

I had to try again, for Kinsey's sake. "Noah, I could call—"

"No."

I tensed. "Why not?"

"Because it brings someone else into this mess we've made ever since Aaron was taken."

"Like telling King to miss me and shoot Teresa?"

He inhaled sharply, practically a gasp. His fingers closed over my shoulder. I pivoted and felt the sting against my open palm. Saw Noah's head snap sideways and the red imprint blossoming on his cheek. Neither of us moved. Seconds passed before I remembered to breathe. I crossed my arms over my chest, as if that could keep my rage tucked inside.

"You ask me to help you," I said darkly. "You ask me to trust you. Then you fucking lie to me. Again!"

"Dahlia, I'm—"

I held up a silencing hand. "If you say you're sorry one more time the next place I hit you will not be your face. The only words I want to hear from you, Noah, are why. You barely knew me. You could have let King kill me, done your other favors, paid the money, and had Aaron back by now. So why?"

A storm of emotions brewed behind his eyes. Emotions I simply could not interpret—would not. He needed to say it, damn him.

"Any explanation I could give you," he finally said, "will just sound like a worn-out cliché."

"Sure, right, because feelings are clichés."

Anger broke to the surface, seeming to darken his green eyes. "Tell me what you want me to say, Dal. What do you need to hear?"

"Nothing." If he had to ask, I didn't want to hear it. Not now, not ever. "Do you have a phone?"

"For what?" he asked, narrowing his eyes.

To shove up your ass.

"I need to call Gage and let him know I'm alive, for one thing. And maybe I can find out exactly what happened at the parking garage."

He hesitated, and I was glad. I didn't even trust myself always to do the right thing—as if I knew what the right thing was in this situation—so he had no business doing so when I couldn't. I had no clue what I'd really say once I got on the phone.

Noah reached into the back pocket of his jeans and produced a cell phone. I took it and slipped past him into the hallway. He didn't follow.

I walked into the other bedroom and closed the door, aware of the power in my hands. Power over his family's future with a single call. Only that wasn't true, was it? He hadn't followed me to listen in or monitor my conversation. He'd trusted me not to betray his family. Then again, he could have just asked Jimmy to read my mind.

I flipped a light switch. A single, bare bulb hung from an exposed ceiling fixture. The bed was neatly made. A suitcase had been shoved haphazardly into a corner, near a broken wooden chair. The furniture was younger, the bed smaller. A child's room at one time, probably a boy.

I sat on the edge of the bed, but instead of dialing Gage's private com, I dialed Ethan's. It rang half a dozen times, and just as I resigned myself to leaving a message, the line clicked over.

"Hello?" Ethan's voice, uncertain and curious. Noise in the background was intermittent and hazy, as though he was in a car.

"It's me," I said.

"Dahlia? Where the hell are you?" The concern I detected was genuine, the question immediate.

"I'm safe."

"Gage has been on a rampage about—" He stopped, muffled the phone. Voices spoke, him and someone else. Someone male. He must have moved his hand from the speaker, because I heard Marco's distinct voice demanding to know where I was. "She's fine," Ethan said. "Calm down a minute."

Back on the line with me, he said, "Okay, so we've all been on a rampage about you."

"What happened this morning?" I asked. "We were talking, I was starting to get through to them, and then the gates of hell erupt and gunfire starts. Who was it?"

More muffled conversation. Then Ethan said to me, "It was Detective Forney and a SWAT team. Look, Gage called Pascal and told him about your lead with the cell phone."

A sudden flash of red burst behind my eyes, rushing straight to my cheeks. My hands started to shake. Gage had betrayed me to the police.

"Pascal told Gage to go ahead with what *we* had planned, though, without police backup," Ethan continued. "Then Forney shows up less than a minute after you walk into the garage, and she takes over the scene. Onyx tried to get over there and warn you, but it was too late. They opened fire before we could stop them. For Christ's sake, Dal, we thought you were dead when we didn't hear from you."

I clenched my left hand, unable to keep my rage under control. It vibrated in every muscle. "I couldn't call before now," I said, amazed at the restraint in my voice, when the rest of my body was helpless. "I'm not hurt, but they shot Dr. Kinsey. He's in pretty bad shape."

"Why didn't you—"

"We can't go to a hospital. Noah won't allow it, and I think those were Kinsey's wishes, too. There's too much at stake." The words came out unedited: "I can't turn them in."

"We can help—"

"No."

Ethan grunted. "Gage thought he was doing the right thing by telling Pascal, and Pascal wasn't even at the parking garage. No one's seen him and he isn't answering his phone."

Strange. Pascal hadn't ordered the police hit, but his partner had—why? A late reaction to the bad breakup with her now jailed boyfriend? And where the hell was Pascal? Far from painting a clearer picture, the new facts only further muddied the palette. "Ethan, I need you to do something for me."

"I'll do what I can, Dal."

"Find out who this other guy is that Liza Forney is seeing." I had no recollection of his name, just that someone else had been beaten the night she was attacked by Bates. "Name, occupation, the works. And then go talk to Bates."

"We already tried. He's at the courthouse for a hearing today. We can't get to him."

"Dammit."

"Why is Bates important?"

"I have a hunch he knows why Forney is acting so oddly."

"Of course he does; he beat her up."

"That's not what I mean."

"I'll do what I can, but after the stunt at the garage, Gage said some choice words to Forney, and we're personae non gratae with the LAPD right now."

"Really?"

"Yeah, he was livid." Whispering. "Marco said Gage's head almost spun in a complete circle. Teresa's, too."

The mental images almost made me smile. "How is Teresa otherwise?"

"She's doped up on pain meds, but the doctors are all positive that she'll be fine. The worst is over."

Relief reached into my chest and released the strangle it had held over my heart for the better part of two days. The flood of peace also set loose a deep-seated well of tears. My vision blurred. "That's the best news I've had all week," I said.

"It is," Ethan agreed. "Look, I have to go. Are you sure—Marco, what's that?"

Something squealed—brakes? The phone went dead.

Twenty-two

Boiling Point

The phone cracked, alerting me to how tightly I was gripping it. I dialed again—no answer. Every number I knew, all with no response. Each failure ratcheted my fear up another notch. My stomach twisted a bit tighter until all that existed was a frozen knot of fear.

Noah took the phone and clasped my hands between his. I hadn't heard him come in. "Dahlia, what?" he asked.

"Hey, guys!" Jimmy shouted. "Get in here!"

We thundered into the living room. Jimmy pointed at the television screen. King had closed in on the set and turned the volume up. On the black-and-white monitor, a news anchor sat primly behind her desk with an inset photograph of Gage over her shoulder.

". . . to our continuing story," she said, voice tinny and devoid of emotion. "The former Ranger known as Cipher has been arrested and officially charged in the attempted murder of a Los Angeles city police detective."

My mouth fell open.

"Detective Lieutenant Peter Pascal was reported missing this morning by his partner when he failed to show up for a joint operation with the former Ranger Corps members." The inset of Cipher disappeared, replaced by a frozen image of the escaping food truck. "This was the scene earlier this morning." The image began to play. Our truck sped toward the exit ramp, taking bullets from half a dozen hidden cops.

"The escaping truck was thought to contain two suspects wanted in a series of horrific murders. One patrolman was injured by returned gunfire—"

"That's a lie," Noah roared. "We never shot back, God-dammit."

The video switched to a long shot, taken from the opposite side of the parking structure. In it, Cipher could be seen arguing vehemently with Detective Forney. Both appeared to be shouting, using wide hand gestures to make their points.

"The sting did not go as planned," the anchor continued. "The Ranger known as Ember was active in drawing out the two suspects. Once believed to have been taken hostage by the fleeing suspects, we are now told that she is, in fact, aiding the fugitives. If you have any information . . ."

A buzzing sound filled my ears as my image appeared on the screen—a freeze-frame shot from the night of the warehouse fire, out of uniform and streaked with ash and soot. My knees wobbled. Noah's arm slipped around my waist, and I didn't fight him.

". . . Detective Pascal was later found in the back of a sport-utility vehicle owned by Cipher, bound, gagged, and presumed dead. However, EMTs managed a miraculous resuscitation on scene, and Detective Pascal is now listed in critical condition at Cedars-Sinai Hospital. The remaining Ranger team members are being sought for questioning in the Twenty-second Street fire that left two people injured and caused hundreds of thousands of dollars in property damage. Police have offered a hotline if you have any information regarding the—"

"This is bullshit," I said. "Gage did not beat that detective nearly to death, and I am not in collusion with murder suspects." Three heads swiveled toward me. "Okay, kind of, but they make it sound like we're all a bunch of criminals. And what fire on Twenty-second Street? Shit."

The newscast switched to regular programming. King turned the set off. The bungalow vibrated with the sudden, intense silence.

"On the upside," King said, "sounds like most of your friends are still out there."

"I lost contact," I said. "I was talking to Ethan, and then we got cut off. No one's answering." I told them what I knew about the parking garage and was met with matching stares of disbelief—or what King's blank face managed as disbelief.

"Didn't you say that Detective Forney's name came up in one of your leads?" Noah asked.

"Tangentially, yes. The video clue you left led to a man named Alan Bates. He was arrested last week for beating up his ex-girlfriend, Detective Liza Forney, and another guy. Bates has a hearing today. He's been in jail almost since this thing started, so he isn't involved. We were going to start looking at additional people from the video, but then other stuff happened."

Like escaping from police in a bullet-riddled food truck. Taking care of an injured man. Stealing a car and assaulting a salesperson. Letting friends get arrested for things they didn't do. That sort of other stuff.

"Why did you send me that video footage?" I asked. "What am I supposed to see in it?"

"We aren't sure," Noah said. "Dad said that during one of his phone calls with the kidnapper, they mentioned the incident in an offhand way. It made him wonder, so he got the file. He couldn't make heads or tails of it, and we were honor bound to not talk about it, so he compromised. He thought you would see something in it he couldn't."

I blew out through my teeth. "I think I just made everything more complicated by finding connections where they don't really exist."

"Are you sure?" King asked.

"About what?"

"No connections."

"I'm not sure about much of anything right now, actually. I don't even know the name of the other man Bates beat up."

"You know your friends, Dahlia," Noah said. "What are they doing now? Hiding from the police or turning themselves in?"

Simon would never allow himself to be hauled in for questioning. He hated and distrusted the police, and for good reason. The others I wasn't sure about, but Ethan and Marco were in trouble. Or hurt. Maybe both.

"If they suspected Forney was setting them up, I think they would hide. I just don't know where. Hill House is obviously off-limits. Ethan has a friend who lives in Burbank, but I don't think he would put her in the middle of this."

Noah furrowed his eyebrows. "What about—" The phone in his hand rang, and he nearly dropped it. He looked at the display, eyes widening. Another ring. "It's them."

"Them who?" lingered on my lips for a moment, until I realized. Noah knelt on the floor next to his brothers. He opened the phone and turned it on speaker.

"Yes?" he said.

"You've been making headlines," an electronically filtered voice said. Impossible to tell if it was male or female. "That's not wise."

"It wasn't our fault."

"Where is the girl Ember? Is she still with you?"

Noah's shoulders tensed. "She's here. She was shot during our escape. I don't know if she's going to make it." What was he doing?

The voice laughed, a dreadful, eerie sound. "So the police managed to do by accident what King couldn't manage on purpose. Interesting. Do you have the money yet?"

"It's in a safe place."

"Good, because we're calling in the final favor. Once it's done, you'll receive instructions on where to drop off your three packages and pick up your brother."

"Three packages?" The trio exchanged confused looks

(well, Jimmy and Noah did; I could only guess at King's blank expression). I remained still, afraid to move and give myself away.

"Three," the voice said. "The money, the person you'll be fetching for me as favor three, and, of course, Ember's dead body. Let her die and then bring her with you."

I closed my eyes, staving off a wave of dizziness that threatened to flatten me. Someone squeezed my ankle. I looked down—Noah's hand, offering what silent support he could.

"Fine," Noah said. "What's the favor?"

"Alan Bates has a pretrial hearing this afternoon at four o'clock. After the hearing, they'll take him out the west-side exit. He will have two police escorts, plus one man driving the van. I want Bates removed from police custody safely. He is the other package."

Jimmy paled, his skin taking on a sallow, stretched appearance. King hung his head.

"You want us to break him out of jail?" Noah asked, hints of anger coloring his voice.

"In a manner of speaking, yes. And make it very obvious it was done by Metas and not just some random thugs. Questions?"

"Where do we take the packages once we have them?"

"I'll know when you have the final package. You will be called with further instructions at that time. Better get ready, kids. It's showtime in four hours."

The caller hung up. I dropped to my knees next to Noah.

His hands were clenched, the knuckles white, arms vibrating with tension.

Jimmy reached out to turn off the phone, still deathly pale. "This is really bad," he said.

"Hurray for Captain Obvious," King sneered.

"Eat me." Affection still laced the barb. The brothers were in it together, and while I was their ace in the hole, I was willing to bet no one in our little group had ever attempted to break someone out of police custody. Certainly not in broad daylight.

"So Bates really is a part of this," I said. The kidnappers wanted him out of jail. Either to kill him or because he was in collusion with their efforts to blackmail the Changelings. The first favor was to kill me in a public manner. Could I have pissed off Bates enough that day at the construction site? Had he really hated me enough—obsessed over me enough—to want me dead? To plot something this elaborate?

Maybe.

"Wait," I said, shifting to give Noah my full-on attention. "You never told me what the second favor was. I know one and three, plus the money. What was number two?"

Noah's face crumpled, as if I'd just punched him in the stomach instead of asking a question. The immediate and telling response worried me; I wasn't going to like his answer.

"The day I did the inspection of your house," he said, each word tentative. Measured. "I planted two listening devices. One in the kitchen and one in the upstairs lounge."

My mouth fell open. I couldn't help it. A chill spread

through my chest, tightening it. Of all the things he'd done to me, the lies he'd told and secrets he'd hidden, this one hurt the most. It hadn't just betrayed me—it betrayed my friends. It put our enemy right inside of our most protected place.

His mouth quivered. "I'm so sorry, Dahlia, I had to."

I pushed away and stood up, hands clenched. "Why didn't you tell me that? Tell me so I could warn them away from those rooms? Dammit, Noah!"

Are you sure—Marco, what's that?

Something had happened. Something bad.

"Where would your friends go?" King asked.

"I don't know." Someplace safe, where they could regroup and rethink. Familiar, maybe. A place everyone could get to, if they were separated. And suddenly, I did know. It made perfect sense. "I need to go."

"You can't," Jimmy said.

"My friends need me. They're in trouble because of you three. I can't contact them, and I need to know if they're okay."

"What about Aaron?"

I shook my head. "I'm sorry, Jimmy."

"Can't we compromise here?" Noah said. "The same person or people are hunting us. We have a common enemy, so let's fight them together."

"No."

"Why not?"

I narrowed my eyes; he clenched his jaw. I planted hands on hips; he stood up, keeping his ground. Point for point, he matched me. Not backing down. Not this time. I didn't want to hate him. I didn't want to challenge him. I just didn't know how much longer I could keep trusting him, when he seemed intent on breaking me at every turn.

"Please, Dahlia," he said.

"We both know you can force me to stay. Will you?"

"Of course not." He seemed offended by the question. Too damned bad. "Please, just work with us."

I resisted because I desperately wanted to hurt him, wound for emotional wound, the way he'd hurt me—intentional or not. Just not with so many lives at stake. I had watched my mother get sicker and sicker until cancer had all but eaten her away. Caliber died because I was afraid to try to stop the fire from spreading. Teresa almost died, and now Abram Kinsey . . . no one else. Not because of me.

"No," I said. Noah looked crushed until I added, "This time, you're working with me."

"Okay," he said without hesitation.

"I need to get across town."

"We dumped the car," Jimmy said.

"No kidding. Thoughts?"

"We could take a bus," King said.

"A bus?"

He had no face at the moment, so I couldn't tell if he was joking or serious. Noah, though, seemed to think the latter. "Are you nuts?" he said.

"No one will be looking for us on public transportation," King said.

"He's got a good point," Jimmy said.

"You don't get to vote on this, because you're staying here."

I raised my hand to silence the protest about to issue from his open mouth. "Someone needs to look after your dad, and we can't haul him across town in his condition."

Jimmy glared at me without protesting further. He understood his role. I hated leaving any of them behind, but Kinsey's wound meant he had to stay immobile. He needed time to heal, and he couldn't be left alone.

To King, I said, "You'll need a face if we're going out in public."

He tilted his head to the side, thinking. His entire body shimmered, going out of focus. Smaller, thinner, darker. He refocused, wearing the illusion of Nadine Lee. The same skirt and tank top I remembered from two days ago, hair long and straight. It was effective. Until he spoke in his mechanical, not-quite-right voice, and said, "How's this?"

"That'll do," I said. "Noah?"

He shimmered immediately, someone already in mind. I watched him morph into a completely different person. Not just anyone, but the gum-smacking, pink-haired waitress from Mallory's Table, wearing the same outfit I'd worn to the restaurant, all the way to the sandals. He didn't miss a detail.

Noah squeezed Jimmy's shoulder. "We'll call when we know something." To me, he said, "Are you sure about this?"

"No," I said. "But we don't have a choice."

King sashayed over to us, "her" heels clicking on the wooden floor. "Where are we going?"

"Century City," I said. "Apparently on a bus, unless anyone has a better suggestion?"

No one did.

Noah and I sat together, with King in the seat in front. Passengers boarded and disembarked the bus at steady intervals, providing us with a rotation of grins and winks from the men (and the occasional woman).

The bus approached our stop and slowed. I nudged Noah, who smacked King on the shoulder, and the three of us exited the bus. So far so good.

I led them to the corner of the next block, glad the city streets were relatively quiet. The neighborhood was seeing a growth spurt, with many older buildings being torn down in favor of low-rent housing, which meant most of the activity was construction related. We had to disappear fast.

Another block away, our destination came into view— the high security gates of the old Ranger Corps Headquarters, itself a renovated movie studio lot. Beyond the twelve-foot, razor wire–lined fence, I saw the rising edifices of the Housing Unit and the Base. Two of the three buildings to survive January's battle with Specter.

"Are you sure they'd come here?" King asked.

"No," I said.

"Great. How do we get inside?"

"There's only one way in." I started across the street. "We try the front door."

Twenty-three

Century City

The intricate iron gate stood chained and locked. Rusted hinges showed neglect, unused since we abandoned it six months ago. Down the main avenue, past an untended hedge, were the charred remains of the Medical Center. It was never cleaned up after that fateful day when the Ranger Corps ceased to exist—when we pulled away and became . . . well, whatever it was we were.

If they were inside somewhere, they hadn't come in this way.

"Should we say 'Open Sesame'?" Noah asked.

King grasped the gate chain in his hands. Nadine's mouth twisted into a grimace, the strain creasing "her" smooth forehead as "she" pulled. Grunted. Pulled harder. A link snapped. The metal chain fell away from the gate. He yanked, forcing it open against the will of the automatic device long locked against entry. The hinges screamed, then gave.

We slipped inside the gate, and King pushed it closed. He wrapped the chain back around to offer the illusion of not being altered. Once inside, both of them dropped their glamours. Noah seemed to have a harder time letting go, and the change left him red-faced and breathing hard. He shrugged off my questions, and we walked down the main avenue, sticking close to the hedge.

Two options presented themselves: the Base or Housing. The Base had been the world's most intricate gymnasium, with exercise facilities for any type of power imaginable. Self-defense classes, stamina testing, even fun activities for the child Rangers (five of whom were now my partners). The roof had a helicopter pad, the basement two thousand square feet of storage.

The Housing Unit looked like an apartment complex, and really, that's what it was: eight stories of facilities that ranged from single-room dorms and communal bathrooms to single-family apartments that comfortably fit adults and their children. The cafeteria was there, on the first floor, along with conference rooms and a social lounge.

My friends had grown up here, as had their parents and mentors, and generations before them. I'd never been here during the heyday of the Corps, when the halls were bustling with activity. Adults and children of all ages, living and working in a safe environment; never imagining it would one day look so abandoned, so forlorn. So foreboding.

I'd never shared their common history.

"Which one?" Noah asked.

Overhead, a raven squawked, loud and long. I looked up, shielding my eyes against the glare of noon sunlight. The ebony bird circled low. I caught a flash of glowing green eyes, and my heart leapt. The raven swooped down, cawed, and flew off toward the Housing Unit.

"It's Onyx," I said, and began to run. Across the empty parking lot and a small grassy lawn, I finally burst through the downstairs doors.

The lobby was dusty and smelled of must and disuse. Marco stood there, in his human form, smiling like a thirsty man who'd just seen water for the first time in days. A handful of scratches littered his face, but he seemed otherwise unhurt.

I fell into his arms, never so glad to see him in my life. He returned the fierce hug.

"We were scared for you, *Ascua*," he said. "Everything happened so quickly, and we were unable to call."

"Coming here was a lucky guess."

Marco glanced over my shoulder. If King's odd appearance surprised him, it didn't show on his face. "And them?"

"It's another long story, but please, trust them. We're all after the same enemy right now, and we need every advantage possible. Is everyone else okay?"

He blanched. Bad sign.

"What?"

"Come on." He grabbed my wrist and pulled.

I let him lead me down the dim corridor toward the conference rooms; Noah and King kept up. We passed the first door and stopped in front of the second. Marco knocked twice, then opened it. The conference room had a long bank of windows, allowing in good light and giving a view of the front parking lot. He'd seen us coming easily enough. The table was pushed to the far wall, chairs stacked on top of it. A cot had been installed in the far corner, hovered over by a figure on a stool.

That figure spun the stool around—Ethan. He stood up when he saw me. A fresh burn covered his left cheek, as glaring red as his hair. His left hand was bandaged in white gauze and hung limply by his side. He blocked the figure on the bed. Cold fingers skated down my spine.

"What happened?" I asked, stepping into the room.

"They blindsided us," Ethan said.

He moved aside, giving me a good view of Renee. My face crumpled. She lay flat on her back, eyes closed, a thin blanket pulled up to her waist. Her arms and chest were covered with bandages, all oozing red and orange in various places. Two spots on her throat and cheek sported dark, blistered burns the size of apples, an oddly purple color on her smoky blue skin. More than that, though, was the loss of her long, shiny blond hair. It had once hung to her waist, and now it curled close to her chin in dark, singed tendrils.

A heavy sob stuck in my throat. I inhaled several times, trying to unstick my voice.

"Who did that?" Noah asked, saving me the effort.

"Some sort of firestarter," Ethan replied. "A Meta."

"A Meta?" I said. "Are you sure?"

Ethan furrowed his eyebrows. "Yeah, Dal, I'm sure. The bastard had flames flying from his fingertips. He grabbed Renee from behind and held her while he burned right through her clothing. I heard her screaming."

Oh God.

"We were on our way to the police station to speak with Gage when you called," Marco said, circling around to stand next to Ethan. "We were forced off the road and into a telephone pole. The driver got out of his car and began shooting fire at us."

"Sent a building up," Ethan said. "Hit a civilian. He knocked me for a loop, so Renee tried to wrap the pyro up in her body." He winced at an unspoken memory. "We heard sirens, and then he bolted. We shouldn't have run, but we did."

"And now the police want you, too," Noah said.

"These people have a pyro working for them," King said. His odd voice made Ethan cringe. I had gotten used to it.

"Who are these people?" Ethan demanded. "All of this crap with Pascal and Forney, and now a pyro tries to kill us. Not to mention everything else you haven't told us yet."

"Look," I said, "I'd love to go through the long version of events with you, but we're in a time crunch. Renee and Dr. Kinsey both need real medical attention, but we can't get them to hospitals until this thing is finished. We're on a three-and-a-half-hour deadline, so the blame game needs to wait until—" Only three faces accounted for. "Wait, where's Simon?"

"We don't know," Ethan said. "He went to the police station right after Gage was arrested by Detective Forney. I think he wanted to get a bead on things and see what he could glean from everyone. Haven't seen him or heard from him."

"Has anyone tried reaching Agent McNally?"

Ethan shook his head. "We're not bringing her into this, not this time." His attention turned to Noah. "Where are the rest of your people?"

"In a safe place," Noah said. "And I want them to stay there."

"Fair enough."

This was it. Our fighting force. Five minds to come up with a plan to save Aaron, catch the kidnapper, and stop a pyro. No more clues. No leads.

No problem.

"Did you ever get that name?" I asked.

Ethan tilted his head to the side. "What name?" His eyes widened. "Oh, you mean the name of the guy with whom Forney was supposedly cheating on Bates? Name's Ken Dawson."

"What?" King and Noah said in tandem.

I gravitated across the room toward Ethan and Marco, a completely subconscious action I didn't comprehend until I was standing there, watching Noah and King look at each other. Only Noah had a readable expression, and I didn't like what I saw there—recognition.

"Who's Ken Dawson?" I asked. Noah looked at the floor, his hands, the ceiling, everywhere but at me. The niggle of worry planted in my stomach. "So much for no more secrets, huh?"

His head snapped up, eyes meeting mine. Seething and angry. "I'm not keeping anything from you," he said. "Ken Dawson was one of our tutors at Weatherfield. He taught us for four or five years, back when we were still kids. He was reassigned. We saw him around the complex a few times over the years, but had no actual contact."

His glare deepened the lines around his eyes, and I regretted my initial reaction. Distrust came too easily nowadays, no matter how much faith he continued to have in me.

"He had a connection to Weatherfield," Ethan said. "Which means Forney has a connection to you and your project."

"It's a stretch," I said. "What could she possibly gain by teaming up with Ken Dawson and putting Bates in jail?" The logical response came as I asked those questions, and I ended up giving myself the proper answers: "Except for a huge wad of ransom money, and a problem boyfriend behind bars."

No one refuted the theory.

"Dawson would have known about our existence, but not our escape," Noah said. "No one knew. Our father was very careful in planning it."

"Someone found out," Ethan said. "Either Dawson or someone who passed it along to Dawson. They knew you escaped, got wind of your plan, and got to Aaron Scott before you could. Dawson and Forney have to be working together on this. Why else interrupt the meeting this morning, put Pascal in a coma, then get Gage arrested?"

"They're trying to keep us off-balance," I said. "Everything in their plan started to unravel when King didn't kill me the afternoon of the warehouse fire. They've been improvising, just like us."

"But why kill you, Dal?"

Right. We hadn't gotten that far yet. Had it really only

been an hour since I'd learned it myself? "Killing me was part of the kidnapper's ransom demands. And it makes sense now, especially if Bates was involved."

"How's that?"

"The interview, that day at the construction site. Bates got fired over it, and he couldn't get a decent reporting job afterward. Some people just fixate on what they decide is the source of their misery, and in his case, that source was me." I ran my fingers through sweaty, tangled locks. "What better opportunity for revenge than when you're already blackmailing three people with preternatural abilities?"

Noah exhaled hard through his clenched teeth. "And now she wants her boyfriend back."

"Precisely."

"Then why get Bates arrested in the first place?"

Good point. "Maybe he wasn't supposed to be arrested. Maybe Dawson was just a means to an end, Bates thought it was more and got jealous, and then Pascal stepped in to protect his partner. Now she needs us to get Bates out."

"What did we miss here?" Ethan asked. "Get Bates out of what?"

Noah filled them in on the phone call and the demand to break Alan Bates out of police custody. It only served to illustrate the theory, and that Bates was in jail for just one reason: Peter Pascal. Pascal was the one who arrested Bates for assaulting Forney and put the first kink in the plan. He started the long line of improvisation that had haunted this little epic for the last week.

Pascal had no idea what his partner had been up to behind his back. He'd tried protecting her, and now labored in a coma for his troubles. Poor guy.

"None of this explains the pyro," Ethan said.

"No, it doesn't," Noah said. "Because Dawson didn't have powers. He wasn't a Meta or a Recombinant, just a tutor."

"A fourth person helping them?" Marco suggested.

"Likely," Ethan said. "But even with all of this information, we don't have any clearer an idea what to do next. Any step we take against Detective Forney will just put Aaron Scott in greater danger. And that's what all of this is about, right?"

"First things first, though," I said. "We need to keep our wounded together. This isn't exactly a low-profile hideout. Can we get Renee to the house where we're keeping Dr. Kinsey?"

"She is in excruciating pain," Marco said.

"Do you have a vehicle we can move her in?" I asked again. Willingly causing Renee more pain was not my objective, but we had no choice.

"No," King said. His grating voice rose above ours, commanding and firm. We paid attention. "No, they need real doctors. Your friend. My father."

Noah turned, hands clenched. "They'll arrest him, King. He's not safe with them."

"King's right," I said, slipping my hand around Noah's wrist and squeezing. "He could die out there and leave Jimmy alone. Your dad needs to be in a hospital. Renee needs fluids and antibiotics and proper treatment, and so does Dr. Kinsey."

Noah closed his eyes briefly. Resolve resided there when he opened them again. "What's your plan, then?"

"We pick a new meeting place, somewhere inconspicuous," I said. "Then call Jimmy, tell him to call an ambulance, and to run when they arrive. Meet us at the new location. We'll do the same here. Marco can stay with Renee until help arrives, and then meet us. In the meantime, the four of us work on how exactly we're going to spring Alan Bates from custody without looking like a bunch of criminals ourselves."

"Is that even possible?" Noah asked.

"Which part? Springing him or not looking like criminals?"

"The second one."

"I don't know, but it's going to be interesting finding out."

"What's our meeting place?" King asked. He had his cellular out, ready to dial and alert Jimmy of the developments.

"Pascal's apartment?" Marco said. "I cannot imagine they will be watching it. Not with him in intensive care."

"Could be bugged, though," I said, thinking of our mansion. "We need someplace central and quiet."

"I think I know a place," Ethan said. "Totino's Restaurant in Studio City. A friend of mine is the manager. She said they moved locations last week, but the owner still has a two-month lease on the old place, so it's sitting empty."

"Think Jimmy can find it?" I asked.

King nodded, fingers hitting speed dial. He put the call on speaker, for which I was grateful. Jimmy picked up on the first ring.

"It's me," King said. "We found the Rangers. We have a plan."

"Good, 'cause I think Dad's bleeding again," Jimmy said, panic in his voice.

"We need you to do something, Jimmy. Call an ambulance."

"What?"

"An ambulance."

"I thought we agreed—"

"I don't want him to die. Do you?"

Silence. Then: "No."

"When the ambulance gets there, you need to run. Get a cab or bus or just run for it, but meet us at—"

"Hold on, someone's at the door."

Noah jerked toward the phone, eyebrows arching high. He looked at King, whose expressionless face seemed more pale than usual. I clutched Noah's arm, sure he'd jump through the phone if he could.

"Who's there, Jimmy?" King asked.

Sounds of scuffling footsteps. "Oh, it's okay, it's just Dahlia."

"What?" I squawked.

Jimmy made a soft, choking noise. "Dahlia?" The thunder of snapping wood and tinkle of shattering glass were punctuated by a short scream.

"Jimmy!" King shouted, holding the phone close to his mouth. "Jimmy?" Heavy, labored breathing was the only sound coming from the phone. Then two deliberate footsteps. Boards creaked. Laughter, high-pitched and feminine. A second crunch, and the connection was gone.

"No, no, no!" Noah said. He snatched the phone from King. Redialed. Tried again to no avail. "Shit!" His arms trembled. Rage radiated in the clenching of his fists, the sweat beading on his brow, the intense snarl of his lips. I backed away, pushed by the physical intensity of it. A stack of chairs rattled, shaken by some unseen force—Noah's power.

"We have to go," King said. "Now."

The cell phone rang, a shrill tone that startled Noah into dropping it. King reached out with lightning speed and snatched it inches from the ground. He looked at the display with eyes I couldn't see, annoyingly void of expression. He pressed speaker.

"You're changing the rules," the filtered voice said, same as before. "So our deal has altered to reflect that. Remember the money, boys?"

"Yes," Noah snarled.

"Double it," the voice said. "Now you have two brothers to pay for." Click.

King pocketed the phone, his movements stiff and mechanical—the only sign that any of this was still affecting him. Must be nice to keep your emotions so hidden. With his nonexistent face, he'd make a hell of a poker player.

"They didn't say anything about Dr. Kinsey," I said. "But they had to have seen him."

"Keep with the plan," Ethan said. "Marco will stay with Renee until an ambulance shows up. We'll head back to your safe house and see if they left any sort of clue behind. He can meet us there."

"It could be a trap," Marco said.

"We'll go in prepared," I replied. "For anything." Somehow the enemy—who I increasingly believed to be Liza Forney—had found Jimmy and Kinsey. Stashing them in the former residence of one of their victims had seemed smart at the time. Now it just felt incredibly dumb. Like leaving a neon street sign that said: Criminals Here! Come And Get Us!

We were going into battle without any idea of the field or the players. I was unused to such a predicament; the boys seemed likewise on edge. Noah was frozen, silent. I touched his shoulder. He looked up. Something wild and fearsome was in his eyes. He searched my face for something.

"What?" I asked. I had to know what he was thinking.

"Didn't you hear what Jimmy said? He said you were at the door, Dahlia."

"Yeah." So what did—? Understanding hit like ice water, chilling me to my very core. He nodded when he realized I'd figured it out. Stricken, I turned to Ethan and Marco, who stared at me as blankly as I'd done moments ago.

Mouth dry, I swallowed several times to find my voice and say, "They have a Changeling, too."

Twenty-four

Changeling

I mpossible," King said.

"Are you sure?" I asked.

"Yes. Our fath—Dr. Kinsey told us only five survived the Recombinant in vitro process and were born. Our two sisters died young. He would have told us if Weatherfield had continued the Changeling research."

"Would he have necessarily known about it?" Ethan asked. "Weatherfield is a big place."

King grunted, folding meaty arms over his chest. "We were his project. His research. His children."

"What about your sisters?" I asked, hoping my next question received a great big positive response. "Did you actually see them die?"

Noah and King exchanged looks, unreadable to anyone but themselves. A silent, tense moment passed before Noah shook his head. "No," he said. "We were told they died. They never let us see their bodies. There wasn't a funeral, because we don't technically exist."

"So your sisters could be alive?"

"We'd know," King said. "We can feel each other when we're close. We have a bond, Dahlia. Do you understand that?"

I persisted, undaunted. "You have a connection because you grew up together, King. If they know who you are, they'd be careful to stay away, right?"

"Could one of them be the pyro who attacked us?" Ethan asked. A stomach-twisting question. "Kinsey said each Changeling has a unique, additional power."

"Our hybrid powers didn't manifest until around age seven," King said.

Ethan tilted his head. "But it's possible?"

"Yes, it is."

"So who are we looking for?" I asked. "Crooked Detective Forney and Ken Dawson, her creepy tutor accomplice? Or a pair of Changeling girls, one of whom can manipulate fire?"

"Both," Ethan said. "If those girls are really alive, they could be anyone, including Detective Forney."

"It doesn't make sense," Noah said. "Even if they were alive, why do this to us? Why torture us like this when all we want is to be left alone?"

"I don't know," I said, determination sparking in me like red flame. "But when we catch them, remind me to ask."

"Why wait?" Marco asked.

The question caught me off-guard. Noah tensed. I spun toward the bank of windows, alert for some sort of immediate attack from the outside. A bird flew low across the lawn, but I saw nothing out of the ordinary. The ground trembled with a slight vibration—enough to notice, and enough to fear its source.

"Marco, what—?" I turned as I spoke, but stopped mid-question. Gasped.

Marco Mendoza was gone. I knew it, even though someone bearing a striking resemblance stood in his place, arms by his sides, smiling with such amusement it seemed a cruel joke. His glowing eyes were replaced by empty whiteness. He radiated power, and the floor beneath his feet spiderwebbed.

Ethan backpedaled, taking a defensive position in front of Renee's prone body. He stared, wide-eyed, mouth open.

I tried to move. Utter shock rooted my feet to the floor. My mind raced.

No! No no no no. Not Marco.

"For someone who calls herself a hero, you're pretty dumb," not-Marco said to me, his voice an amalgamation of his own and someone else's. Someone almost female.

"At least I'm not a murderer," I snarled, rage vibrating through my arms and legs and chest. My heart thudded hard and heavy.

"Murder is a human concept," the Changeling said. "Our kind is above that. We have the power to make our own rules."

"We also have the power to restrain ourselves."

Noah took a step forward. His eyes were focused and intent. "Deuce?" he asked.

Not-Marco shifted his attention to Noah, regarding him with outright amusement. Not-Marco's form shimmered, unfocused. Color tones changed. His body shape slimmed.

He refocused, now a young woman. Somewhere in her twenties, with short brown hair and narrow brown eyes. Pretty, but generic. Her features were not quite pronounced—lips were skin-tone, the nose a bit too flat.

"Hi there, Brother," she said. Her voice had a similar quality to King's, but had been sanded enough to lose the harshest edge.

Ethan roared, his battle cry preceding a blast of air that slammed into the unsuspecting Changeling. Deuce flew backward and hit the edge of a conference table with a crack. She slid to the ground and lay still while a rush of air continued to swirl around the room, coming off Ethan like waves of physical fury.

Noah rushed forward. I caught his arm and pulled him back. He couldn't protect her now, not if she'd killed Marco. King didn't try to interfere. He seemed the most shocked, and the least able to react quickly to learning that at least one of his supposedly dead siblings was very much alive.

Tentative steps drew Ethan forward until he stood over Deuce's supine body. He nudged her arm with his toe. "So much for asking her why," he said.

As if on cue, the ground vibrated. The air crackled with energy. Something deep in the belly of the earth rumbled. Groaned. The floor beneath Ethan exploded upward in a whirlwind of cement, wood, and dirt. He flew, propelled sideways, his cry cut short as he smashed through the windows in a shower of glass.

"Ethan!" I screamed.

Deuce stood, her brown eyes radiating power. She raised

one hand and a ball of earth rose up with it. The ball hovered by her side, waiting for a target. She cocked her head in Renee's direction. "Make me kill her," she said. "I dare you."

I slowly drew heat from the air, but I knew it wasn't enough to propel a good blast. I needed more fuel.

"Why are you doing this?" Noah asked. "We're your family."

She scoffed. "You're not family. You share my genetic material, nothing more. You're a job, Ace."

"Job? Who hired you?"

"The Overseer, who else?"

Who else? Who the hell was the Overseer? Judging by the pull of Noah's mouth and dip of his eyebrows, he didn't know, either. I stole a look at the broken window; nothing moved outside. Desperation pulsed in my heart, constricting my throat. *Come on, Ethan, be okay.*

"Who's the Overseer?" Noah asked.

Deuce's face went slack, her surprise quickly replaced by amusement. "I forgot. You've been kept sheltered in that lab for so long you don't know anything Dr. Kinsey didn't teach you. Let me tell you, dear brother, we may be the only Hybrid Changelings to have survived, but there are dozens of other Recombinants out there."

She glared at me. "Not everyone was satisfied by the return of the Metas' powers. Some people still need us."

"Where's Queen?" King asked, growling his way into the conversation.

"With your brothers and Dr. Kinsey." She reached into her right ear and produced a tiny mike, which she displayed briefly before tucking it back in. "We've been in constant contact. We're smarter than you think. We received proper training."

We couldn't keep bantering like this. As much as I appreciated the big "villain revelation speech," I had to check on Ethan. Get Renee out of there. Warn Gage. Find Simon. A whole host of things impeded by Deuce's need to explain things. I had to throw her off-guard.

"Training in what?" I asked. "Patricide and long-windedness?"

Her mouth quirked. Was she laughing at me? "Hardly, girl. Abram Kinsey is no more a father to me than he is to them. He's a genetic-material donor, just like our mother was. She said so herself when we met."

"Mother?" Noah said. "You know who she is?"

Deuce arched her eyebrows. "You don't? You still haven't pieced this together?"

"Why don't you explain it to me?"

Too much talking. I latched onto the nearest heat source—which happened to be Noah—and tried something new. I simultaneously pulled heat from him, combined it with the power I'd already drawn from the air, and pushed it outward in a neat little package. Right at Deuce.

She manipulated her ball of dirt, tossing it at me the moment my heat wave smacked her to the ground. I ducked and let go of Noah at the same time. The corner of the dirt ball clipped my hip and sent me spinning. I hit the floor hard on my left side, smacking the air out of my lungs.

Deuce shrieked, a sound full of rage and disgust. Beneath

me the ground rumbled furiously. I rolled to the other side in time to see a cloud of dirt sailing toward me like buckshot. I closed my eyes, no power left to propel it away. I heard it hit, a thousand pops of air, but felt nothing.

Hazarding one eye open, I saw Noah. He was crouched in front of me, skin pale and lips trembling from the sudden rush of cold I'd caused. His hands were raised in front of him. He'd stopped the dirt shot, using his own hybrid power against his sister's.

"How can you keep protecting her?" Deuce asked, voice shrill. Beyond furious. "Don't you know what she is?"

"She's mine," Noah replied. Dark, dangerous. An edge I'd never seen before.

I'm—what?

I peeked past Noah's foot and spotted Deuce on her knees by the far wall. Blood dripped from her mouth. She didn't look away from Noah. I took a glance behind me. King was gone. Uh-oh.

Please, God, let him be calling for help or tending to Ethan. Please, please, please.

"What do you think I am?" I asked Deuce, pulling my knees up and rolling into a kneeling position next to Noah. Confident he could shield us from another dirt attack. I'd never met someone who could manipulate the very earth itself.

"A mistake," Deuce said.

I blanched, confused—horribly, utterly confused.

She sensed my befuddlement and regarded me silently for half a minute. "You really don't know?"

"Know what?" I swallowed against a sudden, consuming urge to cry. I felt helpless under her scrutiny, unable to make sense of her words or insinuations.

She opened her mouth to respond, but stopped, her attention stolen by a new sound. Approaching thunder, growing louder and louder. It was not natural thunder. The sky outside was blue, the sun shining bright. Something else, louder still, like a freight train bearing down on our position.

"Oh, hell," Noah said. He tackled me to the floor.

The train tore into the room, gusting wind knocking the door from its hinges with a crash. The dark blur sped past us and smashed head-on into Deuce, propelling her into the wall, through the cement and brick with a sound like a gunshot. She left a gaping, human-size hole.

Human.

He can run upward of eighty miles an hour given an open space and lots of room.

"Was that King?" I asked, nudging Noah off. He obliged and offered me a hand up. I coughed, waving away a cloud of dust that wafted into the room on a warm breeze.

"Yeah." He bolted toward the hole in the wall.

I followed him out into the sweltering afternoon. King sat hunched over on his knees a few dozen yards ahead, a debris trail following him across the untended lawn. Deuce was sprawled on the ground in front of him, bloody and still. I bolted to the left, circling the building to the side where Ethan had come out.

He lay on his back in a sea of broken glass, blood oozing from a dozen small cuts and gashes on his face, hands, and chest. His shoes had been nearly destroyed by the blast, and the legs of his jeans were shredded. Dirty, torn flesh peeked through the flaps of denim. His chest rose and fell evenly, and his eyes were open, staring blankly at the sky.

"Ethan?" I crouched next to him, mindful of the glass. "Ethan?"

He angled his head just a bit to look me in the eye. "That . . . hurt."

The simple statement flooded me with relief. "Can you move?"

"Only if I have to."

"I think you have to, pal, we need to get the hell out of Dodge. That sonic boom is going to make people suspicious, if they weren't already."

"The girl?"

Over my shoulder, Noah and King were kneeling by Deuce. Hand gestures punctuated a heated argument. I couldn't tell if she was alive or dead, but I had to give King credit for his ingenious solution to our standoff—even if it stopped Deuce from answering my question. Something about me bothered her, and it bothered her enough to make her order my assassination.

"Out of the game for now," I replied. "But we have her and that's leverage."

"Against whom?"

"Queen, I guess. Come on, Windy, you've taken worse than this."

He sat up, and with a little help, stood. I slipped one arm around his waist, taking as much of his weight as I could manage. My bruised hip protested. He winced with each limping step forward, every muscle taut and straining. Noah met us halfway, his face pinched and pale.

"She's unconscious," he said. "I don't know for how long. What do we do now?"

"We change the rules," I said.

"What do you mean?"

"I mean we have something they want now." I pointed to Deuce. "So he, she, or it doesn't get to make the demands anymore. We have leverage to make a few of our own."

"What do you have in mind?" Ethan asked.

I traded off with Noah, who took my place supporting Ethan, and then I strode over to Deuce. King watched me, curious and silent. I crouched down and plucked the mike from her ear. It didn't appear to be damaged. "I hope you're listening, Queen," I said, putting the right amount of snarling indignation into my voice. "Because if you are, you know we've got your sister. She's alive, and if you want her to stay that way, you've got five minutes to call King's phone."

The phone rang ten seconds later. King fished it out of his pocket, checked the display, and then nodded.

Showtime. He pressed Speaker.

"How dare you—"

"Shut up," I said, interrupting the angry female voice. "You aren't in control anymore, Queen."

"You're bluffing."

"How do you know? You've attacked my friends, *my* family. What makes you think I won't hurt Deuce to get to you?

Or that I won't kill her if you let anything happen to Jimmy or Dr. Kinsey?"

Something in my voice must have convinced her: "I guess I don't. I know what you're capable of, Ember, even if you don't. That's why you were tagged as a threat."

Tagged? It made me sound like a prize cow.

"What do you want?" Queen demanded.

"I want Cipher out of jail right now, all charges dropped. You've been masquerading as Detective Forney for a while, so I know you can do it, and do it within the hour."

Silence. I looked over my shoulder at Noah. He half-shrugged. My first real bluff worked, however, because Queen said, "Fine. And?"

"Confirmation that Dr. Kinsey has been delivered to a hospital for proper care, same time frame as Cipher's release."

"Done. Anything else?"

"A neutral meeting place where we can make the swap," I said, my confidence growing. "Your sister for Jimmy and Aaron."

"Now, that's hardly fair. One person for two isn't a good deal, and I'm still annoyed at Noah for lying to me about you being shot. I'm willing to trade Jimmy and Aaron for both Deuce and you, Dahlia."

"No," Noah said. I flashed him a withering glare, but he ignored me.

"What's wrong, dear brother?" Queen asked, her voice singsong and full of disdain. "Still not willing to give her up to keep your family safe? I don't know how many more times

I have to taser Aaron to make you understand that killing Dahlia Perkins was never optional."

I shivered and a bitter taste invaded my mouth. Over the phone line, I heard footsteps shuffling. Someone whimpered, and then began to scream. Noah choked. The faintest buzzing sound filtered into the scream; they silenced together. Heavy breathing followed.

"Want me to do it again?" Queen asked.

"Bitch," he ground out.

I could hear the smile in her voice when she said, "Do I make my point? Dahlia and Deuce for your family, Ace. You can't have both."

"Why?" he asked. "What the hell does Bates or Forney have against her that you're so adamant about this? What?"

She laughed. Honest to God, amused laughter. "You have no idea what this is about. Rest assured, Alan Bates would have made a good scapegoat, if you'd just stuck to the plan. This whole exercise has been amusing to me, but it's time to end it. Deuce and I have a life to return to."

"Don't count on it," I said.

More laughter. "Enjoy the next two hours, Dahlia, because this is all going to be done over your dead body. And I don't mean that as a metaphor. I'll call you with a meeting place when my tasks are done."

The line went dead.

Two hours was plenty of time to . . . do . . . stuff. Figuring a way out of offering myself as a human sacrifice was high on the list. We also had to ensure that Queen and Deuce didn't disappear once they were back together and the brothers were safe. With the hell we'd gone through these last few days, we could not risk their escape.

Footsteps shuffled across the grass. A hand reached down and squeezed my shoulder. I looked up, expecting Noah, but found Ethan. Pain and grief swirled in his eyes.

"Did she really kill Marco?" he asked.

Slowly I stood up and clasped both of Ethan's hands in mine. I wanted to say no, that he was tied up in a closet somewhere and we'd find him soon, alive, maybe unconscious. That he wouldn't end up a pile of discarded skin once Deuce came to and dispelled him.

My chest ached. Comforting words fled, chased away by grief. "I think so, Ethan." I hated myself for voicing it, and for making it seem so real. "I think he's gone."

He choked. "Just like that?"

I threw my arms around his neck, ignoring the slick heat of blood. He returned the embrace, pressing his cut face into my shoulder. Marco Mendoza was our friend. Teammate. Brother. For a little while, a stranger had walked among us, secure in his body and knowledge, and used him to betray his allies.

"They'll pay," I said. For Teresa. For Marco.

For all of us.

Twenty-five

Revelations

Three phone calls later, King tossed the trussed-up, still-unconscious Deuce over his shoulder, and we sneaked off the old HQ grounds. Between his burden and Ethan's pronounced limp—he denied any sort of ankle sprain or break, but his left foot was already swelling—our progress was slow. We managed to cross the street and make it down a block to the somewhat protected courtyard of an abandoned office building. Twelve stories tall with its own underground parking garage, the building had a huge For Rent banner strung across the decorative courtyard gates.

Gates that King opened without breaking a sweat.

I helped Ethan sit down on a cracked stone bench, beneath the welcome shade of a half-alive juniper tree. Perspiration rolled down the sides of his face. Pain etched lines around his eyes and mouth. If he ground his teeth any harder, they would snap.

King dumped his package next to a putrid fountain that hadn't run in years. The stone was stained with algae. A few centimeters of rainwater clung to the bottom of the last tier.

In the distance, sirens wailed. Good. Phone call number one had been a success: the ambulance for Renee would be along shortly.

Call two was a message left on Gage's voice mail, giving him the number of King's phone and asking him to call the moment he got it. I wanted him with us during this final fight. Encounter. Whatever it turned into. I needed his advice.

Noah hovered by the gates, watching the street intently. I approached in a wide arch, giving him advanced warning of my presence. We were all on edge. Needless startling should be studiously avoided. His hands were tucked beneath his armpits. Small shivers still racked his body, raising goose bumps up and down his arms, even in the oppressive heat.

"I'm sorry about that," I said.

Without tearing his eyes away from the street, he asked, "About what?"

"Stealing your heat. The cold chill. Not realizing one of my dearest friends wasn't who I thought he was. Pick one."

He turned his head, skin so pale. Almost fragile. "It's not your fault. I'm beginning to think none of this could have turned out okay, no matter what we did or didn't know." He leaned against the gate, facing me full-on. "You heard what Queen said. It was never about Forney or Bates. Or maybe it was at first, but when Queen and Deuce got hold of them, they turned it into something else. Something twisted."

I shoved my hands into the pockets of my jeans, wanting to hug him and somehow provide some warmth. His stance practically screamed *Back Off*, so I kept my distance. "Putting a contract out on me because of professional jealousy and a sense of vengeance, that I could handle," I said. "I understand it, even if it scares me to death. Bates I get. I don't get Queen or what she wants."

"I don't, either." Noah dropped his hands and opened his arms. I fell against his chest, grateful for the simple physical contact—I thought at any moment I might collapse under the weight of my fear and grief. Noah's skin was so cool, almost clammy. I had done that to him.

"Deuce said you don't know what I am," I said, resting my head on his shoulder.

"She was just trying to get to me."

"Are you sure?"

He pressed one finger beneath my chin, urging me to raise my head. I met his stern gaze. At least one of us was confident about something. "I know what you are, Dal."

She's mine. I shivered, as scared by those two words as I was tempted by them.

The ambulance tore past our courtyard, sirens wailing and lights flashing. We watched it drive through the open gates of the old HQ and disappear inside. One nugget of fear began to dissolve. Renee would be taken care of, but a dozen more fears remained.

"Guys?" King said.

He stood over Deuce's body, hands on his hips, dressed up again as Ortega. We had no real way of keeping Deuce under control, so on a hunch that she needed her hands to throw more dirt at us, we'd tied her arms behind her back. And her ankles together. For good measure we'd also rolled her up in a section of old carpeting, partly inspired by my own imprisonment in a wrestling mat back in January. She looked like a brown sausage and was probably hot as hell, but her comfort was of no consequence to me.

It had been strange, watching the tender way King and Noah trussed her up and wiped blood from the cuts on her face and throat. Very gentle, almost caring. They identified her as their sister, their blood, while treating her like the enemy she was. An odd dichotomy. Even though I'd have rejoiced in her immediate and painful death, part of me wanted her alive. Somewhere inside her, Marco still survived. If what Kinsey said was true, then the experiences and memories of the host lived on inside of the Changeling, becoming part of their personality. An amalgamation.

Noah had chosen that life. But would Marco want it, too?

"What is it?" I asked.

"I think she's waking up," King replied.

I waved at Ethan to stay put on his shady bench. Noah followed me. Deuce blinked against the glaring sunlight, her face flushed. Pain pulled her mouth into a straight line. Her eyes flickered back and forth between our backlit silhouettes. I didn't feel the least bit sorry for her.

"How does it feel to be bait?" I asked.

"I told her this was a stupid idea," Deuce said in her half-formed voice. "But Queen wanted to play, and I went along like the obedient girl I am. The Overseer teaches us to obey."

"You mentioned this Overseer before," Noah said. "Who is he?"

"There is so much you don't know, dear brother. So much about the Recombinants and our long history. So much that even your beloved father does not know. Weatherfield is only a small cog in a much larger wheel. All you need be aware of is that the Overseer turns the gears of the wheel, and if you fail him, you are crushed."

"He sent you here to kill Dahlia."

"Yes."

I shuddered. Noah put his hand on the back of my neck—a centering touch. "Why?" he asked.

"You ask why," Deuce said. "We do not. This is why we were taken from Weatherfield, and you three were not."

"Do you have to speak in riddles?" I asked, growing frustrated with the circular conversation. This was impossible. I wanted to reach into her brain and yank out every single bit of pertinent information she was so reluctant to share.

"Did you know we were alive this whole time?" Noah asked, redirecting the conversation.

She blinked. "Of course."

"We were told you were dead."

"And we were told you were weak."

I snorted. "Yeah? Who's the one tied up in a rug?"

Deuce's dark, unfocused eyes latched onto mine, shimmered, then turned a brilliant, luminescent green. The same shade as Marco's eyes. Was he in there? Fighting against the Changeling's control? Fighting to be free of her? Kinsey told us the Changeling always overpowered the host. Dominated. Was that true even if the host was a Meta?

Her eyes changed back to flat brown. It broke the spell, making that momentary glimpse of a friend seem like nothing more than a heat-induced hallucination.

"How long?" I asked.

She arched an eyebrow. "How long what?"

"How long ago did you take Marco? How long have you been spying on us?"

The irritating woman took the time to yawn. I fisted my hands, restraining myself from kicking her in the head.

"The parking garage this morning," she finally said.

My temper cooled a few degrees. The apology in my room had been Marco. We'd forgiven each other, been friends again. It hadn't been a trick.

"Why does the Overseer want me dead?" It felt strange asking about a person I'd never met and didn't know from Adam. This mysterious Overseer seemed to be the one who handed out death warrants to whacked-out female Change-lings.

"You were a mistake," Deuce said. "He doesn't allow mistakes."

Mistake. There was that word again. She said it as though it explained everything, when it explained nothing. Not to me. Not about me.

She blew out hard through her nose, sending a cloud of dust flying across my sneakers. "You truly have no comprehension of any of this, do you?" she said. "Not a single doubt about your past. Your origin. We could have left you alone, and you never would have known differently." Her eyes widened, filling with something akin to amazement. Shock. "The Overseer was wrong."

A gong of doom hung in those four words. She could have been speaking heresy in front of the Pope from the dread in her voice. In the downturn of her mouth and arched eyebrows. Her chin quivered.

"I take it this Overseer isn't wrong very often," I said.

"I have never known him to be wrong."

"So I'm not a mistake?"

"Yes, you are."

My head spun, dizzy from Deuce's flurry of double-talking. "You said—"

"I said the Overseer was wrong, but not about what," Deuce said. She twisted her neck to look at me. "You are still a mistake, but you did not require termination."

That should have made me happy, overjoyed even, but it didn't. It was her opinion of the facts, and she was just a lackey. Maybe she didn't think the mysterious Overseer required my termination, but His Highness did, and she was trained to follow his orders. I wanted to trust that Deuce no longer believed I should be killed. However, doubt niggled in the corner of my mind. Doubt about how much her conscious mind was affected by Marco and his memories of me. How much of him colored her judgment and influenced her rationalization?

"How does the Overseer even know about her?" Noah asked. "What gives him the right to police Metas and decide their fates? What could she possibly have done?"

Deuce rolled her eyes, bored with our questions or maybe our inability to grasp some simple concept. I didn't know which and I didn't care. My patience was stretched thin and about to snap. Whether I lashed out or lashed inward remained to be seen. I was hoping for out.

"The Overseer cares nothing for Metas or their squab-bling," she said, eyes drilling through mine, right into my skull. "Are you truly this naïve, girl? So wrapped up in your existence you cannot see the ocean for the waves? Haven't you ever wondered about those earliest childhood years where the memories are fuzzy? Why you're obsessed with Weatherfield? Why you feel so comfortable around Ace and King and Joker?"

My insides clenched, squeezed flat by a frozen fist of fear. I didn't want to hear anything else. I wanted to clamp my hands over my ears, hum *lalalalala*, and pretend she wasn't there. Anything to prevent her from saying it. "No," I said, tak-ing a single step backward. "I'm a Meta."

"You're not," Deuce said, smiling as though we were about to share a private joke. "You're like us, Dahlia Perkins. You're a Recombinant."

Blood rushed through my head, roaring like a freight train and blocking out all other sounds. Even after hot cement scraped my elbows raw and sharp stones dug into my shoul-der blades, I didn't stop struggling. Someone was holding me down, saying something I couldn't hear. I couldn't hear much of anything over the thundering in my head and shattering of my heart.

Lies, all lies. She would tell me the truth. I'd make her tell me. That's what I'd been doing when Noah knocked me down. Noah.

I stilled, no longer fighting my captor. I closed my eyes

and inhaled deeply. Exhaled. The roaring ceased, allowing words to filter in and make sense again. Noah loomed above me, backlit by the bright sun. My hands were pinned by my sides, and the entire weight of his body pressed down on mine.

"Calm down, for Christ's sake," he said.

I twisted my head around, past the length of our bodies. Deuce was unconscious again, her head lolling to one side. Blood dripped from her nose and from a gash on her forehead. The toes of my right foot ached. I'd kicked her. I'd hurt her just like she wanted me to hurt her. If I had killed her, we would have lost our bargaining chip. We'd have lost his brothers.

Noah's liquid eyes burned into mine. "Can I let you up now?"

"Yes."

He moved. The loss of his still-too-cool body wrapped me in a swirl of humid air. Perspiration broke out across my forehead and throat. I sat up, wincing as my raw elbows twinged and burned. My stomach gurgled, as much from lack of food as from the stroke of sudden, overwhelming terror—and understanding. I wanted Deuce to be wrong, but something deep down, buried below instinct and reason, told me she was right.

Footsteps shuffled. A shadow fell across my lap. Ethan squatted in front of me, groaning at the strain on his battered legs. Blood had dried on his face like garish war paint. He radiated calm, muddled with just a tinge of worry. Worry for me, or *because of* me, I didn't quite know.

"She's lying, Dal," Ethan said. "Trying to keep us off-balance so this doesn't go down in our favor."

"No." I shook my head. "No, Ethan, I don't think she was lying. I don't think I'd feel this way if she was."

"Feel what way?" Noah asked.

"Relieved."

Noah stared. "Relieved?"

I didn't realize I felt it until I voiced the emotion, and then it hit me full force, like a slap in the face. Total and utter relief that I wasn't targeted for death because of a stupid grudge; relief that my sense of misplacement among the Rangers stemmed from being completely different from them, and not just new to the group; relief that I finally—finally!—knew the real agenda behind the mayhem of the last few days.

As frightening as Deuce's announcement had been, I felt liberated for the first time in years. An impossible thing to describe, I could only sit there and feel it, let it wash over me like warm water, caressing away the soil of doubt, leaving only certainty in its wake.

"It's hard to explain," I said. "But it makes sense. I don't have anything from my life before the age of four. No proof I existed in the outside world."

"You said a mudslide destroyed everything," Ethan said. "There was a slide that year, Dal, your mom didn't make it up."

"I don't think she did." *Mom, oh, Mom, how much did you know about this?* "I'm just saying I think Deuce was telling the truth."

Ethan shook his head. Hard. "No, it can't be true. You reactivated at the same time as the rest of us. How is that possible if you aren't a Meta? Some very freaky cosmic co-incidence?"

"I don't know, Ethan." The first time my powers had mani-fested, it was out of self-preservation and the need to stop a grease fire. I hadn't experienced the same gut-twisting agony the others described on the night the Metas' powers were returned; Dr. Seward has attributed it to my being young and new to my powers, but now—"It makes sense, doesn't it? I mean, I never felt the reactivation the same as you guys."

"You didn't?"

I met Ethan's blank stare, surprised and a little confused. "I told you that."

"No, you didn't."

"I—oh God. I told Dr. Seward during my first exam. I just assumed he mentioned it to the rest of you."

Ethan snorted. "Probably didn't cross his mind, being so busy trying to kill us all." He still seemed wary, but at the same time sympathetic.

Was it possible the timing of the grease fire and discover-ing my powers really was some sort of cosmic joke, and that I wasn't a Meta? Yes, it was possible. Was I something com-pletely unnatural? I had no idea.

Unfortunately, Deuce was still unconscious from my hasty response to her announcement. "I guess we'll have to wait and ask Queen when we see her," I said.

"Someone's coming," King said. Silent up until now, he bolted to the courtyard gates and peered through.

I scrambled to my feet, wobbling a bit on unsteady legs, and latched onto Ethan for support.

The rumble of a car engine fast approached. "You know someone who owns a green sedan?" King asked.

"Agent McNally," Ethan said.

The third phone call. We both hated involving her in our current problem, but we needed a vehicle. She hadn't asked for details, for which I was eternally grateful, and had agreed to meet us at our current location. Good timing, too, because our debate on my supposed genetic history was going in circles. Second-guessing Deuce's motives and her words wouldn't help us. We needed to find Queen, get the Scott brothers back, and then get the answers I so desperately craved, and not necessarily in that order.

King pulled the gate open wide enough to allow the car entrance. It wasn't exactly subtle, but most passersby in this neighborhood wouldn't think twice about such an odd sight. Agent McNally left the engine idling, opened her door, and climbed out with a first aid kit in one hand.

"Always prepared?" Ethan asked.

"Good thing, too," McNally replied. Her mouth twisted into a frown, and her age-lined eyes took stock of his injuries. "What happened to you?"

"Took a flying leap out a closed window."

"Next time I recommend opening it first."

Ethan smiled.

"Have you heard from Gage or Simon?" I asked.

"No," McNally said, "but I did hear part of a retraction on the radio. Cipher was released and the rest of you are no longer wanted for questioning in the near death of Detective Pascal."

"Good, then she's keeping her part of the bargain."

McNally cocked her head to the left. "She who?"

"Really long story, and I promise we'll fill you in later, but we have to go." I snatched the first aid kit from her and tossed it to Ethan. She started to protest. I put my hands up to ward it off. "I'm so sorry to scoop and run like this, Agent McNally, but the less you know right now the better off you'll be."

King and Noah started loading Deuce into the backseat of the idling sedan. I'd have preferred the trunk and crossed mental fingers no one pulled us over (or attempted to pull us over, because no way would I stop for a cop today). Ethan dug into the medical bag, probably in search of high-potency painkillers.

I grabbed McNally's arm and tugged her a few feet away. "Can you promise me something, Agent McNally?"

"Of course, Ember."

"If anything happens to me today . . ." I had a hard time getting past those words. It voiced my greatest fear: I might not pull this off. The only way to save Jimmy and Aaron's lives might be to sacrifice my own.

"Ember, you don't—"

"No, I do. If anything happens to me, please tell Teresa I'm sorry. About all of this."

"It isn't your fault."

"Believe me, it is. If I weren't a part of her life, of all of their lives, none of this would have happened. Teresa wouldn't be shot. Marco wouldn't be, uh, missing." Shit, I hadn't communicated that part. I didn't really want to think about it; I was much too close to falling to pieces as it was. Reliving his loss (it seemed such a stupid, unworthy word for what had happened to Marco) hurt too much. A person could only handle so much pain at once without imploding.

"Please," I said. "Just promise you'll tell her."

She furrowed her sleek eyebrows and nodded. "I promise. But you promise me you'll do your damnedest to tell her in person. Tomorrow. When all of this is over."

I forced a smile. "Promise."

"Okay."

King and Ethan had already overtaken the backseat, their rug-rolled burden propped between them. Noah stood by the passenger-side door, leaning on the roof of the car. Watching. Waiting.

This ends today.

With that mantra in mind, I strode toward the driver's door. It was time to get this started, because Ranger or Recombinant, lives were on the line, and nothing was more important than that.

"Dahlia?" Agent McNally called out.

I stopped, turned. "Yeah?"

"Where's the nearest bus stop?" she asked, so deadly serious in tone I just stared for a long moment.

And then I started laughing.

Twenty-six

Home Invasions

A quick inspection of our previous hideout uncovered nothing more useful than a broken kitchen door, an overturned chair, and the rumpled sheets and an empty bed where Kinsey had been. A thin trail of blood stained the hallway carpet. He and Jimmy had been taken quickly and without fuss, thanks to my stolen image—an image gleaned after a chance jostling the day we answered a summons to Sunset Boulevard. Had I ever met the real Liza Forney?

Gage called back as we returned to the car. He was out of jail and not being followed, which was good news for us. I turned the call over to speaker mode and gave the cell to Noah so I could back out of the driveway.

"What about Simon?" I asked. "Have you seen him?"

"No," Gage replied. "And if anyone else has, they aren't saying. Cleared or not, everyone is still suspicious of me."

"They're going to be." I shifted back into drive and coasted down the quiet street. We'd seen no sign of Simon since the parking garage incident. Only a few hours had passed, but it felt like a week. A terrifying thought wormed its way into the front of my mind—what if he was a Changeling this whole time, too? Maybe the real Simon Hewitt had been absorbed into the body and consciousness of Queen or even Deuce, and he was lost to us, as well. Just like Marco.

I squeezed the steering wheel, squeaking the smooth leather beneath my hands. Noah noticed and put a gentle hand on my shoulder. I couldn't entertain those thoughts right now. I had too many other things to entertain. Simon would turn up in an unexpected place. Isn't that how these things worked? You lost a friend, thought you lost another, and everyone ended up safe and sound, after all?

You've been to the cinema too many times, Dal.

"Dahlia?" Noah asked, nudging me.

I snapped out of it, returning to the problem at hand. "What?"

He gave the phone a gentle shake.

"I'm sorry, Gage, say again?" I said.

"I asked how you got Forney to drop the charges," he said.

My mouth became so dry I had to swallow twice before managing a response. "We made a convincing argument."

"You're lying."

How could he tell over the phone? Could he really hear the way my heartbeat sped up? Oh, wait. I was a terrible liar. Even I heard the way my voice cracked.

A stop sign came out of nowhere. I smashed my foot on the brake pedal. Something thumped hard against the back of my seat and made an angry grunt. Noah braced his hands on the dashboard, dropping the phone in the process. The odor of burning metal tingled my nose; McNally needed to get her brake pads checked.

Pay attention, dammit. You're going to get someone else killed.

"What was that?" Gage asked, the sound muffled from the floor.

Noah felt around beneath the seat and retrieved the phone. "Dahlia needs to go back to driver's education," he said.

"What about Forney, Dal?"

I checked both ways, even though it was a four-way stop, and then proceeded. I felt eyes on my back and looked up, catching Ethan's steady gaze in the rearview mirror. Silent and supportive, sad and strong, and urging me to tell him.

So I did, starting with the escape from the parking garage, my car theft, regrouping at the Jarvis house, and setting out to search for the others. I told Ethan's side of things: the fight with the pyro, Renee's injuries, and meeting up at the Base. Our new plan and the call to Jimmy. The realization that at least one other Changeling existed, besides the brothers.

After a moment's consideration, I decided to alter the events slightly. "One of them attacked us at the Base," I said. "She has some sort of control over the earth, but we managed to subdue her. She's tied up in the backseat. There are two of them, though, and we used her for leverage against the one who's been masquerading as Liza Forney. That got her to let you go."

Silence for two more blocks, and then Gage said, "Well,

that's starting to make more sense. I didn't buy her almost killing her own partner just to set us up, but now I do." *Now that it's not really her.* An implicit statement with which I agreed.

"Hey," Gage said, as if it had just occurred to him. "Is Marco with you?"

My hand jerked, nearly taking the car off the road and into someone's hedge. I looked into the rearview, at the half-image of Deuce's sleeping face. Speckled with dried blood, her nose swollen. Technically? "Yeah, he's with us." I winced just saying the words.

"Okay, then." Either I was a better liar than I gave myself credit for, or he was distracted. "So what's the plan?"

He was asking me? "I'm still waiting to hear back from the other Changeling—Queen—" I said, "about where to trade her sister for Jimmy and Aaron." And me. "We need to get you."

"Listen, Liza Forney's apartment isn't far from where I am. We might as well kill two birds with one stone. Meet me there. If your contact hasn't called yet we'll check out the place and compare notes."

I looked at Noah; he nodded. "Okay, what's the address?" Gage gave it to me. "We're only a few blocks from there. Wait outside, and I'll see you in a minute."

"Okay."

Noah closed the phone. A tremor danced up my spine.

"Why didn't you tell him?" Ethan asked.

"Because," I said, negotiating a right turn onto a busier street, "no one should be alone when they hear this kind of news."

———————

Gage took it well. Or he simply refused to process it and locked the pain deep down where it couldn't bother him. Either way, he stared blankly at me for several long, tense seconds, absorbing the fact that one of his oldest friends was hidden somewhere deep inside of the unconscious Changeling called Deuce. Hidden and likely gone forever.

He closed his eyes and worked his jaw. He took a deep breath in and exhaled hard. "I see," he said, opening his eyes. Anger radiated from their silver-flecked depths. Fatigue drew dark circles beneath them, accentuated by the shadows of the underground parking garage. We had met on the lowest level of Forney's building, and I'd taken a moment to spill my guts on the things I couldn't say over the phone. Everything except the massive reboot of my own personal backstory. "How long?"

"The SWAT incident," I said. "I'm not sure how. We didn't really get into specifics before she tried to kill the rest of us."

"How could we not have known?"

Noah found it necessary to reply to the rhetorical question. "It wasn't an illusion you could see through. I know how it works when I do it, and the girls seem even more powerful. More in control of their abilities. You become that person. There's no distinguishing the bodies from each other, and the stronger of the two minds is always in control."

Gage pivoted toward Noah, raising one hand as if to poke him in the chest. He stopped, holding back at the last minute. "Is there any way to reverse it? To release a host intact?"

Noah frowned, looked thoughtful a moment, then glanced over his shoulder at King, who still sat in the backseat of the car, babysitting our hostage. King lifted one shoulder in a noncommittal shrug.

"I don't know, I'm sorry," Noah said. "If there is, we were never taught how. I can't separate the absorbed mind from my own."

Gage wilted in a heartbreaking transformation. I reached out. He jerked away, striding halfway across the parking garage. He stopped, hands on hips, shoulders hunched. Shaking. Ethan brushed past me and limped to his friend's side. They conferred quietly, a conversation not for my ears. I wasn't one of them anymore, was I? No longer a Meta, never a Ranger—my entire history altered in less than an hour with heartbreaking finality. I hadn't asked Ethan to keep it a secret, but would he really hide something so important from Gage?

Noah's hand slipped into mine. Our fingers twined. I held on tight, fighting the overwhelming urge to curl up in a little ball and sob until the pain in my gut went away. Until I was numb and nothing hurt anymore.

"We're running out of time," he whispered.

"You're right," Gage said, looking over his shoulder at us. He must have been using his hearing to its fullest to have caught that. He rubbed his eyes. "Let's go check out Forney's apartment."

King stayed behind with Deuce. Ethan needed to rest his injured legs, but he refused to stay in the car. Our quartet rode an elevator up to the eighth floor. The building was well maintained, while showing signs of age—worn carpet, stained chrome, peeling paint, and rubbed varnish. The elevator chugged along slowly, creaking its way from floor to floor, making me wonder if it would ever get all the way to eight. Like many other buildings on this side of West Hollywood, it was an old hotel converted into cheap flats—the only way many of them survived after the tourist industry went kaput.

Gage led the way down the hall, and I was eager to let him resume command. I preferred following orders. In that way, I supposed, I wasn't unlike the two female Changelings, blindly following orders from their mysterious Overseer. Was that a Recombinant trait?

A television set blared through the door of a neighboring apartment, vibrating the floor with the sound of a car chase and flying bullets. My skin crawled. After being in one of my own, I could never think of those sorts of chases the same way again. Not without remembering the overwhelming fear, the sight of broken glass and blood, the burning brakes, and the ping of bullets off reinforced metal.

In front of Forney's apartment door, Gage closed his eyes and let his senses loose. His nose wrinkled and his nostrils flared. His mouth twisted into a grimace. "There's a body in there," he said. He tried the doorknob, but it didn't turn.

"Want me to get the door?" Noah asked.

Gage stepped aside. "Be my guest."

Noah pressed his palm flat next to the brass knob. Wood crackled, metal squealed. The entire locking mechanism shot backward into the apartment, leaving a gaping hole the size of a fist, and the door swung open.

The air was hot and stuffy, closed up without ventilation. We followed the faint odor that had offended Gage into the one-room apartment. A single bed and two-seater sofa took up most of the space on one side of the room. A small refrigerator and two-burner hotplate served as the kitchen. Heavy blue curtains blocked out light from the room's balcony doors. Old food had gone to seed on one corner of the cheap dining table, contributing to the funky odors. Clothing spilled out of a scarred wooden dresser, and more still from the mirror-door closet.

There was no body, though, which became more apparent as we moved into the center of the room. It had one other door, across from the closet.

"Bathroom," I said.

Gage squared his shoulders and opened the door. I stayed in the middle of the room, uninterested in seeing another dead body (or human slipcover). I'd had my share, thank you very much. He pushed the door open halfway, reached in to turn on the light, and peeked inside. The odor became stronger. My stomach gurgled.

"It's a man," Gage said. "Another skin. I don't know who."

Ethan squeezed through, peering over Gage's shoulder. He backed out quickly, followed by Gage. "Looks like the pyro who attacked us in the street earlier," Ethan said.

Queen had been here in the last two hours. I shuddered, dread dragging cold fingers up my spine.

"Noah," Gage said, "is that Ken Dawson?"

Gage and Ethan stepped out of the bathroom doorway, allowing Noah to go inside. He crouched down and poked at the skin's face with the end of a toilet brush. When he stood up, his face was dark, angry. "I'm almost positive it's him," he said.

"Queen used your old tutor to attack us?" Ethan asked. "She's not leaving any loose ends, is she?"

"No, she's not."

"If she's . . ." Gage paused, his nostrils flaring. "Do you guys smell—?"

The explosion sounded like a muffled shotgun report. Blazing air and smoke belched forth from the far wall, next to the outlet feeding power to the refrigerator. Flames erupted, sneaking up the wall on fast feet, bubbling paint and scorching wood, reaching orange and red tendrils to the ceiling.

I gaped. It wasn't a large explosion. If Queen had meant to kill any of us with it, she had sorely misjudged her fuel source. We stared as a group.

"Anyone else a little underwhelmed?" Ethan asked.

"I guess you can't win every time," I said, taking a few steps closer to the small fire. My right hand reached for it. I concentrated, drawing the heat and flame away from the wall and into myself.

"Dahlia," Gage said. "Wait!"

Too late. The instant the flames absorbed, my insides burned. I screamed and pulled away. The fire came at me anyway, scorching, scalding, like boiling water injected into my bloodstream. Like the chemicals in the warehouse fire, whatever sourced this fire was similarly tainted.

Arms circled me, holding me tight against a hot, muscled chest. I pulled, yelled, clawed to get away from the heat and the intense agony of being boiled alive from the inside out.

Tears spilled down my cheeks, sizzling hot, evaporating before they reached halfway.

I was lifted, carried away in strong arms, and taken to the cooler air of the hallway. My mouth was parched, too dry to produce any more screams. Sensations assaulted me from all sides, every angle, inside and out. Pain and heat and cold. Rough skin and a gentle voice. Soothing. Calming.

The pain receded, leaving behind only a memory of the initial agony. Every extremity trembled. Cold air whirled around me. I forced my eyes open and looked right at Ethan. He knelt in front of me creating the wind. I inhaled, forcing the air into my starving lungs. Familiar hands clutched me from behind. Noah. I pressed back; he tightened his hold.

"Stupid," I said, shivering.

"It was a trap," Gage said, somewhere on my left.

"Smart trap."

"Maybe."

I relaxed into Noah's chest and let the others deal with the apartment fire. I just concentrated on breathing and getting my body temperature back to normal. Fine tremors ran up and down my legs. My insides felt numb, not quite there. The sensations were different from the warehouse poisoning—more concentrated.

My stomach twisted. I lurched out of Noah's grip and vomited murky liquid onto the hallway carpet. I retched until I collapsed and my chest ached. Once again enveloped in the safety of Noah's arms, I began to cry. Unashamed and exhausted, tears of loss and anger spilled in equal measure.

He held me and I sobbed it out, though I knew I should

stop; my body couldn't afford to lose the moisture. Then I was aware of being picked up again and of forward movement. We were leaving. Voices spoke, but I didn't listen. The sounds created no coherent words in my addled brain.

King's voice, booming in the cavern of the parking garage, finally made it through. "What happened?" he asked.

"Booby trap," Gage said. "Is she still out?"

She who? Me she?

"Yeah, she hasn't even twitched."

Oh, Deuce.

Noah deposited me on the front passenger seat. I relaxed into the soft leather, finally regaining my mental faculties. Outside the car, the four men stood in a circle, apparently unsure of their next step. Before they could reach their own conclusion, King's phone rang, its shrill tone cutting across the lot. He pulled it out of his pocket.

"My, we're impatient, aren't we?" Queen asked, crackling over the speaker. "How'd you like my present, Dahlia?"

I hadn't the wits to answer. "Fuck you, Queen," Noah said for me.

She laughed, a frightening sound that set my teeth on edge. "Fuck me, dear Brother? My kinks go in different directions. However, I've done what you asked. Your precious Dr. Kinsey is now in a hospital."

"Good."

"Well played, I must say. But so far in this game, we've been busying ourselves with knights and rooks. Let's see what happens when your queen is left unprotected." The final barb was punctuated with the familiar click of a finished call.

"Knights and rooks?" Noah asked.

"Chess pieces," Gage replied. "Your queen is unprotected. Our queen."

Dread blossomed in my chest, radiating outward like a thousand tiny needle pricks. "Teresa," I said. Four heads swiveled toward me, wearing matching expressions of confusion and shock. "Our queen. The hospital, Gage. Teresa."

Faster than I'd ever seen him move, Gage was in the driver's seat and revving the engine. The others barely had time to climb into the backseat with the rolled-up Changeling before he peeled out of the garage.

Please, God, let me be wrong about this.

Prayers often go unanswered, especially when you are praying to someone who tends to ignore your prayers on a regular basis.

We arrived to find City of Angels a flurry of activity. Police cars and a firetruck, plus a crowd of reporters and onlookers, swarmed the main parking lot. We hit a roadblock just before the entrance turnoff, so Gage pulled around to the next block. Safe from the onlookers. He parked, and we got out. The short drive had given me time enough to recover my leg strength, even though the trembling weakness remained in my arms and chest.

In the distance, four floors up, one of the hospital windows was completely busted out. The majority of the rescue workers had gathered beneath the destruction. Patients' rooms were on that floor. Hadn't Ethan said Teresa was moved out of ICU the previous day? It was all so fuzzy.

With no patience for the police, Ethan swept me and Gage up inside a whirling vortex of wind and carried us into the air. I'd never flown with him like this, with nothing around me but the wind and sky, feet dangling over the ground with no net to catch me. I looked straight down. Noah, King, and the car shrank in size as they were left behind.

Spectators shouted and pointed. Police officers reached for their holstered weapons but then watched without drawing. We flew upward, toward the broken window. Through it, ducking low to miss any jagged edges of glass, right into a patient's room.

A white-coated doctor and two uniformed police officers jumped back at our sudden appearance, their hair and clothes flapping in our wake. Ethan put us down and let the air dissipate. The nearest patient bed was empty, the mattress neatly folded over backward. The curtain surrounding the second bed whispered, slowly settling as the breeze died down.

As I adjusted to having both feet firmly on a solid surface, Gage strode toward the curtain. He ripped it back with one solid tug and yelled out in shock and rage.

Queen had, indeed, kept her word and deposited Abram Kinsey in a hospital bed. He lay there, on his back, still in his street clothes and makeshift bandages, safe now among hovering hospital personnel. On the bedside table was a vase of flowers with a Mylar Get Well Soon balloon attached with a pink ribbon. Nestled among the flowers was a card, a name scrawled across the matching pink envelope: Teresa.

I fell to my knees, unable to breathe, as panic mingled with pure terror.

The opposite wall displayed a single word scratched onto the wallpaper in black charcoal. The chunk of charred wood used to write the message lay on the floor like a silent challenge. Five letters. One implicit meaning.

CHECK.

She'd captured our queen—a devastating move against our side.

Too bad she wasn't smart enough to get her chess rules right.

Twenty-seven

Duality

E than flew us back to the car, armed with confirmation from Dr. Shelby that Kinsey would survive. The bullet had missed all major arteries and organs, and the wound was free of infection. I relayed the information to the brothers as soon as we returned, trying to drum up some measure of happiness for them, but feeling only rage. I clenched my fist around the stick of burnt wood as I spoke. Noah's relief was tempered by our collective anxiety, though, and he tried—he really tried—to be a comfort.

I didn't want that; I wanted to be angry. Furious. At him and at Queen. At this human chess match we were caught in the middle of, with human lives as pawns and the winner allowed to live. Two sides striving for checkmate. A move I planned to make first.

"Why do that?" Gage asked for the sixth or seventh time since flying back from the hospital. He was trying to find sense in a senseless act, and it played on my high levels of frustration.

"Because of me," I said, practically screaming the words.

"To make sure she has something personal to use against me, so I don't renege on our deal."

Gage stilled. He cast a confused look at Ethan, who dropped his gaze to the sidewalk. "What deal? What didn't you tell me?"

More than you know. I don't know how I thought I could have hidden it.

"I'm their assignment, Gage," I said. "Everything the two female Changelings have done is because of me: the slipcover bodies, the things the brothers have been manipulated into, the warehouse fire, and Teresa getting shot. All of it."

A muscle twitched in Gage's clenched jaw. His expression remained otherwise flat. "I still don't—"

"To kill me, Gage, their assignment is to kill me. She"—I pointed at Deuce—"told me those were their orders. Period."

"What was the deal you made?"

I shuffled my weight from foot to foot, hoping for a well-timed interruption. The cellular, though, remained quiet. "Just giving Deuce back wasn't enough to get both Scotts, Gage. She gets me, too."

He bristled. "Absolutely not."

"This isn't open for discussion now that she has Teresa. I know Queen has no qualms about killing, and I can't risk the deaths of three people for my own life. I won't."

"We can come up with an alternative to this, Dal. We can do something."

"No." I shook my head hard—bad idea. Any chance I had of convincing Gage fled when I wobbled, overcome by dizziness, and almost fell. I caught myself on the edge of the car before a rush of helping hands swooped in to save me. Again. I pushed away from the car and away from them. "Goddammit, you guys, I'm not going to break!"

Noah backed up a step, his eyes going wide. I surprised myself with the vehemence in my voice. I drew up to my full height—still several inches shorter than everyone, except Noah—and squared my shoulders.

"I got all of you into this," I said to Gage. "I got Renee burned and Teresa shot and Marco killed."

Gage winced and started shaking his head. "You don't know—"

"Yes, I do. How do you separate two souls who've become one?" I cast a pleading look at Noah. He held it a moment, and then looked away. "Marco's dead, and it's my fault. I need to take responsibility."

"By getting yourself killed, too?" Gage asked.

"They'll never stop hunting you," Deuce said, her unmistakable voice cutting through the conversation like a rusty saw blade. She peered out of one eye; dried blood sealed the other shut, giving her the appearance of a psychotic Cyclops. She made no move to attack or attempt escape.

"Who won't stop?" Gage asked.

"The people who sent her," I said.

Deuce nodded. "The Overseer will never admit to fault or failure, no matter our report. Kill us and others will come. Hide and they will seek her out. Sooner or later, she will die, even if all she cares for must die first."

Her final declaration was directed at Noah. The estranged siblings measured each other up. A flicker of uncertainty tempered her glare. Noah didn't blink or look away, and I knew with perfect clarity that he would face death with me—whether I wanted him to or not.

She's mine.

"That's insane," Gage said. "What the hell did Dahlia do to you people?"

We were so not going there. I couldn't tell him yet—that I wasn't human. I wasn't even MetaHuman. I was some sort of Recombinant-DNA project gone awry that had to be wiped out of existence, because someone called the Overseer said so. "It doesn't matter anymore," I said. "I don't want to die, but if it means saving three lives, I'll do it." The words came easily, spoken from the heart without pause or doubt.

I would die for them.

Ethan and King remained silent spectators to the entire production. I felt their intense stares burning into my back, thinking questions and not asking them, and I was grateful. I had enough trouble wrangling Gage's questions and challenges, and I almost regretted picking him up. Almost. Now I was glad, because I would need him to take care of Ethan.

They weren't coming with us. They just didn't know it yet.

I crouched by the back door, gazing in at Deuce. Her left eye blinked, while the other worked to open. "Will Queen keep her word? Will she let the others go if I give myself up freely?"

"Yes," she replied.

"She's lying," Gage said. "Her heart rate just spiked."

Okay, so I *was* glad to have Gage around. "Will she kill them anyway?" I asked, rewording the question to something simpler. A point-blank query.

Deuce squeezed her eyes shut, mouth puckering, as if trying to force a horrible image out of her mind. Or fight off a bad cramp. I inched forward. Was she having some sort of fit? She'd been rolled up in that rug for the last hour, stuffed in the backseat of a car, on one of the hottest days yet. Anything was likely.

She jerked upright, both eyes flying open. They flashed a shimmering green. Dark, deep slits ran the vertical length of them, just like Marco's panther-form eyes. The skin on her face darkened, pale pink mottling with brown and black smudges of baby-soft fur. My heart jackhammered. The struggle between two dominant personalities played out in a series of facial tics and twitches, and somewhere deep inside of her came a low, feline growl.

"Marco?" I said in a near whisper, afraid to break the spell and scare him away.

Familiar eyes moved, their direction shifting around the interior of the car, looking without understanding. Taking in unfamiliar details. Seeing for the first time. Her head turned and those haunting eyes finally looked at me. Saw me.

"Dahlia?" s/he said. Two voices vied for dominance, coated with Marco Mendoza's subtle accent.

"It's me." I had to remind myself to breathe.

"Do not trust Queen. She will kill them for spite. Deuce knows this, but will not say it. She will not turn against her sister."

"How did you come back?" I wanted to ask a hundred questions, but didn't know how long he had before Deuce's personality beat him back. He'd been strong enough to surface and feed me a hint, and I desperately wanted to hold on to him any way I could.

His/her eyebrows furrowed. Sweat poured down the sides of Deuce's face. Marco's eyes remained. "Should not have taken a Meta. Cannot absorb us. I am as strong as she."

"Can you get out?" Gage asked, startling me. I'd forgotten about the others and found him hovering over my shoulder.

Friendly feline eyes shifted focus to Gage. A spot of fresh blood dribbled from Deuce's left nostril, the stress of dual personalities taking its physical toll. "No," s/he said. "Make her let me go. Please. Let me go."

The anguish in his voice broke my heart. The host retained the memories and experiences of the possessed host, even though the distinct personality died. She couldn't absorb him. He wanted out, and while part of me could have accepted him living on in someone else's head (the part of me that kept saying "at least he'd be alive"), he could not accept it.

He would rather be let go.

"I'm so sorry, Marco," I whispered, unable to raise my voice for fear of its breaking, of letting myself shatter into a hundred little pieces. I didn't want to fight. I didn't want to die. I wanted to live. I wanted my friends back whole and happy. I wanted things back to normal, like they'd been just a few days ago.

What's done can never be undone. You should know that by now.

"Not your fault, *Ascua*." He cried out and squeezed his eyes shut. His mouth puckered. Blood dripped in a steady stream, coating Deuce's lips and chin. The coloration on her skin faded, returning to its original shade. Another shriek came, this time more feminine, and when she opened her eyes, Marco was gone.

"He's getting on my nerves," she said.

Noah shouldered his way past Gage, earning a grunt of annoyance, and crouched next to me. "Why didn't you just absorb him?" he asked. "Why keep his personality compartmentalized if he causes you so much trouble?"

"I couldn't absorb him. His memories would have impaired my judgment. His love for Dahlia is strong enough where it is and provides constant irritation. To take it into myself would be suicide."

His emotions would have overthrown hers. If Deuce had tried to amalgamate Marco into herself, she would have been lost to his loyalty. His love. He would have become the dominant personality, making Deuce useless in her assigned task. She'd worn him and done a good job of it, without actually becoming him. The Changelings had a weakness, after all.

"Why don't you dispel him, then?" I asked. "If you can't take him on, why not get rid of the problem?"

Her nostrils flared. "Because keeping him hurts you."

"Seems to hurt you, too."

"Yours is a more delicious hurt."

"She's lying again," Gage said.

Deuce shot him a poisonous glare. Through clenched teeth, she said, "I can't get him out, all right? I can't absorb him, and I can't get rid of him. He's like an itch that stays just out of reach and burns to be scratched."

"What if we can help?" Gage asked, nudging Noah over this time. Those two were going to end up in a fistfight if they weren't careful.

"Help how?"

"We have a friend with abilities that may be of use to you."

I could have slapped myself. Simon's unique telepathic powers allowed him to sense and control other people's conscious minds. If he could locate and isolate Marco's consciousness, perhaps he could draw our friend back out of Deuce—free them both from each other.

We had to find Simon first.

Deuce seemed to consider the offer, her unfocused brown eyes shifting from Gage to me, and back again. She waged her own internal battle, a choice between living with another mind at constant war with her own and potentially betraying her sister.

"How much is your own life worth to you, Deuce?" I asked. "Do you want to live forever with someone else vying for control of your brain?"

"Can he really do it?" Her eyes glistened. "Can he separate us?"

"We don't know for sure until we ask him." Which led us back to another problem: we didn't know where Simon was. No one had seen him since the morning, and he didn't have an active com.

"Then let's ask him," she said.

"We would, but—"

"I know where he is."

I stared. She winced, tried to shrug.

We should have known.

Queen still hadn't called by the time we arrived back at Hill House. She was either taking her time choosing a meeting location, or still hadn't committed to a plan of action. No matter. We needed all the time we could get.

It made sense to stash someone in our home; since we weren't likely to go back there while under the threat of immediate arrest, it was the perfect hiding place. Gage took Noah in first so they could locate and deactivate the bugs. Gage took that particular revelation better than I expected, considering he'd read Noah's vitals the day he came to inspect the house. I knew firsthand how good an actor Noah was, but it was rare to get one over on Gage.

Once they declared the house clean, King slung Deuce over his shoulder and the rest of us went inside. As promised, we found Simon tied up in the courtyard, awake and a little sunburned, but otherwise unhurt.

I hung back with Noah, waiting in the interior hallway while Gage untied Simon, not daring to hope that this would work in Marco's favor—just hoping it would release them both, and that Deuce would honor her promise to help.

King put Deuce down and started to unroll her from the rug. Ethan oversaw the process, pale and unsteady on his feet. I wanted to tell him to sit down and rest, but knew he wouldn't do that until this was finished. He and Gage wouldn't let me blunder into this on my own.

As if they had a choice in the matter.

"Do you believe in heaven, Noah?" I asked.

"I don't know," he said. "I guess I do, because I believe in hell. Maybe not the biblical heaven and hell, but something."

In the courtyard, Gage and Simon were arguing. A loud, hand gesture–filled argument. Snippets of words filtered through the closed door. King helped Deuce stand up, her hands and feet still tied. Her entire body glistened with sweat, her skin angry and red.

"What if this doesn't work?" I asked.

Noah's arm snaked around my waist. "We'll figure it out, Dahlia. We'll get through this." He kissed my cheek, just a brush of his lips. A gentle reminder that I wasn't alone.

"I haven't forgiven you for lying to me."

"I know."

The cell phone rang. My heart slammed against my chest, and I jumped away from Noah. No one in the courtyard had heard it. Everyone was intent on Deuce and Simon, who stood toe-to-toe. Simon radiated annoyance.

Noah handed me the phone.

"Yes?" I said, turning my back to the courtyard windows.

"I've fulfilled my part of our bargain," Queen said. "You ready to do yours?"

"Your interpretation of fulfillment is hilarious."

"How's my sister?"

"Annoying. How are my friends?"

"Squirming. Joker really should learn it's impolite to peek into people's heads without permission. I'm afraid I had to punish him a little."

I bristled, my hand closing tight around the phone. "If you hurt any of them—"

"Can we please skip this, Dahlia? The part where you issue threats, I issue threats, and neither of us feels threatened by the other? It's tiresome. We both know how this is going to end. You die, your friends go free, and Deuce and I go home for our next assignment."

I glanced at the courtyard, stalling now. Simon's hands were cupped around Deuce's face. Their eyes were shut, both of them concentrating. A sparkle of energy surrounded them, like a shimmer of heat off hot pavement.

"Is this your idea of a happy ending?" I asked.

"This isn't a fairy tale. Happy endings don't exist for people like us."

"I beg to differ."

"Planning to prove me wrong?"

"Definitely."

She scoffed. "You certainly have balls, I'll give you that. If they'd kept you around, instead of erasing your memory and giving you to a human family, you might have amounted to something."

Anger bubbled to the surface as heat rose in my cheeks. I forced my hand to loosen its death grip on the phone. "I did amount to something, you absolute shit." Another look: more energy and a thicker haze of it. Ethan, King, and Gage had retreated to the corner of the courtyard, watching.

Noah's hand slipped into mine; I held it tight.

Queen giggled. Actually freaking giggled. I shuddered. More than any of her threats, uttered or implied, her giggling frightened me the most.

"One hour, Dahlia. Just you and my siblings. No one else."

"Where?"

"Where they failed to kill you the first time." She hung up.

The first time they failed—oh, right. The factory fire. I had a location. Now I had to figure out how to ditch my friends.

Noah slipped the phone back into his pocket. "Well?"

"An hour, and now I know where."

I turned back to the courtyard and froze, dumbfounded by what I saw. Deuce was completely out of phase. I could have been looking at her through an unfocused camera lens. Two distinct shapes meshed together in that blur: one male and one female. One dark, the other pale. Two bodies coexisting in the same space, but neither truly there.

Simon stood in front of them, hands splayed by his sides, eyes closed and forehead wrinkled. Concentrating so deeply I couldn't tell if he was still breathing. He was frozen in place. The three of them seemed to exist in a separate world, out of synch with ours.

Someone screamed, a high-pitched wail that set my teeth on edge, even through the protection of the windows. Gage clamped his hands over his ears, falling to his knees under the echo of it in the enclosed walls of the courtyard. Ethan and King winced under the auditory assault but stood fast. Waiting.

Time stood still. The air crackled and snapped. A flash

of white light obscured the unfocused forms and knocked Simon backward. I raised my hand to shield my eyes. Simon rolled to an ungraceful stop a few feet from Gage. The light died as abruptly as it appeared.

Two figures lay crumpled on the grass, one perpendicular to the other. Deuce was still tied up and fully clothed. She coughed and blinked up at the sun. At her feet, Marco's motionless body lay facedown, completely nude, but whole and not a jumble of empty skin.

"Oh my God," I said. Hope blossomed in my chest. I shoved the door open, ignoring everyone around me except for the one person I never thought I'd see again.

I fell to my knees next to Marco and rolled him onto his back. His eyes were closed, lips slightly parted. I pressed my ear to his bare chest, listening for the elusive heartbeat that would announce partial success. So far away, but it was there—one soft thump, and then another. I sat up, but the cry of victory died on my lips.

No rise and fall. No intake of air. *No, no, no.*

"He's not breathing," I said.

Twenty-eight

Chessboard

I held Marco's hand, offering comfort the only way I could, until the paramedics shouldered me aside. They loaded their gurney into the back of the ambulance, which had arrived relatively quickly after being called. One uniformed girl, who looked too young to be out of high school let alone a practicing paramedic, rhythmically squeezed an Ambu bag. She breathed for Marco, as we'd taken turns breathing for him in the too-long minutes between his separation from Deuce and the ambulance's arrival. The paramedic was keeping him alive with the faith of someone who'd seen miracles before.

I envied her for her faith.

Ethan went with him, as much for company as to get his own injuries tended. We had supplies at the house, but without the medical knowledge of a trained physician, they were mostly useless, and I was glad to see him finally out of direct harm's way.

The ambulance tore down the driveway, lights flashing and siren wailing. I watched from the porch, chilled inside and out. I squashed any lingering threads of hope. A heart-beat was good, but if Marco couldn't breathe on his own . . . no, no doubts. No more wondering.

It was getting late. At least fifteen minutes had passed since the phone call.

Footsteps behind me. I sensed Noah before he spoke: "Deuce wants to talk to you."

"Good for her," I said.

"Dal?" He turned me to face him.

"At least Ethan is away from this," I said, unable to meet his gaze. "They'll be safe at the hospital, I think. It's not City of Angels."

He fought a small smile at my own black humor. "Do you have a plan?"

"You mean besides getting our people back and trying not to die?" He stroked my cheek with his fingers. My stom-ach coiled into a knot of . . . something. "What did you mean when you said 'she's mine'?"

His fingertips skimmed across my throat, around to cup the back of my neck. "When this is all over and everyone's safe, I might ask you to forgive me for lying to you. And if you do, I might then ask you out on a date."

I licked my lips. "Somewhere nicer than Mallory's Table?"

"Yep. Think you might say yes?"

"Just maybe."

He drew me closer, and his mouth covered mine in a gentle kiss. Warm and yielding, promising without pushing. Heat burned in my chest. I memorized the curve of his lips and the subtle, sweet taste of him, the soft abrasion of his unshaven skin on my cheeks. I wanted to savor every detail of our first kiss.

Just in case.

He finished by crushing me in a hug. I rested my chin on his shoulder. Past him, just inside of the porch door, King watched us. He'd abandoned Ortega's shadow, and his expressionless face gave away nothing. I looked where I supposed his eyes were, and for a moment, I saw him. Saw a man behind the blank slate. A man who'd done terrible things in order to protect his family and the great weight resting on his shoulders.

King turned and disappeared into the shadow of the house. I pulled away from Noah. "We need to get King and Deuce and go," I said.

"What about Simon and Gage?" Noah asked.

"I'll take care of them."

For the second time today, I tested my ability to draw energy from living people. I found Gage in the War Room, sifting through a stack of files. He looked up when I entered, shifting from concern to curiosity as I stalked right up to him, clamped my hand down on his arm, and held tight.

Heat pulled out of his skin, absorbing through mine and curling into a ball of energy deep in my chest. He paled, stumbled. Tried to say my name. With a question on his lips and fear in his eyes, he passed out. I tried to catch him and break the fall, but only succeeded in getting tugged down to my knees by his weight.

His head lolled to one side, skin ashen and clammy. He had a strong pulse, though. He'd be cold and pissed when he woke up.

"Dahlia? What happened?"

Bingo. Simon darted into the room and dropped to his knees on the other side of Gage's prone form. Dark smudges colored the skin beneath Simon's eyes, stark as black eye shadow against the pallor of his face. The pull of his thin lips evidenced the strain he'd felt while separating Deuce from Marco. I hated to hurt him more.

"I'm sorry, Simon," I said.

His eyebrows furrowed. "For what?"

I grabbed his wrist. Seconds later, he collapsed on top of Gage. The energy from Simon was somehow stronger than Gage's, more powerful. It roiled and spun, heating my insides. It gave me strength and fueled my determination. I rolled Simon over so he wouldn't wake up in a compromising (and uniquely embarrassing) position.

Noah came with blankets, and we covered them.

Deuce was still tied up in the courtyard; she glared as we approached. "About time, Dahlia," she snapped.

"Shut up," I said. She blinked. "Your sister is the pyro, right? She can control fire?"

"Yes."

Good. Barring any more accelerant poisoning, I could absorb huge amounts of regular fire. "What about you, Deuce? You control earth?"

"Yes."

"If I untie you, are you going to smash me into the ground?"

"No."

She seemed sincere, but I'd have preferred Gage verifying my opinion. "Are you going to behave until we get to the warehouse? Play on our side, since we helped you out with your multiple-personality disorder?"

"As long as you don't hurt my sister, you have my word. I don't want to kill you, but I won't let her die, either."

A little bit of hurt was necessary in subduing Queen, I had no doubt. I could always settle it by knocking Deuce out, too. One less potential enemy to worry about. The only thing stopping me was Queen's reaction if her sister appeared injured. Queen could take it out on one of her hostages.

"Then let's go," I said.

I parked a block away from our destination, and we walked the rest of the way. My entire body thrummed with energy and anticipation, dread and terror. Noah walked next to me, his hand grasping mine in a death grip. Behind us, King led Deuce by the forearm, not seeming to care that his mannequin-like face made him stick out from the crowd. The street was pretty quiet, and we'd not seen another car in two blocks.

Yellow police tape still cordoned off the ruined warehouse and its narrow parking lot. The exterior walls remained intact, bricks blackened and cracked. The interior gaped like a monster's maw, dark and wide and treacherous.

The site hadn't been cleaned up. Debris lay scattered around the perimeter of the building. Chunks of scorched boards and cement, shattered glass and bent beams, all seasoned with the suffocating odors of burnt wood and metal.

The distant rumblings of a train broke the oppressive silence, chugging toward us along the tracks that ran behind the warehouse. It seemed so different now. Less angry, less dangerous.

We slipped beneath the police tape, making no sound as we crossed the parking lot. My eyes never stopped moving. Watching. The side entrance doors were busted down, allowing us easy access through the blackened frame, into a dim room. Overturned filing cabinets spilled burned paper and water-soaked folders across soiled industrial carpeting, which even two days later squished wetly beneath my feet.

I stopped to listen, but heard nothing. No subtle clues or hints. Noah squeezed my hand. I returned the gesture and released him, moving forward on my own. Sunlight sparkled beyond a doorless entryway, hinting at an open area ahead. I stepped over a fallen support beam. Froze.

Somewhere ahead, soft and far away, someone was crying. I maneuvered through the narrow hall, toward the shaft of light. At the end of the pathway, as suspected, the hall opened into the main warehouse.

Blue sky and sunlight glared down, illuminating the rubble-strewn main floor. Overturned metal shelving lay in twisted piles, half melted and misshapen. Heaps of ash sat quietly, undisturbed by the still air. Four central support pillars stood like sentinels, reaching four stories into the sky and touching nothing. Visibility was bad, my view constantly marred by the wreckage.

Something pricked at the back of my mind. A small voice, whispering.

"Jimmy," Noah said.

"I hear him, too," I replied. The crying had stopped and even small noises resounded like a shotgun report. "Stay behind me."

Each step forward was a deliberate action. I hated leaving the safety of the hallway for the open jungle of the warehouse. Attack could come from any direction. The air around me crackled, raising the short hairs on the back of my neck. A quick check over my shoulder revealed Noah as the source. He walked with eyes half-lidded, mouth twisted in concentration. Some sort of telekinetic shield, I guessed.

Good thinking.

A dozen or so yards through the maze of wreckage, the floor opened up. Uneven streaks in the floor's ash coating indicated someone had manually shoved aside the trash and debris to create an open floor space roughly fifty feet in diameter, right in the middle of the central pillars, like a gladiator arena of yesteryear. We found the edge by the southernmost pillar. I held up my hands, keeping my companions back.

"She's here," Deuce said, keeping her voice low.

I nodded.

"Send out Deuce!" Queen shouted. Her voice boomed around the room, vibrating and echoing, making the source impossible to locate.

"Not until I see my friends," I yelled right back, wincing at the result. The acoustics in there were insane.

Queen laughed. "Take a look around, Dahlia. You'll see them."

I inched forward and took a moment to examine the perimeter of the arena. Gazed over piles of wood and metal and cement blocks, charred and broken and strewn about. Nothing to indicate the presence of other people, but there were dozens of holes and breaks. Perfect hiding places.

"Holy shit," Noah said. His hand rose into my peripheral vision, pointing up and to the left.

I followed his direction to the pillar farthest from our position. Ten feet from the ground, Jimmy was bound to the pillar, arms and legs secured by thick ropes. Mouth gagged, eyes open, he struggled against his bonds. Blood stained his sandy-brown hair and coated one side of his face.

Don't trust her! Jimmy shouted, his voice searing through my head. Noah inhaled sharply; he'd heard it, too.

The next pillar over, diagonal from our position, was a man I'd seen only in photographs. Aaron Scott, pale as death, hung limply, similarly secured with rope. He had no outward injuries I could see from a distance. He wasn't conscious and could easily have been dead.

He's alive, but he's hurt, Jimmy said.

"Can you talk back to him?" I asked Noah. He nodded. "Ask him about Teresa and Queen."

Noah squinted. Concentrated. From somewhere in the wreckage below the pillar, the twin prongs of a taser sprung upward and attached to Jimmy's leg. He shrieked, shook, and went limp.

I grabbed Noah around the waist before he could blindly bolt out into the open area. "Don't! It's what she wants."

"I'll kill her for that," he growled.

Deuce grunted. The ground began to rumble and groan. *Uh-oh.*

I whirled, but was too slow to stop Deuce from bashing a chunk of cement block into the back of King's head. He fell like a stone. Blood trickled from the fresh wound in his skull.

Noah raised his hand and splayed his fingers. The air seemed to condense and wave. It pushed forward like a living thing. The invisible force slammed Deuce in the chest and propelled her backward. She hit a wooden beam, cracked it in half, and lay still.

He crouched next to King. "He's alive," he said. "Dammit, I didn't think—"

"Too late now," I said, turning back to the arena's entrance. A figure had emerged from the wreckage beneath Jimmy's pillar. She wore a gray gown that contrasted with the fine purple strands of her hair and coloration of her face. She wobbled, took a step, and stumbled two more. Twenty feet away and moving closer.

Teresa.

I held my breath. She raised her head and our eyes met. Pain, relief, and determination sparkled there. Another step. She swayed. Fell. Shrieked in pain when she hit the ground on her wounded side. Panic squeezed my heart. I raced to her, heedless of my very exposed position, and skidded to a slippery stop by her side.

Thick ash coated her arms and legs. I gently rolled her over. She blinked up at me, tears streaking her cheeks. Fresh blood stained the bandages on her chest, peeking through the smudges of gray ash. Her pained grimace twisted up into an agonized smile. And then to just a smile.

A warning hammered in my head.

Teresa's grin became a leer. "Stupid girl," she said in Queen's distinct voice.

A glamour.

Shit.

From beneath the gown, she produced a handgun, pressed it against my abdomen, and fired.

Twenty-nine

Checkmate

White-hot agony exploded in my stomach. Metallic heat filled my mouth. I smelled scorched cloth. Ozone. The world tilted, and then I was looking up at the sky. The overwhelming pain calmed to a faint numbness. I couldn't feel my legs. Couldn't sit up.

Oh God, this is it.

Energy crackled around me. Someone screamed. Female. A thud and then a second shout—my name this time.

Twin emeralds obscured the sky, so wide they should have fallen out. Plopped to the ground. The emeralds blinked, swimming in liquid. Warm skin touched my cheeks. Something wrapped around my hand.

Noah.

I tried to say his name. Acknowledge him. The sound gurgled in my throat, blocked by thick liquid. It trickled over my lips and down my chin.

"Please no."

Two words made it through the roaring in my ears. I was going to die. Queen had won.

I squeezed the hand in mine, trying to communicate that it was okay. I wasn't scared, just numb and tired. An electrical surge danced up my arm, through my chest. It tickled its way up my spine and set my brain on fire. A tidal wave of emotion poured over me, crushing in its purity.

Fear. Love. Hatred. Dread.

Hope. Above all, hope rose to the top like a buoy, guiding me toward it. Memory swirled around me in a white mist, waiting to be let in. Consumed. Shared. My heart hammered. So loud. Another heart pounded in the distance, soft and gentle. But close, and growing closer.

All at once I understood. I stopped fighting.

I fell into the mist.

I hurtled forward like a shooting star. The pain ceased and all I knew was the fall. An overwhelming pull to another place. My heartbeat faded, going, going. The other pounded harder, louder. Beat in its place, strong and virile. Thrumming with life.

Power rippled around me. Enveloped me in its embrace. I settled in, finding an unoccupied spot in a small, dark corner. Content and safe there, I waited. Time seemed to stop.

Dahlia?

Noah's voice, all around. Inside of me. Part of me. I had no mouth to speak with, no corporeal form at all. Not if what I thought happened had truly just happened.

I'm here.

I'm so sorry. I couldn't let you die like that.

I felt his pain as he felt it, cloying and unruly and very unwanted. He loved me and hated me for the attachment. My heart soared—quite metaphorically, since I had no heart of my own now—and he shivered. Felt it right back. *Is Queen down?* I vaguely sensed our position, but could not see. I had no idea what was happening outside him.

She's getting up and looks pissed. "Shit!"

The last word was spoken aloud. We surged sideways. His panic became my panic. Gunshots pinged around us. We came to a rest. I offered whatever calm I could muster. He took it, used it. Our heartbeat continued to thrum, too fast. Much too fast.

Noah, when she runs out of bullets, she'll use fire. Give me control. I can protect us with my power.

He never hesitated. I surged upward, my senses tingling to life. I smelled the tang of ash and of scorched metal. Saw the glare of sunlight. Heard the creak of wood. Felt the floor, cold and slick beneath my hands.

My hands. Not Noah's hands, but my very own. I flexed the fingers, cracked the knuckles. From the scar on my pinkie courtesy of a jagged can of instant soup, to the mole on the underside of my right wrist. My hair was long and dirty. I touched my face—high cheekbones and flat chin. I was on the outside. Me again, but not really.

Energy crackled all around, snapping and popping like an effervescent froth. Intangible, but malleable. Invisible, but every color of the rainbow. In the floor beneath me, in the clothes surrounding me, and the objects towering over me. Kinetic energy everywhere.

Do you always feel this? I asked.

His answer came from deep within, distant and soft: *Always. Use the power, Dahlia.*

I will.

The energy shifted, swirling coldly just out of sight. I ducked and rolled, and another gunshot shattered a hole into the wooden support beam instead of my head. Outside of the cleared arena, the warehouse presented a treacherous landscape. Spikes of metal and charred wood, overturned shelving units, brick fragments and piles of unidentifiable junk. Sharp corners and edges, snatching and tearing at cloth and flesh.

I ducked behind a cluster of metal pilings. Heard scuffing, a click, and then several tinkling sounds. She was reloading. I crouched low and peeked beneath. Spotted a black shoe and a handful of empty shells. A golden glow encompassed each of them, a tiny promise of movement. I focused on the shell nearest the shoe. It shimmied, then darted sideways. I slammed it into her ankle, piercing flesh and bone and tearing through the other side.

Queen howled and fell. She dropped the gun. It skittered away. I caught onto it and gave it a hard mental shove, pushing it until it disappeared beneath the rubble.

Score one for the good guys.

"You'll pay for that!" Queen screeched.

"Like I haven't heard that before," I retorted.

She was up and running before my voice stopped echoing. I crawled out of my hiding place and found room to stand up. Just in time to see a pillar of fire burst from the ground a dozen feet ahead, somewhere near the perimeter of the arena, and arch skyward. On a collision course with Jimmy.

My protective instinct combined with Noah's, producing a rage unlike anything I'd ever felt. I reached out with two great powers, pulling at the fire with invisible fingers. Mere inches from Jimmy's unconscious form, the fire changed course. It pinged sideways, hitting an invisible barrier.

Queen shrieked. The fire fought me, trying desperately to change its course back toward its intended target. I pulled harder. The plume of fire zoomed toward me like dragon's breath.

Dahlia?

Trust me, Noah.

My powers absorbed the fire into our shared body, tucking it away and storing it. It energized me like a narcotic. Made the world a little brighter, the sky bluer. Odors sharper. Instinct continued bending the arch of the fire, pulling its searing heat away from Jimmy's reddening face. Down, down, toward the ground.

All at once, it ceased, cutting the tether to my energy source. The absorbed heat thrummed through my body. Our body. The kinetic energy around us sparkled, made more clear by the infusion.

We could beat her.

The ground trembled. Earthquake? No, too concentrated. The cement floor beneath my feet crackled, broke. I stared at it, understanding too late.

Dahlia, let me—

He took control. The floor exploded upward in a deadly shower of stone and dirt, the sheer force of it throwing us into the air. I expected pain, the sensation of rending flesh and breaking bone, but felt only the vaguest impression of flying; being tossed and sailing ass over teakettle, unhurt by the exploding floor.

A pocket of kinetic energy enveloped us, protecting us from the explosion. I understood it as we hit and bounced, coming to a soft stop a few feet from the smoking crater. The bubble disappeared, but the memory of it remained.

Nice one, Noah.

Energized and angry, I concentrated those emotions into a single burst of power. It shot forward, sending a pile of debris the size of a sports car careening forward across the floor at thirty miles an hour. It squealed like fingernails down a chalkboard, and it set my teeth on edge. I kept pushing.

Queen screamed (a sound I was starting to love), and was cut off with a thud.

"No!" Deuce this time, the cavernous space making it impossible to source the shout. At least I'd been on target with Queen.

We need to get Jimmy and Aaron down. They're sitting ducks.

"Agreed," I said.

Our fastest path was across the open arena, which left us exposed. The time I'd waste picking a path through the scattered debris was worth risking exposure. I ran faster than I'd ever run in my life, sneakers slipping a bit on the messy floor.

Chunks of rock peppered the ground every other step, trying to connect and failing.

The floor erupted directly in front of me like a land mine and showered me with more stone and dirt. I zagged to the left. The heavy, choking odor of damp earth filled my lungs. Another explosion, almost under my right foot, knocked me sideways. I landed on my shoulder and gasped at the instant pain.

The floor trembled. I scrambled, rolled, and barely missed losing half of my face in the third blast. Another tuck and leap, and I came up on my feet, moving with someone else's skill—Noah's training at Weatherfield. I unleashed a blast of telekinetic energy. It sailed across the arena like a comet.

Deuce stood near the center of the open space, next to the ball of junk I'd pushed out and above Queen's crumpled body. The comet hit Deuce square in the chest and smashed her backward onto her ass. She landed with a pained screech.

I dove behind a nest of twisted shelving and picked my way toward the base of Jimmy's support beam. I concentrated on the knots in the rope. Noah's power let me loosen them enough for Jimmy's weight to pull him down the pike. His eyelids fluttered.

"Jimmy," I said. "Jimmy, wake up."

He did, seeing me for only an instant before he looked over my shoulder. His eyes widened. Something buzzed past my head and slammed into Jimmy's chest. Blood splattered on my face, into my eyes. The jagged edges of a walnut-sized rock poked from the frayed edges of his shirt. He gasped.

Deep inside of me, Noah roared.

The ropes ripped from the pole. Jimmy fell. I barely caught him before he hit the ground. He gasped, hands flailing. I caught them and squeezed. The wound wasn't bleeding. The rock had embedded so hard and fast, it plugged the hole it made. But he could still be bleeding internally.

Noah clawed his way up, fighting to take over. I gave him a mental shake and pushed him away hard.

You can't help him, Noah, stop it!

He stilled. His rage continued—pure, energizing fuel. Jimmy blinked, trying to focus. His jaw trembled.

I touched his cheek. "Hang on, Jimmy," I said.

He nodded, and a single word rang through my head: *Aaron.* Even Jimmy was prodding me away, to do what we'd come here to do: rescue their big brother.

"I'll be back in a minute, you just hold on." I let go, and the pang of regret from Noah nearly buckled my knees. I stumbled, hating to leave Jimmy behind, but we had no choice. Queen and Deuce weren't down yet.

Further proof came as a hail of sand and stone battered the rubble to my left, and tiny particles peppered my arms and legs. Mosquito bites hurt more, but the grit dug in and held. I climbed over a stack of wooden pallets that had made it through the fire. They stood unburned, stable. At the top, I surveyed the warehouse.

A brown-haired head poked out from behind the center debris. It ducked back before I could see which sister was watching me.

Dal, concentrate on the energy inside of that pile. Make it explode.

Worth a shot. I drew on Noah's experience and felt the telekinetic energy inside the wreckage. Felt it swirl and glow, churning into a bubble. It grew. An arm of fire erupted behind the pile and shot toward me like a rocket. I ignored it too long. It struck the pallets beneath my feet and ignited them instantly. I pushed. Their cover exploded in a shower of sparks and metal and screams.

Flames leapt at our ankles, catching the fabric and scorching skin. I refocused and pulled the fire inward to the center of my power. It went out fast. Either I was getting better at this, or Queen was getting weaker. Both were comforting thoughts.

On the arena floor, two bodies lay among the smoldering rubble. The odor of scorched metal tingled my nose. Tears sprang into my eyes, stinging them. Across the open space, a new figure limped out of the shadows.

King!

He stared at the fallen bodies. Looked up. I waved, and he started running.

Down I climbed, back to the warehouse floor. I picked my way across to Aaron's pillar. Just as I had done with Jimmy, I loosened the binding ropes enough to allow him to slip down. Arms around his waist, I managed to lower him to the ground.

Aaron Scott looked like death warmed over. Skin stretched too tight across his cheekbones and forehead, thin and delicate. A fading bruise colored his jaw, stark against the pallor of his skin. Multiple splits marked his chapped lips. Dried blood dotted his dirty T-shirt.

His breathing was labored, shallow.

Noah's fury compounded. Like before, he tried to push to the surface and take control. I held tight and kept him back. His anger could be an asset, but it could also get us killed.

King pushed his way through the debris, knocking it aside like it was cotton batting. He came to a sudden halt and fell to his knees next to us. An eyeless face fixed first on Aaron, and then on me.

"Where's Noah?" he asked.

"Here," I said, pointing to my chest. I half-expected to see the bullet wound still on my body, but it wasn't. I was in full uniform, which surprised me. It shouldn't have; I was just an image now, a glamour of my old self. But who still saw me as a Ranger—me or Noah? No time to ponder that right now. "Short story, no time. Are they dead?"

"Dunno," King said. "Are you dead?"

"I'm not sure. Maybe." Couldn't think about that now. "We need to get Jimmy and get out of here."

King nodded, seeming to understand that the time for questions was much later. He reached for Aaron with shaking hands, seeming nervous now that he was finally presented with the thing he'd been waiting on for so long. It was time to take that final leap into the last body he would ever possess. Into a life he'd chosen to embrace.

I looked at the burn marks on Aaron's bare arms, the dark circles under his eyes. The hell he'd put himself through, and the hell Queen had put him through. Dr. Kinsey believed this was the right thing to do. Noah believed it. Noah *chose* it, and his brothers had agreed. I realized then, even without Noah's underlying emotion, that I believed it, too. It wasn't our job to judge Aaron's life, and perhaps we would see our own judgment for it one day, but I would fight for what I thought was right. Giving the Changelings a chance at a life was right.

Morally ambiguous? Absolutely. It's why so many shades of gray exist in the world.

King grabbed Aaron's shoulders. Both men shimmered and unfocused into a haze of color that meshed into a single blur. The air sang and hummed with power, with life anew. The colors reformed on the ground as one person. Heat rose in Aaron's cheeks. The dark lines disappeared. His skin no longer seemed so breakable. All visible hints of abuse were gone, save the shirt stains. His chest rose and fell evenly, without struggle.

Aaron's eyes flew open, as green as his siblings'. They locked onto mine, swimming with doubt and confusion. He licked his dry lips and tried to speak.

"Can you sit up?" I asked.

He nodded, tried, then flopped back to the floor. I took his hand and tugged, and got him halfway vertical.

"Queen," he said, voice dry and raspy. "She set explosives. I remember her talking. Gotta get out of here."

Getting out of there was at the top of my priority list as soon as we had everyone. "Do you know where Teresa is?"

"I don't . . ." He squinted, thinking. Searching through

memories that still hadn't fully integrated into those of King and the three (at least) other people he'd possessed lately. "No, I don't know. I've been unconscious for a while. Where's Jimmy?"

"Back there."

We cut a fast retreat path. Aaron moved with the grace and agility of a gymnast, very at home in his new body. My arms burned, irritated by the sand firmly shoved beneath the skin. The center of the warehouse remained quiet. Noah shuddered. Homicidal or not, Queen and Deuce were still his kin. In a very strange, body-share kind of way, they were mine, too.

Jimmy had tried to crawl away and now lay on his right side, cheek flat on the cement. The rock had shifted and blood pooled on the ground beneath his left hand. Aaron rolled him onto his back. He saw the wound, and a strangled cry caught in his throat. Jimmy grunted, his eyelids slitting open.

"Hey, big brother," he whispered.

"Hey, Jimbo," Aaron said. "We gotta go, pal, no time to lie around."

Jimmy smiled, displaying red-tinged teeth. "I was supposed to rescue you, you know. Not the other way around."

Something inside Noah broke and sent waves of grief careening through both of us. We hadn't fought this hard and come so far only to lose one of his brothers. I knelt next to Aaron, sought his hand, and squeezed tight.

"You did rescue me, pal," Aaron said.

I slipped back, allowing Noah to rise to the surface. My

hold on his body fell away, and I retreated into the shadows of his mind. Our appearance must have changed as well, because Jimmy blinked sleepily at us. He recognized his other big brother.

"Trance," Jimmy said, voice barely audible. "Van outside. Didn't need her in here."

The news came with only a small measure of relief. It was beaten back by sorrow. Noah nodded our understanding.

Peace flittered across Jimmy's face. Soft words of comfort whispered through our heads, spoken in Jimmy's gentle voice. Three hearts beat as one and, for one brief moment, the Scott brothers were together again.

And then death ripped Jimmy away in its unbeatable grasp and tore their hearts to shreds.

Aaron cried out, his wail beating back all other sounds. He reached for his baby brother. Took him into his arms. He tried to keep hold, but Jimmy was already gone. Noah fell away from the surface, shock setting in so hard and fast I almost couldn't retake control. His emotions and thoughts were so distant, so protected, I couldn't be certain he was still conscious.

Tears streamed down my cheeks, bitter and hot and anchoring me to the present. Air swirled around us. No, not air. Kinetic energy. The short hairs on my arms tingled. I tackled Aaron to the ground. The scorching heat of the fireball zoomed over us, fluttering my hair. It smashed into the base of the support pillar. The iron structure groaned.

Hatred and grief fueled the ball of kinetic energy I blindly threw behind me, toward the wreckage. Metal squealed and banged. Wood clattered. Debris became shrapnel.

"Get Jimmy out of here now," I said into Aaron's ear.

Without waiting for a reply, I scrambled to my feet and plunged into the open arena.

Queen stood in the middle of the cleared area, hands by her sides, breathing hard. Blood coated her throat and her right arm. A sliver of metal stuck out of her left calf. Her eyes blazed with an unnatural—and quite literal—fire. The air around her shimmered like a heat mirage.

To her left, Deuce sat propped up against a bit of wreckage. Two shards of wood protruded from her chest. Blood pooled on the ground around her. Her eyes were closed, her chest still. No, there it was—a faint rise and fall.

I paced forward, circling around until only ten feet separated me from Queen. The heated air rippled.

"How's your sister?" I deadpanned.

Her eyes narrowed. "How's his brother?"

Noah jerked, growing more aware of what I was doing.

"You're very hard to kill, Dahlia," she said. "Harder than I would have expected from an untrained Recombinant."

"See, Queen? That's why you haven't won. You can't see past your own damned pride."

"Maybe, but I'm not as shortsighted as you think."

Her left hand twitched. The north corner of the building erupted with fire and flame, throwing rubble and debris high into the air like a volcano. Three more in quick succession lit up the other corners of the burned-out warehouse. The ground thundered with the sheer force of the detonations.

Smoke thickened the air and drifted high, blotting out the waning sunlight.

There was little left to burn, but Queen hadn't left it to chance. Fire raced along the standing walls of the warehouse, so straight and fast she must have left an accelerant. The familiar odor of gasoline—something I should have smelled sooner—rose on the condensing smoke. Fire surrounded us in a fearsome circle.

"Come on, Blondie," Queen said. "Give me your best shot."

Glad to oblige, Noah said.

Together we unleashed a cloud of telekinetic energy at her. She countered by raising a wall of fire and pushing. The two opposing forces collided in a blinding glare of light. The feedback hit like a kidney punch and knocked me to my knees. Instantly, fire surrounded me, licking and leaping.

I invited the fire inside. It swirled around us, red and orange and yellow, but did not burn. I took its heat, absorbed its energy. Drew it in, deeper, deeper, coiling hot and tight as low as it could go, making room for the continuing assault.

An assault that grew steadily stronger. Fiercer. I couldn't counter the attack. Too much came at me at once. I could only absorb, and even that grew painful. Too much.

Share with me, Dahlia. Give me some control.

No, the fire will hurt you.

Give me.

Damn him, he wrestled for it. My mind and body were consumed with Queen's onslaught of pure fire, propelled by her rage. Control slipped to Noah. Pain prickled, barely there at first, but growing. Intensifying.

Step by step, we moved forward. Taking the fire to Queen. The inferno blazed around us, controlled and contained by Noah's power. Queen screamed. Flames leapt. I reached deep down and pulled power from its storage place. Gave the power to Noah. He took it. Transformed it. Sent it straight back to Queen.

It slammed into her like a carving knife, cleaving skin from muscle. Muscle from bone. Bone from marrow. Endless shrieks blended into the tornado of power and flame and flesh. Pain erupted in my very soul, spreading outward. Touching limbs I no longer possessed, searing flesh I did not wear. It consumed me. Held me in its terrible embrace.

The fire died away; the agony remained. I fled from it, shrinking down as far as I could go. Exhausted. Finished.

Queen was dead, destroyed by her own power. Noah could get the others to safety. He would explain.

Dahlia? Where are you going?

I need to rest, Noah. I'm done.

No! Keep talking to me. Stay here until we can get to Simon.

I'll always be here.

Dahlia? Dahlia!

I held on to the sound of his voice as long as I could, and then let go of that last, delicate thread. I fell. Down, deep down into emptiness.

And peace.

Thirty

New Game

Always with hints of consciousness came agonizing pain. It fogged over everything, thick and murky, harsh and scalding. I fought against it, struggled to pass through it and failed. Voices called to me in words that made no sense—sometimes urgent and fearful, sometimes calm and reassuring. I tried connecting the voices to names without success. Coherent thoughts escaped me. It seemed enough that I wasn't alone.

Time and again, I lost the battle to wake and slipped back into darkness. Pinpricks of light and those distant voices were my only company. They existed together in a haze of passing time. Immeasurable and never-ending time.

Through it all, I was aware of a constant presence. He stayed close, his voice warm and friendly, even when he wasn't talking to me.

After a while, memories surfaced with the pain. Images of faces, both loved and hated. Past and present, alive and dead. My mom, smiling through her agony as cancer ate her from the inside out. Always believing in me, even when I did not. Had she known my secret? Kept my past from me? Did it matter?

Queen, as plain and half-formed as her sister, radiating rage as she died. Disintegrated by her own flames. Destroyed by hatred and blind allegiance to an unknown master. Jimmy Scott, so gentle and undeserving of death, and the rage I'd felt as he was ripped away. Had that been my rage?

Teresa and Marco and Renee . . .

A spike of pain shot through my head. Someone was calling me again, urging me out of the dark. I retreated deeper, away from him.

Teresa. Did they find her?

If I stayed in the dark, I'd never know. I had to know. Agony consumed me as I clawed upward, my entire existence a single, constant throb.

Marco. Did he survive regaining his own body?

I shoved hard against the overwhelming blackness, numb to the pain. Close by, someone sweet and loving caressed my soul. We seemed to pass each other, like wisps of clouds in a bright, blue sky. He didn't speak; he didn't have to.

Renee. Burned and disfigured, her stunning beauty marred by vengeance.

Through the thick haze and daggers of pain, I surfaced. Felt flesh and bone, both foreign and familiar. Heard a voice, steady and pattering, close to my ear. I latched onto the sound. Listened for words I knew. Something about the woods. A staccato rhythm. Poetry?

Ethan. I knew his voice.

He stopped speaking. I lost my lifeline and nearly tumbled back into the abyss. Warmth latched onto my hand and hauled me forward. I concentrated. My fingers twitched around his. No, not really my fingers, were they?

"Dahlia? Christ, there you are. Guys!"

I winced at the volume of his voice—too loud. Everything ached. My mouth was dry, full of cotton balls and sawdust. A warm hand caressed my forehead, while the other squeezed my hand tight. I tried to squeeze back.

"Come on, Dal, open your eyes," Ethan said.

Obeying his request was the hardest thing I'd ever done. Eventually, my eyelids accommodated my wishes and peeled apart. Ethan hovered above me, his eyes wide and shiny. Dark smudges beneath both betrayed his fatigue. Something else was off, though—where were the scratches on his face?

I grunted, unable to make my vocal cords produce actual words. I had so many questions and needed to know so many things.

"We thought we'd lost you for good, Dal."

Yeah, me, too.

I blinked at the obtrusive thought—not my own thought, but a rich voice deep inside. And I suddenly understood. "Noah," I rasped.

Ethan winced. "You're still inside him." His voice broke, and his eyes became impossibly shinier. "Simon tried for weeks, but he couldn't get you out. He thinks it's because you were shot. Your, ah"—he swallowed hard—"body died when Noah absorbed you. He doesn't think he can separate you without . . . killing you for good."

Liquid heat spilled from the corners of my eyes, and I

couldn't distinguish my emotions from those rising up below me. My own shock and grief at knowing I'd never be the same person I'd once been was caught in the whirlwind of Noah's shock and grief from having lost both a brother, two sisters, and a woman he'd cared about to the point of risking his family. Ethan's shock and grief spilled out of his expressive face like a tidal wave.

I'd never be free of Noah's body. Letting me go meant . . . well, I didn't know what it meant. Noah said part of the other person was absorbed into his consciousness, even though the body—skin—was discarded. My stomach gurgled and flipped at the image of my skin crumpled on the ground like an old sheet.

Never happen, Dal. Noah's words were fierce, though distant. He was giving me space, letting me be with my friends now that I'd found my way to the surface. Could we possibly exist like this?

"Teresa?" I asked, redirecting to more pleasant things. I needed to get the information before I exhausted myself and lost my tenuous hold on this body.

"Right here, kiddo," she said from behind Ethan. One person's voice had never sounded so sweet.

He let go of my hand and stepped back. Teresa moved in and perched on the edge of the bed (I realized then that I was in the infirmary at Hill House), her arm in a sling and a wide, sad smile on her face. She looked healthy, if tired—a fatigue that was all my fault.

"You're okay," I said.

"Yeah." She brushed a lock of hair off my forehead.

"Queen stuffed me in the back of a van and left me there high on morphine. I wish I could have done something to help."

"You lived. Almost died because of me."

"No, Dal, I almost died because of the Overseer that Queen and Deuce worked for."

She knew about the Overseer, which meant she knew what I was. I wasn't one of them, and never had been.

Something in my expression must have alarmed her, because she gave my hand a squeeze. "Dr. Kinsey is okay. He and Aaron have been staying here at the house while . . . for now. Marco, too. He started breathing on his own a day after he was released from Deuce. Physically, he's almost one hundred percent."

Aaron? It took me a moment to remember—King and Aaron were one person now, just as Ace/Noah were one. But Jimmy/Joker was dead.

I wanted to be happy for the good news, but so much of it was tempered with unspoken grief. Dr. Kinsey and Aaron were still fugitives from Weatherfield; they had nowhere to go. And what about me and Noah? His place was with his family, but where was my place now? Marco was alive and healing, but had he been changed by sharing a body with Deuce?

God, nothing made sense anymore.

My hold over consciousness was slipping. The slope I'd struggled up earlier was turning to pudding, making it impossible to stay up and alert. I'd have to let go soon. Just not yet. Someone was still unaccounted for. "Renee?"

Teresa's chin trembled, and I thought she might burst

into tears. My heart slammed against my ribs. Oh God, no.

She didn't die, Dal.

"She might be able to come home at the end of the week," Teresa said, her voice husky, broken. "Some of the burns were pretty bad. Because of her ability, the doctors are hesitant to try skin grafts."

I closed my eyes and tried to picture Renee with her long, straw-colored hair and bright smile, the way her energy filled a room, and her absolute confidence in her sex appeal. All I saw clearly was how she'd lain on that pallet in the conference room, unconscious and still in agonizing pain. More tears trailed down my cheeks. I'd failed all of my friends.

You didn't fail them, Dahlia. They're alive. You're alive.

Jimmy died.

I felt Noah's grief in a bitter flash of regret. *I was responsible for Jimmy, not you. We lost Jimmy, but we saved Aaron, so that's something. I could have done a lot of things differently, better, but Ace never understood attraction or love. And Noah's first battle with cancer started in the middle of eleventh grade, so he didn't date. I didn't understand my feelings for you, Dal, not until I saw Queen shoot you. I couldn't just let you die in my arms like that.*

He didn't say it, but I felt his love. We'd certainly created the mother of all complications to our relationship, and I thought back to our only kiss. A warm flutter in my stomach came on the heels of the memory. It would have to do.

"Dal?" Teresa asked, thumb stroking the back of my hand. "Are you going away?"

"For a while." I struggled to get my eyelids open and focus

on her. I was definitely going back to sleep. Whether or not "going away" included leaving Hill House with Noah's family, I couldn't say. The decision was far beyond my limited faculties.

"Simon wants to keep trying to separate you two," she said softly. "He won't give up. None of us will."

I smiled. "Thanks."

I closed my eyes and drifted. Letting go was easy, and I slipped down, into darkness and warmth. Noah passed by me in another cloud-whisper as he rose to the surface, and I thought I felt our fingers brush. I wrapped myself in a cocoon of love and safety, content to rest for a while. It was finally over.

And only just beginning.